LIZ GRZYB was born in the middle of a thunderstorm in Perth, Western Australia. She is the award-winning editor of acclaimed paranormal romance anthologies *Scary Kisses* and *More Scary Kisses*, the Orientalist pantomime *Dreaming of Djinn*, steampunk romance *Kisses by Clockwork*, co-editor of the paranormal noir *Damnation and Dames* and *The Year's Best Australian Fantasy and Horror* series from Ticonderoga Publications. Liz is often to be found sipping champagne and debating the fate of the Oxford comma.

TALIE HELENE is a musician and writer, from Melbourne, Australia. She writes poetry, fiction, and songs. Talie is horror editor for the anthology *The Year's Best Australian Fantasy and Horror* (Ticonderoga Publications); she was news editor for the Australian Horror Writers' Association for four years (2006–2010). She is a member of the SuperNova writers' group. Talie has a background in music journalism, various music industry roles and fine art event management. She performs as a singer/songwriter, and has performed with many artists including The Tenth Stage, Wendy Rule, Saba Persian Orchestra, and Eden. For the latest updates, visit www.taliehelene.com

Also edited by LIZ GRZYB

Scary Kisses
More Scary Kisses
Damnation and Dames (with Amanda Pillar)
Dreaming of Djinn
Kisses by Clockwork
Hear Me Roar

Also edited by LIZ GRZYB & TALIE HELENE

The Year's Best Australian Fantasy & Horror 2010
The Year's Best Australian Fantasy & Horror 2011
The Year's Best Australian Fantasy & Horror 2012
The Year's Best Australian Fantasy & Horror 2013

THE YEAR'S BEST AUSTRALIAN FANTASY & HORROR

~ 2014 ~

THE FIFTH ANNUAL COLLECTION

THE YEAR'S BEST AUSTRALIAN FANTASY & HORROR

~ 2014 ~

EDITED BY

LIZ GRZYB & TALIE HELENE

T☵
þ☵

Ticonderoga
publications

for

Cat Sparks
(L.G.)

Rocky Wood
(T.H.)

The Year's Best Australian Fantasy & Horror 2014
edited by Liz Grzyb & Talie Helene

Published by Ticonderoga Publications

Designed by Russell B. Farr
Typeset in Sabon and Poor Richard

A Cataloging-in-Publications entry for this title is available from The National Library of Australia.

ISBN   978-1-925212-18-1 (hardcover)
        978-1-925212-19-8 (trade paperback)
        978-1-925212-20-4 (ebook)

Ticonderoga Publications
PO Box 29 Greenwood
Western Australia 6924
Australia

www.ticonderogapublications.com

10 9 8 7 6 5 4 3 2 1

The editors would like to thank Alan Baxter, James Bradley, Imogen Cassidy, David Conyers, Terry Dowling, Thoraiya Dyer, Jason Franks, Michelle Goldsmith, Michael Grey, Stephanie Gunn, Lisa L. Hannett, Gerry Huntman, Rick Kennett, David Kernot , Charlotte Kieft, S.G. Larner, Claire McKenna, Andrew J. McKiernan, Faith Mudge, Jason Nahrung, Emma Osborne, Angela Rega, Tansy Rayner Roberts, Angela Slatter, Cat Sparks, Anna Tambour, Kyla Ward, Kaaron Warren, and Janeen Webb.

Liz would like to thank Talie Helene, Russell B. Farr, Amanda Pillar, Kate Dunbar-Smith, Deb Wilson, Jacinta Rosielle, Angela Challis, Shane Cummings, Andrea Orlowsky, Jacintha Bell, Ruza Foster, Frankie Nathan, Kate Williams, Andrew Williams, Carol Ryles, Nicole Murphy, Alan Baxter, Anthony Panegyres, Ambre Hillier, Michael Hillier, Tasmar Dixon, Mel Donald, Phil Ward, Lina Piscitelli, Kim Astle, Helen Grzyb, Marianne de Pierres, Isobelle Carmody, Helen Stubbs, Trudi Canavan, Sue Bursztynski, and the Department of Fabulous.

Talie would like to thank Liz Grzyb, Russell B. Farr, Rocky Wood, Julia Svaganovic, Yaritji Green, Gillian Polack, Sharyn Lilley, Jenny Blackford, Lee Murray, Helen Stubbs, Sean Bowley, Andrew Kutzner, Matthew Sigley, Samantha Escarbe, Josephine Wilson, Leigh Irwin, Sonia Tamarri, Deborah Crabtree, Joanna Girardin, David Schembri, Adrian Bedford, Aaron Sterns, Martin Livings, Sophie Yorkston, Alisa Krasnostein, Jason Fischer, Geoff Brown, Deborah Biancotti, Cameron Trost, Christopher Sequeira, Tim Barsby, Giovanni Raggi, Stacey Palfreyman, Felicity Dowker, Ana Ravic, Lucy Sussex, Sarah Endacott, Jamie Reuel, Chuck McKenzie, Kirstyn McDermott, Ellen Gregory, Deborah Kalin, Tessa Kum, Tracie McBride, Jane Routley, the SuperNova Writers Crew, Charmaine Calaitzis and Adam Calaitzis.

CONTENTS

THE YEAR IN REVIEW

LIZ GRZYB & TALIE HELENE

THE YEAR IN FANTASY

2014 was a year where yet again, many Australasians made their mark upon the world stage. The antipodes were well-represented at the World Fantasy Awards, with nominations for Kaaron Warren in Best Short Fiction, and both Janeen Webb and Angela Slatter in the Best Collection category. Amidst the Sad/Rabid Puppies furore surrounding the Hugo Awards, there was still great news for Australian speculative fiction, as Galactic Suburbia Podcast won Alisa Krasnostein, Alexandra Pierce, Tansy Rayner Roberts and Andrew Finch the Hugo for Best Fancast, and long-running co-operative *Andromeda Spaceways Inflight Magazine* was nominated for Best Semiprozine.

Many Australian fantasy authors featured in international publications this year. *The Mammoth Book of SF by Women*, edited by Alex Dally MacFarlane, included Thoraiya Dyer's "The Second Card of the Major Arcana" and Lucy Sussex's "The Queen of Erewon". Dyer also had stories published in Apex's *War Stories* and Crossed Genres' *Long Hidden* anthologies, and *Analog* magazine. Anna Tambour's "The Walking-Stick Forest" (reprinted in this volume) and Rjurik Davidson's "Night-Time in Caeli-Amur" were released on Tor.com. Suzanne J. Willis was published in the *British Fantasy Society Journal* and in *Postscripts 32/33*, and Deborah Kalin released the Aurealis-nominated "Teratogen" in *Cemetery Dance* #71. "All the Wealth in the World" by Alan Baxter was featured in *Lakeside Circus* and he also sold a story to Red Penny Papers' *Superpow* anthology and *Postscripts*. Lisa L. Hannett also appeared in *Postscripts*.

Fantasy luminary Garth Nix had an amazing year. His short story "A Cargo of Ivories" appeared in George R. R. Martin and Gardner Dozois' mixed-genre *Rogues* anthology, and he published a tale in Ellen Datlow's *Fearful Symmetries*. Nix also had a story alongside Isobelle Carmody, James Bradley and Kaaron Warren in Jonathan Strahan's *Fearsome Magics* anthology from Solaris Books. Kathleen Jennings' delightful "Skull and Hyssop" was included in *Lady Churchill's Rosebud Wristlet* #3, and Gerry Huntman's "Husks" appeared in *Sword and Sorcery Magazine* #2. Angela Rega chalked up a number of international sales, with stories appearing in *Black Apples* anthology from Belladonna Publishing, *Postscripts*, and her disturbing story "Shedding Skin" being published in *Crossed Genres Magazine*, as well as Australian publications in *SQ Mag*, and *Kisses by Clockwork* from Ticonderoga Publications.

Marianne de Pierres was awarded the Curtin Distinguished Alumni Award for significant and valuable contributions made to society, recognising her shining light as an Australian author challenging stereotyping. She also sold her fabulous chick-lit-slightly-paranormal-detective-fiction Tara Sharp series (written under the pseudonym Marianne Delacourt) to Twelfth Planet Press. Nicole Murphy sold her second romantic fantasy trilogy set in the world of Gadda, People of the Star, to Ticonderoga Publications.

Acclaimed horror and fantasy author Angela Slatter was incredibly prolific in both publications and awards this year. Her stories were included in a number of international titles, such as PS Publishing's *Postscripts 32/33*, Stephen Jones' *Zombie Apocalypse! Endgame* "The Badger Bride" in *Strange Tales IV* from Tartarus Press, which is reprinted in this volume, was nominated for the Aurealis Award for Best Fantasy Short Story; "Home and Hearth", which was released as a chapbook from Spectral Press, won the Aurealis for Best Horror Short Story and was listed on the Locus Recommended Reading List; and the intricate "St Dymphna's School for Poison Girls", in *Review of Australian Fiction*, added the Best Fantasy Short Story Award to Slatter's Aurealis haul. In addition to her many original publications this year, her stories were reprinted in many 2014 Year's Bests, such as *The Year's Best YA Speculative Fiction* from Twelfth Planet Press, Paula Guran's *Year's Best Dark Fantasy and Horror* and Stephen Jones' *Mammoth Book of New Horror*. Slatter's stories were also translated into such diverse languages as Polish and Romanian.

Slatter's boutique collection, co-authored with Lisa L. Hannett, *The Female Factory* from Twelfth Planet Press won the Aurealis Award for Best Collection, as well as garnering an Honourable Mention in the Norma K. Hemming Award. Her two other collections published in 2014, *Black Winged Angels* from Ticonderoga Publications, and *The Bitterwood Bible and Other Recountings* from Tartarus Press, were both shortlisted for Best Collection at the Aurealis Awards, and *Bitterwood* also gained Slatter a World Fantasy Award nomination as well as being listed on the Locus Recommended Reading List for the year.

Crowdfunding continued to grow in importance worldwide, and made a large impact on the independent publishing industry in 2014, with a number of anthologies and other publications gaining significant backing and audience before their release. *Cranky Ladies of History* from Fablecroft Press was a noteworthy Australian player in this field, which reached one and a half times their projected goal in their crowdfunding campaign during March, Women's History Month in 2014, ahead of the anthology's release in 2015.

NOTABLE NOVELS

Allen & Unwin released a number of fantasy novels this year, primarily aimed at young adult readers. Garth Nix added the fourth volume to his high fantasy Abhorsen/Old Kingdom Chronicles with *Clariel* which was long-listed for the Inky Awards and shortlisted for the Aurealis Best Young Adult Novel, Locus Awards Best YA Novel, Ditmar Best Novel and ABIA Older Children Award, as well as being mentioned on the Locus Recommended Reading List. Amie Kaufman & Meagan Spooner followed up their Aurealis Award-winning *These Broken Stars* with *This Shattered World*, the second in their adventurous fantasy/science fiction Starbound trilogy, which was shortlisted for both the Best Fantasy and Best

Science Fiction novel at the Aurealis Awards. Justine Larbalestier released her crime/fantasy/horror novel *Razorhurst*, which was shortlisted for the Victorian Premier's Awards, Queensland Literary Awards, The Norma K. Hemming Award, longlisted for the Inky and Sisters in Crime Davitt Awards and won the Aurealis Award for Best Horror Novel. Lynette Lounsbury brought out *Afterworld*, her adventure/fantasy novel, which was shortlisted for the Aurealis Award for Young Adult Novel.

Hachette Book Group published a number of Australian speculative novels, continuing in their tradition of supporting fantasy series. Glenda Larke and Trudi Canavan shared the Ditmar Award for Best Novel for each of their first titles of new series, *The Lascar's Dagger* and *Thief's Magic*, respectively. Larke's *The Lascar's Dagger*, the first in her Forsaken Lands series, was also nominated for the Aurealis Award for Best Fantasy Novel and won Best Professional Long Work in the Tin Duck Awards. Canavan's *Thief's Magic* is the first in her Millennium's Rule trilogy. Karen Miller continued her long association with Orbit, releasing the first in her Tarnished Crown Quintet, *The Falcon Throne*. Prolific paranormal author Keri Arthur rounds out the Hachette Group writers embarking on new series this year, as she released the Aurealis-nominated *Fireborn* to open her urban fantasy Souls of Fire series.

Like most of the big publishers, many of HarperCollins' fantasy novels this year were series related. The three novels of Alan Baxter's Alex Caine series were released, bringing *Bound*, *Obsidian* and *Abduction* to the table. The series started with a bang, with *Bound* introducing Alex's struggle with unleashing his magical power, getting mixed up with a cursed grimoire and a formidable bad guy, and balanced out with a dose of attraction for the powerful Kin fighter, Silhouette. And that's only the first novel! *Bound* was nominated for a Ditmar for Best Novel, while *Obsidian* was nominated for the Best Horror Novel in the Aurealis Awards. Many Harper Collins authors also released their second or third installment of their series this year. Those adding their third title to series were: Duncan Lay, who continued his Empire of Bones series with *Wall of Spears*; Jo Spurrier with *North Star Guide Me Home*, which continued Children of the Black Sun; and KJ Taylor released the third in the Risen Sun series, *The Shadow's Heart*. Kylie Chan released her second book in the Celestial Battle series, *Demon Child*, and Traci Harding also continued her Timekeeper trilogy with Book 2, *The Eternity Gate*. Will Elliott released his quirky novel *Inside* Out, and Dani Kristoff published steamy fantasy *The Sorcerer's Spell* with Harper's digital Impulse imprint.

Pan Macmillan released the delightful *Dreamer's Pool*, the first novel in a captivating new series from Perth author Juliet Marillier. The novel tells of Blackthorn and Grim, two prisoners locked up in a hellish prison for questioning Lord Mathuin's despicable actions. The two escape from wrongful incarceration when a mysterious fey lord offers the prickly Blackthorn a very difficult choice. The story is full of surprises from the first page, but the intricate worldbuilding and intense prose will certainly not surprise Marillier's fans. *Dreamer's Pool* justifiably won the Best Fantasy Novel Aurealis Award and was nominated for Best Novel in the Sir Julius Vogel Awards. Marillier also satisfyingly concluded her young adult fantasy trilogy Shadowfell with *The Caller*, which won the Sir Julius Vogel Award for Best Youth Novel. Both of Marillier's novels this year were nominated for the Tin Duck Award for Best Professional Long Work.

Jay Kristoff released the third in his mythical Lotus War series, *Endsinger* with Pan Macmillan. Jaclyn Moriarty continued her Colours of Madeleine series with *The Cracks in the Kingdom*, which won the Aurealis Award for Best Young Adult Novel, and the Queensland Literary Awards Young Adult Book Award. Ben Peek's first book in his Children trilogy, *The Godless*, and Rjurik Davidson's first novel of Caeli-Amur, *Unwrapped Sky*, were both mentioned in the Locus Recommended Reading List, and *The Godless* was also nominated for the Ditmar Award for Best Novel. K.A. Barker's young adult adventure novel *The Book of Days* was released. It had won Barker the John Marsden Prize in 2010 as an unpublished manuscript.

The digital arm of Pan Macmillan, Momentum Books, has continued to build on their library of speculative fiction. Donna Maree Hanson released two installments of her epic fantasy Dragon Wine series with Momentum: *Shatterwing* and *Skywatcher*. Adina West released the second Omnibus edition of her paranormal Dark Child series, *Covens Rising*, which collects as a novel-length work the episodes she released periodically. Matthew Reilly was another author who serialised his work with Momentum before releasing it as an omnibus in 2014, with *Troll Mountain*. Felicity Pulman released her Arthurian tale *I, Morgana*. Sophie Masson introduced her urban fantasy Trinity series with the first book, *The Koldun Code*. Trent Jamieson added to his excellent urban fantasy Death Works series with Book 4, the novella-length *The Memory of Death*, which raises as many questions as it answers.

Harlequin Australia published some romantic fantasy titles this year. Kim Wilkins' *Daughters of the Storm*, the first in her Blood and Gold series, was released, along with the e-chapbook of her novella *The Crown of Rowan*, which was first published in the Dann/Strahan *Legends of Australian Fantasy* anthology in 2010. *Daughters of the Storm* was shortlisted for the Aurealis Award for Best Fantasy novel. Harlequin's ebook Escape imprint introduced Dani Kristoff's Spellbound in Sydney series, with the saucy *Bespelled*. Daniel de Lorne also opened his erotic vampire Bonds of Blood series with Escape, releasing *Beckoning Blood*.

Angry Robot continued their association with Australian authors in 2014, releasing Craig Cormick's first novel in his Shadow Master series, *The Shadow Master*, and Marianne de Pierres' urban fantasy western *Peacemaker*. *Peacemaker* tells the story of Virgin Jackson, a Ranger, and her new partner, U.S. Marshall Nate Sixkiller as they investigate a dead body mysteriously found in Birrimun Park, the last natural landscape. This is the first in de Pierres' new series of the same name, and was awarded Best Science Fiction Novel at the Aurealis Awards.

Walker Books released Tony Thompson's novelised account of Mary Shelley, *Summer of Monsters*. Tonya Alexandra also introduced her Greek mythology-inspired young adult Love Oracles series with *Nymph*.

Australian independent and boutique presses expanded on their novel releases this year. Satalyte Press brought out the first in Satima Flavell's high fantasy Talismans series, *Dagger of Dresnia*, which was nominated for a Tin Duck Award for Best Long Professional Work. Ticonderoga Publications released the first of RJ Ashby's young adult Kingbreaker Chronicles, *The Assassin of Nara*, and Pantera Press featured Wanda Wiltshire's *Allegiance*, the second story in her Betrothed series. Relative newcomer, Hague Publishing, published Janis Hill's *Isis, Vampires and Ghosts—Oh My!*

M.C. Planck released the first in his World of Prime series, *Sword of the Bright Lady* through Pyr. Penguin brought out Scott Westerfeld's ghostly new novel *Afterworlds*, and Random House released Keith Austin's horrifying young adult fairy tale retelling *Snow, White*. Andrez Bergen released the coming-of-age story *Depth Charging Ice Planet Goth* with Perfect Edge Books.

Jaffa Books published *Impossible Magic*, which is the second in J.F.R. Coates' Destiny of Dragons series. Ben Langdon had his novel *The Miranda Contract* published by Kalamity Press. Tracy M. Joyce opened her Chronicles of Altaica series with *Altaica*, through Odyssey Books. Hoa Pham released *The Other Shore* through Seizure Press, and *City of Masks* by Ashley Capes was brought out by Snapping Turtle Books. D.K. Mok's *The Other Tree* was published through Spence City, and Wilde City Press released Kevil Kiehr's *Drama Queens and Adult Themes*. Keith Shaw Greenwood published *The Clueless Dead* through Xlibris.

COLLECTIONS

Victorian-based Satalyte Publishing released a number of collections this year, including Adam Browne's *Other Stories and Other Stories*. Andrew McKiernan collected a number of his dark fantasy and horror stories in his Australian Shadows Award-winning *Last Year, When We Were Young*. Dirk Strasser's science fiction and fantasy collection *Stories of the Sand* brought together eighteen of Strasser's tales and also included illustrations from Andrew J. McKiernan. M. R. Cosby released the dark fantasy/horror collection *Dying Embers*.

Ticonderoga Publications continued their focus on single-author collections, releasing three. Angela Slatter's Aurealis-nominated *Black-Winged Angels* is a limited edition hardback release of fairytale retellings, illustrated by the magical Kathleen Jennings who was nominated for a Ditmar for this artwork. *Death at the Blue Elephant*, a collection of Janeen Webb's deliciously dark tales, has been nominated for a World Fantasy Award and was mentioned in the Locus Recommended Reading List. Ian McHugh collected a number of his internationally published stories in his Aurealis-nominated collection *Angel Dust.*

Twelfth Planet Press released the Aurealis Award-winning collection *Female Factory* from powerhouse duo Lisa L. Hannett and Angela Slatter, which was also Honourably Mentioned in the Norma K. Hemming Award. The title story was also nominated for a Ditmar Award for Best Novella/Novelette. Rosaleen Love's collection *Secret Lives* was also nominated for the Aurealis Best Collection, with the story "Qasida" being shortlisted for the WSFA Small Press Award. Both collections were listed in the Locus Recommended Reading List.

Angela Slatter had her third collection for the year, *The Bitterwood Bible and Other Recountings* published with Tartarus Press in the UK. *Bitterwood Bible* was nominated for a World Fantasy Award, and an Aurealis Award for best collection, as well as being mentioned in the Locus Recommended Reading List, with illustrator Kathleen Jennings receiving a second Ditmar nomination for her illustrations.

Simon Petrie's mix of new and previously published stories, *Difficult Second Album: more stories of Xenobiology, Space Elevators, and Bats Out Of Hell*, edited by Edwina Harvey, was released by Peggy Bright Books. The title gained Petrie an Aurealis Award nomination for Best Collection. Simon Dewar published *Suspended in Dusk* with Books of the Dead Press.

Angela Meyer released her unsettling *Captives* collection through boutique press Inkerman and Blunt. Queenslanders Vision Writers released 18, their eighteenth anthology of short fiction from active members. David Conyers released *The Shoggoth Conspiracy*, the first volume of his Harrison Peel omnibus collections.

ANTHOLOGIES

The very busy and very talented Jonathan Strahan again dominated Australian anthologies this year. He was nominated for a Locus Award for Best Editor, and edited a number of Locus Recommended Reading Listed anthologies. Solaris Books released the SF anthology *Reach for Infinity*, which was also nominated for a Locus Award, *Fearsome Magics*, which along with *Infinity*, was nominated for an Aurealis Award. Strahan also edited *The Best Science Fiction and Fantasy of the Year: Volume Eight* for Nightshade Books, which was nominated for a Locus Award. Strahan also edited *Subterranean, Winter* 2014, for Subterranean Press.

Twelfth Planet Press had a very successful year with Alisa Krasnostein and Julia Rios' *Kaleidoscope* anthology, which won both the Ditmar and the Aurealis Award for Best Collection, the Tin Duck for Best Professional Production, and was listed in the Tiptree Award honour list and the Locus Recommended Reading List. Amal El-Mohtar's story "The Truth about Owls" from the anthology won Best Short Story in the Locus Awards, and Sean Williams' "The Legend Trap" won the Ditmar for Best Novella/Novelette. Dirk Flinthart's "Vanilla" won Best Young Adult Story at the Aurealis Awards, as well as many of the stories being shortlisted for the WSFA Small Press Award, Ditmar and Aurealis Awards. Krasnostein and Rios also released their first volume of *The Year's Best YA Speculative Fiction.*

Ticonderoga Publications released two anthologies in 2014, the Aurealis and Tin Duck-nominated steampunk romance anthology *Kisses by Clockwork*, edited by Liz Grzyb, which contained the Ditmar-nominated novelette "Escapement" by Stephanie Gunn and the Tin Duck Best Short Written Work story "Siri and the Chaos Maker" by Carol Ryles. The Ditmar-nominated *Year's Best Australian Fantasy and Horror* 2013, edited by Liz Grzyb and Talie Helene was also released.

Tehani Wessely edited two anthologies at Fablecroft this year: the second volume of digital year's best *Focus* 2013 and the fantasy anthology *Phantazein*. *Phantazein* deservedly collected a number of awards and nominations this year. It was nominated for the Aurealis Award for Best Anthology and the Best Collected Work Ditmar, and Charlotte Nash's "The Ghost of Hephaestus" was shortlisted for Best Fantasy Short Story in the Aurealis Awards as well as Best Novella in the Ditmars. Cat Sparks' "The Seventh Relic" won Best Short Story in the Ditmars, and "Bahamut" from Thoraiya Dyer was shortlisted. Kathleen Jennings also won the Ditmar for Best Artwork for her gorgeous cover.

Keith Stevenson edited *Dimension 6*, the Coeur de Lion annual anthology. Dominica Malcolm edited *Amok: An Anthology of Asia-Pacific Speculative Fiction* with Solarwyrm Press, which was nominated for an Aurealis Award for Best Anthology. Simon Petrie and Edwina Harvey edited *Use Only As Directed* from Peggy

Bright Books, which included Stephen Dedman's story "Large Friendly Letters" and was nominated for a Tin Duck Award for Best Short Written Work.

MAGAZINES

ASIM was nominated for a Hugo Award for Best Semiprozine, a fitting acknowledgement of the co-operative's longevity. *Andromeda Spaceways Inflight Magazine* released two issues in 2014: #59 and #60.

Australian-run *SQ Mag* became a paid market in 2014, released six issues, and included stories gaining much critical and popular acclaim. Alan Baxter's story "The Darkness in Clara" was nominated for a Ditmar Award, Michelle Jager's "Bones" was shortlisted for an Australian Shadows Award, and Rhoads Brazos' story "Tread Upon the Brittle Shell" was chosen for inclusion in Ellen Datlow's *Year's Best Horror vol. 7*. Issue 14 of the magazine won the Australian Shadows Award for Best Edited Work.

Review of Australian Fiction releases an issue with two short stories every fortnight in electronic subscription format. Angela Slatter's Aurealis Award-winning, Ditmar-nominated story "St Dymphna's School for Poison Girls" and Deborah Biancotti's Aurealis-nominated "The Executioner Goes Home" were two notable fantasy inclusions.

Aurealis Magazine released ten issues in 2014: issues 67 to 76, each fiction and non-fiction pieces. *Antipodean SF* released 12 issues in 2014, providing flash fiction in web-based and ebook format. David Conyers became the Arts and General Editor of Irish magazine *Albedo One* which released Issues 44 and 45 in 2014. *Dark Matter Zine* regularly publishes reviews, interviews, opinion pieces and guest blogs.

PODCASTS AND OTHER MEDIA

Impressively, *Galactic Suburbia* won the Hugo Award for Best Fancast this year, and was also nominated for the Ditmar and Tin Duck for Best Fan Production for Alisa Krasnostein, Tansy Rayner Roberts, Alexandra Pierce and Andrew Finch.

Kirstyn McDermott and Ian Mond's *The Writer and the Critic* won the Ditmar for Best Fan Publication. Gary K Wolfe & Jonathan Strahan's *The Coode Street Podcast* was nominated for a Tin Duck, and Sean Wright, Helen Stubbs, David McDonald, Alexandra Pierce, Sarah Parker, and Mark Webb were nominated for a Ditmar for *Galactic Chat*. Ion Newcombe's *Antipodean SF Radio Show* became a weekly podcast in March 2014, giving multiple flash fiction stories each week.

Kathleen Jennings' Aurealis-nominated "A Small Wild Magic" comic strip story was published in Kelly Link and Gavin J. Grant's *Monstrous Affections* anthology, released by Candlewick Press. She was awarded the Ditmar Awards for both Best Artwork and Best Fan Art, after all three shortlisted pieces in the Best Artwork category were Jennings'.

Shaun Tan was nominated for the Locus Awards Best Artist, and his picture book *Rules of Summer* (which was released in Australia in 2013, but in the US in 2014) was nominated for Best Art Book in the same awards. Fantasy/horror graphic novel *Mr Unpronounceable and the Sect of the Bleeding Eye* won Tim Molloy the Aurealis Award for Best Illustrated Book. *It Grows!*, Nick Stathopoulos's short film, was nominated for a Ditmar Award for Best Fan Production.

THE YEAR IN HORROR

NOVELS

2014 was an interesting year for horror novels in Australia, with some new authors breaking through with first publications, and some high profile cinema tie-ins with the *Wolf Creek* franchise. *Alice Through Blood-Stained Glass* (HarperCollins) by Dan Adams is a horror-rollick zombie retelling of *Alice in Wonderland*, released as an e-Book. *The Last Shot* (Allen & Unwin) by Michael Adams is a Young Adult adventure, continuing the narrative of psychic teen Danby in a post-apocalyptic world. Goldie Alexander published the YA verse novel *In Hades* (Celapene Press); driving recklessly in a stolen car, 17 year old street boy Kai and his young brother Rod, die and descend into the underworld. Keri Arthur's *Darkness Falls* (Piatkus) is the conclusion to the seven book *Dark Angels Series* centred around half-werewolf, half-Aedh Risa Jones. Keith Austin's *Snow, White* (Random House) is a YA twisted fairytale retelling. *Suicide Forest* (Ghillinnein Books) by Jeremy Bates is Book 1 in the *World's Scariest Places Occult & Supernatural Crime Series*; a legend is awoken in the Aokigahara forest outside of Tokyo. Alan Baxter's dark fantasy *Alex Caine Series* saw prolific publication with three titles—*Bound, Obsidian* and *Abduction*—being released by Harper Collins. Greig Beck published two novels with Momentum—*Gorgon* and *Book of the Dead (Matt Kearns 2)*; the latter is a Lovecraftian romp as protagonist Professor Matt Kearns investigates sinkholes that open to infernal realms and primordial monsters, and unravels the prophecies of Al Azif. *Depth Charging Ice Planet Goth* (John Hunt Publishing) by Andrez Bergen is a weird fiction murder mystery wending through the 1980s Goth scene. *Empties* (White Cat Publications) by Jay Caselberg sees a man investigate the abduction of his comatose wife by strange smiling men. *One Shot* (Arrant Press) by Tom Conyers is an apocalyptic thriller in which a virus turns the infected human population into crazed cannibals. *Uncle Adolf* (Ginninderra Press) by Craig Cormick boasts the strange blurb: "1982 and Adolf Hitler has been living anonymously on the south coast of New South Wales for almost thirty years." *Beckoning Blood* (Escape Publishing) by Daniel de Lorne is a Gothic vampire romance, the second in the *Bonds of Blood Series*.

Nathan M. Farrugia's *The Phoenix Variant* (Momentum) is a technothriller in a viral apocalypse. *Secrets Room* (Seven Tides of Nyx) by Kim Faulks; an abductee wakes trapped in a mysterious cell where torture and shock are used to manipulate a group of captives into revealing their darkest secrets. *Blood Work (Night Call 1)* by L.J. Hayward is an urban paranormal romance following the exploits of a vampire slaying hit team. Janis Hill's *Isis, Vampires and Ghosts -Oh My!* (Hague Publishing) is a light paranormal adventure with a smattering of horror tropes for flavour. Justine Larbalestier's *Razorhurst* (Allen & Unwin) is a highly original YA adventure set during the 1930s razor gangs of Sydney's Surrey Hills; street urchin Kelpie and beautiful, ambitious prostitute Dymphna are guided by the ghost of Dymphna's dead beau. 2014 saw the anticipated release *Origin—Wolf Creek 1* (Penguin Books Australia), the first of the Wolf Creek prequel novels, authored by film writer/director Greg

McLean and Aaron Sterns, and *Desolation Game—Wolf Creek 2* (Penguin Books Australia), the second Wolf Creek prequel novel authored by Greg McLean and Brett McBean; both exploring the formative crimes of fictional serial killer Mick Taylor made infamous in the 2005 feature film. *Origin—Wolf Creek 1* won the Australian Horror Writers' Association's Australian Shadows Award for Best Novel. *Desolation Game—Wolf Creek 2* was originally to be co-authored by Greg McLean and Paul Haines, who lost his battle to cancer in 2012.

Cassandra Page published *Isla's Inheritance* (Turquoise Morning Press); a teen psychic's powers are unlocked at a Halloween séance. Hoa Pham saw publication of *The Other Shore* (Seizure), winning Seizure's *Viva La Novella* competition; when the dead begin speaking to sixteen-year-old Kim Nguyen she is meshed in a web of adult and supernatural exploitation. *Devil City (The Lark Case Files 2)* published by Gestalt Publishing, is Christian Read's second book in a series about occult investigator Lark. Avril Sabine published two YA horror/paranormal romances, both with Broken Gate Publishing; *Retribution—Demon Hunters 2* concerns a demon hunter named Scarlet, and *Whispers in the Dark* is an urban paranormal with elements of romance and same sex relationships. Nova Weetman published a YA ghost story *The Haunting of Lily Frost* with the University of Queensland Press (UQP); a girl moves to a new town, new house, with a haunted attic . . . *Dark Child: Covens Rising*(Momentum) by Adina West is the second book in the Kat Chancer series, following the adventures of half-vampire pathologist protagonist; originally released as a five part serial. Justin Woolley's *A Town Called Dust* (Momentum); a YA thriller set in a walled city called Alice, with two teen protagonists battling hoards of undead ghouls.

COLLECTIONS

Collections in 2014 authored by a single author or a team of co-authors were frequently devoted to horror genre, or had a significant amount of horror fiction mixed with other genres. Ron Barton had two horror stories, "You'd Be Paranoid If You Knew You Were Next" and "Parent-Teacher Night of the Living Dead", in his *Paved With Words* collection. Morgan Bell self-published *Sniggerless Bondulations*, a debut collection of fifteen flash fiction stories. Greg Chapman's debut collection *Vaudeville and Other Nightmares* (Black Beacon Books), edited by Cameron Trost, is entirely devoted to the dark side. New Zealander William Cook saw publication with the collection *One Way Ticket: Suspense Crime Horror Thriller & Mystery Short* 2 (King Billy Publications). The prolific David Conyers released "The Elder Codex" and "The Spiraling Worm" (with John Sunseri) collected together in *The Elder Codex (The Harrison Peel Files Book 3)*. M.R. Cosby's *Dying Embers* (Satalyte Publishing) edited by Stephen Ormsby; tales of urban strangeness and transformation. New Zealander Sharon Hannaford included two horror tales, "So This Is Hell: Fergus's Story" and "Blood and Thunder: Razor's Story" in *A Short Trip to Hell—Hellcat Series Origins Volume* 1.

The Female Factory (Twelfth Planet Press) by Lisa L. Hannett and Angela Slatter was a dark fiction tour de force, with four stories, particularly noteworthy for the titular novella that combined a harrowing picture of early convict settlement with evoking Mary Shelley's *Frankenstein*. Brett Kiellerop's *The Cursed, Volume* 1 (Brevid Books) charted an ambiguous dark territory with several horror tales. David McDonald's *Cold Comfort and Other Tales* (Clan Destine Press) included his horror story "Our Land Abounds". Andrew J. McKiernan's stunning collection *Last Year, When We Were Young* (Satalyte Publishing) deservedly won the Australian Shadows Award for Best Collection. Angela Meyer's *Captives* (Inkerman & Blunt) collected flash fiction stories of misfortune, brushing darker themes such as Alzheimer's and electrocution. Ben Peek's collection *Dead Americans and Other Stories* (ChiZine Publications) included the dark "There Is Something So Quiet & Empty Inside Of You That It Must Be Something Precious". David Schembri released the substantial collection *Unearthly Fables* (The Writing Show and David Schembri Studios). C.M. Simpson self-published no less than four story collections, three of which contained some horror content: *365 Days of Flash Fiction, Short Stories and Poems from* 2013, *Vol. 2: The Year Just Gone, and Short Stories and Poems from* 2013, *Vol. 1: Remnants to Recent Years*. Angela Slatter saw publication of another excellent collection, *The Bitterwood Bible and Other Recountings* (Tartarus Press); the collection was nominated for a World Fantasy Award in the category of Best Collection. John T. Stolarczyk published the collection *Mist and Mirrors* (iUniverse); dark fantasy stories with strong horror themes. Janeen Webb's beautiful complex collection *Death at The Blue Elephant* (Ticonderoga Publications), edited by Russell B. Farr, included the original dark story "Skull Beach" and novella "The Lady of the Swamp"; the collection was nominated for a World Fantasy Award in the category of Best Collection.

STAND ALONE HORROR STORY PUBLICATIONS

An emerging trend in 2014 was the publication of short stories and novellas as stand-alone titles, the trend tracking with an increasing reader market for electronic editions. New Zealander William Cook published *Dead and Buried: A Supernatural Young Adult Thriller* (King Billy Publications); stand-alone e-book containing a supernatural coming-of-age ghost story that deals with the consequences of bullying. *Dreams of Destruction* by Shane Jiraiya Cummings, a Lovecraftian novella published as an e-edition, won the Paul Haines Award for Long Fiction (novella) awarded by the Australian Horror Writers Association (AHWA). Nick Falk published a children's comedy fantasy of novella length, *Billy is a Dragon 2: Werewolves Beware* (Random House Australia) incorporating the werewolf trope. Dirk Flinthart's novella *Sanction—Night Beast* 1.5 (FableCroft Publishing); the technothriller sequal to *Path of Night* concerning former detective Jen Morris. Jason Franks published two related stand-alone story titles both with Possible Press; *Hellhound on my Trail (Bloody Waters Book Two)* details how bluesman Bad Jack Saunders meets a mysterious stranger at a crossroads at midnight, and *The Martyr and the Qarin (Bloody Waters Book Three)* continues the story of shred guitarist Clarice Marnier. *Dead Lucky* by Rebecca Fung was released as part of the *One Night Stands Series*, published by Perpetual Motion Machine Publishing. George Ivanoff's novella-length story for children *The Haunting of Spook House: You Choose . . . 4* (Random House Australia) is a haunted house adventure for children, in the "choose your own adventure" style of branching narrative. Trent Jamieson's novella *The Memory of Death (Death Works 4)* published by Momentum continues the story of corporate Grim Reaper Steven de Selby, as an addenda to the *Deathworks Novel Trilogy*. R.R.Lang self-published the stand-alone story *Army Dreamers* as an e-book. Theresa A.

O'Dea's *Professional Bitches* is described by the author as "a horror fiction novella . . . about how two close girlfriends get involved in the sex industry." Birch Plaise saw publication with *Beauty's Curse: A Horror Novelette* (Bowman Press) a historical horror romance. D.L. Richardson's novella *Poison in the Pond* is a paranormal psychological thriller about abduction and obsession. Angela Slatter's *Home and Hearth* was released as a chapbook from Spectral Press. J.M. Thorne's *Watching* (Infinity Dreaming) is a horror novella about alien invasion.

ANTHOLOGIES—ANTIPODEAN

2014 was another massive year for anthologies, with many produced by Australian publishers, including some interesting regional publications. 18, edited by Belinda Hamilton, was published by the writers' group Vision Writers; the anthology included horror tales "Low Life" by Allan Walsh, "The Black Queen" by Melanie Bird, and "18 Barr St" by Christopher Kneipp. *Amok: An Anthology of Asia-Pacific Speculative Fiction* (Solarwyrm Press) edited by Dominica Malcolm, featured a number of horror stories including the editor's own "When The Rice Was Gone", Robert Mammone's "Suffer the Children", Barry Rosenberg's "The Dead of the Night"and David Kernot's "The Lost People". Jenny Blackford's poem "An Afterlife of Stone" appeared in *A Slow Combusting Hymn: Poetry from and about Newcastle and the Hunter Region*, edited by Jean Kent and Kit Kelen (ASM and Cerberus Press). Another major regional anthology, *Novascapes: A Speculative Fiction Anthology from the Hunter Region of Australia* 1 (Invisible Elephant Press) edited by C.E. Page featured writers living in or having originally come from the Hunter, Newcastle and Central Coast regions of New South Wales; the anthology included stories from Margo Lanagan, Kirstyn McDermott, Jenny Blackford, Janeen Webb, Russell Blackford, Danuta Electra Raine, Catherine Moffat, Andrew C. Jaxson, Willie Southgate, Blake Liddell, Bethany Kable, Thoraiya Dyer and editor C.E. Page; this was funded by a Pozible campaign that raised $3,000.

Coeur de Lion published *Dimension6* in several editions in 2014; edited by Keith Stevenson, *Dimension6 speculative fiction* 1 featured Jason Nahrung's "The Preservation Society";

Dimension6 speculative fiction 2 included "He Ain't Dead" by Robert N. Stephenson and "Upon a Distant Shore" by Alan Baxter; *Dimension6 speculative fiction* included the "New Chronicles of Andras Thorn" by Cat Sparks and "The Shark God Covenant" by Robert Hood.

disquiet edited by Tracie McBride and John Irvine, was dedicated to dark fiction by Australian and New Zealand authors; published by Finnish publisher Creativia, notable stories include editor Tracie McBride's stories "Riding The Storm" and "The Truth About Dolphins"; Peter Friend's "Lightning Ridge"; Charlotte Kieft's "Chiaroscuro"; Ryn Lilley's "The Rainbow Effect"; Eileen Mueller's "The Watch Serpent"; Lee Pletzers "Water"; A.J. Ponder's "The Collector"; and "Tracks" by Tim Jones.

Fearsome Magics (Solaris) edited by Jonathan Strahan included the horror stories "The Nursery Corner" by Kaaron Warren and "The Changeling" by James Bradley. *Kisses by Clockwork* (Ticonderoga Publications) edited by Liz Grzyb had a few darker moments with "The Tic-Toc Boy of Constantinople" by Anthony Panegyres and Angela Rega's "The Law of Love".

Christopher Marcatili saw publication of "The Necrophage"in *Site Lines* (Xoum); Site Lines is the University of Technology (Sydney) Writers' Anthology. FableCroft published *Phantazein* edited by Tehani Wessely; this included dark moments with "The Seventh Relic" by Cat Sparks and "Kneaded" by S.G. Larner.

SNAFU: An Anthology of Military Horror (Cohesion Press) edited by Geoff Brown and Amanda J. Spedding; this eight story anthology includes Australian writer Greig Beck's "The Fossil". Cohesion Press also released *SNAFU: Heroes: An Anthology of Military Horror*, again edited by Geoff Brown and Amanda J. Spedding, a supplemental volume to *SNAFU*, with more short stories and novellas from four military horror writers (no antipodean contributors).

Black Beacon Books published *Subtropical Suspense* edited by Cameron Trost. This anthology included a number of very fine stories of supernatural horror or horror-tinged realism, including: "The Deluge" by Gerry Huntman, "Blood on the Ice" by Helen Stubbs, "The Final Cut" by Linda Brucesmith, "Downpour" by Sophie Yorkston, and the compelling "Scarlett Fever" by Alice Godwin.

Suspended in Dusk (Books of the Dead Press), the editorial debut from Simon Dewar, included notable Australian contributors: S.G. Larner's "Shades of Memory", Angela Slatter's "The Way Of All Flesh", Tom Dullemond's "Would To God That We Were There", and Alan Baxter's "Shadows of the Lonely Dead"; the latter won the Australian Shadows Award for Best Short Fiction. Dark Continents Publishing released *The Sea* anthology, edited by Nerine Dorman, with noteworthy dark tales "The Wire Bird" by Simon Dewar and "A Drought of Tears" by Rob Porteous. (Porteous won the Conflux 2014 short story comp with the story "Death Watch".) Dark Continents, which was run by a team including Australian writer Tracie McBride, closed their doors in 2014. Spineless Wonders published *The World to Come* edited by Patrick West and Om Prakash Dwivedi; notable antipodean contributions were "When The Birds Come" by Emily Riches, and Leah Swann's "Of Life Below". Busybird Publishing released *[unititled]* 6 including D. Robert Grixti's "Pretty Birds" and Adrienne Tam's "The Human Child". Peggy Bright Books published *Use Only As Directed* edited by Simon Petrie and Edwina Harvey, with darker tales being Alex Isle's "The Kind Neighbours of Hell", Claire McKenna's "Yard", Michelle Goldsmith's "The Climbing Tree", Janeen Webb's "Future Perfect", and Charlotte Nash's "Dellinger".

ANTHOLOGY PUBLICATIONS—INTERNATIONAL

Antipodean authors saw considerable success with publication of short stories dispersed across a wide array of overseas anthologies in 2014. Paul Mannering's "The Princess and the Flea" was published in the charity horror anthology *At Hell's Gates: Volume One: Existing Worlds*, edited by Monique Happy and James Crawford; all proceeds from sales of this anthology went to the Intrepid Fallen Heroes Fund. Lee Pletzers published "SARAH" in the *Bellator* anthology. G.N. Braun saw publication of "Happy Hour" in *Blood Type: An Anthology of Vampire SF on the Cutting Edge* (Nightscape Press), edited by Robert S. Wilson; all net proceeds went to The Cystic Fibrosis Trust. David Grigg's "This Too, Too Solid Flesh" was published in *Cadavers* (KnightWatch Press) edited by G.P. Stratford. Michael Grey published the irreverent Lovecraftian steampunk tale "1884" in *Cthulhu Lives!* (Ghostwood Books). The *Demonic Visions* anthology edited by Chris Robertson saw three in the series published in 2014: *Demonic Visions: 50 Horror Tales 3* included from Rebecca Fung's "Anything for Love", and Raymond Gates's "Show and Tell"; *Demonic Visions: 50 Horror Tales 4* included Rebecca Fung's "Snake Season" and Raymond Gates's "The Mind of an Artiste"; and *Demonic Visions: 50 Horror Tales 5* included Raymond Gates's "Continuity" and Rebecca Fung's "The Eleventh Piper". Rebecca Fung also saw publication with "The Mummified Monk" in *Daylight Dims: Volume Two* (Stealth Fiction) edited by Kristopher Mallory. Angela Slatter published the classic "Let the Words Take You" in *Dreams of Shadow and Smoke: Stories for J.S. Le Fanu* (Swan River Press) edited by Brian J. Showers.

Equilibrium Overturned (Grey Matter Press) edited by Anthony Rivera and Sharon Lawson included Australian contributions— Jay Caselberg's "Compartmental", and S.G. Larner's "Perfect Soldiers". Chaosium's *Extreme Planets* anthology, the follow up to the 2013 *Call of Cthulhu* anthology, edited by David Conyers, David Kernot and Jeff Harris, featured "The Hyphal Layer" by Meryl Ferguson, and Conyers and David Kernot's own "Petrochemical Skies". David Conyers saw publication with "Downsizing in the Technopoly" in *Tides of Possibility* (Slipjack Publishing) edited by K. J. Russell. *Fearful Symmetries* (ChiZine Publications) edited by Ellen Datlow included Terry Dowling's "The Four Darks", Garth Nix's "Shay Corsham Worsted", and Kaaron Warren's confronting "Bridge of Sighs". Barry Rosenberg published "Finding His Roots" in *Growing Concerns* (Chupa Cabra House), edited by Alex Hurst. Rebecca Fung saw publication of "Everywhere Eyes" in *Her Dark Voice* (Knightwatch Press); edited by Theresa Derwin, this selection female speculative authors was a fundraiser with the proceeds going to a Breast Cancer charity. Angela Slatter's "Only the Dead and the Moonstruck" appeared in *Letters to Lovecraft* (Stone Skin Press) edited by Jesse Bullington. Barry Rosenberg's "Dread Man Walking" appeared in *Life of the Dead* (Martinus Publishing). Terry Dowling's "Corpse Rose" appeared in *Nightmare Carnival* (Dark Horse Books) edited by Ellen Datlow. The *Night Terrors III* (Blood Bound Books) anthology, edited by G. Winston Hyatt, Theresa Dillon, and Marc Ciccarone, included "Of The Color Turmeric, Climbing on Fingertips" by Gerry Huntman and "Sailor's Rest" by Jay Caselberg. Caselberg's

"Bite Marks", appeared in *Noir* (NewCon Press), edited by Ian Whates. David Grigg's "The Miracle Cure" appeared in *NovoPulp Anthology Volume 2* (Hermit Studio), edited by H. David Blalock, Emil Hugo, Charles Barouch, Chris Capps, and Zachary Seibert.

Cameron Trost's "Lauren" was published in *Of Devils and Deviants: An Anthology of Erotic Horror* (Crowded Quarantine Publications), edited by Adam Millard and Zoe-Ray Millard. Ron Barton's "Parent-Teacher Night of the Living Dead" saw publication in *Paved With Words*. Havva Murat's "Where Once Were Hearts" appeared in *Portals* (Roane Publishing). Rebecca Fung's "Eyes" appeared in *Potatoes* (KnightWatch Press). Ashlee Scheuerman's "Dyscrasia" saw publication in the anthology *Qualia Nous* (Written Backwards). Jeremy Szal's "Contact Zero" appeared in *Quantum Fairy Tales*. William Cook's story "Pretty Boy" appeared in the *Serial Killers Quattuor* anthology edited by James Ward Kirk (James Ward Kirk Publishing). Kaaron Warren's "Death's Door Café" was published in *Shadows & Tall Trees* (ChiZine Publications), edited by Michael Kelly. Havva Murat's "Encantado" appeared in *Spooktacular Seductions* (Roane Publishing).

G.N. Braun's "Junksick" was published in *Tales from the Lake Volume 1* (Crystal Lake Publishing) edited by Joe Mynhardt. Gerry Huntman's "The Past Catching Up" appeared in *The Badlands* (Dead Guns Press). Rick Kennett's "Dolls for Another Day" was published in *The Ghosts & Scholars Book of Shadows: Vol 2* (Sarob Press) in a limited and numbered edition hardcover collecting 'prequels and sequels' honouring eleven classic ghost stories of M.R. James, edited by Rosemary Pardoe. "The Optimist" by Kaaron Warren appeared in *The Many Tortures of Anthony Cardno*, edited by Anthony Cardno for Talekyn Press. Angela Slatter's "The October Widow" appeared in *The Spectral Book of Horror Stories* (Spectral Press) edited by Mark Morris. Kaaron Warren's "The Lantern Men" appeared in *Two Hundred and Twenty-One Baker Streets* (Abbaddon Books) edited by David Thomas Moore.

"Not as it Seems" by Lee Pletzers was published in the *These Vampires Still Don't Sparkle* anthology (Sky Warrior Book Publishing) edited by Carol Hightshoe. "To Not-Be Or To Not Not-Be" by Barry Rosenberg appeared in *Vampires*

Suck: Alternate Hilarities 2 (Strange Musings Press), edited by Giovanni Valentino. "Darkness In The Mountain Of Light" by Gerry Huntman appeared in *What Lies Beneath* (Horrified Press), edited by Dorothy Davies. Co-authored story "The Bullet and the Flesh" from David Conyers and David Kernot appeared in *World War Cthulhu* (Dark Regions Press), edited by Brian M. Sammons and Glynn Owen Barrass. Shauna O'Meara's story "Beneath the Surface of Two Kills" appeared in the competitive *Writers of the Future Volume 30* (Galaxy Press). Angela Slatter's "Red Dust, White Earth" was published in *Zombie Apocalypse! Endgame* (Constable & Robinson) edited by Stephen Jones. Anthony Ferguson's "The Ardent Dead" was published in *Zom Rom Com: A Zombie Anthology* (KnightWatch Press) edited by Stewart Hotston.

MAGAZINES & JOURNALS—ANTIPODEAN

Antipodean magazines continued to be a central market for horror short fiction publication in 2014, with one notable year-long publication lapse: *Midnight Echo* magazine, published by the Australian Horror Writers Association (AHWA) had an intermission to reconsider the viability of the hardcopy print format; during this time of restructure Cassie Britland handed over the role of *Midnight Echo* Executive Editor to Daniel Miller, and then opted to retain the role. The magazine moved to digital formats only, and the guest editor working with AHWA on *Midnight Echo* in a pre-production capacity during 2014 was Kaaron Warren. Dan Rabarts story *Children of the Tide* was published on the Midnight Echo website in January 2014; the story was the winner of the Melbourne Zombie Convention Short Story competition in 2013.

Andromeda Spaceways Inflight Magazine published some horror fiction in their genre mix. *Andromeda Spaceways Inflight Magazine* 59 included "That Which We Believe" by Steve Cameron (a novelette work-shopped by the late Paul Haines during Cameron's AHWA mentorship) and Caitlene Cooke's "The Zombie Haiku". Michelle Goldsmith's story "Of Gold and Dust" was published in *Andromeda Spaceways Inflight Magazine* 60. *Aurealis* magazine (Chimaera Publications) also included some darker offerings with David Stevens's "Avoiding Gagarin" in *Aurealis* 68, Matthew J. Morrison's "The Stain on the Lake" in *Aurealis* 70, Allan Chen's

"Kisses with Teeth" in *Aurealis* 73, and Leife Shallcross's "Music for an Ivory Violin" in *Aurealis* 74.

The *Review of Australian Fiction* continued to prove a welcoming market for dark genre fiction, with a number of prominent horror writers contributing; Deborah Biancotti saw publication there twice in 2014, with "No Mercy for the Executioner" in *Review of Australian Fiction, Volume 11, Issue 6*, and "The Executioner Goes Home" in *Review of Australian Fiction, Volume 9, Issue 2*. Thoraiya Dyer's story "Burning the Lady's Bones" also appeared in *Review of Australian Fiction, Volume 11, Issue 6*. Lisa L. Hannett's "The Beat That Billie Bore" appeared in *Review of Australian Fiction Review of Australian Fiction Volume 11, Issue 1*. Kirstyn McDermott's novella "By the Moon's Good Grace" was published in *Review of Australian Fiction, Vol.12, Issue 3*—a dark feminist retelling of the "Little Red Riding Hood" tale, reflecting the author's PhD focus on fairy tales. Jason Fischer's "Percy's War" was published in *Review of Australian Fiction, Volume 12, Issue 2*.

SQ Mag (IFWG Publishing Australia), edited by Sophie Yorkston, had a massive year, publishing six online editions in 2014, a number of which featured Australian horror, including an Australiana Special Edition. The online magazine won an Australian Shadows Award for Best Edited Work. *SQ Mag 12 (January 2014)* featured New Zealander Lee Murray's unsettling boarding school vignette "Inside Ferndale". *SQ Mag 13* (March 2014) included the horror story "Keeping an Open Mind" by New Zealander Dan Rabarts, "The Girl in the Glass Bottle" by Brian G. Ross, and "The Church of Asag" by Cameron Trost. *SQ Mag 14 Special Edition: Australiana* (May 2014) included some stellar Australian fiction—"The Darkness in Clara" by Alan Baxter, "Eleanor Atkins is Dead and Her House is Boarded Up" by Kaaron Warren, "Chasing the Storm" by S. G. Larner, "Bones" by Michelle Jager, as well as an interview with Wolf Creek prequel authors Aaron Sterns and Brett McBean, and an opinion piece feature "State of Play of Australian Speculative Fiction" in two parts, with "The State of Science Fiction and Fantasy in Australia" penned by Tehani Wessely, and "The State of Horror Literature in Australia" authored by Geoff Brown; the latter generated some critical discourse about omissions and balance, a discussion comported in the very civilized manner of Australian genre debate. *SQ Mag* 15 *(July 2014)* included "Metempsychosis" by Jason Franks. *SQ Mag* 16 *(September 2014)* included "The Nanofabricated Truth" by David Conyers.

A number of other magazines and journals featured a smattering of horror offerings during the year. Cassandra Downie's story "The Driver" was published in *Dark Matter Zine: Unmasked Special Edition* edited by Nalini Haynes. S.G.Larner's 'Banned Girl' appeared in *FictionVale Episode 4*, edited by Jodi Cleghorn. Jenny Blackford's poem "I made myself a lover" was published in Melbourne-based new publication *Gargouille Literary Journal, Issue 1*, December 2014. James Bradley's creepy "Skinsuit" was published in *Island 137*. Lucy Sussex published a flash vignette "The Grave of the Barbie Doll" on Nike Sulway's website perilousadventures.net. David Stevens saw publication of "Good Boy" in Perth-based *Regime Magazine of New Writing* (Regime Books), edited by Peter Jeffery and Chris Palazzolo. Rebecca Fraser's "Peroxide and the Doppelganger", a hallucinogenic punk rock trip to the shadow-self, by was published in *The Quarry Journal* 4 a student-edited annual journal published with the support of Macquarie University's Department of English.

MAGAZINES & JOURNALS—INTERNATIONAL

Authors continued to look to overseas magazines for publication with great success. The prolific David Conyers saw publication of "The Shaping Man" in Irish magazine *Albedo One #45*, edited by Robert Neilson. Emma Osborne's "Zip" appeared in *Bastion Science Fiction Magazine, Issue 5, August 2014*, edited by R. Leigh Hennig and William Delman. Jeremy Szal's "The Rainmaker" was published in *Bewildering Stories Issue 578*, flash fiction edited by Charles C. Cole. Brian G. Ross saw publication of "A Week in the Life Of . . . " in *Dark Moon Digest, Issue 15* (Perpetual Motion Machine) edited by *Lori Michelle. Daily Science Fiction* edited by Michele-Lee Barasso and Jonathan Laden published "Mephisto"by Alan Baxter in *Daily Science Fiction, June 23, 2014* and "Eight Pieces of Losing You" by Samantha Murray in *Daily Science Fiction, 2 April 2014*. S.G. Larner's "Labyrinth Hope" appeared in Ontario-based YA magazine *Inaccurate Realities 5: Monsters*, edited by Christa S.

Lovecraft eZine, edited by Mike Davis, included Australian works "War Gods of Men" co-authored by David Conyers and David Kernot in *Lovecraft eZine* #31, *June* 2014, and "The Eldritch Force" co-authored by an ensemble comprised of Peter Rawlik, Glynn Owen Barrass, Brian M. Sammons. Bruce L. Priddy, Robert M. Price, Rick Lai and David Conyers, in *Lovecraft eZine* #28, *February* 2014. Jeremy Szal sold "Without a Trace"to *MicroHorror*, edited by Nathen Rosen. Ben Peek's "Upon The Body" was published in *Nightmare Magazine* #23 *(August* 2014*)*, edited by John Joseph Adams.

Postscripts 32/33: *Far Voyager* (PS Publishing) edited by Nick Gevers included "A Girl of Feather and Music" by Lisa L. Hannett, "Winter Children" by Angela Slatter, "Thirty Three Tears to a Teaspoon" by Alan Baxter, "Rusalka Salon For Girls Who Like To Get Their Hair Wet" by Angie Rega, and "The Psychometrist" by Suzanne Willis. Willis also saw publication with "The Rattenfänger's Pipe" in the re-imagined *Schlock Magazine February* 2014 *Issue*. Ben Peek published "In The Broken City" in *Shimmer* 18, guest edited by Ann Vandermeer. Emma Osborne's "The Box Wife" appeared in *Shock Totem: Curious Tales of the Macabre and Twisted* 9.

Brian G. Ross published "The Beast of Broken Rock" at paying market *T. Gene Davis's Speculative Blog.* "The Last Door: A Prelude—The Five Arches" by David Conyers was published at the website of independent video game studio *The Game Kitchen* (Spain). Lee Pletzers published "Two Kinds of Animal" in *The Literary Hatchet* #10 (Pear Tree Press), short story editor Eugene Hosey. *Tor.com,* webzine department of the genre book publisher, included Australian contributions with "The Walking-Stick Forest" by Anna Tambour, and "Night-time in Caeli-Amur" by Rjurik Davidson. Lloyd Connor's "Some Corner of a Dorset Field that is Forever Arabia" appeared in *Three-Lobed Burning Eye* #25, edited by Andrew S. Fuller. Rebecca Fung's "Little Nightmare" appeared in *Voluted Tales* 14 *(June-July* 2014*)*, edited by Becca Butcher.

Spectral Realms No. 1 *Summer* 2014, edited by S.T. Joshi for Hippocampus Press, featured an extensive array of Australian weird poets in the table of contents (not all contributions were the first publication): Leigh Blackmore contributed "Emeraldesse" and

"In Splendor All Arrayed" and "Lines on a Drawing by Hannes Bok"; Kyla Lee Ward contributed "Necromancy"; Margaret Curtis contributed "The Witches' House"; Charles Lovecraft contributed "A Weird Tale" and "Night Visit'" and "Afrasiab Down the Oxus"; David Schembri contributed "Beneath the Ferny Trees" and "Note of the Executioner"; Phillip A. Ellis contributed "As Told to My Infant Grandchildren" and "Omens from Afar".

ANTIPODEAN HORROR FILMS

2014 saw the production of many feature length Australian horror films. Australian-Canadian psychological horror film, *The Babadook*, in which a troubled widow, and her six-year-old son, are menaced by an evil entity; written and directed by Jennifer Kent, the film was shown at the 2014 Sundance Film Festival to critical acclaim. *Lemon Tree Passage*, the directorial debut by David James Campbell, was based upon an urban legend about a haunted road in New South Wales. *Plague*, directed by Kostas Ouzas and Nick Kozakis, written by Ouzas; a couple struggle to survive the zombie apocalypse. The film premiered at the Fantastic Planet Sci-Fi, Horror, and Fantasy Film Festival; Screen Media Films bought US distribution rights after the film played at the Marché du Film at Cannes. *Wyrmwood* (alternative title *Wyrmwood: Road of the Dead*), an action-horror film and the feature directorial debut of Kiah Roache-Turner; the film tells the story of an outback mechanic battling through the zombie apocalypse; the film debuted at Fantastic Fest in Austin, Texas. *I, Frankenstein*, directed by Stuart Beattie, in which Frankenstein's monster is caught in a war between two immortal clans; the film was nominated for the Australian Screen Sound Guild Feature Film Soundtrack of the Year award. *Charlie's Farm*, directed by Chris Sun; four friends venture into the outback to explore the site where a family were killed by an angry mob. *Apocalyptic*, directed by Glenn Triggs; a news crew is ensnared by a doomsday cult; winner of the Haunted Award at the British Horror Film Festival.

Inner Demon, directed by Ursula Dabrowsky; in the follow up to *Family Demons*, a teenage girl abducted by serial killers discovers their killing ground is haunted by a malevolent spirit; the film won in three categories at A Night of Horror International Film Festival; Best Australian Feature; Best Australian Director;

Best Female Performance (Sarah Jeavons). *The Fear of Darkness*, directed by Christopher Fitchett; a psychiatrist must confront a creature dwelling in her unconscious as she investigates a supernatural disappearance—winner for Best Sound in FilmQuest Cthulhu, FilmQuest Film Festival, USA. *Throwback*, directed by Travis Bain, in which explorers tangle with a Yowie in Far North Queensland. *There's Something in the Pilliga* directed by Dane Millerd; an indie film crew seek out the legendary Pilliga Yowie,—or "Jingra"—in a remote part of New South Wales. *Into the Deep*; American college students making an audition tape for an extreme game show find themselves stranded in baited water surrounded by Great White Sharks. *Beckoning the Butcher* directed by Dale Trott; teens in an isolated house summon an evil spirit. *Killervision* directed by Dale Trott; a brain-injured man is tormented by visions of his friends being murdered while watching B grade movies. *Infected Paradise* directed by Julian Cheah; holiday makers on Seagull Island, a paradise off the north coast of Western Australia, have their serene retreat interrupted when a soldier infected with an experimental virus washes up on the beach. *Silent Eyes* directed by James Peniata; a serial killer rampages unchecked. *The Ghost of Victoria Park* directed by Matthew Dixon; paranormal investigators explore a crossroad on an abandoned train line where a series of mysterious murders and unexplained deaths have occurred. *Escape to Entrapment* directed by Carolyn Harris; a retelling of historic events when seven escaped convicts resort to cannibalism in the Tasmanian wilderness.

Housebound, the New Zealand horror comedy feature film written, edited, and directed by Gerard Johnstone, had a world premiere at South by Southwest in March 2014. *ABCs of Death 2*, sequel to the 2012 film *The ABCs of Death*, is an international (New Zealand/Japan/American) anthology horror comedy showcasing twenty-six short films by different directors. *I Survived a Zombie Holocaust,* directed and written by Guy Pigden, premiered in Dunedin, New Zealand. Comedy vampire mockumentary *What We Do in the Shadows*, directed and written by Taika Waititi and Jemaine Clement, premiered at the Sundance Film Festival in January 2014; the film had a limited US release and drew $6.9 million at the box office.

2014 also saw many short horror films completed and released; from Australia notable works include: B-grade horror comedy *It Grows!*, directed by Ryan Cauchi & Nick Stathopoulos, in which a cyberchondriac with a floundering relationship with his girlfriend (played by writer Cat Sparks) has something weird growing in his garden; the film was nominated for the Aurealis Convenors' Award for Excellence, and won the Ditmar Award for Best Fan Publication in Any Medium. *Dark Origins*, in which a psychologist discovers the terrifying trauma haunting her young patient, directed by Evan Randall Green, saw stunning success in overseas showings— winner of the Audience Choice Award: Best Short Screenplay at the International Film Festival of Cinematic Arts Los Angeles, winner of Best Actress (Rosie Keogh) and Best Narrative Short at the Los Angeles Cinema Festival of Hollywood; winner of Best Actress and Best Narrative Short at the Louisville Fright Night Film Fest, and winner of Best Performance (Rosie Keogh) at the Route 66 Film Festival. *Salvage*, directed by Daniel Flood; a lone rescue worker scours an abandoned region. *The Waiting Game*, directed by Jerome Velinksy; a girl leaves a house party & walks home alone. *Schoolies Massacre*, directed by Benjamin Morton; a masked killer crashes schools festivities.

In New Zealand horror short films, the undead were popular! In *Clear Eyes: Scourge of the Zombies*, directed by Fred Potts, a 14 year old girl encounters a kind of fast intelligent sub- species of zombie, nicknamed the "clear eyes". *Outer Darkness* directed by Aaron Falvey; a small group try to survive the zombie apocalypse. *A Love Story* directed by Steven Baker; a woman in a remote location retreats into a fantasy world, while her zombie husband is tied to a tree outside their house. *Umbra*, directed by Bryn Tilly, depicts the 'tenebrous fever dream' of a transforming vampire. *Cry Wolf* directed Aaron Falvey; a posse of drunken revelers encounters a mythological wolf creature. *The Pale One* directed by Luke McLean; pale spirits (Patupaiarehe, Turehu, Ngati Hotu and Urukehu) from Maori mythology dwell in the forest and mountains. *The Malthouse* directed by Phil McKinnon and Aaron Falvey; partying kids at an abandoned malthouse awaken a supernatural presence. *There Are No Robots* directed by Stephen Ross; a man seeks psychiatric help for his morbid aversion to robots. *Jelly Tip Jimmy*, directed by Scott Satherley; the story of a nightmare neighbour. *Another Mouth to Feed* directed by Cameron Pitney; psychological thriller about impossible geometry and madness. *The Intruder* directed by Léah McVeagh; two selfie videos uploaded to Instagram document a girl's demise. *The Mirage Complex* directed by Justine Law and Mark Strachan; a comedy horror animation depicting a psychotic episode whilst watching horror movies.

•••••••••••

REMEMBERED

Graham Stone, 88, bibliographer, Australian SF authority and recipient of the A. Bertram Chandler award; Rocky Wood, 55, New Zealand-born Australian Bram Stoker Award-winning writer and researcher, President of the HWA; Brian Clarke, Western Australian book collector and fan; Mel Tregonning, 31, Western Australian genre artist; Graham Joyce, 59, British World Fantasy Award-winner; Matthew Richell, 41, Hachette Australia CEO; Jay Lake, 49, American award-winning fantasy writer; Lucius Shepard, 70, American multiple World Fantasy Award-winning writer; Michael Shea, 67, American World Fantasy Award winner; Neal Barrett, Jr., 84, American SFWA Author Emeritus; Gough Whitlam AC QC, 98, former Australian Prime Minister, established the independent Australia Council for the Arts; Ida Elizabeth Osbourne, 98, founder of ABC's Argonauts Club.

ROCKY WOOD

19 OCTOBER 1959 – 1 DECEMBER 2014

Rocky Wood, born in Wellington, New Zealand, and raising his own family in Melbourne, Australia, has the distinction of being the first author to be President of the Horror Writers' Association from outside of North America and Europe—a far too dry way of saying that the affable, quirky Rocky was an "international guy" and he derived *so much fun* from being involved in the horror writing community on the biggest scale. His great passion for researching and publishing about the works of Stephen King also spoke of his mind gravitating to *towering* talent; you figure out what makes Stephen King's lexicon tick, and you hold the Rosetta Stone to appreciating horror of the late-twentieth and twenty-first century.

Rocky's legacy to the HWA, which he developed without fanfare, political or critical discourse, was to build greater diversity into the association. He built bridges between Australia and international horror markets, by actively recruiting Australian writers to participate in the Bram Stoker Awards Committees—notably many of those writers were women. (If you have met Rocky's very impressive partner and daughters, his affinity for valuing strong women makes personal sense.) When Rocky's illness robbed him of the ability to move and speak, he continued to put tremendous energy into corresponding with both the elite professionals and the aspiring and emerging writers; regardless of how advanced they were in their publishing journey, he was *interested* in everyone.

Rocky Wood was a writer, researcher, and a leader, but the talent that seems to overarch the others, in speaking to his compatriots both in Australia and overseas, is there is an entire community of horror writers who regarded him to be their individual mentor—and are bemused to discover he invested time and interest in a staggering number of writer's careers. As King himself paid tribute to Rocky—"Man, I really liked that guy."

— Talie Helene

THE
YEAR'S BEST
AUSTRALIAN
FANTASY
&
HORROR
~ 2014 ~

THE FIFTH ANNUAL
COLLECTION

CORPSE ROSE

TERRY DOWLING

Not counting the viewports in whatever Apollo CSMs were attached to it during its short active life, Skylab only had the single window in its main wardroom. And when the mission crew finally departed in 1974 and the first US space station was officially abandoned in space at last, the light of Earth shone through that window for more than five years before the station fell from orbit in July 1979, lighting a chill silence broken only by the vagaries of temperature and the occasional peppering of micro-particles against the hull sounding in whatever unvented gases remained, in many ways the noises most human habitats make. For a time Skylab became the newest kind of haunted house, though all stories of the face peering in that solitary window—and, worse yet, peering out—are merely that, stories, with no possible basis in fact. But peering in or out, it is one of the world's oddest supra-urban myths: this notion of a face in the wardroom window of Skylab before it fell and, yes, *as* it fell.

—Heinrich Fleymann

The day Jeremy Scott Renton turned eleven, a circus ran away to join him.

Not all at once, mind, but the thirteen members of the Corpse Rose Heirloom Carnival and Former Circus (to give it its full name) came to check him out and give their approval, arriving secretly in their ones and twos, never making a fuss, never drawing too much attention. They stayed long enough for the troupe to gather once more, doing the usual mufti work in bars, stocking supermarket shelves, cleaning swimming pools until they had finally assembled, all thirteen, then confirmed him as theirs and them as his, and went their various ways again.

Every single one had to approve, of course, theirs being one of the seven great lost and hidden carnivals of the world. Things were done differently in the Heirloom Carnivals, or the Sly Carnivals as they were sometimes called—and the Corpse Rose Heirloom Carnival and Former Circus followed the old protocols to the letter.

As for Jeremy Scott Renton—Jem to his friends—he wouldn't learn that it had happened at all for another twenty-five years, eleven days after a carefully placed operative persuaded both a doting grandmother and fond older sister in Perth that a round-trip ticket on the Indian-Pacific and a week at Cottesloe Beach would be the perfect birthday gift for a 36-year-old grandson and younger brother just back from five years with the Australian Design Council in London. The Indian-Pacific running from Sydney to Perth via Adelaide was one of the remaining great train journeys in the world, all 2698 miles of it, and it seemed like a grand idea.

Jem had five weeks' leave owing and was glad to spend part of it with his west-coast kin before settling down to his new posting. He thoroughly enjoyed the Sydney to Adelaide leg of the journey and had every expectation of enjoying the longer haul across the vast Nullarbor Plain as well. Outback Australia was one of the no-time, slow-time places of the world and, by association, so too was the inside of the Indian-Pacific when it made that crossing.

It was when the train made its customary stop at the not-quite-ghost-town of Cook, 513 miles north-west of Port Augusta in the middle of the Nullarbor, population anything from four to fifteen on an Indian-Pacific day, that what had been set in motion twenty-five years before reached the end of this particular recruitment phase, and the next part of the old Sly Carnival spell that had planted the seed of an idea with grandmother and sister was engaged.

Jem was standing with a hundred or so other passengers by the trackside stalls and pull-up shopfronts, stretching his legs in the heat and glare and examining the souvenir tea-towels, velveteen cushion covers, and other handcrafts with half a mind of getting something for his Gran. The long blast of a car horn made him look up to see a battered old Jeep Cherokee arrive in its cloud of dust, making him immediately think that some last-minute passenger was joining the train.

Jem noticed two things then: the weathered, thirty-something brunette in work shirt, jeans, and boots who climbed out from behind the wheel, a tall, solidly built woman—statuesque was the word—and the motif on the vehicle's door: a coffin with a bright red rose laid across it, with maybe half a dozen words underneath.

It was that motif—coffin and rose inside its faded rondel—that did it, triggered an all-purpose compulsion spell, what's called an obligato in the old Sly Carnival speak.

When the Indian Pacific pulled away twenty minutes later and the town settled back into its usual silence—just the murmur of the tea-towel brigade packing up and the sound of crows and currawongs out on the flats—Jem was standing beside the track, and more than happy to climb into the Jeep alongside the woman and set off into the northwest.

He wasn't thinking too clearly right then, but it was his first *official* contact with the Corpse Rose Heirloom Carnival and Former Circus.

• • •

They were ten minutes along a dirt road stretching across land as flat as a table when he finally drifted back.

"How did you manage that—?"

"Mally," she said, warmly enough. She had a tanned pleasant face, a good smile. "Short for Millicent Quinn, at your service. We've got tricks we can use."

"I'll say. I don't feel pissed off but know I should."

"Part of the package. You can get even later."

"Figure you won't let that happen. So where we going again?"

Mally gave him a long hard look. "Usually we just say you're going to a carnival for a day or so, and leave it to what we call an obligato to keep it foggy for the sake of a quiet drive out. But Mr F. said you'd probably be special, and I could make up my own mind. We're going about a hundred miles or so."

"So the name on your door there? The Corpse Rose Heirloom Carnival and Former Circus. What's with the *Former* part? How does that work?"

"Once the animals are gone a circus automatically becomes a carnival. That's what Mr Fleymann says, though there's no single ruling. Gipsy carnivals do it different. Taureg carnivals."

"Are there Gipsy carnivals? Taureg carnivals?"

"Hard to say. Put up a tent. Tell a fortune. Juggle some balls. When does it become official? Sometimes there's a clear business plan. Sometimes it's just passed on."

"The heirloom part."

"See. You're getting the hang of it already. Mr F. did pick well this time."

This time, Jem noted, but wanted to keep it light, get his bearings. He wasn't in the train anymore. Something extraordinary had happened yet didn't *feel* like it. He knew that should bother him as well, his *lack* of concern, but felt no alarm whatsoever, which, somewhere back in there, was dimly, remotely troubling. It had to be what Mally had said, part of the package.

Jem went along with it, sat scanning the distances. "So, hey, look where we are."

"Exactly. Can't think of a better thing for making a body really see the world than flying at three thousand feet or spending time in a desert."

"Unless it's spending time at a carnival in a desert."

Mally struck the steering wheel in agreement. "Right you are, Jem Renton!"

"Or maybe flying over a carnival in a desert in the middle of nowhere. That'd really make you curious, really make you want to go down and check it out."

Mally's grin held but she gave him another hard look, as if he had just said something profound, then went back to playing her own part in keeping it light. "Works for us, Jem. Never short of people dropping by."

"So why out here?"

Mally kept her eyes on the road. "Now that's *the* question. Part of it's about words. Names for things. Where they come from. What they mean. *How* you say them."

"Like Heirloom."

"There you go. Used to be the name for an important family entitlement. Something passed on in trust. From the word for a tool, an instrument. Ask Mr F."

"Right. And Corpse Rose?"

"What it says. Plant a rose bush on someone's grave and you get a very strong-smelling rose. Very sweet. Beauty from corruption. A special fragrance with a hint of carrion, some say, but that's nonsense."

Jem considered that, then gathered his thoughts enough to ask: "Mally, why am I here?"

"Can't say too much, Jem, but some people have a special gift they're never aware of. The thirteen in our troupe, well, it's our job to find these gifted ones, set up ways to bring them to us and use that gift while it's good and strong. They enable us, see, let us do what we do."

"And I have this gift? This power?"

"Right." And she told him how he had been chosen all those years ago, appointed, seconded, whatever it was, making it seem casual but no doubt proceeding according to a careful script.

Jem sat smiling and nodding in the pleasant buzz of wheels of sand, sun on his face, and accepted it all. These sorts of things had to happen all the time. People just never knew.

But he made himself keep at it. "So once they've found someone what do these old Heirloom Carnivals *do*? Apart from running away to join people."

Mally grinned again. "Like that, do you? Well, for a start we keep some things to ourselves. We appreciate things done right, using the old traditions. There's at least one Sly Carnival on every continent, tucked away, making do, getting by, can you believe it? Lots of friendly competition."

"And what? They *stay* hidden?"

"Enough people find them."

"You're not telling me much."

"Just what so many words do, Jem. Don't tell you much. Make you go deeper. But you'll see for yourself. Not long now."

• • •

For the rest of the drive it was just flat horizon in every direction under a hot blue sky, long sweeps of red earth, stretches of sand and salt pan, scraps of saltbush and bluebush on what modest dunes and ridges there were. Then there was a crusting of something off to one side, a few uncertain shapes that grew to be a clustering of tents and vehicles near what might have once been a watercourse of some kind.

Mally pulled up, opened her door and jumped out. "I'll go find Mr Fleymann and tell him you're here," she said, and set off amid the tents.

Jem sat a while listening to the day, watching the spot where she had disappeared. It occurred to him vaguely that he should call his Gran and Lucy, though he felt little urgency about that. Still, he was missing from the train. When he did try Lucy's number there was no signal, hardly surprising, so no way to check in, check facts, confirm terms like Heirloom and Corpse Rose, the rest of the world for that matter. And Mally had taken the keys. He really was cut off from everything.

Except this.

Jem didn't like the feeling it gave him. It made him decide that, since Mally hadn't actually told him to stay in the car, he'd take a look around. If this was all he had then he'd have it.

He opened the door and started toward the tents. As far as he could tell there were maybe ten in all, three impressively large, the size of modest family homes, the rest no larger than the average one-car garage. No real fairway running between either; it was much more haphazard than that, more a series of narrow alleys snaking between guy-lines to where some well-used caravans, a few vans and two weathered SUVs were parked.

Jem studied the scene, listening for voices. The tents stirred in the afternoon breeze, bellying now and then so the entry flaps showed glimpses of darkness. Sand hissed against the canvas. Stays thrummed a little, but as the softest, listen-or-you'll-miss-it sound.

It was starting to spook him, though Jem told himself that thirteen in the troupe didn't mean they were necessarily on site. Maybe they were off in a town somewhere or sleeping out the hottest part of the day. The *effect* was of no-one-at- home quiet, but he sensed he was being watched all the same, that if he turned quickly enough he'd see someone before they pulled back out of sight, maybe catch them peeping out of tents.

At least Mally's Jeep was still where she had left it. At least there was one other person besides himself.

Had been.

So where on Earth was she? Going to find Mr Fleymann, she'd said. Surely no *finding* was involved, although, going by what she'd said about words, maybe there was.

We appreciate things done right.

Jem shook his head, worried by how easygoing, how *unworried* he kept feeling about all this. He'd been abducted, tricked, conned. Things were seriously wrong, though it all seemed harmless, no big deal.

And maybe they wanted him to get a sense of the place on his own, check out the different tents, see which ones he'd try. There weren't that many. That had to be it.

Part of the package.

He moved towards the caravans, taking the alleyway with at least four tents opening onto it. They all had signage of some kind, wooden display boards above the entrance flaps, though most with words so faded he could only make out the nearest. THE WAIT, it said in bleached gold on weathered blue, which made him chuckle since that was exactly what he was doing. Still, hardly the name for your usual fairground attraction.

Maybe the Tauregs and Gipsies did better.

Jem was summoning up the nerve to enter, actually reaching to lift the flap, when Mally appeared at the entrance to the last tent in the row, the big one nearest the vehicles.

"Jem, over here! Come meet the boss!"

He waved in acknowledgment, as if he were the one who had *chosen* to interrupt his train journey and pay a visit. He stepped over guy-lines to the largest tent of the lot, probably the closest thing to a big top the carnival had. There was no signboard above the entrance this time.

When Jem stepped inside he saw two masts supporting the canopy, though, again, there was no sign of Mally. It was frustrating, annoying somehow—welcome feelings after the buzz of the drive out from Cook. The world was slowly becoming real again, his again. He blinked, kept allowing that he was being tricked, not seeing people who were right in front of him. The space looked completely empty but for a large display case between the masts, an old waist-high museum-style thing on four wooden legs, the size of a kitchen table, glass top and sides lit from above by a powerful spotlight that created a dazzling pool of light where it stood.

The obvious thing to do, the only thing really, was go see what it contained. Which had him smiling again. All part of the show.

The case held a model of the carnival itself, miniature versions of the tents, caravans and vehicles, even Mally's Jeep, showing the alleys running between, the adjacent sand flats, the tiniest tufts of scrub. The spotlight was like the blazing sun outside, and Jem could even imagine the tents stirring ever so slightly in an impossible breeze. It looked so real that it made him wonder if he'd be shown in the diorama if he stepped outside again, which meant he'd have to be out there for it to happen, of course, which meant he could *never* be in a position to see it. But that was the sense he got, that he'd be shown, that it was all shown in miniature here: a lizard scurrying by, a bird flying through.

"That's us," an elderly male voice said, and Jem looked up into shadow to see Mally standing with a tall lean man in an off-white three-piece suit, one that looked bleached and quaint as if made of canvas or sailcloth. It had eccentric pleats and odd little tucks and ruffles like compressed fans, even a rolled cravat of the stuff at his throat.

Mally gestured grandly. "Jem Renton. It's my great pleasure to introduce our Ringmaster and Master of Ceremonies, Mr Heinrich Fleymann, originally of Gutenberg. Mr F. as we call him."

"Good to meet you, Jem Renton," Mr F. said. "It's been a while."

Twinkling dry was the right term for him, Jem decided as they shook hands. Dry skin, dry voice, all with a sheen spilling from the eyes, which in themselves looked dry. An old painting of a man, complete with an explosion of white Mark Twain hair and wearing a raw canvas suit waiting for colors, highlights, flourishes.

Obligato courtesy came easy. "I'd say thanks for the invite, Mr F., but I had no choice in that."

Mr Fleymann spread his hands. "Sorry to say. But we'll set things right." His words held only the slightest trace of his German ancestry.

Jem found it easy to play along. "I thought weird carnivals came in on trains."

"Well, we're Down Under, see, so it's all ass-about. We join you. *You* come to *us* on the train." Dry voice, dry smile stretching back, bushy white hair catching the light.

"So *why* am I here? Mally said I have a hidden power you mean to use."

"Straight to it, good. You check out the attractions on offer. We have nine tonight. You get to pick three."

"Pick as in try those tents?"

"Pick as in they're your three. You try them all. Think of it as partly a fortune telling thing."

"That's what my gift's for? Lets you read the future?"

"Most surely does. Lets us *determine* the future, if we're lucky. It all depends on what choices you make. Life's about choosing. No point otherwise."

Jem remembered what Mally had said about words and wondered what Mr Fleymann *wasn't* saying. That was the game here. "You picked me. Joined me. How does that work?"

"Checked you out. Laid the old Sly spell, part of it in Perth with your Gran and sister, part when you reached Cook. Other folk drop by, see the tents, decide to check us out. That's the gravy. *We* chose you. Makes all the difference."

"But you're still not saying why."

"Hey, no sir! We've waited years for your visit. It's *our* reward for all the effort."

"You've chosen others? Visited others?"

"We have. We did. We do. Constantly. Got people out scouting right now."

"Finding new blood."

"Not our choice of words. Some duds, some misses, but all considered it averages out. It's how we do what we do."

"Come on, Mr Fleymann? You've got me here. Just what do you do. I don't see any trade dropping by."

"Not today, Jem! Not tonight. Tonight *you're* here! It's your turn. You're the main attraction! We perform for you. Not just anyone can make us cross half a continent scouting."

"I just visit the tents?"

"Pay each of the nine a visit, yes. Meditate. Reflect. Choose your three. They'll be the ones we use."

"For a fortune telling."

"At the very least. For whatever comes."

"Mally says there are thirteen in the troupe. Will I get to meet the others?"

"They wouldn't miss this for the world. Though, like I say, we got some off scouting. Half-Bottle Johnny and Swallowed

Girl can't be here, and one of our two Kabuki Crows sends his apologies."

"Finding my replacement if I don't cut it."

"Your successor whether you do or don't. It never stops. They find someone, we shut up shop and go check them out like we did you."

"And if I refuse?"

Mr Fleymann's face locked. The smile gleamed above the fan of his cravat, hinted, promised.

"Then we lose out this time. You lose out."

"You have that spell thing going. You could force me."

"Not how we like it to be. Keep that as one of our Get Out of Jail Free cards. We all get them. Even you get one."

"You're serious?"

"Old rules. You could guess our secret name, our special name of power. Every Heirloom Carnival has one. Some visitors get lucky. Most don't. That let's you cut and run."

"Can't be too obvious."

"Has to be in plain sight."

"So I've seen it already?"

"Most likely. But best you choose your three. Spend time with them, then come tell us. Have a bit of a debriefing on what you've understood. Answer a few questions."

"Then I can go?"

"How it works. Jeremy Scott Renton goes Scott free. He's off our books."

"But with no memory of having being here."

Mr F. snatched dazzle from the spotlight, grinned like a brand-new scimitar. "Still deciding about that. But, hey, Jem, you're looking tired. Why don't you go have a nap till later?"

"Thanks, Mr F., but I'm not—"

The third part of the obligato kicked in then. Jem collapsed where he stood, and Mally was there to catch him, every bit as strong as she looked.

• • •

When he woke it was evening and he was lying on an old car seat alongside one of the SUVs. To his left the western horizon was a band of gold over a vast blackness, sweeping up to become crimson passing through aqua into richest indigo overhead, already filling with early stars.

To his right the tents were so many jewel boxes, Chinese lanterns, shifting cabinets of light, sides stirring in the breeze off the desert. Daytime drab had become evening miracle, the easy magic of carnivals and circuses everywhere. The heat was going out of the land, but seeing the softly glowing shapes stopped Jem minding too much.

They had deliberately planned it this way, of course, provided the comfortable shift, the right segue from one mode to another. All the tents were illuminated internally, Jem noticed; all had lanterns atop poles by their entrances, a few left dark, most lit to show their signboards. There were people about too, not Mally or Mr F. as far as he could tell, but others, the rest of the troupe, doing last-minute errands, taking their places. There was music playing as well: pipes, Gipsy violins, some light percussion, probably a recording rather than live musicians but muted, far-off, entirely appropriate.

In spite of the circumstances, Jem felt genuine excitement, obligato effect or otherwise, though again with a stab of something else behind it, also muted and far off, which, in another time, another place, might have been panic. But he *felt* excited was the thing.

And here was Mally, wearing finery of her own: the cheekiest, flimsiest, most unlikely ingénue shift that clung to her full body way too well.

"Aren't you cold?" was all he could manage.

"Surely will be. But, hey, I've been in jeans all day. This is playtime! And time to start your tour."

"What, I just go wandering?"

"Take your time. Any order you like. It's all about you now."

"You're not coming?"

"I'm part of the performance, ninny. Off you go."

Jem had thought there'd be more to it, more fanfare, more of a fuss. But he stood and stretched, then started for the nearest attraction, half-intending to do a clockwise circuit.

The first tent he reached was warmly lit but empty, its lantern and signboard dark. After peering in at the single mast and the small patch of desert under a single yellow spot, he moved on to the next in line.

This one's lantern showed a single word on its signboard: TIMEWISE, and the smiling long-jawed man in straw boater, plaid jacket, slacks and the shiniest shoes to one side of the entrance immediately greeted him.

"Evenin', guv. Welcome to the show."

"I just go in?"

"Do as you please, guv."

Jem entered the warmly lit space, saw the single yellow spot illuminating a wooden stand a bit like a lectern. Its only feature was a single throw switch set into a vertical board at the top. The labels ON and OFF were marked clearly in black letters on white.

"What do I do?" Jem asked. "Throw the switch?"

"Do nothing, if you've a mind," the man said. "Or throw it. Some do. Some don't. Makes some folk feel things are happening if they do."

"There's no wiring."

"There's always wiring, guv. Could be hidden in the stand, under the sand. Could be a placebo. Makes some folks feel good to throw it. Empowered, you know."

"But they waste time deciding."

"Clever, but there's more to it. They stand to get forever. We're dripping with clocks. Got 'em all over us. Fingernails growing. Hair. Whiskers. Hunger. Lots o'clocks. Constant reminders. It's a Yes/No. Throw the switch! Stop the clocks! Maybe that's it."

"Live forever!"

"Free of time! Absolutely!"

"But the heart is a clock. That'd have to stop too."

"Got me. It would."

"So much for forever."

"We're all just hydrogen atoms being clever, mate. Being this or that. We all go there."

"That's the forever?"

"Surely is."

"No choice at all really."

"None I'd make. But face it. Some people are thoughtless, careless. Don't know why we have seasons. Why planes fly. This is for them. You always get some."

"So you're culling."

"Trimming the bush."

"No thanks."

"Come back anytime."

Jem left the tent, moved on to the next. Its signboard read MUM ON THE SOFA, and there was no one by the entrance this time. But when Jem looked inside he saw exactly what the sign promised: a woman in her late sixties wearing a house dress and apron sitting on a sofa knitting and watching an old-style television set. The sound was turned right down, the screen showed only static, but the woman seemed to be watching it intently until she saw him. Then her eyes lit up and she smiled broadly.

"Come in, dearie! Big night ahead. Set a spell. Plenty of room."

Jem stayed where he was in the entryway. There was something in how the woman's eyes had brightened too gleefully, in how her grin had spread and locked in the flickering light of her TV, so much like Mr F.'s. Overdoing it, but intentionally, he suspected, and Jem had the sudden notion that if he sat down beside the woman, started watching her white TV snow, he'd never get up again.

"Maybe later," he said. "Lots to do."

"Always is," the woman said, sounding genuinely disappointed.

Jem moved on, passed another empty tent—same lonely spotlight, same spread of empty sand and scrub—then found himself outside one of the larger attractions.

SKYLAB LAND, the sign read, and when Jem stepped inside he saw four tall box pedestals, two to each side of a throne-type chair towards the rear. On each rested what looked like a piece of old grey-white insulation paneling, presumably meant to be scrap salvaged from Skylab when it came down in the late seventies. The figure on the throne was tricked out in what was meant to be a spacesuit of the stuff: incongruous pieces glued and wired over an old ski-suit, complete with a makeshift helmet. The pitted and frosted face-plate concealed the wearer's face entirely.

As Jem moved between the pedestals, the figured stirred, started his spiel. "Skylab was the United States' first space station." It was a male voice, one that sounded a lot like Mr F.'s in fact. "Set in place in 1973, abandoned in 1974, completed 38,981 orbits, finally fell to Earth in August 1979. NASA meant to go back, have one of the new-fangled space shuttles move it to a higher orbit and re-use it, but that never happened. The station came down. This attraction celebrates its homecoming."

"That's it?" Jem asked.

"That's it. You're welcome to examine the exhibits."

Jem glanced at the scraps of metal and plastic, whatever they really were. "Are they genuine?"

"Can't say. I just wear this, give the spiel."

"Maybe another time then. Other sights to see."

"Always are."

Jem stepped outside to find the sky completely dark now, all traces of light gone from the western horizon. Without a midway to give him his bearings be became disoriented, found himself in the alley he'd been in earlier in the day, facing the signboard reading THE WAIT.

Now the flaps were fixed back. Warm light shone from within. The stocky man by the entrance had an impressive handle-bar moustache—fake surely—and wore a showman's purple velvet suit with embroidered lapels. He immediately assumed his role.

"Evenin', Mr Renton. I'm Grips Ashton. and this is—"

"The Wait."

"Surely is. Step in."

Jem ignored the invitation, again settled for what he could see from the entrance. In the middle of a space the size of a family living room, a spotlight illuminated a single bentwood chair.

Jem laughed out loud at the absurdity of such a pay-off. Truth in advertising again at least, like MUM ON THE SOFA, though hardly an attraction. Sit in the chair, become the exhibit.

"You're welcome to take a seat," Grips Ashton said with not a touch of irony, voice as smooth as driftwood left in the ocean just long enough. "Rest a bit. Big night ahead."

"Have to check out all the attractions. You know not to slow me down."

The big moustache twitched. "Jem, let a guy do his spiel, okay? I'm meant to say it to anyone who shows up."

"Even specials like me?"

"Especially specials. It's only temptation if it works, right? And I'm a genuine Ashton. Old circus name down under. Give a guy a break! "

"Another time, Grips."

Jem stepped away, tried the next tent along. Again the signboard was blank, the lantern on the pole dark. When Jem peered in, he saw just the central mast, the solitary spot, a sad scrappy patch of sand, its exhibit long abandoned or, as Jem thought about it, waiting to arrive. Another kind of truth in advertising really, the promise of other days, other possibilities, that or a memorial for what had once been.

Jem felt an odd emotion building, realized it was quite possibly dread, though dread as a concept, dread *without* the fear. What was he missing? Things were going on that he wasn't tracking properly.

He kept on to the next attraction in the alley, taking care with the guy-lines and tent-pegs, and it occurred to him for the first time that simply taking care not to stumble was keeping him focused, kept him paying attention, as if to offset the remaining effects of the obigato.

THE THOUGHTFUL GLASS OF WATER this latest signboard read, and as Jem reached it a middle-aged woman in pink tutu, fish-net stockings and black Doc Martins, hair coiffed in the most striking fuchsia dreadlocks, made as if to hold the already open flaps aside, gesturing to the feature within: a wooden pedestal with a single glass of clear fluid resting upon it.

"Time out, luvvy!" she said in a passing imitation of a Cockney accent. "You can pee behind the vans whenever y'like, but we need other kinds of refreshment, right? Dinner's later, all of us together, but for now drink your fill."

"Why the 'Thoughtful'?"

"People ponder it like you're doing."

"Any takers?"

"Rarely. But they don't get the prize."

"There's a prize?"

"Made you thoughtful again, see. Working already. Quench your thirst."

"It's my first time round. Maybe later."

"Right you are. Press on."

Jem did so, determined to get it over with. How long he'd been at it he had no idea. It was full night now, the sky filled with stars, streaked with the occasional tektites rushing down.

The next signboard read THE MERMAID, and this time it was Mally by the entrance, still in her flimsy evening finery.

"You know the drill," she said as Jem stepped inside.

He'd expected someone in a tank, one of the women in a mermaid get-up, so what he saw threw him: a large plasma screen showing stars, space, the glowing curve of the world as if seen from low-Earth orbit. Not a still either, he realized, but possibly recorded footage from a station like Skylab had been. In the soft lighting of the tent the effect was powerful, like looking through a window.

"Mally, I don't get the connection. Where's the mermaid?"

"I keep asking myself the same thing," Mally said.

Jem sighed, tired of the trickery, of how off kilter all this was. Why couldn't they just say what they wanted, spell it out? Let him be on his way?

But there were so few exhibits to go. Without a word he continued along to a signboard reading: THE CHEERFUL EXCHANGE OF GASES, whose "attraction" proved to be just as frustrating, as elusively annoying as the rest, nothing but a small tree in a terracotta pot, one of those topiary things like a green ball on a stick. It stood on a low pedestal inside plastic dust-curtains arranged like a makeshift shower stall.

A man in his forties, looking like a pastor in a black suit and plain white shirt, waited inside the entrance, and gestured grandly towards the booth. "Put your head inside, brother, and take a breath of God's clean air the way it was intended."

"Just take a breath?"

"Easy in, easy out, friend. One of the Lord's sweetest gifts. Clear your head. Won't take but a moment."

Jem said nothing, just turned and left. Two to go. Only two.

Maybe the obligato was wearing thin. He was feeling unsettled, anxious, vaguely frightened now, more and more aware of how wrong it all was, though the next signboard distracted him a bit. THE ISSUS TRIP, it read, which immediately had Jem recalling his high-school history classes, and how Issus was the town in ancient Turkey where Alexander the Great had defeated some Persian king or other. Curiosity had the better of him. What could it possibly be this time?

Inside he found two large art prints side by side on easels, each under a warm yellow spot, and both dealing with that historical event. A mature-aged woman in spectacles and worn dove-grey suit immediately stepped forward like a museum curator or matronly tour guide.

"On the left we have the Alexander Mosaic dating from around 100 BCE," she said, "originally from the House of the Faun in Pompeii but presently in the Naples National Archaeological Museum. It shows Alexander the Great and Darius III in conflict at the Battle of Issus in 333 BCE. On the right you see Albrecht Altdorfer's 1529 painting *The Battle of Alexander at Issus*, long regarded as that artist's best work and presently in the Alte Pinakothek museum in Munich."

That concluded the presentation, though the woman remained to one side as if ready to answer any questions her visitor cared to ask.

Jem studied the prints for a minute or so—the mosaic with Darius in his chariot, the Altdorfer with its grand view of mighty armies locked in battle—then said "Thank you" and went outside, feeling incredible relief when he saw that the next tent along was the two-masted one, the Big Top.

Was this the final exhibit, the ninth, or had he missed one?

When Jem stepped inside, he found it as empty as it had been earlier in the day. There was just the display case under its fierce white spot. Warm yellow elsewhere, dazzling glare for this single display.

He went and studied the miniature again, found it just as unsettling as before. It was *too* realistic, as if waiting to move yet confined by these glass sides. It made Jem feel like he was a god peering down, which brought the immediate "Russian Doll" reaction that such a god might be looking down on him. That had him glancing upwards instinctively, peering first into the terrible glare, then beyond that fierce core of light to what lay in the shadows to either side: dozens, hundreds, thousands of masks, faces, fixed there, staring down, a vast audience.

Jem blinked, strained to make sure what he was seeing.

Then Mr Fleymann spoke. "So, Jem, what's it to be? Which three will you pick?"

Jem looked down to find the whole troupe gathered about him, about the display case: Mally in her shift, the woman in the tutu and Doc Martins, the pastor in his dark suit, the curator woman, all of them.

"Is this one included?"

"Of course. If you need more time—"

"I'm ready." Jem said, and realized he was, that he *could* choose, had already done so.

"Shoot then."

Jem hesitated only a moment, getting the exact names clear in his head. "Right. My choices. Skylab Land, The Mermaid, and The Issus Trip."

Mr Fleymann grinned. Mally did. There were immediate smiles on the faces of the troupe, not just of happiness and excitement, but what looked like genuine relief as well.

Mr F. raised a hand, smoothed his cravat in a nervous gesture. "Now think carefully, Jem. You chose Skylab Land, The Mermaid, and The Issus Trip. Very revealing for us here. Very useful given our specialty. But if you had to pick *one* of the three, just *one*, which would it be?"

Jem thought immediately of the Alexander Mosaic. "The Issus Trip. No idea why."

It was like everyone started breathing again, Mr F., Mally, the whole troupe. There were more smiles, more excitement, sheer relief.

"Good choice!" Mr F. said. "You've turned out to be everything we wanted you to be, Jem."

"What did you want me to be?"

"How we operate, sorry. How we have to operate. All the Heirloom Carnivals."

"Please. What have I just done?"

Mr F. stretched his arms wide in an expansive, almost hieratic gesture. "You've just helped us move ahead. Enabled our next target."

Now it was Jem who went very still. He understood nothing, but sensed that something awful had just happened.

Mr F. could barely contain his delight. "Good thing you didn't pick The Wait. Many do. Looks so easy."

Jem made himself stay with the flow. "Just sit there till you get the joke, hey?"

Mr Fleymann's eyes flashed with a fierce delight totally without mirth. "Sit there till you realize that's all you'll ever do."

"Excuse me?"

"Wordplay again, Jem. How it seems. How it sounds. How it is for us. Names of power every one. That's what we trade in here."

And the grin locked, held. It was a grimace that nudged.

Get it? Ged it?

The Weight.

Jem felt a rush of horror. "You're joking."

"Try it when we're done if you've a mind."

"It looks so innocent."

"So can a throw switch with an electric current running through it. So can a glass of acid looking like water. Need to think a certain way about things."

Like why a carnival would set up in a desert.

That thought flashed through Jem's mind, even as he pictured the humble set-up of The Wait. How many people never left that chair? Had never been able to? Took their ease. Felt the pressure come.

"Come morning—"

"Wouldn't find much. It's exponential."

"The other exhibits—?"

"Have ways of biting."

"My three?"

"The only ones that are genuine. The rest kill. You passed the test."

The implications overwhelmed Jem. The faces on the canvas just now. Visitors dropping by.

"Surely there'd be investigations. Missing person reports."

"Always are. They find nothing. We have ways."

"But why? It can't be just trimming the bush."

"Much more, Jem. We're back to words again, see. Names. Ways of saying, seeing. If trees are solar engines exchanging gases, and people are living furnaces, burning away day and night, making more living furnaces, what does that make a carnival like this one? The Heirloom Carnivals? The Sly Carnivals?"

"Not just entertainments, distractions?"

"Try harder. Go deeper?"

"A machine? A device? A means for catching souls? Making a hell on Earth?"

"Too corny. Too clichéd. Harder. Deeper."

Jem tried to grasp what Mr F. wanted. Completions? Ways of resolving something? He didn't want to say.

Mr Fleymann read that hesitation. "Ever heard of the face in Skylab's window?"

"The what?"

"You picked *all* our space features."

"A face in Skylab's window?"

"Our favorite urban myth. Favorite conspiracy theory so far. Too much time on your hands in space. Lots of boredom. Lots of astronaut humor you never hear about. Pranks among the different mission crews. The Skylab 3 crew leaving dummies wearing flight suits for the final Skylab crew to find, stuff like that. Somewhere in there is talk of a face peering in the single wardroom window, Al Bean seeing it but staying mum, figuring it was just a reflection, rogue optics, then Jack Lousma and Owen Garriott seeing it, which later had them quizzing the other crews, but all agreeing to keep it to themselves. No use drawing bad psych ratings, screwing up re-selection eligibility or their pensions. But somehow it got round, somehow it became a face peering out, of course, which became the face peering out when the station fell."

"Skylab Land!"

"Go on, Jem. It's your pick. Finish it!"

"Where exactly did Skylab land?"

"That's the way! Let's have it!"

"We're in the debris field!"

"Most certainly are. This is where she came down—all the way from Esperance and Ballardonia up to where we're standing right now."

"Then your Spaceman. That get-up!"

"Who knows exactly? Parts of the Multiple Docking Adaptor or the Apollo Telescope Mount. Bits of hull, who can say? We're not about to call NASA and have them verify what's what."

"But the face plate—?"

"Glass burns up pretty quick, Jem. That may not be any part of the actual window."

"But—"

"Let's continue shall we? This is your test, remember. The Mermaid?"

"That view from space. It can't be Mer-maid. It has to be *Mir*-maid, for the Russian space station *Mir* that came down in the late nineties!"

Mr F. beamed his approval. "Well done. In March 2001, to be exact. Following some interesting mishaps: a fire in February

1997 and a major collision with a supply ship a few months later, temporary loss of contact with the station at the end of 2000. But we miscalculated, didn't allow for the extent of official efforts to control re-entry. She came down in the Pacific east of New Zealand. We only managed to secure the tiniest fragments."

"Then the ISS in ISSUS! The Issus Trip has to be the ISS, the International Space Station!"

"Bravo, Jem! You're a true paragon! Worth a thousand drop-ins." And in his near-manic delight he gestured up to where the imaginary audience watched, the faces on the inside of this largest tent.

And no obligato could keep *that* thought from Jem's mind.

"These tents! Your suits!—" He tried to speak it.

"Oldest tradition among the Heirloom Carnivals, yes. Something worthwhile passed on. Probably comes from the steppes of Russia long ago, but who can say?"

Jem looked up, again saw beyond the terrible glare of the spot to what lay in the spread of shadow: dozens, hundreds of masks, *faces*, fixed, peering down. Faces on the canvas. Faces *made* of canvas!

Canvas made of faces!

The display case miniature the bait, a distraction to keep candidates looking down, looking in, looking away. This is what *had* happened to those who failed in their choices, the uninvited, the unsuccessful ones. Those tents, all deadly, all capable of biting.

This was how the Heirloom Carnivals replenished themselves, added to themselves, repaired, maintained, made new tents, new suits.

Mr Fleymann may have regretted his exuberance, though it seemed that he always revealed how it was like this. "One Sly Carnival specializes in the sinking of great passenger ships. I'm sure you remember a certain White Star Line vessel meeting an iceberg, and can recall a rather more recent disaster off Isola del Giglio. Another works at upsetting Royal Houses and world governments. Our specialty is bringing down balloons, aircraft and, more recently, space habitats—the first haunted houses ever to be *off* the planet. A real cachet in that."

"What becomes of me?"

"We keep you on a bit longer. Use your services again."

"*Again*? Why, what have I done?"

"Enabled us, Jem. Given us the power to begin work on our next target. You could be invaluable. Who knows what else you'll help us do?"

"Unless I guess your secret name. Some do, you said. It's likely I've seen it, you said."

"Correct. We keep to the rules."

Everyone had gone still again, holding, waiting.

Jem looked down at the case, at the tiny world contained there, trying to grasp what he'd seen amid the misdirection, the deflections, the word-play, desperately seeking a Get Out of Jail Free Card, some ultimate name of power that compelled obedience.

Maybe it was in old carnival lore, old circus customs, like "Hey Rube!"—the old carnie cry for calling for help in a fight, a special Mayday. And Mayday itself—a distress call in all kinds of emergencies, from *m'aider*—Come help me!—in French. Things meant things. Words mattered here. Things half-heard. Misdirection.

Like Skylab Land!

The Mermaid!

And Mr Fleymann! *Flay*man indeed! Power in names.

Mum on the Sofa. Couch Ma! *Cauchemar*! Nightmare.

And Mally Quinn, for heaven's sake! How could he have missed it? Mallequin! Mannequin!

He looked down at the glare and the dazzle, the tiny world, at everything the world *was* here. The only world.

Corpse Rose!

Could it be? Of course.

That name! That name of power!

That was it! He knew it.

He said it out loud, blurted it, said it a second time.

"Dammit!" someone said, possibly Mally.

"Bugger!" muttered someone else.

Mr F.'s grin held, but the light went out of it like sand sliding around stones. Just the grimace remained, leached and horrid. Finally it relaxed, broke apart.

"Well played, Jem. But no matter. You've set us on our way. Tomorrow, the International Space Station will have a small but annoying toilet blockage, and one of its lesser windows will get the first signs of pitting. Nothing major yet, and a bit theatrical, I know, but it made the folks in Washington and Moscow very nervous when those faces appeared in their station windows. More nations involved with the ISS. Harder to hush up. It's time to bring the house down, but we'll make sure it's haunted first."

"What happens to me?"

"Get Out of Jail Free, lucky boy. You were everything we hoped you'd be."

• • •

Jem woke leaning against a tree in the dusty main street of Cook, legs thrust out in front. Someone was talking to him, a tall weathered brunette who kept glancing at her watch, clearly had things to do.

"Train's in tomorrow," she said, then indicated the old man standing next to her. "Pete says you can sleep on his verandah tonight. You'll be fine."

Jem fought to get his bearings, remember everything, anything, watched the woman walk over to a Jeep Cherokee, climb in and start the engine.

"Heat stroke'll get ya, young fella," the old man said. "Like the lady says, you'll be fine in a day or two."

Jem managed to stand. "Say, Pete, did you see a sign on that Jeep's door? Name of a property or something?"

"Never did. Mally's pretty much a loner. You see somethin'?"

"Not sure. For a moment I thought I saw that old name from the Bible. Lazarus."

"Wasn't he the fella that rose from the dead?"

Jem watched the Jeep driving off amid the dust. "At the very least."

• • • • • • • • • • •

SIGNATURE

FAITH MUDGE

Priya Gowda had never met a book she wouldn't read, and she'd met a lot of them. She was born to sell books, or at least that was what Rieke told her.

"I don't know how you do it," he confessed one Friday morning, while they were unpacking a delivery: six boxes of a new thriller that had the author's name in bigger type than the title. "I feel like a dietician selling chips."

"I like chips," Priya said, slitting the tape on the last box and gathering up an armful of books. "What's wrong with chips?"

"They're the twenty-first century's cigarettes. They have no nutritional benefit whatsoever, and they increase the burden on an already dysfunctional medical system. What's right with chips?"

"They taste nice." Priya shrugged. "Life's not all soul searching any more than it's all salad."

She straightened up, books stacked on her lap, and maneuvered her wheelchair out of the storeroom. Behind her, Rieke paused to check the shelving of the children's section. He hated books being misplaced and took every opportunity to reshuffle them into their proper order.

"Doesn't it drive you mad, though?" he asked. "When you see the classics passed over for an empty fad?"

"The classics are still there if I want them," Priya pointed out. "In the meantime, I'm going to read the heck out of sexy super spies."

Priya had worked with Rieke at Nightingale and Priest for just over two years, and she knew he meant well. He was a fully accredited hipster, a bony young man in his mid twenties with ice blonde hair and thick black-rimmed bifocals, and his favorite authors were all ill-fated poets or nineteenth century social activists. He accepted his duty to sell people what they wanted to buy the way a clergyman might tolerate wayward members of the flock, in the hope of converting unwary customers to greater things.

The bookshop was inner city, between a sushi bar and a bakery, with displays of paper art in the windows and a blackboard by the door listing new releases and discounts. Inside, the floor was glossy black, the walls papered in the design of a seventeenth century map. Sleek red lamps hung from the ceiling at key points, radiating warm light.

A landmark compromise between caffeine-junkie computer programmer Cassandra Nightingale and her indie publisher girlfriend Emilia Priest, the shop was a fusion of their passions. Shiny black shelving overlooked a cluster of red-topped tables, with barstools arrayed along the counter, and there was even a shelf of free books—an eclectic, eternally changing collection, pages dog-eared and margins full of other people's thoughts. Added to wi-fi and Saturday night author talks, it really wasn't surprising that Nightingale and Priest had gained a devoted community.

Cassandra was rarely in the shop, providing funds rather than presence. When she dropped by it was like receiving a visiting dignitary, sending her employees into a delighted panic. Emilia came in more regularly. She liked to arrange impromptu poetry readings and was currently editing an anthology of modern verse, including several original poems by Rieke. He adored her.

Priya loved bookshops on principle, and Nightingale and Priest had always been her favorite. In her last workplace she had been the brown disabled girl. Here, Emilia wanted her marketing suggestions and Rieke was supportive to the point of being overprotective. Later that day when a customer asked Priya where she was from—rather, where she was *really* from—he came barreling out of the aisles like a very tall, thin tank, and Priya had to talk fast to get in first.

"Woodridge," she said brightly, pushing the woman's bagged book across the counter. "How about you?"

"The racism in this country!" Rieke fumed afterwards. "She took one look at your skin and assumed you'd just set foot on Australian soil. How do you put up with people like that?"

Priya sighed. "If I were an ambassador for immigration, I'd have a big fancy car with flags on it. My job isn't to explain myself, it's to sell them books."

"You were born to do this," Rieke said, and Priya tucked the words away in a corner of her memory to savor later on the way home.

Her brother Kabir met her at Central Station, as usual, because her mother worried about her on public transport alone at night. He was not much of a bodyguard, slender rather than toned, boyishly scruffy with his rumpled black hair and electric blue shoelaces, but he worked in the city too, taking calls for the ambulance service. On the way home he told her about the stupid pranks that had wasted his time that day, and she told him about Rieke's latest protest against populism.

"He's got a point," Kabir said. "I mean, maybe the classics need some defending."

"You only say that because you fancy him." Priya glanced at her brother slyly. "Has he made you read Keats yet?"

Kabir went pink. "How did you know?"

Priya settled back contentedly. "I'm your inside woman on this. Trust me, it's a good sign."

• • •

In Queensland, August could be the golden month on the cusp between unnatural cold and unbearable heat. Priya's family spent a lot of time outside in weather like this. Their four-bedroom house was not really designed to accommodate seven people, let alone one with a wheelchair—sometimes the only place to get some quiet was in the street outside. The best space they had was the back deck, where everyone could gather around the same table. After dinner they lingered to talk while the younger kids chased each other around the lawn, but as the others began to drift away, Priya stayed, watching the dusk fall.

"Come inside," her mother called from the kitchen window. "Why must you work out there? You'll be devoured by mosquitoes."

Priya held up a textbook, inviolate armor to her parents. "I'll be in soon."

When she was sure she wasn't being watched, she reached into the book bag at her feet, bringing out a notepad and a sleek white cell phone. She kept an eye on it as she worked. It had been in her possession for well over a year, but it wasn't hers. Every time she wondered whether she was being tricked, all she had to do was look at the phone. It never needed credit, or even signal.

It was dark when the call came, later than usual. Priya answered at the first ring and the voice on the other end purred against her ear like a chilly breeze.

"What have you been up to, my dear?"

"Keeping busy!" Priya said, forcibly bright. "How about you?"

"Don't be facetious, child." The voice sharpened, from a purr to a growl. "I know everything you do. It would not hurt, I think, for you to remember that."

"A good night to you too." Priya opened the notepad to a list of names. "Let's get on with it, shall we?"

The bargain had been a bad idea. Priya had known that from the moment she found the phone and heard her name at the other end, but she had made it anyway. Fate had reached out a helping hand when she needed it most.

The bargain had brought her to the bookshop.

• • •

Emilia was there when Priya arrived the next morning, sitting at one of the barstools and spinning a spoon dejectedly in her empty cup. She was a slight, elegant woman in her late thirties, wearing a pearly chiffon scarf to complement her black and white polka dot dress. It was only close up that Priya realized one spot was spilt coffee.

"Good morning," she said tentatively. "Is everything okay?"

"No," Emilia said. Her voice, still crisply British after eight years living in Australia, was terse with exhaustion. "Things are anything but okay."

"What's happened?"

Instead of answering, Emilia got up and made herself more coffee. She made a cappuccino for Priya too, nudging aside a chair to make space for her to roll up.

"So what's wrong?" Priya asked, breathing in the aroma rising from her cup.

Emilia sighed. "Look. You're a smart girl, Priya, and you know me pretty well, so if I tell you something weird, you'll know I mean it. Yes?"

Priya nodded.

"We're about to be evicted. By a Fate."

Priya opened her mouth at the first sentence. The second froze her in place.

"By Fate," Emilia added, "I mean an actual manifestation of destiny. Go look it up in the mythology section if you like. I have. It doesn't help much."

Priya put down her cup with inordinate care. "Oh," she said. "No." Her voice sounded hollow. *What have I done?*

"It's all my own stupid fault," Emilia sighed. "I'm a stone cold bibliophile, you know that. My press means the world, but you would not *believe* the bad luck . . . I only kept in the black by working around the clock. Eventually Cass gave me a deadline: find a new job or a new girlfriend."

Emilia smiled tiredly. "A bookshop seemed the best balance— that way I could keep up my press on the side—but bookshops aren't exactly hot stuff right now. I couldn't get the money I needed from a bank. Then I met *her.* Imagine a female Rumpelstiltskin in a nice business suit who lends out all the golden straw and makes you sign a contract as long as your arm."

Priya choked. "You've seen her?"

"She gave me three years to figure out her name," Emilia continued, as if she hadn't heard. "It seemed such a long time. I mean, there are books, online databases, census records. I thought I could do it. Three years, and it's up on Monday. I was so *stupid.*"

She lifted her head. "You're taking this well. You must think I've gone crazy."

"I don't," Priya whispered. "I still have a year and a half left."

The bookshop had never been so silent.

"What," Emilia said, at last, very carefully, "did you ask for?"

"I needed a job." Priya looked at her hands while she spoke. "It was—I couldn't afford to keep studying. Either I had to ask my parents for a loan or give up my degree, and they don't have the money to spare. Somehow, she knew."

"She brought you here?"

Priya nodded. Emilia stood up abruptly. "I need more coffee."

One of the glass doors swung suddenly open and both women jumped, but it was only Rieke. He unwound several yards of thin sage green scarf and came over to their table, slowing down as he took in their expressions.

"What's wrong?" he demanded.

"It's complicated," Emilia sighed. "What do you know about Fates?"

Rieke dropped his scarf. He stared at Emilia, panic-stricken. "I didn't have a choice! I had nowhere to go, and she found me—"

Emilia braced herself against the table. "Dear God."

* * *

Priya had been grateful at first. If she could guess the Fate's name within three years, she would be left in peace; if she could not, her degree and all results therein would be forfeit. Like Emilia, she had been sure she could find the name in the allotted time. Like Emilia, she was no closer now than she had been on the day she'd signed the contract.

Emilia paced back and forth, listening as Rieke told the same story. When the old-fashioned station clock above the counter struck nine, though, she pulled herself together.

"We are unspeakably screwed," she said fiercely, "but we can still sell books. Priya, open the doors!"

Saturdays were the busiest day of the week at Nightingale and Priest and this was no exception—the tables were full all morning, and Priya kept busy behind the counter bagging books. Occupied with the familiar pattern of the day, she didn't notice anything was wrong until Emilia suddenly stiffened and leaned over to hiss, *"She's here."*

Priya followed her glare to an elderly woman in a crisp white business suit with a crocodile skin handbag hooked over her arm. Her white hair was twisted into a complicated knot at the back of her head. She met Emilia's glare and smiled sweetly, like someone's executive granny.

"I am *not* serving her," Emilia muttered. "I just *won't.*"

They couldn't kick her out, though, not in front of a whole café of oblivious onlookers. Priya might not know much about magic, but customer service, she understood.

"You go," she said. "I'll do it."

By the time the old lady, or Fate, or whatever she was reached the counter, Emilia had fled to the furthest reaches of the history section. Priya dredged up a smile.

"Hello, ma'am, how can I help you today?" she reeled off. She had said the same words so often that they sounded permanently strung together, like a hackneyed song lyric. The old lady smiled too, her lips pastel pink, her teeth very white.

"Well, I'm not sure yet," she said. "What can you offer?"

"We have coffee, tea, hot chocolate, iced chocolate, fruit juice or mineral water."

The old lady looked at the laminated menu propped up in front of the coffee machine. "A pomegranate juice would hit the spot."

Priya smiled. Maybe she would be losing the best job of her life tomorrow because of this woman, but if it came to a contest, she could out-smile her. She wheeled to the glass-fronted fridge, bringing her legs into full view. Their distorted shape was visible under Priya's skirt; she didn't dress to hide it. When she turned around with the juice in her hand, the Fate looked vaguely horrified, the very picture of a sweet old lady feeling embarrassed for her.

"Oh my," she said. "I'm so sorry."

"It's no trouble," Priya replied, placing the chilled bottle on the counter. "That's four-fifty, thank you."

The Fate opened her crocodile skin handbag. "How did it happen, dear? Your . . . impairment, I mean. It must be so hard."

"Well, it would be nice if more trains connected to platforms properly," Priya agreed. "Do you happen to work for Queensland Rail?"

The Fate gave her a hard look. Priya kept smiling. Her "benefactor" had been more frightening anonymous at the other end of a phone. Priya knew how to deal with people like this, the ones who felt better by trying to make her feel worse. It made sense that the Fate would be one of those. What was the use of people who were content with their lives if you made your living out of desperate souls?

"Thank you, dear," the Fate said, no longer smiling.

"Have a nice day." Priya beamed.

• • •

Priya didn't go home when the shop closed that evening. She called her mother to say she was out with friends and repeated the message to Kabir, assuring him she'd take a taxi later. Then she joined Emilia and Rieke at their table.

Emilia had popped out briefly to fetch supplies from the bakery next door, so there was a bag of cheese croissants amidst the coffee cups. Priya was the only one who had any appetite. She was on her second croissant when the sharp click of Cass's footsteps sounded on the pavement outside.

Cass was not much taller than Emilia, but looked like she should be. Her hair was a dynamic bottle green, cut in a sharp bob, and her sweeping black eyebrows gave all her facial expressions extra drama, making her look annoyed even when she wasn't—though tonight she probably *was* annoyed. She shrugged out of her black brocade jacket and grabbed Emilia's cup of coffee, draining it in one gulp.

"Right," she said. Her Irish accent was much stronger than usual, a sure sign she was angry. "Solutions would be good any time now."

Rieke hunched unhappily in his seat, as though her words had been personally directed at him.

"Do you know anything about creatures like this?" Priya asked, not hopefully.

"What, because I'm from Ireland?" Cass laughed sharply. "When I was little my nan told me not to wear green or the fairies would take me away. That's the sum total of my paranormal knowledge." She glared at Emilia. "I can't believe you didn't even *ask me* before you went and signed your life away."

"Excuse me, you cared? That's news," Emilia snapped. "What happened to, 'it's your mess, sort it out'? You thought the shop was a terrible idea from the start. Why would I ask you for advice when I knew you'd tell me not to even try?"

Cass flinched, color bursting across her cheeks as if Emilia had slapped her. "That's what this is about? Tell me, when was the last time you let me help you with *anything*?"

Rieke looked on in a state of horrified stupefaction. Priya thought about dead crocodiles and eyes that were complacent and hungry at the same time. Maybe the Fate would have called in Emilia's contract anyway, but why come in person?

She slammed her hands down on the table, startling her employers into silence. "Why does she want to close down the bookshop? It's making money, and from the look of things, she likes money. Why does hearing someone else figure out her own name matter more than repaying the loan?"

"I—" Emilia hesitated. "I thought it was just malice."

"This is the supernatural," Cass scoffed. "Why would it make sense?"

Priya chose to ignore that. "The way I see it, she has other plans for this place. Malice doesn't pay for crocodile skin bags."

"She'll probably sell it off to some other idiot," Emilia muttered. Cass twitched her hand, as though she was going to reach out, but didn't.

"Oh, what's the use," Emilia said bitterly, pushing back her chair. "I've gone through millions of names, literally millions, without ever getting the right one. I'm not going to guess it now. I'm sorry, Priya, Rieke. However you got here, you've been fantastic employees. I may not be able to keep the shop open, but maybe the references and experience will help you get a job somewhere else."

She stood up stiffly. "I'm going home."

Rieke unfolded himself abruptly, and gave her a brief, awkward hug. Priya came over to hug her too, then Cass, who looked startled at being included.

"Whatever happens," Priya said, "we'll be okay. Right?"

They all nodded, but none of them believed it.

• • •

Getting home was a pain. Priya called a taxi just like she'd promised, but despite her specifications the first one that showed up was a regular cab and she had to wait another two hours for a maxi-taxi that could take her wheelchair. Rieke waited with her, slumped gloomily against a wall, not talking.

All the way home, she turned the same question over like it was a kind of Rubik's cube and if she just looked at it from the right angle she could make the colors align. *Why?* Priya closed her eyes, trying not to cry.

"What's wrong?" were her mother's first words as Priya bumped through the door. The rest of the family was already in bed, but Priya's mother was waiting up in the kitchen with a cup of tea and the radio turned down low. All Priya wanted was to fall into bed and forget that tomorrow she might not have a job.

"I'm fine," she said. "Really, Mum, I'm fine."

"Nonsense. Come here and I'll make more tea."

Reluctantly, Priya edged into the kitchen, which, with its elderly four-seater table and enormous fridge, was a bit too crowded to maneuver through easily. As she pulled up on one side of the table, Priya's eyes went automatically to the two framed quotes that hung above the sink. *They cannot take away our self-respect if we do not give it to them*, Mahatma Gandhi said in neat calligraphy, and *If you're going through hell, keep going*, Winston Churchill added. They were the sentiments by which Priya's mother had lived much of her life.

"Did you have a nice evening?" her mother asked, watching her narrowly.

"No," Priya admitted. Her mother pushed a mug across the table and she took it with a sigh. "Cass and Emilia are in trouble."

"What kind of trouble?"

"Their lender is a crook. They might lose everything. It's so unfair. Emilia put her heart and soul into that shop."

"What about you?" her mother demanded. "Is there any trouble with the law?"

"No. They've done nothing illegal."

"Can they still pay *you*?"

Priya shrugged. "I'll be fine. It's them I'm worried about. And Rieke." She remembered what Emilia had said about malice and looked at the quotes again. "Do you believe in fate, Mum? That things can't be changed?"

Her mother looked surprised. "Never," she said, without hesitation. "We always have choices. Not all of them will be good, but they are ours to make."

"Yes," Priya said thoughtfully. "I think so too."

• • •

Sunday was not one of Priya's days at the bookshop. She slipped the white phone under her mattress and spent the morning at a nearby internet cafe, trying to define the nebulous shape of an idea. She needed more data.

When she came home, she heard the soft buzz of the phone and pulled it out. She looked at it for a long time, letting it ring in her hand. Then she fetched her father's hammer and smashed the phone into tiny pieces.

• • •

On Monday she arrived early to find Rieke compulsively straightening the shelves as though a precise alignment of spines could prevent anything bad from happening. When Priya called out "good morning!" he turned around and stared.

"Good?" he echoed disbelievingly.

"The shop's still open," Priya told him. "That's a start."

Emilia came out from the aisles. Her eyes were very red. "If you say so," she said. "I've made a sign explaining things—well, what I can—I'll post it on the door."

"Don't," Priya said hastily. "Please, not today."

"Today is the last day," Emilia said tiredly. "Our regulars deserve to know."

"Please, Emilia. Let's go about business as usual. The Fate is bound to come back, she'll want to see the effect this is having on us. So let's show her."

"A brave face?" Emilia smiled grimly. "Well, pride I do have. Or so I'm told. All right, we'll hold it together for one last day. Rieke! Open up. We have books to sell."

Priya was on alert all morning, waiting for a glimpse of crocodile skin or pastel lipstick. Emilia, her smile so determined it looked slightly dangerous, organized an impromptu poetry recital and for the first time ever Rieke did a reading. Priya applauded from behind the till. The crowd of customers clapped too, pleased but bemused by the strangely defiant atmosphere. At the back, clapping thin, beautifully manicured hands, was the Fate.

Finally, Priya thought.

The Fate was smiling, but she wasn't pleased. Priya rolled carefully between the tables until one of her wheels bumped gently against the crocodile skin handbag.

"Back again!" she said, before the Fate could speak. "How can we help you?"

The Fate looked, for the briefest moment, unnerved. Then a deeply unpleasant smile spread across her face.

"You can watch," she said, in a low but clear voice, her eyes fixed on Priya's, "as this little enclave is shut and its patrons are cut adrift in the world. You can watch me drink down its dreams and eat up its hopes. And I will watch *you*, my dear. You'll drift from job to job, never quite fitting in, taken out of pity and pushed out the door when indulging your . . . misfortune . . . becomes too much of a bother. Without my favour, you will become nothing."

Her words hit Priya like venom. She spun quickly to retreat behind the till, but not before she'd caught a glimpse of the Fate's satisfied face. Her cheeks were flushed a healthy pink.

"You see, my dear?" Priya heard her say. "You can help me."

• • •

All day long, the Fate sat in that corner. At closing time, when other customers had made their final purchases and vacated their tables, she remained. Emilia was locking up when Cass arrived. They looked at each other with a taut uncertainty, then Emilia yanked down the shutter and turned on the Fate.

"Well," she said, "you want the shop? You'll have to take it from me."

The Fate stood up, carefully brushing down her jacket. She was smiling indulgently, as if Emilia was a recalcitrant granddaughter.

"I did so hope you would say that. Invitations make it so much easier. These silly rules!" She gave a light, almost girlish laugh. "You painted dreams into the walls, dear. All those things you've wanted for so long and been told you couldn't have. They smell *delicious*. You will chase chance all your life but never taste them again. They're already gone." The Fate's voice dropped to a stage whisper. "After all, what do you love that you have left to lose?"

Cass looked at Emilia urgently, as though waiting to hear that refuted, but Emilia didn't look at her. She had her hands over her mouth and tears welling up in her eyes. Emilia, who never gave up.

Cass rounded on the Fate instead. "Fuck you," she spat, disgustedly. "What are you going to do? Use your great and terrible powers to throw us out? All I've seen are cheap tricks and mind games."

"The best tricks are the ones you don't see coming," the Fate said confidingly. "And you never do, do you! Always blindsided, always left behind. You pretend you *want* to be different, but that's not true, is it?"

"How can you live with yourself?" Rieke stepped forward, his fists balled. The Fate looked at Cass for a moment longer, with the air of someone licking the last dregs of cream off a spoon, before turning her pastel smile in his direction.

"A rhetorical question!" she cried jovially, as if Rieke had made a good joke. "Perhaps what you're really wondering is how it's done? *You've* never been very good at living with yourself, have you, Frederik? Not even your own name! You know that everyone you meet is only ever putting *up* with you, don't you? And when they get tired of tolerating those awful little quirks of yours, it's your own fault. That nice young lad—Kabir, isn't it? He's been so polite, putting up with those strange tics that you think pass for flirting, but you know that won't last."

Rieke's face had gone grey. The Fate, by contrast, was practically glowing with health as she watched him, her skin visibly smoother. Inside Priya's head, the last squares of the Rubik's cube slotted into place.

"Actually," she said, "that's not true."

The Fate began to say something about misery and cripples but Priya talked over her, raising her voice. "My brother has had a crush on Rieke from the day they met. You're not a Fate at all, are you? You're a sort of vampire. And those silly rules count for something. That's why you made Emilia sign the contract. You can lie about everything else, but not—"

The Fate brought up a finger and leveled it like a gun at Priya's head. "You," she said, sweet as poison, "shall. Be. Silent. This is my ground. It was where my maker drank my soul and where I woke, immortal. I was here when carriages rolled in the streets, not pathetic little girls. There have always been broken souls like you, looking for a place to call their own, and there always will be. You know, they say your appetite wanes as you get older, but I am so *hungry*."

She turned back to Emilia, smiling again.

"Who would have thought I would find such a feast?"

Priya shrank back instinctively from those teeth. Her hands tightened on the arms of her wheelchair, but the fight or flight instinct was one she was used to overriding. She chose a third option: think.

"We all signed your contracts," she repeated, doggedly. "Which means they matter. So I name you. I name you . . . " Priya hesitated, then shrugged. It was already too late to help herself if she was wrong—she might as well enjoy the moment. "*I name you* Spot."

The color drained from the woman's face, her skin collapsing into wrinkles as if unseen hands were crumpling her up. She looked stunned.

"You have no power over this place," Priya said firmly. "Or anyone here." She raised her hands in dismissal. "Begone, foul Spot!"

The woman whined, a wordless sound of entreaty, while her eyes blazed with rage. Priya wanted to look away but didn't dare.

The creature *crumbled*, drifting apart like burnt paper until all that was left was dust on the floor.

There was a long silence. Emilia was the first to move, nudging the sad pile with her toe. "How did you do that?" she breathed.

"I didn't expect *that* to happen," Priya confessed. She realized her hands were shaking and squeezed the arms of her chair tightly. She felt horrified and elated at the same time, and rather sick.

"It's like Cass said," she added, "that . . . whatever that was, was all about mind games. If she was really a Fate, she'd know how Kabir felt—and instead, all she had were lies. Saying those awful things was feeding her somehow. She was feeding off all of us. Particularly you, Emilia. This was your dream, and she wanted to eat it whole."

Emilia jerked back from the dust. "She almost did. She almost took everything." She looked at Cass uncertainly. "I suppose that's my fault for not asking for help."

Instead of agreeing, Cass seized Emilia's hands and pulled her into a ferocious hug. "Fuck," she half-wailed. "Did that really happen?"

Emilia hugged her back hard, burying her face in Cass's jacket. "I'm sorry, I'm sorry, I'm sorry," she chanted, her voice muffled. "I dragged you into all this—" She twisted briefly to look over her shoulder. "Priya, consider yourself employed for life, okay?"

Priya laughed shakily. "Is it too soon to ask for a contract?"

Emilia shuddered. "Way too soon."

Priya heard a door open and jumped nervously, but it was only Rieke, returning from the storeroom with a vacuum. They all watched in silence as he ran the nozzle repeatedly over the same patch of floor until long after every speck of dust had to be gone. Then he stripped out the bag, threw it in the sink behind the counter and pulled a box of matches from his pocket, setting the thing on fire.

"Vampires have to be burnt," he said flatly.

Emilia walked over to stand beside him and turned on a tap to wash the ashes down the drain. "And drowned," she agreed.

Later that night, meeting her at the station, Kabir told Priya she looked tired.

"Are you okay?" he asked.

"I'm fine," she said, smiling at how the words sounded in her mouth. "Just fine. Call Rieke and ask him out tonight."

Kabir blinked. "What?"

"I'm your inside woman on this," Priya reminded him. "Tonight's a good time."

Kabir pulled his phone from his pocket and dithered over it for a moment with his finger on a speed dial he'd never used. "Are you sure about this? Won't he think it's weird, me just calling out of the blue?"

"Maybe," Priya said. "Then he'll say yes."

Kabir hit the number.

The train was pulling in. The platform streamed with people who didn't know about a Fate who was a vampire in disguise, who didn't know there was a bookshop called Nightingale and Priest with dreams painted into the walls. Who had no idea how big the world really was.

It wasn't Priya's job to tell them. Her job was to sell them books.

• • • • • • • • • • •

THE BOX WIFE

EMMA OSBORNE

If you run your hands over me you'll be pulling splinters from your palms for days.

I am in a room bare and dark.

"Melissa, oh oh," it says, thrusting. "Kelly, my dear, my love, Kelly." Sometimes I am one or both. Three nights ago, it called me little one, though I am bigger than it by half. I have many names. Each of them, I remember. Each of them is an identity that drapes over me like a mask.

It made me one night from boxes and springs. My joints were screwed in and locked into place with bolts. My boxes were nailed together; each hammer blow like a gunshot. I will always remember the thrill of the drill as it punched through my rough planks to make gaps for the hoses. I have painted toenails, red on the left side and black on the right. My front is covered with a woolly sheepskin. The rest of me is skinned with rubber gloves. I worry that I may crack in the cold.

My room has a window dressed with lace that restrains any errant snowflake that may fly to me. The walls are the pink of new flesh. There is something bundled up in the corner that has the colour and smell of burned hair.

"Madison," it says, choking. "Belle, my sweet, my heart."

It is heavy and stinks of lust. When it rolls on me I flex and shift. I turn my head but it always moves me into its preferred position. I am slick in patches and moist in others. A hank of hair birthed from a hairdresser's garbage bag has been slapped atop my pate and fastened with tape. The lock is of many colors and red.

It built me from flat pillows and rusted clockwork. It painted on eyes so that I may stare at it and glued in teeth so that I may smile. I contain wires that squeal when it lifts my arms. I am voiceless, but for the creak of my parts.

I am obliging.

It slows its movement and begins to oil me. I lay exposed as it pushes warmed liquid into my hollows and cranks with insistent fingertips.

"Holly," it says, as it maintains me. "You can't go. You are here for me, here to stay."

There is someone below us, rattling against bricks and coughing up the water and the bread that it leaves when the pumping is steady. The pumping has to be steady for me to breathe. I am connected by clouded tubes to something below me, far down where I can't see. My circulatory system is squeezed by anonymous hands and this thing that might be blood flows up through the dangling tubes. My cheeks bloom, sometimes, and other times my whole cavity heaves.

The pumper grants me breath, minute by minute. I thank the pumper, silently, every time the sun rises to shine in through my window.

"Geraldine." It names me anew as it finishes its greasing and begins to thrust once more. It drags its fingers through the wool and grips hard with each push. "My sweet, my heart," it calls me, quietly, then louder. "Geraldine!"

I wonder who she is; who they all are. Former lovers? Enemies? Sisters? I try to give them all faces, when I am named for them but I do not and will never know them. All I know is that I am them, for a time, until it changes the name and my identity hastens to the next.

"Jessica, I have always known that it would be you. I have waited for you forever and ever. Jessica, lovely one, Jessica!" It scrapes its cheek against my cheek and I can smell its muggy breath.

I am allowed to rock along with it, when I am being used. Sometimes I make the smallest of unnecessary movements when I think that it is too caught up to notice. It feels like a minuscule act of rebellion. I dare not even tremble when I am in my room, alone. It tells me that if I move when it isn't around, it will come to me in the smallest hours and set me on fire—just burn me up into a crisp. It could be lying. But I don't know anything.

I am just a box.

I could tell you a story. I could tell you about the way that it whispered me to this place, telling me how beautiful I was, oh, how perfect; all the while gouging its fingernails into the parts of me that once had feeling. I could spin you a tale of my life before it, before this room. I could tell you of the time I ran after a dragonfly and skidded through mud until I was wet up to my knees in a creek. I could recount for you the months it took me to learn how to play my favourite song, could show you the guitar-string callouses that emerged. I could count for you the number of rooms that I slept in, from the time I was small until the day that I was installed in this place.

I could tell you how it watched me, found me, took me up from the world that didn't see me for what I was, or what I could become. I could tell you of how I was sung to this room by a poisoned voice, each note another snare to catch me and bind me tight. I could tell you of how I gently resisted, until I didn't.

But the stories would be a lie. I have always been here. I am a box.

I am a wife.

It screams when the pumping dies out and I fade, and its thick boots go *smash smash smash* on the stairs—and then on body and bones. I know that this means no more food for the pumper, stuck far down below me. No sustenance until the lesson has sunk in. And I lay back, deflated, the sheepskin sagging at the corners.

I wonder if this is the time when it won't come back. Maybe today, the pumper will defeat it and we can both leave, together. But no, soon enough it is up and up the stairs and leaning into my corners.

"Jennifer. My sweet Jenny," it whispers at me and my lack of ear. "Jenny, darling, you're here."

I imagine one up above me, hovering in this place in order to keep me safe. I wish to smile when I think of that one, the watcher. Perhaps the watcher is real and has been, always. I can see a crack in the roof through which the watcher could observe me. I have looked and looked. Listened. I'd only need a scratch to know that the room above is occupied; just one faint drag of a nail.

Perhaps the watcher has a window, too. I hope that the watcher can see things, everything, all of the world that I do not know and will never visit. I would give anything—even my sheepskin—for the watcher to come down and whisper to me of the sights and the sounds and the taste of the world, even if it was nothing more than stories of dust and mold. Anything.

I would also like a kiss. Just one.

"Brenda. Glenda. Kate!" it says, hips rolling. It picks up speed, quivering around the throat. Its skin is red and wet. I wonder if this time it will shake me to pieces. If so, I am sure that I will be repaired back into usefulness.

It wriggles like something freshly caught.

"Charlene! Oh, my love, my little one!" It is louder and faster. Drips patter onto my rubber skin. One hand grips my shoulders. The other is lower, moving. I am fortunate not to bruise. I notice, idly, that today the room is fresh with morning sunshine. I wonder if it will go out and live a real life today, after it is finished with its wife.

I do not know what it does when it goes, but it often comes to me smelling of flowers and methanol. Once, it visited me in the smallest hours of the night, near to the dawn. It reeked of cheap perfume and I knew then that it had tried to be somebody else's. It chastened itself, repeated again and again that this was its life now, that I was its world and that it would never leave me, not for anything.

It made promises to me, the kind that you should treasure. And then it started and kept going until noon.

All the while, I stayed perfectly still.

Now it shivers and shakes. It must have built me to be pretty, but I don't know what that means.

I realize that my hair has fallen off. The hank must be huddling on the floor like a lonely spider. It notices, shouting that I have ruined everything, and swings a hard slap. I rock to one side and I know I shouldn't, but I tilt up my hip as I roll and I know I should have warned it with my lipless mouth, but—

The point of the spring is sharp and dips into its upper thigh with ease, cutting into its thickest blood-tube. This metallic slip is utterly silent, but it begins to scream immediately. There are no words, but there is terror. It lays about with its arms, as red comes in spurting throbs. My rubber is drenched with warmth.

It knows that I shifted and it wants to kill me. It screeches with the voice of death and brings both clenched fists down upon my face. My teeth clatter down the back of my throat. The pump of my false-breath sucks them into the dark of my belly. It hits me again, but this time the blow is weaker and I know that I will outlast it.

"Caroline," it sobs, "I only wanted—I wish that you were . . . "

It dies next to me in the bed, the way a faithful lover ought to.

I lay broken for a time. I am not sure what to do or how to be. My false-breath continues to ease in and out of me, slippery and moist. I count the strands of cobwebs that are high in the corners of my room and when I am finished, I start anew. This continues, perhaps for hours, until I hear whimpering from the pumper. My breath continued, even through all of the noise, because nobody has told the one below to stop. The pumper does not know that we are both alone now, together.

I hear another cry, a hungry sound. I know that, somehow, I must go.

Firstly, I must sit. My wired arms are extended above my head but as the cries grow louder, I swing them up so that they clatter down on either side of my sheepskin. My wires thrum as I hoist up my torso. I ease myself forward, dizzy with the tilt of the world. My sheepskin falls off and I can see the worn wool sticking up in bloody peaks.

My displaced teeth rattle in my belly as I stand on sprung legs. The tubes that carry my breath and blood to me pop off the suckers that sit along the ridge of my wooden spine. There is a leak. I lurch toward the door and cogs spill from me like dropped coins.

I realize that I will never hear its voice again.

I do not mourn. It didn't build me to mourn, or to grieve. I was built to be silent and useful.

I move from my room and carefully turn at the top of the stairs. I know that I must go down and down and down.

So much of me has fallen off that I am nearly nothing when I reach the middle of the stairs, but every step has shown me a new thing. I go slowly, relying on stiff knees that were never meant to take weight. My painted eyes would widen if they could, even at the zigzagging strips of crackling wallpaper.

I halt at the window, a full storey lower than my own. I see a yard thick with weeds and broken glass. The sight is glorious.

There are machines laying at odd angles, gutted. I wonder if I carry any of their parts within me. I am rapt, until I see the others. They are scattered about the enclosed yard with a carelessness that speaks of their failures.

Broken wives. Lost wives. My predecessors. I wonder if I hold any of their screws and nails and am all at once sure that I do. I think that I might match at least two of them for paint. My glossy eyes show me ruins and hulks. I trace their frames and feel something that could be horror and something that may be love.

The only thing that could move me is another cry from the pumper.

"Please," comes the call. "Please." I go. I go to save the only one left.

I shuffle down in to the dark and I lose more of myself with every step. I remind myself that they are only fragments and parts. Surely I have a few to spare.

I hear clanging and sobbing, but when I reach the door the pumper goes quiet, perhaps expecting punishment. My fingers scrape at the latch until the door opens. I stand in the frame, illuminated by the light of a new day. I must look a fright, for the pumper shrieks at the sight of me. With great effort, I hold up my hands.

Peace, I am here for you, here to take you away from all of this, I think, though I cannot shape the word with my empty mouth. I wonder if the watcher would say the same to me, if I were the one being rescued.

The pumper runs to me and I grind into a hunch.

I am enveloped by pale arms. They squeeze me tight and I creak.

"You came," says the pumper, breathlessly. "I wished and hoped for you to come. I knew that you would. I knew it."

My bloody shoulder is dampened with tears. I lean forward, pressing my rubber skin to the stark bones of the one who gave me breath. We turn and my knees pop, but I can see freedom and know that I only need to walk a few steps and then we will be outside. I begin to shake and I do not know if I will ever be able to stop.

The pumper wraps a hand around mine, whispers a secret to me and kisses me. Just once. That is enough.

∙∙∙∙∙∙∙∙∙∙∙

THE BADGER BRIDE

ANGELA SLATTER

The tip of the quill scratches its way across the parchment, a sound that sets my teeth on edge.

One might think I'd be used to it by now.

The black marks it leaves in its wake make no sense to me—indeed the entire book makes no sense—then again, I am a mere copyist and mine's not to question why. Although I do.

Frequently.

Much to my father's despair.

When he brought me this commission, I turned the tome over and over—a difficult enough task, for the thing is heavy, aged and fragile, the ebon cover tacky to the touch, the pages brittle—and a smell rose from the skin of the thing that was quite unpleasant. The name of the author and the title of the book were quite obscured, a thick stygian gum had been smeared across them and it was hard to perceive whether this application was intentional or the result of mere carelessness. The inner leaves confirmed any suspicions of intent—no extant title page waited therein, merely the remnants of a folio torn from the binding, tiny sad folds of paper with ragged edges remained.

So, an anonymous book.

"Who is the client?" I asked my father, Adelbert (former Abbot of the monastery of St Simeon-in-the-Grove), who rolled his eyes and bid me *Just do the job.*

"But, Father, it is very old, very frail, the ink is faded—indeed fading as I watch if my eyes don't deceive me." I manoeuvred the article in question so he could better see. "Is it the last of its kind? Who is the owner? What does he expect?"

"He expects, like your father, that you do not ask questions, little prying thing. That you take this volume and copy it as quickly as you might!" He took a deep breath and roared, "Else I'll put you out in the cold, Gytha!"

I made a 'harumph', and left his study. He will not put me out; he will do no such thing. I am the only child in Fox Hollow House who earns her keep, after all. Aelfrith spends her days draped across the couch, sighing for a husband, and Edda spends hers exercising and grooming the six horses in the stables. I alone understood and adopted the scholarly arts Father had tried to teach us; and I alone I adopted the trade he learned in the monastery (and at which, he freely admits, was terrible). People come from all around, from as far away as Lodellan, to have me copy their books, their precious, unique, failing books; to have me adorn and amend them, to add vines and flowers and strange animals in the margins; to change the existing illustrations they cannot bear (modestly clothe a naked Eve, paint out grandmother's warts on her nose, give uncle a chin that does not slope so straight from lower lip to collar bones). Copy, edit, amend, ameliorate, augment and occasionally, if the pay is right, forge.

I will make your book what you want it to be, either more or less itself.

So many since I was very small—so small that Father had to lift me up onto the stool piled with two firm fat cushions that I might be able to sit at the tilted desk and reach the inks and shafts, the paints and tints, the papers and parchments that required my attention.

My fingers are stained from the mixing of hues of slate and blue, flashes of umber and gold, red and green; the same fingers are scarred, fletched with nicks from sharpening my very fine goose feather quills. When I work, I wear white cotton gloves, each pair washed in the hottest of hot water after use. I have spectacles, thick half-moons of polished glass to magnify the things I must discern and craft; these perch on the end of my nose only when I am mid-copy. Aelfrith says I look like someone's granny, for all my smooth skin and dark hair.

"No one," she taunts, "would ever believe you young."

Edda merely grunts at that and adds that I need to get out more—that *both* Aelfrith and I need to take in the healthful air and exercise that she regards as her very own sustenance. We three have different mothers, so we are more like to be dissimilar than if we shared a maternal imprint. Fathers have so much less influence.

The scratching of the nib, which has almost hypnotised me, has a rival: the tap-tap-tapping of a bare frozen branch from the wild cherry tree by the side of the house.

My scriptorium (with a tiny bed cupboard in one corner) is located on the second floor, in the room with the most windows so I might steal in all the light I can. The cherry tree is naked and frosted; it looks dead, as if it will never bloom again. The cold coming from the glass panes may just convince me this is true—this place cannot be too warm, so I may have only the smallest of fires, banked low in the grate. I prefer to not work in winter (hence my interrogation of Father as to the need for urgency and the status of the client—I'd prefer someone I could send away with a flea in the ear until, at *my* convenience, she or he returned when bid).

I have spent the day copying this wretched thing, stopping but once to read a couplet aloud, hoping that speech might add some meaning, but it remained nonsense. Looking up I blink hard until my eyes stop watering at the change in focus, and watch the thin branch as the wind pushes it this way and that; any moment now, any moment, it will snap. But no, the thing is hardier than I would have thought. It endures.

I stand, stretch, arching my back until I hear the four distinct cracks that say my spine is aligned once more. I take stiff steps over to the window (where a cushioned seat awaits, draped with shawls) and survey the garden, white as a fine linen sheet, its purity broken only by the shadowy things there's not *quite* enough fall to cover: the chopping block, the wood pile, the swing we use only in summer and only when we are feeling particularly frivolous. And a dark mobile thing, the size of a small dog or a large cat, which is inching its way forward, terribly slowly, shaking the snow off its gentleman's coat quite determinedly.

Brock.

All stiffness is gone from my limbs and I fly from the room, down the staircase with its carved banister and hideous newel post (the head of a green man, but not as cheerful as it should be), making a great commotion that brings my family from various directions. I don't even worry about a cloak, but fling open the door and charge out into the white.

For precious moments I'm lost, blinded, then I catch sight once more of the determined lope—almost a waddle, with his limbs so chilled—of the black fur and the hoary streak down his back. I stumble through the cold powder and catch up the poor creature. He is heavy; he smells strongly, oh so strongly; he looks at me with bleary-eyed distrust.

"There, there," I croon, stroking one hand over his head and face as I trudge towards the front door, where Father and my sisters wait. "You're safe here, little brock, little badger."

And the poxy little whoreson bites me.

Not viciously—it was merely a warning nip—and only on the one finger but still he breaks the skin and it wells red and stings. Then he snuggles against me, smugly content.

• • •

Edda washes and salves my would. While she applies a bandage to the two sharp punctures, I glare at the animal, curled snug in a blanket-lined basket by the kitchen fire.

His eyes are closed, his breathing is even and he is making a deep throaty noise somewhere between a grunt and a purr. One lid lifts, a brown orb stares at me, then slowly lowers again. In a bowl in front of his basket (both of which items once belonged to Father's long-dead hunting hound) are slices of preserved apple and cherries, tepid milk, porridge and honey. His left hind foot is bandaged; a deep cut slashed its fat pad. The cold had stopped the bleeding, but once inside, the flow started again. He let us bathe the limb with warm water and apply a rosemary salve to it before Edda swaddled him like a baby. He didn't bite *her*.

"He must have gotten lost," says Aelfrith, admiring his coal coat. He is a young male, not a cub, but not a fully grown boar. The streak of white from his snout to his tail is clean as clean can be. All things considered he is a very *hygienic* badger; well, except for the smell, which is not unpleasant, merely strong and musky.

Edda nods. "Yes, he's wandered away from his sett."

"Or perhaps he's been driven out—old boar and new boar can't live in peace," I say, flexing my finger in hope of loosening Edda's tight wrapping. "Especially as he seems to be a biter."

"He only bit *you*, Gytha."

"I'm sure it was just to say *hello*," laughs Aelfrith.

I give my sisters the look they deserve and am about to serve up a retort when Father's bulk hoves into view. "Still fussing with that confounded animal?"

"*O God, how manifold are your works!*" I quote.

"*In wisdom thou hast made them all,*" follows Edda.

Aelfrith chimes in with, "*The earth is full of your myriad blessed creatures.*"

"*Yea, blessed!*" we chorus, our mockery taking on the ring of a hymn.

Adelbert regrets (many times daily, I suspect) teaching his daughters scriptures, for we have ended up with firm beliefs, but also varied means of arguing with him on his own terms.

"Gytha, don't you have work to do? You know the client expects that book by season's end."

"And yes, I've been meaning to talk to you about this, Father. Winter work and no say to me in the deadline! It's not acceptable." I frown.

He sees that bluster and bullying will not get him far this day, so he softens his tone. "Gytha, I am sorry, but this is a special job. No more like this, I promise—but with the coin from this one commission, we need not work for two whole years!"

"*We* don't work, Father. *I* work," I grumble, but turn on my heel and stride from the kitchen.

In the scriptorium, the fire has gone out and I have only a few more hours of usable light left. I poke at the embers and stir them up until flames lick at the twigs I throw on. When it is crackling, I defiantly throw on a larger log than I normally would and watch it catch with satisfaction.

I rub my hands together until they warm, massage the fingers (carefully with the tender one), then sit down to begin once more (page ten: a drawing of a young woman, who seems to be sleeping, but for the fact there is a great tear over her heart; and words in a language I do not understand, but which make me nervous nonetheless).

There is a scratching at the door.

I curse and pull it open. No one is there. Then: a furry weight as Master Brock crosses the threshold and treads over my feet, to sit himself on the rug in front of the fire.

We stare at each other for a moment, until he closes his eyes.

I shrug and return to the book.

• • •

I come down to a scene of high circus the next morning, the badger limping at my heels. I stop in the kitchen doorway and he peeks out from behind my skirts.

"The cheese is gone!" Father shouts.

"The cheese?" I ask.

"All the cheese!" says Edda.

"All our lovely, lovely cheese," wails Aelfrith.

"The cheese?" I repeat, thinking perhaps I am not awake, but still dreaming. I did not sleep well, and the welt on my finger throbbed throughout the night.

Father looks at me as though I am an imbecile. "The cheese has been eaten. Our entire winter supply. Gone."

Father is fond of his cheese.

"And no sign of a thief. No doors unlocked, no windows broken," says Edda knowingly.

"Well, don't look at me." I traipse down the narrow stairs to the cellar, which is a surprisingly small room, half the size of the kitchen, and lined with shelves laden with bottles of preserved fruit and vegetables from last summer, wrapped parcels of salted fish and pork, sacks of flour and sugar, small jars of salt and ground pepper, three kegs of Father's cider, one of his brandy, and a distinct lack of the five large wheels of cheese I set there at the beginning of winter.

I look closely at the walls, the floor, as if I might find a secret passageway heretofore unsuspected, then I shake my head. It's probably Aelfrith, wandering in her sleep again and now feeding her frustrations by eating. She'd best stop or we'll be well out of food before the snows end. Turning to go back up, I find myself pinned by a dark gaze in a curious face. I narrow my eyes and wonder at the badger sitting patiently at the top of the stairs. The cheese was on the highest shelf, my head height, and badgers are not known for their climbing ability, nor for their love of dairy. I shake my head once more and return to the kitchen, wondering how to phrase my suspicions of Aelfrith politely.

But this drama, it seems, has passed and another, quieter one has taken its place. Father is nowhere to be seen, and my sisters have moved themselves to the parlour, where they sit expectantly. Aelfrith, in particular, is preening.

"Where's Father?"

"In his study and not to be disturbed," says Edda.

Aelfrith nods. "He's with a client—*the* client." She takes a deep breath, which she exhales with words riding upon it, "He's ever so handsome, Gytha!"

Even Edda nods and I've not seen her enthused about the appearance of anything but a horse for many a year. Then again, we don't get too many men passing by, only the occasional monk, old friends of Father's, random clients, and tinkers. Certainly none from the burnt-out bones of Southarp village.

I make a move towards the door and Edda leaps up, terribly distressed and barring my way. "Oh, no! You mustn't disturb them—Father said so."

I narrow my eyes and stomp off to my workroom. Honestly, she doesn't know me at all. I sit at the window seat and watch, noting the absence of either horse or carriage. It doesn't take long before I hear the front door open and see a figure step out from beneath the storm porch, firmly settling a tricorne hat upon thick golden hair.

He gets a good head-start while I fight with the frozen casement latch and eventually clamber down the stout limbs of the cherry tree. I follow his tracks, deep footprints, and huddle against the shawls I threw hastily around my shoulders. Soon, I'm into the woods; icicles hang where leaves should be, and the patches of sky glimpsed through the bare tangle of branches are grey and unwelcoming. If I do not find him soon I will give up—I'm no fool. He will visit again and I will be waiting; next time I will charge into Father's study and take the golden-haired man's measure.

I'm cold and shivering. The moment I turn around, there he is, grinning like a wolf.

I see none of the handsomeness Aelfrith was mooning over, merely appetite and a will to do whatever he wishes. In his hands, a knife, long and thin, a stiletto blade; his knuckles are white around the ivory handle.

"The book," I blurt and his expression alters. Ah! Here it is, that beautiful mask. But I've seen what it covers and I will not be deceived. "I wanted to ask you about your book."

Smoothly he hides the knife in the sheath at his belt, tucks it out of sight as if it might be easily forgotten. He is richly dressed, his coat lined with ermine.

"My apologies—I could only hear someone following me and thought to defend myself from footpads. I did not mean to frighten you." He points and I follow the direction of his kid-gloved finger. "My coach is there."

And so it is, on the road above where we stand in a hollow. Black and shiny as ebony, with four black steeds, a driver and a footman, both blank faced as they peer down at us. I find myself shaking and will it to stop. I clear my throat.

"The book—I was wondering if you knew its name and author? Only—I've been wondering. Professional curiosity," I say, trying to look scholarly and serious.

He gives me a brilliant smile and shakes his head. "Afraid not, Mistress Gytha—it is Gytha, yes, my copyist? I am—a collector— the book took my fancy. It's value is purely ornamental and sentimental. It reminds me of someone very dear. But its ink is fading, the cover is derelict. I require a copy."

"But I can re-ink the text, clean the cover, fix the bindings."

"No, no. My memory hinges on the contents, not the container. New is best." His expression tells me that he does not like old things; he is one of those who prefer possessions to be pristine and unused when they come to his hand. An old book is not the artefact for him—the knowledge therein is what he wants, but he desires it in a splendid new *repository*. I notice his clothing—blue breeches, gold and cream waistcoat, white silk shirt, silver-grey frock coat and highly polished boots—not one item seems overly *worn*. Indeed, there is no sign of anything having been worn before at all; there is no fading of colour, nor weakening of nap, no hint of *threadbare* at the collar and wrists, and certainly no wrinkles or folds that might come with habitual attire. This man likes his things *shiny*.

"Where did you find it?"

He smiles again and does not answer, effortlessly striding up the slope to his conveyance. He tips his hat and climbs in. He leans out the window and says, "I shall return in the spring, Mistress Gytha, to claim my book. I trust you'll not disappoint me."

I stand shivering for some time after he is gone.

• • •

St Simeon-in-the-Grove is a small monastery, all things considered. A mere twenty monks, aged from twelve (two boys left on the doorstep some years before) to ninety-five (the librarian).

Edda has let me take our oldest horse, a tall beastie, with feathered feet and a mane like a blanket. Hengroen moves slowly and surely—it's a bit like being on a very sturdy boat, his gait is almost floating, which makes me feel both safe and seasick after an hour on his broad back. My rear protests as I dismount and I groan loudly. The young monk who comes forward to take Hengroen looks astounded as I tip back the hood of my thick travelling cloak—obviously he has been brought up to believe women are crafty creatures, both fragrant and evil, but not given to terrible bodily noises. He should hear Edda after a meal of beans.

"Larcwide will see me," I say, before he begins the speech about how my kind are not allowed in the monastery. A rule instituted since—in fact because of—my father's tenure. "I'm bringing a book."

Of course, I'm *assuming* he will see me as he has done before— that he will not remember that little fracas a few years back. This young man knows the librarian collects books, is consulted on them regularly, is an authority on things that hold words in one place. I'm banking on the very good chance that he has been terrified by at least one of the old man's tirades, and will be too afraid to refuse me.

"Don't worry," I say, and pat his hand. He shivers the way a horse does when a fly lands on its hide. "I'll take the side entrance so as not to cause a fuss."

I'm rewarded with a flash of relief and he nods, leading my great mount to the stables for a rest. I dart across the rectangle of snow that in summer is a patch of green, keeping my head down, but I needn't bother—most of the brothers are at prayer this time of day. At the bottom of a tall tower—not the one with the bell in it, the one opposite—there is a small slender door, overgrown with winter ivy (which in this season looks deceased, as if the wall is shedding its skin), but a sharp eye will note the dry grey handle twisted about with dead vines, almost invisible. I get splinters, but the ingress opens with relative ease. Inside there is a set of black stone steps curving around and up. The air is dry and cold, but warmer as I rise. I can smell ink and paper, and old man.

The librarian is shuffling back and forth between cases, twitching books from the shelves, muttering, sliding them back into place or shifting them to another spot. The shelves climb the walls and in the centre of the tower is a series of platforms, weighted down with even more tomes, reached by a sort of elevator and pulley system, that creaks above. A thin monk steps off on the third platform as I watch, nimbly balancing an armful of volumes. Larcwide glares upward as dust particles drift down.

"I told you," he yells, "to clean your shoes! And did you? Did you?"

There is a muffled and indecipherable reply from aloft, and the old man swears softly.

"Father Larcwide?"

He swings around in surprise and squints at me. He won't rant about me being a woman, although he may well rant about my incursion. He shared in many of my father's adventures, but his continued presence at St Simeon is testament to both his inability to produce offspring and to his unassailed position as bibliognost. By virtue of his irreplaceable knowledge, his transgressions could be overlooked. Unfortunately for Adelbert's career, anyone can be an under-enthused abbot and mediocre copyist.

"Father Larcwide, I need to talk to you," I say and hold up the satchel hanging at my side. His eyes sparkle and he gestures for me to come closer.

He peers at my face and recognition dawns. "Adelbert's girl? The clever one."

I grin and nod. "Gytha. I need you to look at something."

"Why me?" he grumps, contrary for the sake of it.

"Because there's none like you." His ego, duly stroked, allows him to lead me along a maze of shelves to an alcove just big enough for a writing desk and two chairs. He sits and invites me to do the same. I draw the thing out of the bag, and unwrap it from the layers of shawl, then place it on the table between us. Larcwide leans forward to read the now-visible title. I have been working at it, testing out a variety of oils and soft cloths, trying to wear away at the black mess. It was slow toil: if I used too much of the lubricant, too much pressure as I rubbed, the stuff would have simply eaten its way through the cover. It is a capricious mix, with a peculiar personality all of its own (bought from the strange little man who travels in spring and summer and brings me supplies of the things that are hardest to find). One letter at a time. So carefully. So very carefully, until:

Murcianus. A Book of Craft.

Larcwide's hands shake as he reaches out but does not touch the tome. His fingers are blue and brittle, stained with age spots. They hover over what I have so painstakingly cleaned.

"Do you know what this is? Of course you don't," his voice quivers. Then, "Where did you get this?"

No, I don't know, although, I have a suspicion, have had since I reached a page I recognised: a drawing of a hand with candles set in the tops of all the fingers and the thumb. A hand of glory. But I choose to act the innocent and answer only his second question. "A client. A commission my father took on."

He shakes his head. "Oh, Adelbert. Will you never learn?" He closes his eyes, no more than a blink, but he looks exhausted when he opens them again.

"What is it?" I ask.

He nods. "A *grimoire*. A book of craft. And this one . . . " He finally picks the thing up and rubs his fingers on the back cover, in the right-hand bottom corner, finding what I already know is there: the subtle relief of an embossment, *M*. He almost drops the book, so great is his surprise. "Belonged to *him*!"

I want to poke and prod him, extract the information swiftly, but I wait patiently. He looks at me suspiciously, then with judgment. I don't know who *he* is.

"Murcianus. This is the Bitterwood Bible."

And I stare blankly at him and Larcwide's expression rolls into utter despair.

"Murcianus, one of the greatest encyclopaedists ever known. Well, of the arcane and the eldritch specifically. He wandered the world, recording and compiling every strange ritual, every bizarre being, every spell, curse, myth, legend, enchantment, magical locations . . . " the monk seems to run out of words. "Just . . . everything!"

I remain silent.

"Those books, nowadays, are so rare you barely find one outside of a private collection. They are wonderfully illustrated, most erudite and informative, filled with wisdom and wit and scholarship." He turns my tome over in his hands. "But there are other volumes, Gytha, like this one, written in the language of witches, comprehensible to only a few, this one is a rarity. Full of knowledge best left unknown, things too dangerous to be writ down. There are places, Gytha, where his works are banned; where those who carry them are burned, their ashes scattered."

His face reddens and he looks away, remembering to whom he speaks; remembering at last our argument when I asked him for information my father refused. The one occasion I managed to extract the name of my mother from Adelbert, he was in his cups. He'd called her Hafwen and told me she had been so briefly beautiful, then burned. She was his final indiscretion, the one that sent him from the monastery, lucky to leave with his life. That is all I was able to get from him before he passed out; he woke the next day with a sore head and foul temper, and would tell me nothing more. When I asked Larcwide, tried to extract an answer, he banned me from coming to see him. I'd hoped the intervening years and his age had dimmed the memory.

"And the book. Where would *this* have come from?"

He shrugged. "Lost? Left behind? Stolen? Who knows. All I know is this isn't some harmless thing you're working on, Gytha." He pauses, suddenly suspicious. "You haven't read from it?"

I would like to deny it, but my blush makes a liar of me. Larcwide goes pales and pushes the book at me, insistent. "What did you read?"

Flicking carefully through the pages I find the relevant one, with the drawings of wheat sheaves and other plants. The old man's dark eyes skim the words and they seem to make sense to him as he sits back and puffs out a sigh of relief. "Transformation, but it's just a season spell. Not much harm in it."

"What's that?"

"To work change for a few months only, to make an animal change its shape."

"Not a person?" I worry at the bandaged finger, which has not healed these past weeks, but itches still.

"Oh no, that requires far more effort, instruments and ingredients—and if the subject is unwilling? Even stronger items are needed." He rubs his hands together. Larcwide seems to know rather more about magic than he should, I think, but do not say.

"But you have no ability, so I shouldn't worry about it. Just don't do it again—some spells are so powerful they need only be spoken, without intent, for them to effect a change, unwanted or otherwise. You should know, though, that every bit of magic leaves a trace, Gytha, no matter small. Even the tiniest skerrick may rub off, leaving the potential for *metamorphosis* in its wake."

"Thank you, Father." I take the book from him and begin to wrap it up once more. He leans across the table, grasps my wrist and says, "What will you do with this?"

"This is a commission, I cannot simply make it disappear." I lower my voice. "And I fear this client, Father, I fear him greatly. I will not risk my life nor that of my family by refusing to give him what he has demanded."

"But, child, it's too dangerous. If you will not listen to sense, I shall have to tell the Abbot."

"And if you do so, there's every good chance I will be burned—it won't matter that this book is not mine, it will simply matter that it is in my possession." I hold his gaze for a long moment. I do not think he would like to see me as ashes.

"What will you do?" he asks quietly once more, defeated.

I shake my head. "I'll think of something."

• • •

I wipe my hands on a rag, then wash them with hot water and Edda's whortleberry soap, massaging the cramps and the smell of ink and oil out of them. Passing my desk I survey the work: the replica is almost done. I am exhausted and my eyes ache; I have been copying by the light of the fire and as many lanterns and candles as I could find without leaving my family in darkness. Outside the black mirror of the window, the air smells of spring. The days have grown longer, warmer, but I have spent an eternity inside, working on this damnable book. The time is fast approaching and although I have not slept well since the client's last visit, it is not the sole reason for my sleeplessness.

The doors to the bed cupboard are open, just a little, and inside I can make out blankets and coverlets heaped up, mounded over the form of a slumbering young man with the thickest, blackest hair relieved only by a streak of white down the middle. He snuffles and snores, his hands curled like paws, batting at the pillows as he stirs, then stilling as he settles once again.

I struggle with the buttons of my dress, then drop it to the rug, half-undone. Crawling in beside him, I fit myself into the half-moon of his body and breathe deeply. He smells musky, slightly sweet. I close my eyes, nestling as his arms come around me.

"I want peaches," he mumbles, breath warm in my ear.

"You ate them all, remember?" That was how I found him, in his-night-time shape, late on the evening I returned from St Simeon-in-the-Grove, crouched on the floor of the cellar, struggling with a bottle of preserved peaches. His hands seemed not to know quite what to do, and he dropped the bottle, which smashed impressively. He merely gave a grunt and neatly picked slices of the preserved fruit from the glass, carefully examining it for shards, then elegantly chewed it in tiny bites.

"It doesn't stop me wanting them," he points out, in a reasonable tone.

"Ordinary badgers don't eat peaches."

"Well, I'm no ordinary badger, obviously," he says, and shrugs, a movement that takes his whole body, not just his shoulders.

Badgerish.

"You ate plenty this evening. I cannot believe how much food you put away—and Aelfrith insists upon feeding you twice a day. You won't fit in my bed soon."

"Get a bigger bed." As he cuddles comfortably into my back. I take hold of one of his hands, weave our fingers together.

"At least there's no cheese left."

"Oh, that cheese! Terrible cheese. Awful constipation."

"An ordinary badger doesn't eat *cheese*. Or indeed, spend his winter in a girl's bed."

"An ordinary badger doesn't get hit by stray magic." He nuzzles my neck, pauses. "How long will this last, do you think?"

I shake my head, feeling dizzy as if I am dangling over a terrible pit where all the loss in the world resides. "I don't know." I squeeze his hands. "What do you think about, in the day? When you're . . . "

"Four-legged and furred? Badgerish things: about food and warmth, staying safe, about spring and blackberries and wild cherries and windfalls apples." He wiggles against me to suggest the time for talking is done and other activities should be considered.

Here is the problem with raising daughters so far from suitable mates: it makes them prey to roaming, transformed badgers. It makes their hearts easy pickings, like windfall apples.

• • •

I keep my eyes downcast, but watch through lowered lashes. Adelbert is trying to hide his surprise at my seeming modesty. He is also trying to hide his look of suspicion. We sit in his study, all three of us on separate over-stuffed armchairs.

The client has my work in his hands. He is appreciating the fine red leather cover I've added. It is different to the old one, but I see that I was right: this pleases him, this newness. There is neither title nor author on the front.

"Your workmanship is exquisite, Mistress Gytha. I commend you." He tosses my father a heavy bag of coins, and Adelbert's eyes go soft, like a drunk seeing his first drink of the day. "And the original?"

"I burned it," I pipe up and two pairs of eyes turn on me. I hold up a small box and shake it gently. "The ashes. The book—the ink was almost unreadable by the time I finished and I did not think you would care, sir. It was old and not new."

The man stares at me for long moments, then nods and brings out a smile. "Yes, you're right, Mistress Gytha. Although, such a decision I would have liked to make myself."

He does not care the original is gone, he merely cares about my high-handedness. I offer the box and manage to sound sincere, "I apologise, sir. Would you like . . . "

He shakes his head dismissively and I nod. "I *am* very sorry, sir."

"No matter, no matter," he smiles and waves his hand. He places the book into a leather case he has brought specifically for the purpose. "I shall take my leave."

Father sees him to the door, then returns to the study. Through the open windows comes the warm air of the first day of spring. I watch, just as I watched him that first occasion, as the client appears around the side of the house, then disappears into the green of the woods. I do not pursue him this time. I watch until the trees swallow him, until I am sure he is nearing his carriage waiting up on the road, waiting far from us so no one will know he has been here, has brought something here, so no one will question and perhaps hunt here, or suspect him of whatever he is doing.

"Well done, Gytha," says my father. His good mood cannot be contained. He moves around the room, laughing and joking, pouring us both a glass from the last bottle of the summer-berry wine. He counts out my coin into a smaller purse and gives it to me. I sit opposite and stare at him until he becomes uncomfortable. "What is it?"

"Hafwen." I do not say 'my mother' for she has never been that, only ever an absence to whom I was able to put a name a few years ago. He makes a sharp sound and jerks his head to one side before bringing his gaze back to me.

"Well, what about her?"

"Who was she?"

"A girl. Just a girl."

"Was she a witch?"

I have never seen such grief in my father, such a terrible thing clawing its way up from inside and painting itself across his face. He lowers his head so I cannot see, then slowly raises it once more. Everything is gone but an awful blankness. I will get nothing from him.

"Enjoy the spring, Gytha, while there are no new commissions," he tells me and looks away, starring resolutely out the window at the garden, but not, I suspect, seeing it.

• • •

From the blanket box at the foot of my bed, I lift out several coverlets, folded winter dresses and shawls. At the bottom is the original Murcianus *grimoire*, its text and diagrams re-inked each day before I copied it. Each page has been dusted with a setting powder of my own devising. I run my fingers across the cover and wonder how long it will take me to learn the language of witches, to take the knowledge I need for my purpose. I wonder if Larcwide might be prepared to teach me. I wonder if I have any of my mother's blood in me to help.

I notice a four-legged absence. I look around for the badger. He is not in his usual spot, the rug by the hearth, but then as the days have grown longer he has been roaming about the house more, seemingly restless. Perhaps he is in the kitchen, begging food from Aelfrith. He will be so fat soon.

My sister is rolling out dough; a dozen apples sit on the bench, waiting to be peeled. Beside them, a bucket of blackberries, lush and dark. But there is no sign of the badger.

"Where is he? Where is Brock?"

Aelfrith looks at me in surprise. "He wanted to go out."

The kitchen door stands open. From the threshold I survey the green grass and the plants, growing thickly in the house-garden.

There is no sign of him.

No track, no trail, no hint.

I run out, to the stables. Edda has a curry comb and is grooming Hengroen.

"Have you seen him? Have you seen the badger?" I ask, uncaring that my voice is breaking.

She shakes her head, and *tuts.* "You knew he would go, Gytha. I know you're fond of him, but he's a wild creature. It's not as if he's a dog or a horse."

I knew the spell would end. I knew he would change back, but I thought he would stay. I thought he would wait. I thought I could find something in the *grimoire*, some means to make him transform for good, to keep him with me.

A breeze starts up but the dancing air does nothing to lift my spirits. I did not think his badgerish instincts would lead him away from me so soon. The itching of my punctured finger is all I have left.

• • •

It is only three days later that I see the client again.

I thought I would have longer. I had planned to leave when he had gone, when I had both book and badger. I had planned to run and find another life, but with my love departed, I had fallen into a funk. I had lost the will to move. I lost any care that the golden-haired man might try one of his new spells and find it did not work. That he would try another and it, too, would not work. And another and another until he realised that I had copied each and every enchantment, each and every curse, incorrectly. Just a tiny detail in each, a line missing, an ingredient changed, a direction left out, an instrument added.

Sitting on the window seat in my room, I see the man breaking out of the woods, his long knife catching the sun, and I finally rediscover the will to move. I bundle the *grimoire* into a satchel and drape the bag's strap across my chest. I clatter down the stairs, run into Edda, who protests, until I put a hand over her mouth, the bandage still on the finger that will not heal.

"Sister, if you never listen to me again, listen now. Lock the doors. Do not let anyone in, especially not that man, the handsome man. Don't let him in, Edda, no matter what. Keep all the doors locked. I am sorry for whatever I may have brought down upon you."

I flee before she can answer. I tear out the door, creep around the corner of the house, then make sure the client catches sight of me. He gives a sound somewhere between a yell and a scream, but all rage, and pounds after me. It's the only thing I can do, to draw him away from my family.

I know these woods far better than he. I know the paths both seen and hidden, I dart between trees, under hanging mosses, I hurdle over rocks and stiles and rills, but still he keeps on my trail.

Then, all is silence. I stop, wait, turning, turning, turning, trying to see if he is anywhere in sight. From behind a huge oak, he lunges, the knife preceding him and slicing across my left side, not enough to kill, but to wound, to hurt. I swing the heavy satchel up at him and catch him in the face. He goes down like a sack of potatoes. I run.

I keep running, fleeing into the darkest, deepest part of the wood, bleeding, weakening, aching, my lungs burning, my legs shaking. In a green hollow, a spot dotted with mounds and slopes, I trip over a branch and the breath *whumps* out of me. I hit my chin and bite my tongue and iron tastes in my mouth. Behind me I can hear the crashing, the swearing, the inexorable rampaging of the golden-haired man.

My injured finger tingles, twinges, burns. I hear a chittering, a squeak, a growl close by. Searching, I find the mouth of a hole and in that mouth a creature of black and white, a fine well-fed badger, who calls to me. I scramble up try to stand, but my entire body convulses, arcs in on itself. The hand with the injured finger curls beyond my will, as does the other. They turn ebony with fur, the nails elongating, becoming hard horn. I drop on all fours and shudder as the transformation completes. The boar's call changes, the noise more urgent. With the strap of the satchel still around my new shoulders, I scamper up the hillock, and follow my love down the tunnel and into the sett. The book is dragged along behind, getting caught now and then, but the corridors are wide enough for it to get through with a tug or two. We come to a large chamber filled with clean straw; the strap slips from me, the book's progress halting, pushing up a wave of the dry yellow covering that will eventually settle over it.

I can no longer hear the sounds above ground of a man thwarted and driven beyond his patience. I cannot hear the raging and the cries of loss. I lie still and my mate snuffles at the wound in my side, licking it clean. He curves around me, our black and white fur a chessboard match. Even as I hope my family will be safe, I begin to forget Fox Hollow House. Ideas about books and inks and pages and covers all subside into a dim memory place. I begin to think of worms and beetles, of windfall apples, blackberries, and wild cherries. I begin to think badgerish thoughts.

•••••••••••

THE PRESERVATION SOCIETY

JASON NAHRUNG

I

Jack entered last. The darkness closed in on him like a fist. The windowless room had a darkly timbered floor and walls painted so deeply burgundy they could have been black. Candles accentuated the gloom rather than illuminating it. The iron chandelier hung like a dead spider from the decorative rose in the centre of the ceiling; the pressed metal was the colour of bone.

Anticipation sharpened his senses. He had come in through the only door, painted to blend in with the wall. Six chairs surrounded a long, thin table in the centre of the room. The stainless steel shone in the subdued light, a gutter forming a grim depression that led to a glass vial under the drain: not a drop was to be wasted.

Jasmine, a floating pale face with blonde hair piled on top and a voluminous black dress rendered vague and shapeless in the gloom, sat opposite the door and gestured for them to sit. Her fingernails were thin and sharp, glowing at the tips. Her fingers appeared inordinately long where they poked from delicate lace gloves. She had a fragrance to her, a blend of night-blooming flowers and old bookshops.

Leather creaked under him as Jack settled in a recliner. Each chair had a round side table with burgundy cloth and black napkin. The only other furniture was a drinks cart, holding nothing other than a collection of fine crystal goblets; they threw faint orange-red patterns against the wall, like the reflection of sunlight shimmering on water.

Elise sat opposite him, her eyes shining with excitement as she smoothed her skirt. Her mother, raven-like, sat next to her; then the dandy in his long coat, the nob in his business suit. He had already forgotten the men's names. He'd barely listened to the overly polite conversation at the welcome in the drawing room; had said little. Hadn't even minded so much that Elise had given him the cold shoulder under the watchful glare of her mother. Tonight was all about this moment.

Jasmine held up a dainty brass bell. All eyes fixed on that instrument. Jack jerked as she gave the bell a calculated shake and it rang high and clear. His heart thudded. His body flushed hot, as blood surged through his system. He'd been fasting, as instructed, even since he'd left Brissie days ago. God, he was thirsty. His mouth was as dry as drought; his teeth like the bones of dead sheep.

A dark-skinned girl in a starched white nurse's uniform—no cap—entered, leading a shambling woman in a thin, white gown. The transparent material barely hid the radiance of the woman's tanned, finely muscled flesh. Nipples were dark suggestions under the fabric. Her hair, sun-bleached blonde, was cut short to reveal the throat. The overhead candles made dark shadows of her eyes; she had the distant stare of someone under mesmerism. She radiated heat and blood, smelled of saltwater.

Should there be chanting, Jack wondered? The sacrifice had arrived, and he felt dirty, now that he could see her. . . but she was here by choice. He tried to find comfort in that. But did she know that she wouldn't be leaving here, at least, not in the same way she arrived? If she'd been promised eternity, he was fairly certain no-one had told her the *how*. And if she'd been promised an end—there must be some desperation fuelling this act—then she was being cheated. She might not know it, but she would not end here. Someone would take her home with them, a collectable to be masturbated over. He should've been wearing a raincoat, carrying tissues.

The woman stumbled and the nurse helped her, first removing the gown, then holding her hand as she sat on the side of the table. She swung her feet up and stretched out. Her flesh goose pimpled. The room felt warm and close to Jack, but he supposed the metal must be chill. There were straps for ankles and wrists, but the nurse didn't secure them.

The nurse wheeled the trolley over and opened a drawer. Objects glinted silver on a velvet mat.

"The subject," Jasmine told them, "is not drugged, but has been placed under a low-level suggestion to ease the taking. I assure you, there is nothing untoward in her bloodstream. To be certain, I will take the first sample."

Jasmine nodded, a curt starting signal. Jack saw the movement from the corner of his eye; he was focused on what the nurse was doing. He held back a moan of need as flesh was pierced—a shunt sparkled like some exotic piece of body jewellery in the woman's chest. She barely reacted: a slight shudder of the feet, a subtle increase in her anxiety curling into the room. Fresh blood tainted the air as the nurse threw a stained cotton ball into a bin under the trolley.

"The glasses are on a heated tray to maximise taste," Jasmine told them.

The nurse took a goblet and tapped the shunt. He heard the liquid hit the glass, smelt the gush. His parched mouth flowed with saliva that contained both a mild anaesthetic and a highly efficient anticoagulant. Neither would be needed tonight.

The nurse shut the tap and—quickly, efficiently—took the glass to Jasmine, who held it as though it was the holy grail, waved it under her nose to enjoy the bouquet, then sipped, rolling it around in her mouth. It was quite a performance. The stench of desire filled the room. The gent, seated next to Jack, growled.

"Ladies and gentlemen," Jasmine said, her eyes slit in reverie, "the experience is superb. There is no fear to be tasted here. Perhaps the faintest pinch of melancholy, but nothing more. It flavours the experience; it does not pollute it."

She told the nurse to proceed and five goblets were half-filled, then delivered to each of them. Jack's hands trembled as he lifted his glass, so warm in his palms, pink bubbles still dotting its ruby surface. The five of them were dogs, straining at the leash; he was past embarrassment.

"Ladies and gentlemen, I give you Angela," Jasmine announced. "Bon appétit and bon voyage."

He drank.

• • •

In the heat of the day, smelling of horse and sweat and chemicals, they muster the cattle into the yards and dip them for ticks and buffalo fly. The flies are a nuisance but the ticks are vile, buds of stolen blood spotting the herd's necks and guts and legs; rubbery, the ticks burst like bloody berries if squeezed, but the heads, buried in flesh, can infect, and en masse they can make a beast do poorly.

Afterwards, he tries living off cattle by moonlight, but unlike the tick, he finds no nourishment there. Only the two-legged herd can give him what he needs. He feels himself drifting away, like trying to live on air and water. He needs more, and out here with the roos and the gum trees and the beady-eyed crows, there is no more to be had.

He's never met anyone who can so much as stand the thought of ticks.

• • •

Angie wears a silver mermaid on a chain. It catches the sunlight as it dangles below her tanned chest, seeming to swim of its own accord as she dives under the waves. The pendant was a present from her daughter—Richard said Nerida had picked it out herself. She never takes it off.

II

Jasmine rang the bell, jarring them all back to awareness. Angela looked pale, her breath shallow. The bruiser opened the door. He was tall and wide and thick and looked at each of them as though he had metal detectors in his eyes, though he'd swept them all when they'd arrived. It had been a perfunctory act: you didn't spend as much money and surrender a quart of blood simply to cause trouble. Besides, any ill intentions would be transparent at the first taste.

"Ladies and gentlemen, let us adjourn to the drawing room," Jasmine said, motioning them out. "It is time to bid."

They reluctantly pulled themselves from their chairs—Elise actually swooned. She looked radiant, lips ripe and red, eyes bloodshot, flesh rosy with blood and remembered sunshine. The thought of tasting her made him hard.

Jack took a long time to walk past the woman on the table, feeling her life already slipping from his veins. The cool of seawater, the salt crusting on his skin, the delicious heat. . .

He trailed after the others. The guard shut the door and took his station, leaving only the nurse in the chamber. Mundane worldly odours—eucalyptus, brine, petrochemicals—encroached from the outdoors. The cloying miasma of the human condition crowded Jack like ghosts: sweat and food, detergents, piss. Blood.

Jasmine left them "to savour and anticipate" and they spread around the drawing room, jealous even of sharing space. The nervous bonhomie of their brief pre-aperitif meeting had been left in the tap room.

"This is my third blood walk," Mrs Winterbourne announced, her voice slicing through the stillness. "I got to keep the last one." A hand touched her breast, her lips; her lashes flickered as though a movie was unreeling on the backs of her lids.

"Geez, Mother, rub it in, why don't you?"

Mrs Winterbourne flashed a sharp-toothed smile at her sparrow-faced daughter. Elise appeared old enough to be Mrs Winterbourne's younger sister. Jack couldn't be certain just how long ago Elise had been preserved—her blood hadn't revealed that fact to him when they'd been swapping claret in her Brisbane loft, and it wasn't polite to ask—but it'd been well before his time. No amount of hip threads or jargon could hide the age in their eyes. The tedium wore them all down eventually. Tonight proved just how far they were prepared to go to hold it at bay, and he was hardly in a position to judge: he was here, wasn't he? But he'd had no idea . . .

Mrs Winterbourne caressed Elise's cheek with the back of her hand. "Don't worry, sweetheart. You might be more fortunate this time."

Elise stared, furious, out the window, where there was nothing to see: the dark of hillside against the dark of sky, a glow suggesting the city of Cairns nestled out of sight between mountains and mudflats. The house was so still, so quiet, they could have been the only people left on the planet.

Except that, no-one in this room had been a person in a very long time.

Jack was the youngest here, of that he was certain. The country had been in the grip of the Depression when he'd opened the farmhouse door to the wrong swaggie. Jack had been lucky, according to some he'd met since. There were a lot more rules these days about who got preserved and who didn't. A lot more regulation. Australia wasn't as carefree as it used to be.

Neither was he.

• • •

The watercourses are as cracked and dry as pine bark. The sky is gritty with dust. Dawn and sunset bleed over the parched country. Spirits wither, hearts shrink, the hot westerly picks up dreams and lives and blows them all to hell along with the topsoil. The molasses runs out and only the mustiest hay remains in the shed. The cattle are little more than hides stretched over skeletons. Sometimes a dying cow's skull is particularly thick and it has to be shot twice. When the pyres have burnt cold, Jack and his father dig a hole and bury the bones. The bank sends letters.

When the drought breaks, only a couple of years after his father's death, and the paddocks are thick with green grass, they are too understocked to take advantage and the bank won't extend their debt to buy more. They are—his day foreman tells him when they meet at the cracked Formica table in the kitchen one night— royally fucked, and Jack thinks the foreman is almost relieved not to have to deal with the daylight-shy boss any longer.

Why is it, he wonders, that regret sticks like a burr, but joy floats away like a dandelion seed?

• • •

His name is Richard, never Dick—NEVER Dick—and he's absolutely everything to Angie; him and Nerida. Absolutely everything.

Richard. Such dark eyes and dark hair, tanned skin so warm, as though it contains all the sun it's felt. The black curls so thick around his cock, the little tuft between his pecs. Curling her fingers through his hair. Holding his back, feeling the muscles moving, the solid weight of his thighs between hers.

Campfire heat keeping the night chill at bay. Stars sparkle overhead. Wine in his mouth, salt on his skin, sand on their bodies. She clings and she clings and she never wants it to end.

The dawn, when it inevitably comes, red fingers shimmering to gold and silver on the water, is the most beautiful she has ever seen. There will never be another one like it.

III

The dandy stood by a bookcase, leafing through one of the volumes. How long had it taken to perfect that stance? One leather-booted foot out just so, the hips and shoulders angled to make that frock coat fall just—God, everything was so. . . so *so*. He drew in a breath, making a nasally whine, and slammed the book shut. "I am *still* burning." He held out one hand, looking at the pink tinting his flesh. "How *does* Jasmine do it? It's like nothing else I've felt."

Elise turned from the window, suddenly animated. "It's amazing, isn't it? It's like—you know how when you feed, you get little bits and pieces of their lives, mouthful by mouthful; death stuff, mostly, or sex stuff? It's like that, isn't it? Like, 3D cinema compared to black-and-white telly. It's as if Jasmine can distil their feelings—physical as well as emotional: the whole works—and squeeze it out like. . . like juice from an orange. It's even better than you said, Mother."

"And if you win the auction, you get to keep it," Mrs Winterbourne said. "Their lives always fade with time, but not when you take the last drop: the life drop."

The nob adjusted his almost not-there glasses as he stared at Elise. "Quite remarkable."

"*Quite* remarkable," Mrs Winterbourne said, and scanned Jack again, her lip curling. Apparently she didn't approve of his jeans, his scuffed leather jacket. Or maybe the still-healing bite marks he'd left on Elise during the tryst that had revealed this little blood klatch.

It had taken every cent and every favour he had to be here. He'd had to pay a blood bond to Jasmine, a specimen squeezed into a bottle from a cut on the wrist. He didn't care if she sifted it—he had no secrets.

Elise sauntered around the room, her hips swinging to set the part in her skirt swaying, revealing black stocking and white thigh. She settled, dove-like, on the thickly stuffed arm of the antique armchair in which he sat. Though her arm was draped around his shoulders, he saw the glance she shot at the nob. Jack turned away—he'd known there was nothing for him there, but still, he'd hoped for longer. For more.

Foolish him. Eternal life was the absence of hope; only cunning remained. Jack realised that now. Hope was for the humans like Angie, strapped down and bleeding out so the monsters like him could steal a taste of what they'd lost. Her trust had been misplaced. She was a trophy and he was vying with these four to be the repository. He tasted bile.

"It's all about the blood," Elise said, stretching to show off her marked throat, and he remembered her moaning as he worked his way down to suck on the femoral, her blood squirting into his mouth like milk from a cow's teat. "It contains everything we need. I mean, we call it blood memory, but that's not really doing it justice, is it? Memory—you can't trust memory. What happened, and what we remember happening, they're two different things."

"The blood knows," Mrs Winterbourne said, and there was a sharpness to her tone, like scissors snapping shut. "You can't fool the blood."

Elise turned, all attention on her, hunger a palpable sensation in the room. She looked deeply into Jack's eyes and asked, "Have you ever killed someone, Jack?"

Under those combined gazes, he confessed, "Yes."

"Well, I bet taking the life drop is like that, only better."

"Much better," Mrs Winterbourne said, regarding him with eyes snake-hungry and unblinking.

• • •

A literal roll in the hay with Deborah Burt. Spiky stuff, and dusty, and the sun frying on the tin roof and making laser lines across the bales and in the dusty air, their skin and lips tasting of dirt and straw and sweat, and he shoots before he barely has it in her, and she says it'll be better next time, but the swaggie's at the door and the next time he sees Debbie Burt, well, it sure is better, but it isn't sex. It all happens so fast, he spills more than he drinks, and although she remains, her life, so short, is barely there. She remembers their tumble in the hay, though, and seeing it from both sides is intriguing at first but ultimately unsatisfying: he doesn't look good naked and he didn't do much for her at all and she was covered in scratches from the hay for days with a rash across her arse and shoulder blades and she was kind of grateful it had ended quickly because she'd have hated to have had a kid with him.

• • •

Sun spears through water the colour of dust. Coral glimmers, striated with sunlight. Angie's skin pimples, but the chill of the water fades as she splashes towards a massive outcrop of brain-patterned coral, its mushroom top a quilt of pinks and blues and greens; fingers stick up amid plates and bowls and swaying fronds. Darting fish sparkle. One big one, yellow and blue, takes a leisurely cruise around the edge. Two little red-and-white ones hunker down in the centre of one formation, charging at any fish that comes close.

Her snorkel breath whooshes in and out past her ear. Her heart thumps. Legs kick, hands flapping leisurely from time to time for extra stabilisation as she floats with the current, eyeing the world below. She floats, sun warm on her back as she rises and falls with the waves.

IV

Jasmine rejoined them. She placed a small casket, like a ballot box, on the table, and next to it, five pens, five slips of paper, five envelopes.

The Winterbournes were the last to take their bid forms and huddled together by the fireplace. The dandy took a stance by the window, looking like some kind of Romantic poet contemplating the love that was just out of sight. The nob sat in a chair, tapping his pen against his pursed lips as though the blank paper in his hand were a spreadsheet of profit and loss.

Jack scribbled his bid, sealed the envelope and placed it in the box. The others all stared at him. Jasmine gave the faintest of nods.

"Is there somewhere I can stretch my legs?" he asked. "While I wait?"

"Of course." She smiled ingratiatingly as she indicated the door. "It's not unusual to want some solitude after the blood walk. I find the east garden is an ideal place for digestion. Someone will fetch you when it's time."

• • •

One day at noon, when all he can see is darkness till the end of time, he walks naked into the house paddock and embraces the sunshine. He's well alight by the time he changes his mind. It takes his father the whole afternoon to contain the grassfire he's caused. It takes him weeks to recover. The pain isn't as bad as he expected, but the smell never leaves the house.

• • •

Angie pulls her cardigan tighter around her shoulders against the cold wind as they arrive back at the dock, sunset spreading like a wound across the clouds, all blood and bruises reflecting on the gunmetal sea. Sadness sweeps over her as she soaks up the view;

she's faintly annoyed when Richard hugs her, blocking her sight of it: those last precious drops of colour fading fast as the sun sinks behind the mountains and blinking aircraft fly in and out from the airport and the parrots race in squawking flocks down the esplanade and cars drive blithely by and joggers huff past in iPod isolation and there's the smell of barbecue and the sound of laughter from a picnic table crowded with people in shorts and t-shirts and don't they feel the cold?

V

Jack reached the corridor to the sacrifice room and slowed his nonchalant pace. The guard watched him, his crossed arms unfurling to hang at his sides. Jack faltered. 'Um, east garden?'

A massive paw pointed back the way Jack had come.

The guard's headset crackled; he kept an eye on Jack as he answered. Jack turned away and then—and then, Jack felt it, heard it—the guard walked away down the corridor, his back to Jack, as though Jack was already gone. Jack turned and, oh so quiet on the tips of his sneakers, ran to the door and slipped inside.

The nurse looked up, eyes wide.

They locked gazes.

He asked her, "Please."

"You can't escape," the nurse said, battling his compulsion.

"What?"

"Jasmine knows. She has your blood. She knows you're here."

"Please," he said, and she succumbed, and left the room in a daze. "Five minutes till visiting time is over." She held up her hand, fingers spread wide. Her nails were so white. Shiny like moonlight. "Five minutes."

Angie had been covered with a blanket. Her eyelids jumped with dreams. There was gloss on her lips; someone wanted a beautiful corpse. Attention to detail—part of the reason Jasmine could charge so much. And all the knowledge she gleaned from her guests' blood: priceless.

Jack stroked Angie's face, her hair, her throat. There would be one more feeding and then . . . nothing. Her life fading from their veins, except for that one lucky blood walker who could offer the most. How often could they do it, he wondered, before all those stolen lives melted their brains? How much memory and experience, joy and pain, could a single person carry with them before it was all too much? For some, one was enough. More than enough.

Had Jasmine opened the bids yet? His hastily scrawled FUCK YOU wouldn't curry any favour.

For Winterbourne, that shrew, a collector, enough was never enough. Junkies all, heading for that eventual overdose.

She wouldn't have this one. Angie would not be banished to the dark of Mrs Winterbourne's soul, nor that of her inconstant daughter. None of them would have her.

He ignored the shunt, used his fangs to open her throat, and drank from the carotid. Angie sighed as her life flowed into him, a crimson sea white-capped with memories. Brimming, storm-tossed, he wrenched himself from her ebbing vein and fell like flotsam on the floor. Blood collected in the vial under the table and overflowed, at first a stream, then drips, puddling at his feet.

• • •

He offers to preserve both his parents. They both say no.

• • •

She and Richard go upstairs and pop in on his parents who are babysitting Nerida. She clings to her daughter who smells of chlorine and sunblock from a day in the pool, then hooks her mermaid necklace around her daughter's throat; it's way too long. She tells them she needs something from her room and at the door she—click—freeze-frames the sight of her husband and daughter before she pulls it shut. She goes downstairs to find Jasmine in her very black, window-tinted BMW waiting for her with her legs crossed and a clinical smile on her face. Jasmine's eyes seem very big and very bright and after that, there isn't much else at all.

VI

Angie was dying. Cancer. All that sun. It giveth and taketh away, Angie; he'd seen enough drought to know what too much could do. Now, of course, it only took. At least for those like him. Jasmine's offer had come as a reprieve; that suggestion of never dying, though at cost. Angie would miss out on the suburban home and the surfing safari—the diving paradise of Guam a sight unseen. Those things, she would have to bequeath for another to know. And she couldn't comprehend the pain of watching Richard and little Nerida living long, comfortable lives without her, of watching them age and die. Or did she really think that she'd be allowed to share Jasmine's promise of immortality with them?

"Well, haven't you made a fine mess," Jasmine said from the doorway.

Jack staggered to his feet with the ungainly stance of a newborn calf, hanging on to the table for support.

"Lap it up, bitch," he said. "She's gone." He winced, Angie's life still roiling through him. "Going. She's going—going free."

The nurse came around from behind Jasmine and held two fingers to Angie's throat, then her wrist. She met Jasmine's inquiring look and gave a single shake of her head.

Jasmine told her guard to fetch the others. She had the age advantage; she could take Jack. He didn't need to taste her blood to know that.

"You don't actually do anything, do you?" he asked, pointing at Angie, aware of the slur in his voice. Blood drunk. "They do it all for you. Their last day on earth. Intense. Every minute, clung to. Do they ever regret? Do they ever realise what it is they're giving up?"

"There can only be one *last* day." She stood near the door, arms folded, a disquieting smile on her lips. "They revel in it. And they tell themselves it's for the best. It can only work once—like any drug, if you abuse it, it loses its magic."

"How many repeat customers do you get? How many Winterbournes chasing the rush before the thrill wears off?"

"More than you might think. I vary the experiences, but the emphasis is always on what my clients feel the most loss of. And I do my best to keep the subject's regret to a minimum. Accentuate the positive," she said, a lilt in her voice.

"You lie to them."

"What did you tell your cattle when you sent them off to the abattoir?"

The others crowded around Jasmine. The nob stared at the body, the blood, with naked disappointment.

"Not quite how I expected, but still, it'll do," Mrs Winterbourne said, and Jasmine returned her smile. Encouraged, she announced: "I do like the young. So bold. So passionate."

"So fucking wasteful," the dandy said.

"I have passion," Elise said.

"No you don't, dear," Mrs Winterbourne replied. "You have the memory of passion. The *boy*, however . . . "

Jack sized them up. The men, confused, angry; Elise, petulant. And she'd brought him here, to this abattoir. Could he tear her head off, before they dragged him down?

"I'm sorry that you won't be able to bid," Jasmine said to Mrs Winterbourne, a hand on her forearm. "It wouldn't be proper."

"I appreciate that, but I don't mind." She gripped Elise's shoulder. "This was for my daughter."

"What?" The girl looked shocked.

Jasmine, with a glance at Jack, explained, "When your mother became aware of your interest in this . . . gentleman . . . she came to me with an idea for a very special auction."

"Auction?" Jack said. "We don't do that to each other!"

The dandy interrupted: "Can we? Won't we, you know, *overload*?"

"He's only young, not even a hundred," Jasmine reassured him. "He is—was—a farmer. Think about that."

"A farmer? Like, tomatoes and stuff?"

"No, as in cattle," Elise explained. "I've seen it. Lots of cattle. All that drought and rain." She bit her lip, faking coy. "That girl in the hay."

The nob understood. "Long days in the saddle." He rubbed his jaw as he stared at Jack, measuring.

"And so much more," Jasmine said, her eyes shining with gentle mockery. "From dawn to dusk, a farmer's day is never done."

They all looked at Jack, hunger and guilt plain on their faces.

Jack looked for an escape. He'd expected daylight, maybe decapitation. An end. Him and Angie, going out together, their lives their own and no-one else's.

"And he still has the swimmer inside of him," Jasmine told them. "Think of it as a two-for-one."

"I'm in," the dandy said.

"Me too," said the nob.

Elise pouted, her fingers fluttering to the scars on her throat, pushing her skirt against her groin.

"Jack, my darling, you didn't have to make me bid. I would've taken you for free."

Mrs Winterbourne embraced her daughter from behind, her expression triumphant and hungry over Elise's shoulder.

Elise held her mother's hands against her. Her voice was husky when she continued, "Or were you afraid I'd share?"

Jack managed two steps before they had him. Jasmine didn't even need to get involved.

They strapped him to the table, Angie's body dumped on the floor in their haste.

He'd hoped for a day in someone else's sun. A sun brighter, happier, than his own. Had that really been too much to ask for?

The nurse loomed over him and he concentrated on the memory he most wanted them to have.

Sunburn. All the way to the bone.

•••••••••••

THE OUD

THORAIYA DYER

My dead husband's demons are seeking to sink into my daughter's bones.

Inside our stone hut, Ghalya is yet to wake. Outside it, the pine forest also. Sunrise catches dewdrops hanging from dark needles. Gazelles slip through shadows and wildcats settle silently in tree forks to sleep.

But pebbles roll where there are no feet, human or animal, to disturb them. Cracked shapes shift, breaking free of their concealment against scale-patterned bark.

The morning steals the feeling from my fingers as I pluck the strings of my oud with a risha of smooth bone. The music of grief emerges, keeping the demons at bay. Legend says that the ribcage-like shape of the instrument was inspired by the bleached, hanging bones of a grandson of Adam. The dead boy's father constructed the wooden skeleton of the oud in imitation of the terrible source of his mourning.

I have not worn mourning colours, for the Christian villagers must not know that my husband has died. They would send another family to take my place in this part of the wood. That family would collect the unopened cones of the wild pines, extracting the nuts when the dried cones open, cutting the dead wood to keep the forest healthy. It is food, it is income, it is safety for a larger family than mine—now just Ghalya and me—but they do not know of the dozen others I must feed and keep hidden.

They do not know that the secret cave where a Druze leader died is now a refuge for his defeated son.

At last, the demons lie still. Rays of light touch the tree bark and it is only bark, again. I hold the instrument in the moment of quiet before the birds swoop in, to quarrel and to sing, now that the sense of unease which warns them of demons is lifted from their thin, feathery skins.

I can keep no tame fowl in the forest. The goats, in contrast, never shrink from looking a demon in the eye. I pack the oud away in its leather case and sling it across my shoulder as I move to unlatch the gate of the goat pen. As time goes by, as my grief fades, the song becomes less powerful. Sometime soon, maybe even now, it will not last a full day.

The oud must be within arm's reach when that time comes.

Inside the hut, bags of straining yoghurt make the same milky *drip, drip, drip* as the limestone daggers of the cave. It makes me shiver in foreboding but I cannot falter. I pack my hand cart with flat loaves of bread, pastries stuffed with goat meat and pine nuts, soft cheeses, cucumbers, sesame seeds, and olive oil.

When the Janissaries raid the village, they take great casks of wine. Those elite infantrymen serve the Ottoman Sultan, Murad IV. I do not take wine with me, to the place where I am going.

"Time to wake, little squirrel," I whisper into the soap-soft scent of my sleeping child. Ghalya frowns and tries to turn her back, but I shake her shoulder until she's awake enough to ride on my back without falling, her five-year-old fingers knotted around my neck.

We set off with the goats trailing after us. If any early risers from the village of Bkassin see us, they will think we go to the base of the terrible north-facing cliff to fill waterskins from the mineral waters. Or to let the goats find what nourishment they can from the mosses growing in the southern end of the valley. It is perpetually in the shadow of the mountain, pounded by waterfalls in spring when the snow melts.

When we reach it, I pay no attention to the goats as they scatter. They know how to find their way home. A thin spray of water from the stream, which winds its way through the village of Jezzine and then falls off the edge into emptiness, seeds my shawl fringe with diamonds and rouses Ghalya.

"Are we there?" she murmurs. "I don't like the men. They smell bad. I don't like the dark."

I wish I could leave her at the base of the falls. I wish I could trust in the song. If the demons come when I am not with her, they will sap the strength of her muscles, as they did with Hisham, so that he could not rise from his bed.

They will take her mind, as they took Hisham's, so that he could not recognise anyone. He screamed satanic songs until his eyes bulged and his lips turned blue.

Ghalya is heavy. Healthy. Strong. But her legs aren't long enough to cross the broken gaps in the mountain path. I hitch her up higher; I must carry her, despite the ache in my back and the burning in my thighs. The cart I hide in its usual place behind the bushes.

"Not yet, little squirrel. Hold on tight. Don't let go until I say."

Only I can see the firebirds, with their great hooked beaks and flames for feathers. Each one is ten times the height of a man. The pair are petrified, part of the cliff face, one on either side of the waterfall. They are the guardians of Jezzine. Mother warned me they could be woken by my sorrow.

The song I am giving to you, she said sharply. *You must never sing it near the firebirds. It is for holding back the stone demons. The bone demons. Not for holding back the Ottomans. Not for setting the firebirds against the Sultan. You understand?*

What did I care about Ottomans? I had cradled the oud as if it was Hisham's sweating brow, and cried and cried under the critical, dry eyes of my mother. Her face was framed by the fall of the black veil from the inscribed silver tower of her tantoura and her robes were belted with silver, too. She had risen far in the ranks of the Knowledgeable since I had disobeyed her and fled the foothills to marry a Maronite Christian.

If this can keep the demons away, I sobbed, *why didn't you bring it while Hisham was alive?*

He was not my blood. She shrugged. *He was not mine to save. In a dream, I saw my hands putting the instrument into your hands. Your father taught you how to play. You haven't forgotten. All you need is the right risha with which to pluck the strings.*

You didn't have a dream! Admit it. You wanted him to die because he was not a Druze. You sent the demons!

Silence! Her voice was an avalanche. *Your false baptism was blasphemy enough without such accusations. And do not let me hear this word, Druze, pass your lips again. We are the Muwahhidun. Ad-Darazi was a heretic. Do not call us after him. He interpreted the Koran poorly. We do not need the sword to spread the faith.*

No, I whispered. *Only to cut off your hands and feet when they do not obey you.*

You cut yourself off, Zahara. From me and from God. For now, your grief will keep Ghalya safe, but when you finally forget your husband—and you will forget him, forget his smile, forget the sound of his voice, forget the shape of his face—then you must come home to us, to forge a new sorrow with which to fight.

I do not wish to forge any new sorrows. I have had enough of them. Instead, I will borrow the sorrow of others. I am not as ignorant as Mother thinks. It is not because I care, as Fakr-ad-Din does, about my country becoming united—Sunni Muslim, Christian, and Druze—that I feed the fugitives in the cave. Nor do I feed them in order to defy the Ottoman Sultan, nor the Pasha from Damascus who rules with the Sultan's authority.

No. I feed them because Fakr-ad-Din's son has been recently killed. His grief is raw. His grief is new.

Hisham's demons are old. They were his mother's. I don't know how long they have been in his family and I don't know any way in which they can be destroyed. All I know for sure is that my song of grief has lasted almost three years and is beginning to fade. Might the song of a prince, even a prince defeated and in hiding, not last for thirty years, or more?

God loves Fakr-ad-Din, I think, or he could not have been the Prince. He could not have conquered from Palmyra to the sea, built mighty castles, or beaten the armies of Damascus.

"It is the woman," calls a low voice from the mouth of the grotto.

"Weapons away," another voice murmurs. "It is only the woman. Come. We will go down to the valley and unload the cart."

I hesitate at the cave mouth. Inside, it is cold. Wet. Dark. A screen for the bloody shadow-puppet show of my unexorcised memories. Hisham died in a cave like this one. The Jesuits chained him to the wall. In the Cave of the Mad, they said, the healing powers of the saint would save him.

The saint did not save him.

"The beautiful Zahara," says the man who can only be Prince Fakr-ad-Din. Each time I have come before, it has been full dark, and the prince has been engaged in secret meetings, but his supporters do not dare visit in daylight.

He takes my hand, kisses it. Christian women permit such things. My mother would have clawed out his eyes.

The prince has a woman's height. He has a curling white moustache and a waist-length beard that obscures the thread-of-gold embroidery decorating his silks. He carries a lantern in his left hand. A scimitar hangs at his waist. "It is a gift of heaven to meet you at last," he says. "My nephew told me the story of how he shot one of your goats. Instead of bringing the Janissaries, you vowed to keep us from starving, and here you are, true to your vow. Is your husband in good health?"

God loves Fakr-ad-Din.

"My husband is blessed with excellent health," I say by rote.

See me, God. I give bread and cheese to the one that you love. Will you give me some crumb in return? Or has my baptism truly cleaved me from you? Can you truly be turned aside by water?

"And your children?"

"My daughter is also blessed, your Highness. Is your royal family well?"

There it is. The mouth slackened by distress. The tic in one eye. The breath in his lungs that is suddenly not enough. Finally, he wets his lips and speaks.

"My . . . my nephew is well. Nephew!"

The middle-aged cavalryman who killed my goat comes out of a side-passage. He carries a Turkish bow and a musket. It has been three months since I first saw him and though he still wears the same brown tunic, baggy black trousers, and knee-high boots as he did on that morning, his neat black beard is no longer neat.

He quirks an eyebrow that is sliced in half by an old scimitar scar.

"Yes, Uncle?"

"You did not tell me that the talented Zahara is also a musician. You did not tell me she carries an oud."

"Do you think music is prudent in this place, Uncle?"

"She will play for me in the inner chamber. My soul is weary."

"As you wish, Uncle."

If Fakr-ad-Din fears his father's demons, it does not show. He leads me deeper and deeper into the cave. My foot slips on uneven ground and the jostling wakes Ghalya fully. Though soldiers cannot, in general, be trusted, I have no fear that these will harm her. They depend on me.

"I don't like the dark," she says in a frightened voice by my ear.

"Hush, little squirrel," I say, struggling wearily to find my balance. "I will play some soothing music, soon."

"But Aunty Rafqa says—"

When we reach the inner chamber, I let Ghalya slip down to the carpet. She stretches, but stays hiding behind me, peeping around me as I unsling the oud case and sit with my legs crossed beneath my many-layered skirts. White beards frighten her.

"What would you hear, your highness?" I ask.

"You hold your head tilted back," Fakr-ad-Din observes lightly. "You wore a tantoura when you learned to play."

"Conversion is permitted, O Prince of the Druze."

"This Prince of the Druze only wonders if the talented Zahara knows any verses of the Koran."

"Yes. Of course."

I begin to play, with the risha I made from my husband's breastbone, and to sing, with a voice that the Sunnis would say— and this is a belief shared by Hisham's sister Rafqa, a Christian—is heretical. To them, the voice of a woman is the voice of temptation. The Muwahhidun, on the other hand, do not care, so long as the songs are not sung to outsiders.

Until al-Hakim returns, the curtain is drawn, the door closed, the ink has dried up in the inkwell and the pen is broken. At first, I think the howling is the howling of my husband as the demons torture him in the Cave of the Mad. Then, I realise it is Ghalya.

"No!" she scolds, little fists on my back. "Aunty Rafqa says God wishes women to be silent. You must not sing God's songs, Mama!"

"Ghalya," I hiss. "You are angering the prince! Be quiet or I shall slap you, hard!"

But the prince is smiling.

"Never mind," he says. "Hush, child. Hush, Zahara. It was wrong of me to ask. You are a Christian woman now. I only thought to distract myself from dark thoughts with prayers from my childhood. They make me feel a boy again, playing warlord in my father's jewelled costumes."

I understand with a thrill that this is the key to my new song. The black, unshelled kernel of his grief. If he will only show it to me, I can weave it into my protective music. Then all I will have to do is steal one of his son's bones for my new risha, and Ghalya will be safe.

No pine nut was ever shelled without first hitting it with a rock.

"Did your son dress in your robes, as a boy?" I ask with false hesitancy, my heart galloping.

"Yes, he did," Fakr-ad-Din says hoarsely.

"In your castle by the sea?"

"No. In the Palace of the Moon. He laughed, even when he grew tangled in them and fell. He cut his lip. Kept laughing, even as he bled."

"Is that where you buried him?" I prompt softly, dangerously.

But Fakr-ad-Din's gaze is vacant. He travels along the river of his grief. I must put my waterwheel into that flow. I must harness the power of it.

The Prince's nephew returns and the moment is lost. He guides me out of the Prince's inner sanctum and pays me for the food in gold coins I can never use, never show to anyone. I carry them back down the cliff face with my dangle-legged daughter, my oud, and my frustration. I am so close.

Next time. Next time, he will tell me.

When I get back to the stone hut in the pine forest, half my goats have been trussed and slaughtered. My jars of flour and oil have been loaded onto donkeys for transport to the town.

Bristling with edged weapons and hostility, the Janissaries are waiting.

• • •

The pasha's narrow face is impatient.

He taps his palm with a riding crop. The end of his jewelled turban tucks under his grey-bearded chin. The beard boasts to all who see him that though he leads the uniformed Janissaries, he is not of them.

He is a pasha of Damascus, a Muslim and a free man, not a Christian conscript sworn to celibacy, trained for war and severely disciplined since childhood to owe their loyalty to the Sultan alone.

"I told you, I haven't seen anyone," I say again, my throat shrivelled with thirst. Forced to kneel before the pasha with a yatagan sword resting lightly on the nape of my neck, I glance at the huddle of villagers behind the pasha's retinue, Ghalya among them, restrained tightly by her terrified Aunty Rafqa and Uncle Estefan.

"Where is your husband?" the pasha demands. "Consorting with the rebels, no doubt."

"He is a woodcutter, my lord! He is cutting wood in the forest!"

"We will see. Take the instrument from her."

The sword at my back slides beneath the knot of the sling. If they take the oud, it will mean my daughter's death. My fingers fly over my shoulder to the knot, to seize the sling, and are sliced through for their troubles.

My blood is everywhere. Men are shouting. I am frantic.

"No, my lord! Please, my lord!"

Somebody kicks me between the shoulder blades. Somebody else drags me away from the green where the Pasha holds court. I smell incense and fowl droppings. My right hand, before my eyes, is a fountain of red. The fingers do not function.

They have taken my oud. I will never play again.

Stones are cold against my back. Rafqa and Estefan have propped me against the side of the little church. Bkassin's church was paid for by the coins dribbling back to the village from all the sons taken to be Janissaries.

Sons like Rafqa and Estefan's son. His name was Yusuf. Now it is Mehmed, but I still recognise him. I remember how Rafqa cut her hair when he was taken, as though he had died. Now, his face swims in front of mine.

Young. Handsome. A bare, cleft chin.

"Wind it tighter to stop the blood," he tells Rafqa. "I will beg my lord for the use of his Jewish physician."

I realise Rafqa is ruining her best striped sash by binding my bleeding hand with it. Estefan looms behind her, muffling Ghalya's face against his paunch.

"Kill her," I gasp to my dead husband's brother. "Kill her, or find a way to bring my oud back to me."

"You should not have been carrying it, Zahara," Estefan answers, stricken. "You gave up women's witchcraft when you married Hisham. Music is for men only."

"My son risks his life for you," Rafqa says, crushing my hand between both of hers. "He betrays a lingering affection for his former family simply by speaking to his own mother, and now—"

I watch her mouth moving but the sounds lose their meaning. In the white clouds overhead, I see the shapes of snow-covered pine trees, and Hisham standing beneath them, swinging Ghalya into the sky. I see him drinking from the mineral spring.

Then the spring dries up. Hisham digs a well behind the stone hut. Down in the dark, that is where the demons find him. They slip from the stone into his bones. They make him scream and writhe.

The Jesuits hear him in passing. They hold long conversations, not with me, but with one another and with the God they say has led them through the valley. I don't hear their God speak, but the brothers say that Hisham must go with them to the monastery.

I trail after them with Ghalya like a milk goat with a kid at foot, ignored by them, until they are forced to bar me from the Cave. My woman's blood will pollute it, they say.

"Run away, Ghalya," I try to say. "Run away. Don't go to the cave. Don't go to the cave, Hisham. You'll die there. You'll die in chains."

Whiteness is everywhere. The clouds have come down. They are all around.

"Which cave is she talking about?" Rafqa says sharply.

"My God," Estefan says. "She is speaking of the grotto. The grotto of Fakr-ad-Din's father. She knows where he is. The pasha spoke true. Hisham is a traitor."

"We must tell the pasha, right away. With this information, we can protect our son. We can protect the village."

And then I do not hear or see anything at all.

• • •

When I wake, frogs are crooning to a crescent moon.

The bed by the open window is a lump of layered blankets on a swept clay floor. My right hand is a heavy lump of bandage and clotted blood. I can't feel anything inside. There is no sign of Ghalya, but then, she would not be allowed to sleep with me. I am a bad influence. Rafqa will be her mother, from now on.

For as long as she has left to live.

Crawling to the storage shelves behind the closed door, I take Rafqa's funeral garb from its wrappings and put it on. My husband is dead. I have never worn mourning colours for him, but the night is black, and the robes are black, and I must reach the grotto to warn Fakr-ad-Din of what I have accidentally done.

Is that why? Mother's voice demands in my imagination. *Is it to warn him, or to find out, at last, where he has hidden the bones of his son? Is it to warn him, or to beg him to bring his soldiers down into the valley and murder the pasha, murder all his Janissaries, including your own nephew, so that you can have your oud returned to you and save Ghalya from the stone demons?*

I climb out of the window. Take the forgotten road out of Bkassin, far enough that the pasha's guards will not see me, before circling around, heading for the southern end of the valley where the mighty cliff waits.

It takes hours to cross the valley floor. There are no wolves in the pine forest. They will not come where there are demons.

I see no demons.

"Where are you?" I wonder aloud; I wonder if I am still delirious. Or walking in a dream, for I do not grow thirsty, or tired.

I find the base of the waterfall by its spray on my face, and climb the perilous path between the sleeping firebirds. The path is treacherous enough by day. It is foolhardy to attempt it by moonlight. Yet I make no missteps in Rafqa's curled, black satin slippers, and when I find the grotto I call Fakr-ad-Din's name into its empty depths.

For, of course, it is empty. There were no scouts to give warning of my approach. No lanterns live in the dripping dark.

I stand there, a pillar of futility and pain, wondering if I should simply throw myself off the edge. It is a long way down. There is no chance I would survive.

• • •

When I arrive back at the village, it is emptied of the pasha and his soldiers.

I realise that the shapes of men I avoided on my way to the valley were the bodies of villagers who had defied the pasha, tied to upright halberds before being stoned to death.

Placing one foot after another, one ruined slipper after another, between the uneven stones of Bkassine's main street, I collapse by the building that houses the village spring, drinking spilled water from broken buckets out of a dust-flecked pool while reflected sunlight spears my gritty eyes. The village water is tasteless. Not like the mineral water that rushes from the mountain.

After a short rest, I stagger back to Rafqa's house.

"I curse the day that Hisham ever laid eyes on you," she cries. "I curse the day your house was joined to mine."

Ignoring her, I seek another source of crying, one that comes from a room that once belonged to Rafqa's son. His toy wooden animals still sit on the window sill. Ghalya lies limply in a bundle of furs. Her face is flushed and her eyes are staring.

I see the stone demons move inside her. I see them eating her from within. Estefan moves back from her. His eyes are wild.

"We should not have done it," he says. "We should not have helped the pasha. Now the girl has no father to guide her. No wonder she has gone mad."

I feel my knees touch the floor beside the bed. I gather Ghalya into my arms.

Let them leave her body, I beg wordlessly. *Let them leave her body and enter into mine.*

But they do not leave her body. Three days later, she is dead.

• • •

Standing before the stone firebirds, I take the oud out of its sling.

Every movement that I make is slow and deliberate. I have only half a thumb and my two smallest fingers remaining on my right hand.

It was months before my wounds healed and I was able to steal the oud back from the wedding celebrant who had taken it. After that, it was only a matter of desecrating Ghalya's grave. The stone cover, placed there to prevent her demons from infecting anyone else, was no barrier to the demons, though it was to me. I used a woodcutter's axe in my left hand—the hand furthest from God, the hand closest to the Devil—to break through the stone, and then through the ribcage of the perfect daughter I had borne.

With her breastbone for my risha, I knew the song of my grief would be powerful enough to move mountains.

I look up at the firebirds. When they open their eyes, fire will cover everything that falls into their line of vision. The pine forest will burn. Gazelles and wildcats will flee for their lives. Villagers, too.

My mother told me the music was not for setting the firebirds against the Ottomans, but that was before they murdered my child. Her granddaughter. She cannot stop me.

She will not stop me.

"Awake, spirits of the mountain," I sing. "Children of the sun. Fakr-ad-Din is taken to Constantinople. There is work to be done."

The great birds shiver. They ripple. They begin to glow.

In the always-shade of the cliff face, the firebirds open their eyes.

• • • • • • • • • • •

THE LADY OF THE SWAMP

JANEEN WEBB

Detective Inspector David Dyson shrugged into the jacket of his too-tight suit. He straightened his tie and squared his shoulders before he stepped outside to face the waiting crowd of journalists. The summer sun was high: the day was a scorcher. Dyson missed his air-conditioned city office—he was sweating before he had even made it to the end of the corridor of the country church hall he had commandeered for his search headquarters. The questions began before the heavy door had closed behind him, the reporters shouting over each other to bid for his attention. Television cameras winked on, microphones were thrust at his face.

"Come on, Dyson," one of the older men yelled. "It's hot out here. Give us a break!"

"Yeah!" said another. "The public has a right to know about this swamp massacre. How bad is it?"

Dyson held up his hand for silence.

"I know you are all anxious for answers," he said, getting a general laugh. "You all know me. I'm a cautious man. I don't jump to conclusions, no matter how tempting a quick solution might be."

"Was it wild animals?"

"There are rumours . . . "

"Patience," Dyson said. "It's early days yet. I will now read a prepared statement." He cleared his throat, his cough loud in the sudden silence.

"As you know," he said, "the remains of several bodies have been found in the swamp. At this stage, the forensics team is still working to establish the exact number: I am sure you will appreciate the delicacy of the process. DNA tests take time. My officers are checking the list of missing persons against the records of the Company concerned, in an effort to establish which unaccounted-for employees may have been in the area at the time to work on the access road. Obviously, not all of the dead are necessarily Company employees, so we are asking anyone with missing friends or relatives who may have been in the vicinity of the swamp to come forward."

He paused for breath.

"What about the old lady? What about the diaries? Why are you keeping them secret?"

Dyson shrugged. "Word travels fast," he said.

"It's a country town," one of the women said, smiling.

"All I can tell you," Dyson said firmly, "is that yesterday when we widened our search one of my officers found a cave. The only artefact in that cave was an old biscuit tin, and in that tin were a number of exercise books—the sort that kids use in school—and a bundle of loose papers. They were mostly just records of bird and animal sightings, dating back for about twenty years."

"But?"

"But the most recent notebooks contain some pretty weird stuff. I have no reason to believe they will shed any light at all on the massacre. But we are checking them out, just in case there's a speck of something useful."

"Have you found her? The old woman, I mean?"

"So far, there's no trace of her anywhere. The townsfolk here confirm that an elderly lady did have a beaten-up plywood caravan out there beside the swamp, but nobody has seen her lately. There's no caravan there now. If the journals hidden in the cave really are hers, they will almost certainly turn out to be nothing more than the ramblings of an eccentric old woman who lived rough in a swamp and spent too much time on her own. And until the forensics team is through, we can't know whether she died there—as part of the massacre or from other causes—or simply moved away."

"But . . . "

"No more questions: that's all I have for you, for now. There'll be further bulletins as and when more information becomes available."

Dyson turned to leave.

"Will you release the diaries?" one of the journalists shouted.

"All in good time, my friends," Dyson said. "I'll release them when our people are through with them."

• • •

Back in the relative coolness of the office at the rear of the hall, Dyson gulped down two painkillers with a mouthful of tepid bottled water. The very thought of releasing those journals had made his headache worse. He intended to do no such thing. He had enough trouble to contend with. He hoped—would have prayed if he'd been a religious man—the things recorded in there had not really happened. He felt in his bones that the diaries must belong to the old lady, and he'd been profoundly unsettled by what she had written. He, who prided himself on being one of the toughest in the force, had had nightmares after he'd read them. He told himself that the old biddy had probably been cooking up those magic mushrooms he'd heard grew around that particular swamp, and recording her hallucinations—that, at least would explain it. The problem was that she sounded sane enough when she wrote about verifiable events—the town meetings, the Company and so on. But then, she also recorded other things, terrifying things that could not—must not—be true.

Dyson went back to his borrowed desk. He sighed deeply as he opened the hinged lid on the big, old-fashioned tin once more, resigned to taking another look at the diaries. Some of the old schoolbooks had fallen apart when they were opened, scattering papers. Dyson decided, on reflection, that he was not being paid nearly enough for this. He settled down, unwillingly, to read, shuffling backwards and forwards through the pages of spidery handwriting, trying to figure out a plausible sequence of events.

• • •

JUNE 21ST

Today, I found a cave, a very special cave. It has been a chilly day, a day of biting winds and slippery ground. I was walking along a ridge when I skidded, lost my footing, slid down the bank. I turned my back on the wind to get my breath and wipe my muddy hands, and I was amazed to realize that I was looking at a well-preserved midden—a mound of bones and shells and debris that spoke of occupation.

I was cautious, careful not to disturb the pile. I edged my way around to see what lay behind. And I found the low entrance. I did not hesitate: I ducked my head and stepped inside, out of the wind. Everything was suddenly quiet. I fumbled in my jeans for my pencil torch, and shone a thin beam into the gloom. I couldn't see very much, but I could make out that beyond its narrow mouth the cave widened and opened into a high cavern, with clean sand on the floor. And on the sand were footprints, dozens of them, of different sizes—and all of them barefoot, except for my own tracks. I tiptoed further in, feeling like an intruder in somebody's home. I couldn't shake the sensation that the inhabitants had just stepped out for a while, that they'd be back any minute. I knew that this was not true—the first people had been cleared out long ago, hunted off their lands, never to return. And yet, I felt that I was being watched.

I explored further, and found a small, sweet-water spring that seeped through the rock at the very back. The cave had formed, I realized, when the river followed a different course. It had been left high and dry when the channel changed its path. These things happened. I tiptoed back towards the entrance and paused to sit for a while, thinking about the tribe who had used this cave. I was overwhelmed by the peacefulness of it: I knew it was a safe haven, a special place. I did not want to leave. I found it very hard to return to the swamp, but I had no camping gear with me, no food. I shall have to go back.

• • •

JUNE 26TH

Last night I found the crystal. I hesitate to write this down, but honesty is one of the privileges of age. I can at least be honest with myself, here, in my own notebook.

I couldn't stop thinking about the cave. I felt compelled to return to it—and this time I took my backpack, camping gear and bedroll. My first new discovery was a moment of pure pleasure: the lamplight revealed a whole wall of cave paintings, scenes of tribal life picked out in browns, reds, yellows and whites on the bare rock. This had been no casual camp. This was a major site for a vanished people. I wondered if it could have been a sacred place. I imagined the paintings were of a dreamtime story, but it was not a story that I recognized. I pottered around for ages, happily exploring.

But what I found next worried me. Further back in the cave, above the sooty indentation where the tribal people had kept their fire, a giant black serpent had been drawn in charcoal—it reared up, its huge maw gaping wide as if to swallow the whole world. It took my breath away. It scared the life out of me. I was shaking, and yet I couldn't bring myself to leave. And then I remembered that the giant snake must be the Rainbow Serpent. That would make sense: I knew that the mythical creation serpent was always to be found close to water—near rivers, creeks, waterfalls, lagoons—so I figured it must have been depicted here to protect the swamp. I liked that idea. I took comfort from it. I forgot that the Rainbow Serpent could also be very, very dangerous. And I stayed.

I built my fire in the ancient fireplace, and tiptoed past the enormous serpent to the very back of the cave to fetch water from the spring. And as I leaned forward to fill my billycan I reached out to the rock ledge to steady myself. My fingertips brushed against a cold, hard shape: without thinking I picked it up. I knew from the feel of the thing that I was holding a crystal—heaven knows I have collected enough of them over the years—and so I slipped it into my pocket without paying it much attention. I was too focussed on the spring's nearness to the menacing serpent: that snake's black image seemed to coil and grow in the flickering firelight.

My heart was in my mouth as I edged past it once more. I made it back to my fire, set my billycan on its tripod to boil water for my tea, and cooked my meal, such as it was. Later, I laid out my bedroll beside the fire and curled up to sleep. And when I slept, I dreamed: it was a vivid dream of the tribe that had lived here, as if the painted fishing and hunting scenes had come to life.

In my dream I was young again. And not just young—I was young and desirable: I was kidnapped by the men from a neighbouring tribe to be the wife of a tall young man with kind brown eyes and the just-healing chest scars of recent ritual. The dream was so real I could smell the camp smoke and the body sweat when I was carried off, slung over a muscular shoulder. I knew, with the certainty of dreams, that I was happy. This was not a violent abduction—it felt stage-managed, as if the elders had orchestrated the whole thing. My handsome dream lover was everything I ever wished for: he satisfied my every desire.

But such sweet dreams do not last. Some hours later, I woke in darkness. I was cold—I needed to put more wood on the fire. I still had water in my billycan, enough to make another cup of tea. I wanted a hot drink to warm me. And as I waited for the water to boil, I glanced through the mouth of the cave, seeing the stars burning bright in a clear, black winter sky: Scorpio was climbing high into the night, blazing cold and brilliant, and the curve of its tail reminded me of the serpent on the cave wall. It was a bad thought.

A sudden gust of cold wind blew through the cave. The fire sputtered, but steadied again. Wood smoke eddied about: my eyes watered, and as I reached into my pocket for my handkerchief my fingers found the crystal once more. I took it out, seeing by re-kindled firelight that I held a fine piece of crystalline smoky quartz. I switched on my lamp, holding up the crystal for a better look.

I wish I hadn't done that.

The crystal was beautiful: it shaded from clear grey through to inky black, and it warmed quickly—too quickly—to my touch. It held me. I could not look away. I shivered, gazing into the heart of darkness. And the Darkness stared back. I felt naked, bare to the bone as a searing intelligence peered into the core of me, stripping me to my very soul. There were no words, and yet I understood that it offered knowledge, and with it power—and that it demanded sacrifice in return. It wanted blood, my blood. I did not want to know. I would not pay the price. My mind was being torn apart. I think I must have screamed before I fell senseless on the sandy floor of the cave.

I do not know how long I lay there. But I remember the dream: no matter how I try, I know I will never forget that dream.

In this second dream, my young lover was back, and I knew I should be happy. But as I offered myself to his embrace, the dream flicked into nightmare. My lover transformed into a demon, his lovemaking becoming insistent, brutal. He was hurting me, devouring me, pounding my body, bruising my bones. And then he morphed again. He turned into the great serpent itself, wrapping his shining black coils around me, crushing the life out of me. I struggled, but I could not pull away. And yet, I would not yield: the darkness that raped my body could not penetrate the core of me, could not take my mind. I absolutely refused to allow it. It was a small defiance, but it was the only answer that was mine to make. I have known despair: it cannot reach me now. I shrieked at the black, starlit sky.

I think it must have been my own cry that jolted me from fevered sleep. I woke up shaking, sweating, crying. As I struggled to sit upright, something dark and misshapen slithered away from my thighs—and my thighs felt sticky. The smell of it made me retch. I grabbed for my bedroll and wrapped the blanket around myself, desperate for cover. My breathing slowed, but I knew I couldn't stay beside the fire. The fireplace was too close to the charcoal-etched serpent. I crawled to the entrance of the cave and sat waiting for the first grey pre-dawn light, huddled into the blanket, rehearsing the nightmare. The nightmare would not leave my mind.

I tried to explain it away. Nothing made sense. All I knew was that I needed to go home. As soon as I could see the path, I gathered my stuff and scrambled down the treacherous bank. I headed back to my caravan. I was relieved to find that everything was as I had left it. The sun was rising as I lit my fire and heated water for my bath. I told myself to get a grip: I told myself that I had had a ghastly nightmare, that I had hallucinated, that I had dreamed the unspeakable incubus—that I was home safe now, and all was well.

But as I began to wash myself, the horror returned. I could see that there was blood on my thighs. I could smell a strange, musky odour on my skin. I scrubbed myself clean, remembering. I knew, then, that the Darkness truly had violated me. I knew that some dark thing had used the black crystal to find me. I was very, very frightened.

• • •

It was late in the day when Detective Inspector Dyson put the journal down, massaging his temples with his fingertips. "Christ almighty," he muttered. "I can't believe I'm sitting here sifting through the sexual fantasies of an old lady." He looked at his watch. *It's almost time for a drink*, he thought. *I could almost risk running into the journo mob down at the pub. I'll have to see them sooner or later—there's only one hotel in this town, and we're all staying in it. God knows I need a drink.*

On his way out he stopped by Sergeant Murphy's desk.

"Yes, sir?" she asked.

"Tell the guys in the field to keep an eye out for a crystal," he said. "A black quartz crystal."

"Sir?"

"It's evidence. If it's out there, I want it found."

Murphy looked sceptical, but did not demur. "If you say so, sir," she said.

• • •

Later that evening, duly fortified by several beers, a decent steak and a half-bottle of red wine, Dyson returned to his task. The revelations of the journal weren't any easier to stomach, but at least he felt stronger. He sighed, and went back to sorting through the pages.

• • •

JULY 17TH

For weeks, I have been afraid to sleep, afraid of what dreams might come. But the dark demon of my dream has not returned, and today I decided that I must take full control of my life once more. I decided I would not let a nightmare get the better of me. I decided that I had enough courage to go back to the cave, to face my fear.

I was shaking when I got there, but I had to do it, I had to go in. I was not surprised to find that the dark crystal was still there, where I dropped it on the scuffed sand. I am as sure as I can be that no one else knows about the cave. I would not look again into the darkness of the crystal's depths, but I put it into my jacket pocket. I will keep it safe.

I built a fire close to the mouth of the cave, and I forced myself to spend another night there, watching the winter stars wheel overhead. I dozed, but I did not dream. There were no nightmares: I began to relax a little. I felt strangely welcome, then, as if I belonged. It seems that the danger has passed.

• • •

SEPTEMBER 25TH

I am elderly, well past childbearing age. I was not looking for the signs. My pregnancy has come as a shock.

• • •

FEBRUARY 22ND

It won't be long, now. I have known, from the moment I first felt the child kick in my belly, that I cannot call a midwife when my time comes. It would be too dangerous if word ever got out. *Devil spawn*, the locals would call it. There are superstitious souls aplenty out there. I am terrified of what my offspring, sired by the incubus, might turn out to be. I will have to give birth alone. I hope I can survive it.

• • •

MARCH 20TH

The child is mercifully small. I woke in the dead of night, my contractions upon me. I knew my time was close. I was ready: I had prepared a pile of clean rags, I had filled my water kettle and set it on my spirit stove ready to boil, I had sterilized my sharpest knife. My waters broke. I steadied myself, gripping the bar that braced my bed. I rode the waves of pain, howling at the moon.

I could sense that everything around my old caravan was still, waiting. The nocturnal animals paused in their routines, listening to my travail. I knew, in my bones, that the Dark was listening too. The Dark was waiting for its child.

It had not long to wait. The tiny dark thing slithered out easily between my thighs. I grabbed it, held it, cut and tied its cord. Its first, unearthly cry split the silence of the night. I felt the tension ease. The child lived. I placed it on my breast to suckle it. It bit. It didn't want milk, I realized. It needed blood. Instinct, and my hormones, took over. I let it feed. Whatever it was, it was mine. I knew, then, that I would care for it.

I did what I needed to do. I cleaned myself up, and when I was steady enough to walk I put the afterbirth out for the scavengers to feed on—it was the best way, the way of the natural world. I swaddled the child and held it to my body to warm it. I have raised a lot of strange creatures, orphaned creatures, out here in the swamp. I would raise this one too. Eventually, I slept.

The child's wail woke me, piercing the night, demanding its next feed. In the lamplight, the eyes that looked up at me were as blue as my own, and the tiny fingers that curled around mine were human enough. But as for the rest . . . I could not pretend, even to myself, that this alien thing could pass for human. My breast was sore where I had been bitten. I took up the sharp knife and sliced my arm, just a little, so that the blood welled up, and I held it out to the child. It sucked greedily. It was the start of a feeding routine that almost cost me my life.

• • •

JUNE 29TH

The child grows very quickly. I am weak from loss of blood. I don't know what to do to wean it.

• • •

JUNE 30TH

The Dark has provided the answer: today a freshly killed swamp rat was left on my doorstep—and the monster-child pounced. I had to turn away as it fed, gorging on sticky entrails. I couldn't watch that. I cleaned it up afterwards.

• • •

JULY 6TH

Tonight, the child left to hunt for itself. It went at dusk, and came back to me to sleep.

• • •

JULY 10TH

I was getting used to this new routine, but last night the child did not come back. I searched for it, fearing the worst. But then I heard it, and I knew it had simply moved on. It's only natural.

• • •

JULY 12TH

I know the child is still out there, somewhere in the swamp. I can feel it when it is near; I will always recognize its howl, this flesh of my flesh that haunts the night.

• • •

Dyson felt sick. He knew he could go no further with this particular line of enquiry, at least for the moment. He put it aside, and switched to safer ground. He could check the Company records that had arrived this afternoon against the old woman's diary entries: that much would be verifiable. He laid the printout of the Company's official account of its interactions with the local community on his desk, and then searched through the journals until he found a matching entry.

• • •

AUGUST 17TH

There is trouble brewing. There has been a public announcement. A coal seam gas facility has been approved in this area. My friends are indignant: they can't figure out exactly why their land should be wrecked to provide power for far-away cities.

I got a lift into town when the Company held its public meeting. I thought I might be able to help. I listened from the doorway at the back of the hall: I watched while the local mayor struggled to referee the confrontation. The community was divided. Landowners who wanted the income at any price shouted economics at conservationists who shouted back about endangering the water table and preserving wildlife habitat.

The local people know about the swamp, about what hides beneath its surface. They say the swamp is haunted. They stay well away from it at night. But nobody listens to the locals. The locals are powerless. The bulldozer men have government contracts. They have bankrolled a huge advertising campaign, extolling the public good of their depredations. I know it is all about money: what they can take, what they can make.

I had already told my friends about the environmental officers who came out to the swamp to conduct a special kind of survey. I didn't know what it was for, until now. The whole thing was a farce. Those men were public servants: they only came during office hours. I watched them crashing about in the undergrowth, putting their feet up in their hide, slurping thermos lattes and leaving behind discarded sandwich wrappers. They knew I was there. They didn't offer me so much as a packet of peanuts. They ignored me.

I did offer to help. "You might like to look at my log book," I said. "I've been recording wildlife sightings here for over twenty years. I know what lives here."

"No thanks," they replied. "We can't be sure it's accurate. The survey has to be done by accredited experts."

"Meaning yourselves?"

"You got it, lady."

So I left them to it.

The birds and animals hid until the interlopers had gone. The dark things were always asleep. And the survey men, oblivious, went home each afternoon at four o'clock. I could have warned them: I *would* have warned them, if only they had not been so busy not seeing what was there.

• • •

The Company spokesman at the meeting was a smooth, oleaginous creep. He never stopped smiling. "The government has already sold us its permission," he said. "Our fracking process has been declared safe. Any chemicals that leak into the swamp will be minimal, practically harmless."

"But you can't really know what the impact on wildlife will be, can you?" one of the conservationists asked.

"We will study the situation carefully," the man replied.

"Can you reverse it?"

"No—but we can take whatever steps become necessary," he said.

"It'll be way too late by the time you do that," another man yelled. "The damage will be permanent. You'll just be dissecting the corpses of the creatures you have destroyed."

"We've done our environmental survey," the Company man said smugly. "We didn't find anything unusual or endangered in the swamp. There's always some damage. But you will find that our projected levels are within acceptable tolerances."

"There *is* no acceptable level for mutation or death. This is a sensitive ecosystem. *Everything* that's out there will be endangered if you have your way!"

The mayor was doing his best to keep things calm. So he asked his next question: "What about the people who live here? How will your processes affect us?"

"We can't drink methane either," the first conservationist said sharply.

The Company man kept smiling. "I can assure you that contamination on that scale just won't happen," he said.

"It already has, in other places. There's a farmer up in the Valley who can light his tap water with a match. His video clip is all over the net."

The Company man ignored this. "We need to progress this industry," he said. He was good at his job: he stuck to his message. "Our development will be good for the economy. It will provide jobs for your community. We have the requisite permissions. The cheapest option is to bulldoze an access road across government land, and that means going through the swamp."

There were angry mutterings at this.

"Arrogant bastard," one of the farmers shouted. "I don't know why you bothered to come here at all. You're not listening. I tell you, that swamp isn't safe."

The Company man shrugged. "I'm a man of science," he said. "I'll leave the superstitious nonsense to you."

"Don't say we didn't warn you," the farmer said. He turned his back in disgust and strode out of the meeting.

I could see that the Company man didn't care. He had made his point. How could I speak up, after that? I know that more things will be endangered than any of them could ever guess. And it won't just be the wildlife that's at risk if they antagonize the Darkness: the Dark owns this swamp. I fear the Dark will fight back.

• • •

SEPTEMBER 28TH

Things just got worse—much, much worse. The Company is pushing ahead with its development. Today, I found out that I am personally involved. They want me out of here. Today, a Company man came to my home. He marched right up to my old caravan with its peeling ply and mouldering annexe. He didn't even knock.

"Move it or lose it," he said.

I could smell his sweat, could see the dark rings under his armpits where his shirt clung uncomfortably. He had had a long, hot walk to my campsite, and he oozed an acrid mix of perspiration and bad temper. His smile was nasty, the smug smile of a man who enjoys the pain of others, the thin smile of a small time bully. Blind Freddy could see I couldn't move it—I have nothing to pull it with, even if the tyres hadn't perished long ago and the axles rusted slowly as they settled into the soft ground of this campsite that I chose so long ago. This is my last refuge, and he can't wait to smash it down. I saw the corners of his mouth quirk again, relishing my distress.

"The access road goes right through here, lady," he said. "You'll have to be out by then."

• • •

There was a single line in the Company records: "Advised residents about route of access road through swamp."

The Inspector looked thoughtful. For the first time he felt a glimmer of sympathy for the old lady. She might have been crazy, and some of the things she'd written were truly shocking, but Dyson was beginning to suspect foul play of the more ordinary, criminal kind. He made a note to interview the Company employee who had visited the woman's campsite.

• • •

SEPTEMBER 30TH

When my friends found out, they were outraged. I told them it wouldn't help, but they called the shock jocks anyway. I listened in on my tinny little transistor radio: I couldn't help myself. It was hard to think it was really about me when the Talkback radio program buzzed with discussion about the eviction of an elderly woman from her solitary caravan on the edge of the wetlands: the morals, the ethics, the economics of it. I was bemused by the support, amazed at the vilification.

• • •

Chief Inspector Dyson paused, clicked on his email. The recording of the talkback session had arrived, as requested. He turned up the volume, listening:

"What was she doing there anyway?" a lot of callers wanted to know.

"In other cultures, hermits are respected," one woman said. "A lot of our saints chose a life of solitary contemplation. We should leave her in peace."

This, it transpired, was a minority view. The caller was howled down: the lady in the swamp was an inconvenience; she was in the way of progress; she was clearly crazy, poor thing, and should be taken somewhere institutional for her own good—perhaps a nice hostel for the homeless.

"Which is what the poor woman will be if you demolish her home," the first caller had replied tartly.

The logic of it didn't matter. The lobby groups got into the act, then the shills for the Company.

Dyson had heard it all before. He wondered how long it would be before someone accused the old lady of witchcraft, imagined her blackened billy into a spell-brewing cauldron. It was that kind of program. He turned back to the diary.

• • •

I switched off the radio, at the last. I couldn't bear it. I felt cold, numb with terror. I know how it will end: I am to be cast out once again, and this time with violence.

• • •

OCTOBER 1ST

The reporters found me, of course. I think I surprised them.

I think they expected a crazed hermit, not an educated woman. They wanted to know why I was living in the swamp at all. I told them the truth, for what it's worth:

"When my husband died, I managed to keep the farm going for a while. But I missed too many payments. The bank foreclosed. They took everything. I wasn't fit for company, then. The doctor diagnosed depression: a compound of grief, loss, and humiliation. I was so ashamed. I didn't want to be in anyone's way, so I brought the old caravan here: I needed to think, to put myself back together. I found the solitude soothing, and I stayed. My husband and I used to come here, bird watching. It was always peaceful here. I didn't drop out—life dropped me."

• • •

Dyson pulled up the transcripts of the interviews. The diary account checked out. These pieces were falling into place.

He read on, still listening to the recordings, cross-checking.

It was a young cadet, clearly embarrassed, who asked the next question. He demanded to know why the old woman was obstructing progress.

"What progress?" she said.

"We need a clean energy future," he replied. "We need new technologies."

"Who's we?" she asked.

"All of us."

"I don't use power. I don't need coal seam gas."

"Nobody should have to live like this, like you!" he said. His voice dripped contempt.

"Millions do," she said mildly.

"But not here: not in this country."

His ignorance was breathtaking.

"Perhaps you should investigate some of the outlying settlements," the woman said. "Perhaps you'd like to put an access road through a humpy."

A senior reporter intervened, diverting the argument. "Let me ask you about the bigger picture," he said hurriedly. "Surely you would agree that we need better energy sources if we are to avert future disasters."

"Of course," she replied.

· · ·

Dyson chuckled. The old woman was no fool. She had seen the trap.

· · ·

"But saving the planet by destroying its wildlife isn't very clever," she went on. "Our beloved leaders have a lot to say about maintaining biodiversity. Surely that means the animals should survive too."

"What would *you* do then?"

"Think smaller," she said. "If every building had solar panels you wouldn't need to pollute these wetlands to feed big expensive power plants."

"Don't you think that's a bit naïve?" It was the cadet again.

She lost patience. "Naivety is believing that power brokers and energy corporations care about anything other than the bottom line," she said. "Politicians can't think small—they want the grand gesture, the big political erections, the large party donations. They want the photo op when cut they cut the ribbon on the next financial disaster."

That did it. The cadet lost it completely.

"What could you possibly know, living rough in a swamp?" he shouted. "It reeks."

"You mistake poverty for ignorance, young man. You're disappointed that I'm not dressed in rags and muttering incoherently. I'm sorry I'm not the story you expected."

"Well," said the senior reporter, wrapping it up. "Thank you so much for your time." And that was more or less it.

· · ·

Dyson skipped the formalities and fast-forwarded to the coverage that had gone to air. As he had expected, there was no sympathy for the woman's plight: she was the shrill, vituperative, opinionated hag in the swamp—a self-confessed depressive, a post-menopausal neurotic who couldn't see reason. She was standing in the way of a carefully orchestrated urban dream. She'd have to go.

Dyson checked the diary again, curious to see her reaction.

· · ·

"The reporters couldn't leave fast enough. I was photographed and thanked for my time. I watched them straggle back to their city-shiny four-wheel drives. I knew I'd blown it. I knew I sounded too strident, but I couldn't help myself. The words just tumbled out. These people were trespassing—they had come to my home, judging me, telling me what to think. Lord knows what they'd have said if they'd found out about the child.

• • •

OCTOBER 12TH

The Company man came back. "The press won't save you," he said. "The road still goes through here. Bulldozers don't care what rubbish they clear away." He poked a stubby finger at my plywood caravan. "This'll splinter like matchsticks."

"What happens if I don't move?"

He smiled his mean little smile. "We'll go right through you," he said.

"Murder?" The word hung in the air between us.

"Let's just say we *will* have you out of here, one way or another."

"I'm not going anywhere."

"In that case, lady," he said, "we know where you live."

There was no mistaking the threat. For the first time in all my years of solitude I feel truly afraid of other people. I am afraid of the Company men.

I was too scared to sleep in my van that night. I packed my rucksack and headed for the safety of the cave.

• • •

And now, thought Dyson, we come to the crux of it.

• • •

OCTOBER 13TH

I have never told anyone about the cave. At first, I thought that if I revealed its existence, if I told the press about its wonderful paintings, the find would be of such significance that work on the access road would stop. But now I know otherwise. Now I have seen what the press will do. Now I have decided to protect this place from a process that would surely end in its destruction. There's been enough desecration already in the wetlands. I cannot save the animals. I will shield this cave, if I can, from industry archaeologists.

The reporters think I am crazy. They won't listen to me anyhow. And after that trumped-up environmental survey, I know what will happen if I tell the Company about the cave. Carefully chosen experts will declare the cave paintings to be of no particular significance, and the bulldozer men will go right ahead. But others will know of it. There will be graffiti here within the week. The cave is almost impossible to see, even close up. And the Company men will not be looking. It will be safe enough. I think, perhaps, that I will hide here, when I am finally hunted out of my home.

• • •

Dyson picked up a folded piece of notepaper that had fluttered to the floor. He glanced at it, about to put it aside. But then he saw the date on the top of it. This note had been scrawled, hastily, and tucked inside the lid of the biscuit tin. He hoped this was what he had been looking for.

• • •

NOVEMBER 15TH

Last night was terrible. I did not dare to light my lamp. I saw flashlights splintering the darkness of the wetlands, and I did not wish to be found by the men who wielded them. I knew I wouldn't stand a chance.

Then I heard the screams. I was lying alone, awake in the darkness when the screaming started. I put my pillow over my head until it stopped, abruptly. I did not go outside to look.

I know the carnage will be terrible. I do not need to find the exact place of it to know what has happened out there. I know that the Company men have trespassed where they should not: they have been setting up their campsite, killing where they pleased, killing for sport. The Dark is angry.

And now the Dark has been hunting: I wonder if those men had a last, terrifying glimpse of fangs and claws and dark muscle before they were torn apart. I can't feel sorry for them. People tried to warn them. They wouldn't listen.

The animals will be feeding now: fresh-killed meat is always a bonanza for scavenging eagles, crows, foxes—and if there's anything in the water, the eels and fishes will be nibbling on the dead.

• • •

Dyson shuddered, but pressed on, hoping for more clues. If the note was right, some of the killings had happened a day earlier than he had thought. There was no phone signal out there—no reason that the other workers heading out to the site would have suspected that anything was wrong until they got there. And then . . . It seemed that the forensic team was right—the massacre *had* occurred over a couple of days.

• • •

NOVEMBER 16TH

Today will be my last day in my old caravan. I will sleep in my old bed for the last time tonight.

The weather is hot. I have tidied my home for the last time. Everything has been cleaned and put away. Nothing is out of place. I have put my diaries into an airtight biscuit tin, in case they may be found, in case they may be of some future use. My diaries are the record of my life in the swamp, and of the secrets I have uncovered but never told. The secrets have been safe with me. I have hidden the tin in the cave, a secret within a secret.

I have decided, now, as the last day approaches, to stay with the animals, to stay with my van. I know that if am seen near the cave, its secret will be out. I feel old, and spent, and defeated. I do not know how to start again. I feel a chill, creeping sort of horror at the thought of being stuck in an institution for the elderly and destitute. I know I cannot survive that. I cut my ties with such close-pressed humanity long ago. I cannot bear to leave the swamp, or the Dark that holds me here—my life is here, my child is here.

• • •

The day is dawning.

Today, as always, the animals come to her, drawn to the familiar cadence of her voice. Shyly, quietly, they approach her where she sits upright on her campstool on the edge of the swamp, reading. She wraps her woollen shawl tightly around her thin shoulders, breathes in the sharp air, and reads aloud in the chilly dawn mist. She is not reading a holy book—St Augustine or Lao Tze. The animals do not need improvement: lumbering wombats, elegant wallabies, shy echidnas, darting quolls, a tubby antechinus, an elderly koala in the fork of a tree—they are all listening. Where the water pools in the shallows there are lizards, frogs, and snakes.

There are other things in the swamp, things she cannot name: older things, darker things. They have had a busy night, hunting, and now they are slithering home, sliding into sleep. They will not attack by daylight—it is not their time. She knows that she is not in danger: in her left hand she holds the smoky quartz crystal that guarantees her safety—a crystal so dark it is almost black, a crystal that draws warmth from her hand, rising quickly to blood heat. She has paid her dues, has earned her place here. Her wrinkled, papery old skin is criss-crossed with scars—she has given blood, she has let her child feed. Even monsters have to feed.

As the sun rises, the air is full of the morning chorus: she hears carolling magpies, the liquid song of a native thrush, the short notes of rosellas and king parrots, the tiny chirruping of fairy wrens and thornbills and spinebills and honeyeaters, and then a raucous wattlebird, sounding like an old motor bike kick-started into morning. Further out in the swamp, black water swirls and eddies and gurgles around a rotting log where something misshapen and muddy has dived to the inky depths. Above it, she hears black swans, and the stirrings of shell duck and black duck and wood duck, even tiny grebes, and the calls of the moorhens and swamp hens and coots. She glances upwards at the piercing sound of thin cries, sees that the raptors are rising: the wedge-tailed eagles are riding the first thermals of the day. There's a peal of manic laughter from the kookaburras, and a tawny owl hoots, once, not yet abed.

Today she is reading Pride & Prejudice. *Perhaps the wombat twins will be encouraged to make good marriages, finding strong partners with glossy coats and superior burrows. She smiles at the thought, knowing that they will be as solitary as the rest. It is a sad smile. Today the bulldozers will come. Animals will die. She will not move. Perhaps she will die too. She hopes she is ready.*

As she waits, she thinks back over her life in the swamp. The animals have grown accustomed to her now. She recalls the testing, early days: the smash and grab raids by possums before she moved every scrap of food into airtight tins; the swooping attacks of territorial magpies at nesting time before her own space was firmly established; the wombat that pushed over a wooden bench every night until they reached an accommodation about its location. For the younger ones, she has always been here. They will even creep towards her fire on cold nights, sharing warmth, sheltering from the denizens of the dark.

She has helped where she could. She remembers sitting up all night with an eyedropper to trickle-feed warm milk to an orphaned baby wombat, found still alive in its road-killed mother's pouch. It lived curled up in a hand-knitted beanie until it was old enough to toddle about her camp, and it stayed with her for a while, until one day it simply left to establish a territory of its own. Since then she has raised a succession of orphans, has often had a joey sleeping snug in an old cardigan slung from a tent pole. She has waded into the swamp to rescue injured wetland wildlife, feeling vaguely responsible for the debris left by human visitors. She has removed hooks from beaks and wings, and patiently extricated tangled egrets and herons from discarded fishing line. But experience has taught her to draw the line at snarled snakes: snakes just aren't grateful.

Today, she has pinned up her long white hair and is wearing her best clothes—her dark blue pants, her cream silk blouse, clasped at the neck with her mother's pearl-and-diamante brooch, the only thing of value that she owns. Her favourite blue shawl completes her outfit—the ensemble of things that she is prepared to be seen dead in. She feels calm now. She clutches her quartz crystal as she sits.

The animals are blissfully unaware of the fate that approaches them. They are busying themselves with the demands of the day— the foraging, the feeding of young, the digging of burrows. Her reading is simply another part of their routines, a gentle morning sound that is familiar, safe. The sun is shining now: the water is smooth, unruffled; there is a faint scent of gum blossom in the air, and the native bees are busy. It is a perfect blue day in the swamp.

As she closes her book and tilts her face upward to feel the warmth on her wrinkled skin, she hears a low rumbling in the distance, the thunder that presages the bulldozers. There will be no more stories for the animals. A wallaby pauses, pricks its ears forwards, bounds away from the sound. A flock of corellas rises suddenly and wheels overhead, screeching alarm to the skies. Behind them, a column of dust is rising, staining the blue to brown. Other birds take up the alarm, and the wetlands fill with warning cries. Black swans, wood ducks, water birds of all kinds take to the air, heading for safety.

The thunder grows louder: the ground is beginning to shake and the still water is rippling with shock waves. The air is sharp with the smell of crushed eucalyptus, and under it the dark stink of diesel. The animals are fleeing in panic now. Their alarm cries are lost in the deafening cacophony of grinding and cracking and tearing as virgin bushland is ripped up by the roots. She feels for the animals: she shares their terror. She wants to run too. She will not.

She bites her lips, tastes blood. She raises the crystal, smearing it with a bloody kiss, summoning the intelligence that rules beyond the Dark. She has made her decision. Now she will pay the price. She looks into the crystal, feels the vertigo as the dark mind sees her, takes her. She senses the Darkness coming. Shadows form and coalesce in the twilight under the trees, watching. She has let it in—whatever the outer Darkness brings here can be no worse than what the Company men will do. It is a choice of evils.

She stares as the scene takes on the slow horror-movie reality of nightmare. The bulldozer juggernaut is rolling towards her, destroying everything in its path. She sees a ti-tree snap and topple, revealing her first glimpse of bright yellow machinery, casting dark shadows in the swamp. Shadow rises to shadow.

The moment is upon her. She squares her shoulders, waiting.

It's a good day to die.

• • •

Detective Inspector David Dyson faced the media once more.

"I think I can be fairly confident that we have solved the mystery of the disappearance of the old lady who lived in the swamp," he said. "We have found the scattered remains of a caravan where it was bulldozed; we have found a brooch that has been identified as belonging to her; we have enough evidence to suggest that the woman's body is among the dead. This appears to have been a straightforward killing. One of the Company employees is helping us with our enquiries."

"What about the other bodies?"

"Our investigations are continuing," Dyson said. "The case is being referred to the Serious Crimes Squad." He allowed himself a tight smile. *I never liked those smug bastards anyway,* he thought. *Let them make sense of it if they can.*

"There are still some pretty dark rumours," one of the reporters said, "about what else might be out there."

"Some of the locals are still convinced the place is haunted."

"There are always rumours and superstitions around cases like these," Dyson said wearily. "I promise you, I haven't seen any ghosts."

The reporters laughed.

Dyson knew they didn't want to believe in anything other than human agency for what had happened out there, any more than he did. "There will be more updates as evidence becomes available," he said.

As he turned to leave, he slipped his hand into his coat pocket, touching the cool black crystal with his fingertips. He closed his hand over it. It warmed quickly—too quickly—to his touch.

•••••••••••

THE CHANGELING

JAMES BRADLEY

Hannah is not certain what wakes her: not a sound, she thinks, more a sense someone or something has passed through the room.

For a space of seconds she does not move, just lies, listening. Outside it is dark, silent save for the sound of the stream. She can smell woodsmoke, the sweet scent of the thyme over the fire; next to her in his cradle Connor sleeps, his breath slow and shallow. Somewhere in the distance an owl cries out.

Rising she crosses to the door, the shock of the cold making her gasp as she opens it. The moon high overhead, darkness pooling beneath the trees, in the runnels of the grass. Although it is still she cannot shake the feeling she is not alone, that a presence hovers nearby. After a moment a fox emerges from the blackberries by the stream, its lean shape separating from their shadow to jog quickly through the moonlight, head lowered; as it disappears again she turns inside again, only to notice the horseshoe that usually hangs over the doorway lying in the dark by her feet; kneeling she picks it up, and places it on the table before she lies down and draws the blanket around her shoulders.

When she wakes again it is already light, the sound of the birds outside loud. Sitting up she is surprised to see Connor is already awake, his eyes focused on the roof overhead. For a few seconds she watches him, wondering how long he has been lying there like that, something in the way he stares suddenly striking her as peculiar. As she reaches for him he flinches, his body stiffening, but as he finds her breast he relaxes, Hannah closing her eyes as the pressure of his mouth opens her inside, the feeling blunt, like desire. Like grief.

Once he is fed she dresses, then, drawing her shawl about herself, heads out into the quiet of the morning with Connor in her arms. Outside it is still, grey mist between the trees, down by the water the shape of a heron is visible and the quick plop of the otters as they flick and dive can be heard, but she barely notices as she hurries on, up the path toward the road.

Now she is alone she is not sure how she feels about living out here on her own. Brendan built the cottage when they were courting, spending his evenings cutting wood and daubing the walls. It had been his gift to her, a demonstration of his belief in their future, yet Hannah had never cared for the house; instead it had been the place she loved, its proximity to the river and the woods, the curling brambles and wildflowers. Although it was only half a mile from the village, it was possible to step off the road and disappear down the path into a secret place, one that seemed to have a life all of its own. This morning she is mostly aware of the damp branches blocking her path, the way they slap her face and wet her sleeves, so that by the time she reaches the road and begins the walk to the fields she is wet and Connor is wailing.

Today they are harrowing, breaking the cold ground for the seed. Sometimes when they work there is merriment, laughter and singing, but not today, for it is hard, dismal work, an icy drizzle misting across them, the freezing soil turning their hands red and aching, so they work in silence, the only sound their breath, the sudden cries of the crows each time one of them rises to cast stones at them.

With Connor's weight against her Hannah works more slowly, meaning the others are already gathered by the fire in the field's corner when she leaves her work and joins them for the morning meal. Ill-tempered with the work, they barely acknowledge her as she seats herself, shifts Connor's weight so he may feed. But as she unties her bodice he suddenly pulls away and opening his mouth begins to shriek.

It is not a sound she has heard before, not a sound any child should make. Not a cry but one continuous note, high, piercing, horrible. Startled she looks up, sees the others staring at her. Unsure what to do she tries to adjust his position, jiggling him to calm him, but nothing seems to work, until at last she stumbles to her feet and retreats across the field, away from the others.

When at last he stops she is shaken, more shaken than she could have imagined. In the sudden silence she sits trembling, frightened to move unless he starts again. Finally she summons the courage to turn him, but as she shifts her weight he suddnely tenses and begins again, the sound louder this time, more sustained, continuing on and on and on until it seems it will never cease.

• • •

In the days that follow the sudden bouts of shrieking grow more frequent, Connor's high, inhuman cry leaving her so shaken she can barely think, barely function, so it is all she can do to draw water from the stream and gather the wool for spinning. On the fourth day it is too much, and she runs from the cottage in tears and stands in the forest with her eyes screwed shut, chanting wordlessly to herself to try to drown out the sound of his screaming.

When she returns he is lying quietly in his crib, his eyes fixed on the ceiling, but as she approaches he flinches away from her, as if frightened she means to touch him, and staring down at him she finds herself certain some distemper has crept into him without her noticing, something she does not know how to name or control.

• • •

She was nine when Brendan arrived in the village. The master had been visiting the Duke at Chatterton and when he returned Brendan was walking behind him. Later they learned there had been an accident in the Duke's stable, that Brendan's father had been killed, and for reasons that were never fully clear the master had offered to take him into his service.

Brendan's father had come from over the water, and Brendan had the dark hair and black eyes of his father's people. Yet he was a good lad, clear and kind and open-faced, and although at first some of the men resented him they could not hate him for long.

The first time Hannah saw him she was surprised by how tall he was, how handsome. He was leading one of the master's bays, moving lightly as the horse danced and whinnied, his face alight. Although the horse had been expensive it had proven wild and unmanageable, refusing all riders and charging at any who approached it. But as she watched Brendan took its halter and pressed his forehead to its face, stroking its neck and murmuring quietly until it finally grew calm.

As Brendan grew he became more handsome, his good looks and graceful charm meaning all the girls wanted him for a sweetheart.

Sometimes Hannah watched the way they fought to dance with him at the festivals, saw the generous way he accepted their hands, his habit of giving each his attention no matter whether they were pretty or not.

Yet somehow Hannah never danced with him. Not because she didn't care for him, but because something held her back. Occasionally she would catch him looking at her, and he would look away, but not before he had smiled.

Then when she was fifteen there came an afternoon when she was out on the road and she heard a horse behind her. Turning she saw it was the bay, Brendan astride it. Reining it in he stopped beside her.

"Hannah Wilkes," he said. "I had not thought to see you out here."

She turned to look at him. He was smiling, carelessly beautiful.

"Then you cannot know this road. I walk this way often."

He hesitated, and for a moment she regretted the sharpness of her tone.

"I'm sorry," he said, dismounting. "I did not mean to offend you."

She shook her head. "You didn't."

"Why do you come here?"

She shrugged. "I like the quiet," she said, aware of the intentness of the way he watched her, his attention to what she said.

"And you?"

He smiled. "She needed riding and it seemed a fine day to take her out."

Reaching up Hannah stroked the bay's long nose. "Is she still wild?"

Brendan patted the bay's neck with one hand. "Not for me."

While they were speaking they had reached the shadow of the great oak that stood between the road and the wood. Looking at it Brendan grinned.

"Come with me," he said, looping the horse's halter over a branch and opening the gate. When she hesitated he held out his hand.

"Don't worry," he said. "There's nothing to be afraid of."

Taking his outstretched hand Hannah allowed him to lead her down the hill into the wood. Beech trees grew there, tall and green, and beyond them a stream. By the stream he slowed, placing his hands on her waist to lift her over, then, taking her hand, he led her on, into the wood.

Beneath the trees it was quiet, the only sound the wind in the trees, the cries of the birds. Brendan moved quickly, quietly, a smile on his face. Then, as they reached the edge of a hollow he stopped, motioning to her to keep quiet.

At first she did not see what he was pointing at. Then she saw a mother fox and her cubs, playing in the hollow. The cubs were small, jumping and pouncing on each other and rolling here and there. Surprised, she smiled, and turning saw Brendan smiling back.

"How do you know they were here?"

He shrugged, then placing a hand on her arm pointed to the ridge behind the cubs where the vixen had appeared, a rabbit in her mouth. Perhaps catching wind of them she stopped, sniffing the air. Down below the cubs began to mewl and cry, racing toward her. Then, as the cubs reached her, the vixen lowered her head, and with her cubs jumping around her, jogged down into the hollow.

"Does Old Hughes know?" she asked, and at the mention of the gamekeeper's name Brendan shot her a conspiratorial smile and shook his head.

"What if he finds out?"

Brendan shrugged. "He'll not mind about a few foxes."

Looking down at the mother tearing the rabbit apart for her cubs Hannah remembered how many times foxes had stolen chickens from the farms nearby.

"Are you sure about that?"

This time he grinned. "No."

That evening, when she arrived home, her father saw something in her manner, and, suspicious, asked her where she had been.

"Nowhere," she said, "just walking."

But her brother, Will, snorted. "Young John Bradley said he saw her walking with Brendan O'Rourke on the village road."

She shot her brother an angry look, but he just folded his arms and smiled unpleasantly. Across the table her father looked up, his face suspicious. The Bradleys owned the farm that bordered theirs, and he had long intended Hannah would marry Old John Bradley's eldest son, Young John. Yet she did not care for young

John, thinking there was a coldness in him, a resentment that made him small.

Her father removed his pipe from his mouth. "Brendan O'Rourke?"

"He was out riding," she said, perhaps too boldly. "It didn't mean anything."

Her father sat staring at her for a long moment. "You be careful of that boy," he said at last. "I'll not have you as some Irishman's whore."

• • •

Sometimes she wonders whether things might have been different if not for her brother and father's determination she wed John Bradley. For as the summer progressed she found herself meeting with Brendan in secret.

It was intoxicating at first, to have somebody so obviously in love with her. He was so handsome, so kind, so in love with the idea of her it was almost impossible to resist. Yet still some part of her held back. It wasn't that she didn't care for him: she did. Nor was it that he didn't make her happy, or that his presence didn't make her spirits lift: indeed when they were together she could almost convince herself she loved him as he clearly loved her. But each time they parted she felt that feeling slip away, replaced by a sick feeling she was betraying someone, although whether it was him or her she was never quite sure.

Sometimes she wondered why he couldn't see it, couldn't tell, and then she felt wicked, certain that it was her doing, that she was deceiving him. More than once she decided to break it off, and once even did, yet each time she saw him again, and her doubts fled. It was as if his love were enough for both of them when they were together.

Meanwhile Will watched her, seeking to catch her out. They had never been close, something in his nature making him jealous of her. Sometimes she wondered what it was that made him want her to marry John at all, although she knew the truth was simple: that he wished her to conform to his wishes, to do as she was bid.

And then, on the evening of the harvest, she and Brendan slipped away into the forest together. The night was warm, and as they walked they could hear the sound of laughter and music from the feast over the back. Yet as they reached the stream they heard a noise behind them, and turning, saw Will standing there.

"Will!" she said, in surprise. "What are you doing here?"

He laughed. "I would rather know what you are doing here, although I do not think it will take much unravelling."

"Where I go is my affair."

"Not when you go with this one."

"It is not your concern, Will. Go back to the feast."

He laughed. "Oh but it is my concern, sister. For you have been forbidden to walk out with this Irishman."

At this Brendan stepped forward. "I have no quarrel with you, Will."

Will looked at him as if seeing him for the first time. "No? Well I have a quarrel with you. Have you forgotten my sister is promised to another?"

"Promised by you," Hannah said.

"Promised by our father. Or have you forgotten him?" Will said hotly, stepping forward. Beside her Brendan extended an arm, shielding Hannah from her brother, and as he did Hannah felt something shift, felt the way things moved around her. Perhaps Will felt it too, for he hesitated, then shook his head, and snorted.

"So it's to be like that, is it? Well you've made your bed, Hannah, I hope you enjoy lying in it."

• • •

As the days grow longer she visits the village less and less. Although Connor's fits of screaming have grown less frequent he has grown increasingly difficult in other ways, only rarely sleeping, his moods alternating almost without warning between jags of hysterical crying and a curious, empty state where he lies staring at the wall or the ceiling, as if seeing something there that she cannot. The nights are the worst, when he will not sleep for longer than an hour, demanding food and screaming in the dark or lying staring into the black in silence. Occasionally she tries to convince him to sit, for he is almost eight months old, and should be crawling soon, but he turns rigid at her touch, or lolls away.

Yet despite it all Connor continues to grow. Sometimes when he is asleep she looks at him and sees the child that was, the beautiful baby she had held the day he was born, and in those moments she is filled with love for him. But when he is awake these moments disappear in the face of his anger and screaming.

In the village it is worse. It is common knowledge there is something wrong with her child, yet no one speaks of it to her. And so she goes through her days alone, tending to Connor and avoiding the gaze of people she has known all her life.

Even when she works alongside them she is like one apart. In the fields, the others fall quiet when she is there, or make awkward conversation, so much so that she takes to working on her own, bent over in a patch of field a furrow or two removed from the others.

And then, one afternoon in July she is with the Widow Thirlwell in the kitchens, preparing the food for the men's dinners. All week they have been bringing in the hay from the western fields, the men and many of the women labouring through the afternoons and into the long, high evenings, eager to take advantage of the warm, dry weather, and although it is hard work there is cheer in it, and in the meals they eat, often after ten, when the sun finally dips low and the dusk comes. As they begin bundling the food the widow pauses and looks at Connor for a long moment before returning to her work.

"You should not blame yourself," she says after a few seconds, not looking up as she speaks. "Some children do not thrive."

Startled, Hannah pauses, a rush of emotion rising in her throat. A moment later the widow lifts her face and looks at her. She has round cheeks that are burnished apple red by the sun, and her eyes are small and bleary blue, yet there is a sharp intelligence behind her laughing manner.

"Some of the women say it was the shock of losing that husband of yours, others talk of bad blood, or witchcraft. Don't listen to them: I had three children who did not thrive and I never lay with the devil or any foolery like that."

Still Hannah does not speak. Part of her wants to weep with relief, but another part is angry and upset she has been a subject of discussion.

That evening, when she takes the food out, she watches the others talking and laughing, sees the children chasing each other, and her head singing with exhaustion, finds herself gripped by a sudden fury, too afraid even to speak for fear she will shout or scream like a madwoman.

• • •

A week later she is out by the field when old Maggie appears out of the trees. Hoping to slip away Hannah averts her eyes but the old woman is too quick, calling her name so Hannah must turn and acknowledge her. As Hannah turns Maggie smiles unpleasantly, aware she has won this small contest of wills.

"What is it?" Hannah demands, although she knows the answer well enough.

"You did not pay me," Maggie says.

Hannah doesn't flinch. "Why should I pay you for witchery?"

"Perhaps you should ask yourself that question. After all, you're the one with a child who will not thrive."

Hannah takes a step toward the old woman, her fists clenching. "Did you curse him, witch?"

Maggie snorts. "Calm yourself, girl. I had nothing to do with what ails your child, though I would have been within my rights"

When Hannah doesn't step back Maggie smiles. "Are you telling me you haven't guessed the truth already?"

'What truth is that, witch?"

"Your child: he is not human."

Hannah hesitates. "Not human?"

"It is the work of the little people. A baby as fair as him is easy prey for them. Was there never a night you did not feel their presence?"

She does not reply, just stands, looking at the old woman. Maggie smiles unpleasantly at her.

"Yes, now you see. The child you rear is no longer yours. Your Connor is gone, stolen away. And in his place a changeling."

"No," she says in a strangled voice. Maggie does not move, just stands, staring at her. Not for the first time Hannah sees the delight the old woman takes in causing pain.

"Is he as other children? Does he speak? Does he walk or play? Does he cry out when you touch him?"

She shakes her head.

"It is because he is not human, he is a thing made of wood by fairy hands."

Something in Maggie's words makes Hannah pause. "Wood?"

Maggie smiles and nods.

"And my Connor?"

Maggie shrugs. "Gone."

"And how do I get him back?"

"Drive out the changeling. They fear fire and water: if you push him under the creature will leap free rather than drown, and once the enchantment is broken your child will return."

Hannah stands looking at the old woman. Somewhere in her she knows this pleases Maggie that the old woman sees a way to have her in her power, that this is itself a vengeance of sorts.

"I must go," she says. "I will be missed."

Connor is sleeping when she returns, although she sees by Jane's face the time he was not was not easy. Taking a penny from her apron she presses it into her hand, but Jane pushes it back, telling her to keep it.

"You have enough to worry about," she says.

She does not argue, just nods, dropping her eyes as Jane leans close and kisses her cheek before she slips out the door and away.

Left alone with Connor she stares at him, hearing Maggie's words echoing in her ears. Could it be that this creature she calls her own is nothing of the sort? That this thing she holds in her arms and feeds at her breast is nothing but a copy of a child? Part of her knows that it is madness, that the old woman's words were meant to disturb and frighten in precisely this way, yet as she looks at him lying there she cannot put the idea out of her mind.

• • •

She and Brendan had been married a year when she went to Maggie. Brendan did not suggest it, nor would he have wanted her to if he had known, but she knew her failure to be taken with child worried him. It was not for want of trying: although afterward she often felt lonely, lost, she could not help take pleasure in the way their bodies moved together, in Brendan's delight with her, the rapt intensity of his desire.

Maggie's hut was quiet when she reached it, although in front of it a fire burned, a pot suspended over it. Over the door hung rabbit's feet, the skulls of animals. Seeing them Hannah hesitated, stepping back, behind a tree, but as she did old Maggie emerged, and looked her way.

"Who's that?" Maggie called. "Don't worry, I know you're there."

A moment passed then Hannah stepped out to find the old woman staring at her.

"So," she said, "it's you. What brings you to my hut?"

Hannah did not answer, just stood rigidly, and after a moment Maggie snorted.

"I see," she said, and turning motioned to Hannah to follow her into the hut.

Inside it was dark, thick with the stink of smoke and herbs and the old woman's body.

"You would be with child?" Maggie asked, and Hannah nodded. For a long moment the old woman stared at her. Then she reached out a hand, quick as a snake, and shoved it into Hannah's skirts. Hannah cried out, in shock and shame, but she did not pull away. The old woman's hand was hard, her fingers rough. As she poked and felt Hannah fought the urge to look away, unwilling to give the old hag the pleasure of seeing her distress.

"He loves you, I think."

Hannah looked at her in surprise and found Maggie watching her.

"And you?" she asked, "Do you love him?"

When Hannah did not reply immediately Maggie chuckled, a cold smile on her face.

"No matter. Here, drink this, then lie with him under the full moon. A child will come."

Hannah took the herbs in her hand. Maggie was watching her. All at once she felt a kind of revulsion toward the old woman, her prying smile.

"What, witch?" she asked, the anger in her voice surprising her.

"You should be careful," Maggie said. "He is touched by the fairies, that husband of yours. And they are jealous of those they favour." As she spoke she reached out a hand for Hannah, but Hannah jerked away, suddenly filled with loathing. Maggie smiled in something like triumph, but shaking her head Hannah backed out of the hut, not turning back when she heard the old woman behind her, calling her name, demanding her coin.

She waited a week, then on the night of the full moon she made the soup Brendan liked and drank the herbs, wincing at their bitter taste. And when they were done she took him to their bed, and with an urgency that frightened her, drew him into herself.. But when they were done and he lay spent on top of her she felt the old emptiness return, and with it a loneliness that sang through her like regret.

• • •

As July passes she works in the fields in the days, sleeps in her cottage at night. While the other children run and play by the hedgerows and on the furrows, chasing the birds under the care of their older siblings Connor lies and stares at the clouds or the leaves overhead. Other children his age are walking, speaking, yet although his body is strong, the muscles in his back and neck holding him rigid when she touches him he does not sit, and on those occasions she rolls him onto his belly the violence of his fury and screaming quickly convinces her to return him to his back.

It is a blessing, in a way, for while he lies still she can work uninterrupted. Once she might have joked and laughed with the others as they worked, but as the months have passed the other villagers have become cautious around her; although they still laugh amongst themselves as they work they keep their distance from Hannah only, speaking to her when they have to.

It pleases her, in a way, to be made separate like this. For she does not seek their company, and in truth she has little energy for it. For although Connor is calm in the daylight, he is not at night. Instead, when the darkness comes he begins to cry and thrash, his voice rising in the high-pitched scream she has come to hate and fear, the sound of it keeping her from sleep night after night.

Were he another child she might be able to comfort him, to lull him to sleep. Yet her touch only makes it worse, provoking cries of fury and distress. The only thing that will work is feeding, and even that only works less often with each passing week. More than once she has found herself seated outside, in the dark, listening to his cries inside, and wishing only for sleep.

Unable to sleep at night she takes to curling up in the shade of the trees during the warmth of the afternoon, while the others rest and talk, dozing amidst the smell of the grass and the soil, the high song of the insects.

Thus it is that one afternoon she wakes to the sound of voices, and sitting up sees the others have made their way to the side of the road. Lifting an arm to shade her eyes she sees a man leading a wagon along the road below, some object secured beneath tarpaulins atop it.

As she hurries across the field to join the others she sees the object on the back is a machine,, a monster of a thing made of metal and timber, with great pipes protruding from it.

"It's the threshing machine for the master," Bill Egan says as she draws level with him, not taking his eyes from the road. Hannah nods, remembering hearing the talk about this machine, the way it has put men out of work in towns all over the county. But as she stands, watching the wagon wind on toward the big house it is not the machine she is looking at, but the young man on the horse, who has stopped and is conversing with old Tom Moore, his face relaxed and filled with an easy good cheer.

• • •

In the days that follow the thresher is the only subject of conversation in the fields amongst the men. The women, by contrast, are more interested by the young gentleman, whose name it seems is Thomas Middleton. He is an engineer, and has the manners of a gentleman, although he is often in the field with the other men. Jane claims to have heard he will be here a month, which means he will be here for the harvest dance, and for a time they amuse themselves by imagining who he might dance with.

She does not join them in their chatter. Yet she watches him. He is handsome, but she does not see that, or not only that. Instead she sees somebody who has come from the town, somebody who moves in a world larger than this one. There is a lightness and an ease to his manner, an openness in his smile she cannot help but notice.

Once, only a few years ago, he would have noticed her. Now though she pauses in her work to stare at him, aware of the way she has been made invisible. One afternoon, down by the road she pauses by the trough where the horses are watered and takes in her reflection, saddened by the sight of her sunburned cheeks and unruly hair, the coarseness of her skin.

But then, a fortnight or so after he arrives, Old Tom Moore calls her to him in the east field and bids her bear a message back to the master's house for the Widow Thirlwell. Because it is hot Hannah takes the path past the old dovecote by the stream, hoping to keep to the dappled shade of the beech trees that spread there. The dovecote has been abandoned for as long as anybody can remember, its structure home to wild birds, disturbed only by the children who come here to steal their eggs. But as she rounds the bend toward the road she is surprised to see Mr Middleton standing in front of it. Suddenly uncertain she comes to a halt, and is about to turn away and up the slope, but as she does he turns and looks at her.

"I am sorry," she says, "I did not mean to disturb you."

He smiles. "You have not disturbed me. I was just wondering how long this has stood empty. Do you know?"

Hannah shakes her head. "It was empty when I was a child," she says. "And even then it was old".

Mr Middleton looks back at the structure, as if considering her answer. "And would the local people use it if it were not abandoned?"

Hannah hesitates, uncertain about what he is asking. "It is not ours to use," she says. "It is the master's".

He nods and looks at her again. "But if it were yours to use you would use it?"

"I suppose."

Perhaps seeing her discomfort Mr Middleton shakes his head and grins.

"I'm sorry," he says. "I sometimes forget myself. It's just it seems strange, you all toiling in the fields while something like this stands empty."

Hannah nods. "Perhaps you should speak to the master."

He looks at her. "Perhaps I should," he says, then pauses, looking at her. "Do you have a name?"

Hannah looks at him. Seen close up he is younger than she had thought, his eyes green beneath brown hair.

"Hannah O'Rourke."

"A handsome name," he says. "And what brings you this way?"

"I am taking a message to the kitchens."

"I see. I am heading back there myself. Might I walk with you?"

For a long moment he stands, watching her. Then, surprising herself, Hannah smiles. "Of course," she says.

• • •

When she returns to the field she does not tell the others of her conversation with Mr Middleton, although she knows some busybody will make sure they hear of it soon enough. But for now it is enough to have this thing for herself, to feel the way it swells within her. Perhaps Connor senses it as well, for as she makes her way back home that evening he lies against her quietly, without fighting or complaining as he usually does, and when it comes to sleep he passes easily into unconsciousness. Yesterday he screamed and fought and moaned and she wept with frustration, until she looked at him and saw what other saw, that there is something unnatural about him, something not-human, as if he were a distorted reflection of a child. Yet now, as she lies on the edge of sleep and hears him breathing next to her she does not know what to think. For although he is barely there, a dumb thing, still she knows somewhere within herself his flesh is of hers, his warmth is wound into her being, and to think otherwise is sinful, hateful, a denial of herself as much as of him.

• • •

July fades into August, the days coming high and hot so they work faster against the threat of the storms they know will come. As they cut the wheat she watches Mr Middleton directing the men, teaching them the operation of the machine. Although they have not spoken again since that afternoon she has seen his eyes seek her out across the field, seen the way his manner changes as she passes. So have others: although they are wary of teasing her about it some of the women have taken to whistling at her when he passes, although she will not give them the pleasure of responding.

The machine is a monstrous thing. Steam-driven, it roars and hisses, belching steam and smoke into the air as it grinds and creaks. The first time it started Connor began to scream, beating his head into the ground so hard she was afraid he would do himself harm. That first day she bore him away down to the stream where it was quiet and spent half an hour trying to calm him, a response that has not altered, meaning she has spent much of the past fortnight with him screaming and beating his head, the merest murmur of the machine enough to make him grow rigid and begin to fight.

For the others the machine is a constant source of wonder. Even though the men still mutter darkly about how many have been put on the road by similar machines this one is a source of constant fascination, so much so that at any given moment a group of them are to be found standing near it, watching as the wheat is fed into its maw and discussing its operations.

And then, all at once, the harvest is over, and the celebrations are upon them. Although it is two years since she went to the harvest dance, this year she finds herself as giddy about it as she was when she was a girl of fourteen.

The Widow Thirlwell offers to care for Connor while she is at the dance, and so, on the evening appointed she brushes her hair and takes the shawl Brendan bought her when they wed and walks the half a mile into the village to leave him with her and then on, to the back barn, where the dance is to be held.

It is a warm night, and although the storm that has been threatening all day has held off clouds are gathering to the west, lightning dancing on the horizon. Perhaps sensing she meant to leave him, perhaps simply because he was uncomfortable in a strange place Connor had begun to whimper as she bid the Widow farewell, and although she hesitated the Widow had placed a hand in the small of her back and pushed her out into the warm night, leaving her anxious, but now, as she approaches the barn that unease falls away, replaced by a strange, giddy delight in the possibility of her freedom.

Although it is still early a crowd has already gathered, some seated at the tables that stand in the yard, others laughing and talking. To one side a group of the younger men are gathered around the barrels, drinking; as she enters she glimpses her brother and Young John Bradley, and for a moment she and Will's eyes meet, before Will looks back to John and raises his mug. In the trees lanterns have been hung, giving the place the feel of a fairy kingdom.

Now she is here she is not certain she should be. Once these people were her friends: now she is a stranger amongst them. For a while she lingers by the oak tree, looking out over the crowd. By the barn Tunny Brown and the others are tuning their instruments, in front of them some of the children are chasing each other, darting back and forth across the area that has been set aside for dancing. From somewhere in the distance thunder rumbles; without thinking she tightens her hand about her shawl.

And then, just as she is deciding to slip away, to go back and spend the evening in the Widow's kitchen, she feels somebody beside her, and turning, sees Mr Middleton, the sight of him causing her to step back in surprise. He smiles.

"I'm sorry, I didn't mean to startle you."

She shakes her head. "You didn't."

"Are you sure?" he asks, and for a moment she hesitates, then laughs.

"Maybe a little."

"Perhaps I could fetch you a drink to make up for my rudeness?"

At first Hannah does not know what to say, then she nods, quickly, as if this moment might end. "Yes," she says. "I would like that".

He extends his arm, and together they walk toward the tree where the barrels stand. As they approach several of the men glance at the two of them and turn away but if Mr Middleton notices he does not show it.

"That man with Young John Bradley, he is your brother?" he asks as they wander back toward the tree.

Surprised Hannah glances over her shoulder. "Yes," she says. "How . . . ?"

Mr Middleton smiles and gives a little shrug. "I heard some of the men talking."

"And what else did they say?" she says, the flash of anger in her voice surprising her.

If Mr Middleton is surprised by her anger he does not show it. "That you were married to one of the stablemen but he died. That you have a child who is touched."

Hannah stares at him, searching for some sign of mockery. "And if it is true?"

Mr Middleton looks at her, his green eyes clear. "All villages are full of gossip," he says, "In my experience it is best not to pay it too much heed."

Still Hannah does not move.

"Although I am sorry you have suffered such grief."

His voice is so calm, so kind that Hannah cannot speak, and so for a long moment they stand in silence. Then over by the barn Tunny Brown and the others strike up a tune. With a smile Mr Middleton extends a hand. "Perhaps we should dance?"

If Mr Middleton is used to more elevated pleasures it does not show, for he is light and quick on his feet, bowing to the women in a playful way that makes them laugh. But it is Hannah he returns to whenever he can, holding her hand and watching her. And when, after half an hour the two of them stumble off again, to lean against a tree, he bows to her with a flourish, provoking her to laughter one more time.

"You dance well," she says, and he laughs.

"And so I should. My father is a dancing master."

Hannah looks at him. "No," she says. "I do not believe you."

Mr Middleton laughs again. "Most assuredly. A good one as well."

"Then how did you become an engineer?"

Mr Middleton shrugs. "It seemed a good profession."

"The men say the machine will put them out of work."

Mr Middleton pauses. When he continues his voice is less careless. "They are right. But it will be for the best."

"How can it be for the best if they are without work?"

"There will be other work in the towns or the cities. But it's not about them, it's about the future. We have the chance to change people's lives, to bring them ease and opportunity. We cannot not take it."

Hannah does not reply, and after a moment he continues.

"This village, your village, it is a good place, but its ways are of the past. People here talk of witchcraft and fairies and ghosts. This machine and others like it are the beginning of the end for those old ways."

Hannah glances at him, looking for some sign he has divined her fears, that he is speaking to her of more than just the village and its ways.

"I am sorry if I have offended you," he says.

She shakes her head. "You have not offended me. Yet I think you underestimate the difficulty of the task you describe. People here do not think their ways are old-fashioned, they think they are right. The idea of changing frightens them."

As she speaks a cry goes up from some of the men, and glancing over she sees the harvest princess has appeared.

"And you?" Mr Middleton asks.

Hannah hesitates. "I do not know. Now come, we must throw flowers with the rest of them".

There are more dances and songs and drinking, so it is after midnight when the storm arrives, the cool air sweeping in over the trees and sending plates and glasses tumbling. Taking Hannah's arm Mr Middleton draws her away, and with his coat over her head the two of them run back toward the Widow Thirlwell's cottage. By the stile at her gate they pause, the rain clattering down around them.

"Thank you," he says.

"For what?" Hannah asks.

"For tonight." To her surprise Hannah laughs, and reaching up kisses his cheek. "You are a fine dancer."

He laughs. "As are you."

She can feel his eyes on her as she runs down the path toward the Widow's door, the possibility of his presence making her step light. But before she is halfway there she hears Connor scream and her belly clenches. On the doorstep she pauses, eyes closed and listening, willing this moment to continue even as she steels herself for the moment when she opens the door and it begins again.

He lies on a blanket, his body rigid and face contorted, his head beating rhythmically on the floor. The air stinks of shit. The Widow is slumped in a chair on the other side of the room, her face pale and drawn.

Crossing to him Hannah kneels, but he jerks his body away from her, redoubling his screaming.

"He's been like this since you left," the Widow says. Hannah does not answer, just nods, and reaching down she gathers him up, pressing his rigid body to her.

"I am sorry," she says but the Widow only shakes her head.

"It's not your fault."

Hannah doesn't answer, just turns toward the door.

"You can't go out, not when it's like this" the Widow says, standing, but Hannah only shakes her head.

"Thank you," she says again, and pressing Connor's stinking form to her chest she hurries out into the rain.

• • •

She was cooking when they found Brendan. She heard the cry, and running out she saw them gathering around the stables.

He might have been asleep, save for the trickle of blood that ran down his forehead, and the way his body lay slackly. As she approached they stepped aside to let her pass, but some impulse made her stop before she reached him, stand looking at him lying there.

Looking up she heard a horse whinny. "It was the bay," she said. "Wasn't it?"

Old Bill Tompkins hesitated. His face was stricken. Then he nodded.

"Aye."

Behind him she could see the horse's face, its eyes calm, unconcerned, as if its actions had barely ruffled its consciousness. Sometimes, in the weeks that followed she would see the horse standing in the yard or grazing in the field. Each time she watched it, waiting for some sign it understood what it had done, yet all she saw was its impassive gaze, the glint of madness that had always been there. Sometimes, when she was alone, she tried to imagine what it must be like to be a horse, a bird, to move like that through the world.

If she had thought Brendan's death would heal the rift between her and her parents she was wrong. On those occasions she saw her mother or her father in the village they would turn away from her, as if ashamed. Her brother did not turn away, instead he stared at her, smiling, as if she had proven him right in some way.

And so when Connor came she was alone, left to fight her way through the labour without help or guidance, his tiny body wrenched into the world in the soft dark of the summer evening, the floor around her thick with blood and fluid, the taste of her own flesh sharp in her mouth as she tore the cord, and afterward, his small, angry life pressed against her as they slept.

It was two days before she was well enough to walk to the village. Her body weak, still thick with pregnancy yet loose and shattered as well. As she entered people stared at her, at the way she bore Connor against herself, and she saw the way she was no longer one of them.

• • •

She is drawing water when Mr Middleton appears, wandering along the path beside the stream in the half-light of dusk. Setting the bucket down she straightens, pleased to see the way he smiles when he sees her.

"Miss O'Rourke," he says, "I had not thought to find you here."

She nods toward the hut. "I live here," she says.

Glancing up at the cottage he nods.

"So far away. Does it not get lonely out here on your own?" As he speaks he smiles, and Hannah blushes, afraid he is teasing her.

"I' like it. Why are you here?"

He glances back the way he came. "I thought to see where the stream led."

Perhaps she looks disappointed because he smiles again. "And you? Are they not working in the high fields today?"

"I'm not shirking," she says, and he laughs.

"I did not think you were." As he speaks she stoops to lift the bucket and he steps forward.

"Let me take that," he says. As he speaks his hand closes on hers, and she looks up, sees his face close to hers. For a second or two they do not move, then he pulls gently on the bucket, and she releases it.

She directs him to place the bucket by the door to the cottage, then turns and looks back down the slope toward the stream.

"This is a fine aspect. A man might do well to look at it in the evening."

Hannah looks at him, sees he is grinning. "I thought you a man of the town."

He nods. "Indeed I miss the town when I am away. But the country has its compensations."

As he speaks he smiles, and she feels herself blush.

"It would be nice to be able to compare them," she says.

He laughs. "Perhaps you could visit me one day."

She stares at him, trying to tell whether he is teasing.

"What?"

"I think you are teasing me"

Again he laughs. "And if I were?"

"That would be most unkind."

For a long moment he stands, looking at her. Then he looks down.

"I am sorry it is only now we are having this conversation," he says.

"Why?"

"Because we shall not have a chance to continue it. I leave tomorrow."

"Tomorrow?"

He nods. "I have been called back unexpectedly."

"But you will be back, will you not?"

He looks at her for a long moment. "I cannot see when."

For a few seconds neither speaks. Then he steps back. "I am sorry," he says, "I have taken up enough of your time already".

"No," she says, surprising herself with her boldness. "Please, stay." But he doesn't answer, just lifts a hand and touches her face with his fingers.

"I am sorry, would that I had come this way sooner. If you are in the town you should look for me though." For a moment she thinks he will lean forward, kiss her, the touch of his fingers on her cheek almost painful. But then he steps back, moving away into the fading light.

For a long time she does not move, just stands, staring down at the stream and the space where he stood. All her life she has wanted a reason to leave, to go to the town, and here, now, one has slipped away from her. Perhaps it might have been different if she were a wanton, if she had convinced him to stay, but somehow she thinks not.

Bending down she places her hand on the bucket, meaning to lift it, but even as she does she feels herself falter, and releasing it leans back against the doorframe. How did she come to be here, she thinks, alone out in the woods, without a husband or a family or anyone for conversation? How is it that she does not live in the town, have fine clothes, live by the light of candles?

It could have been different, perhaps, if she had not married Brendan, if she had simply left, sought a place in one of the great houses or service somewhere, for then she might have met another man, one who might have lifted her out of here, away from here, a man like Mr Middleton perhaps, kind and good and full of life. What a life that might have been. And then the thought comes to her: might that not still happen? After all, he had asked her to call on him; perhaps she might leave too, follow him to the town. There is something between them, she is sure of that, something good and true, and he would make a fine husband.

And then from behind her she hears Connor begin to cry, his high-pitched wail piercing the quiet of the evening, and as he does she knows this is just idle fancy, no matter how fine he is no man would take a woman with a changeling for a child, no man would want that screaming lump of wood if he did not have to. For a moment she imagines just standing up, beginning to walk, the way her steps might carry her down, away from the cottage to the bank of the stream, then on, along, through the forest to the road, and on, to Bath. She could, she thinks, nobody would know, nobody would miss her, she would just be gone, the thought so liberating she actually gasps. Yet as she gets to her feet it is not the quiet she hears but Connor, screaming, on and on, the sound crowding her mind, filling it, and despite herself she turns, goes in to him. When will it stop, she thinks as she reaches out to lift him, when will it ever get better? As she lifts him to her shoulder she hears his breathing change as he gathers himself for another round of screaming, the sound of his cries filling the cottage until she puts him down again, and turning, walks back out into the gathering dark. Yet as she does she remembers Maggie's words, her description of the ways the spell might be broken, the thought stopping her in her tracks, making her turn, walk back in to where Connor lies, his tiny face screwed up in fury. For a long moment she hesitates, not sure what to do, then all at once she reaches down, gathers him up, and half-walking, half-running, stumbles out the door, down the slope to the stream, the shock of the water cold as she hits it and splashes out into the flow, insects skittering before her. In her arms Connor's cries falter in surprise before he begins to scream again, louder this time, but as he does she grasps him by the shoulders with both hands and pushes him down, into the water, his eyes opening in shock as the water covers his face, his mouth opening and closing as he thrashes and pulls, his distress so plain she has to fight to resist relenting, letting him go. It is strange she thinks, the way time has grown elastic, the way she is in the moment and without it, as if she has stepped out of this world and into another. Beneath the water Connor is still struggling, his face contorted and screaming. Any moment now he will change, she thinks, any moment.

Now.

YARD

CLAIRE MᶜKENNA

All it took was a broken street-light two doors down, and in the murk of just-dark she mistook the shadow of the two-door coupe for Noel's sedan, him home early from work, their relationship having taken a turn for the better since the money started coming in.

Had she identified the car correctly she might not have walked in the front door with such a huge smile, only to feel it frost-over and die at the shock of seeing DeDe Barker and the friend she had brought with her instead.

The friend slouched in Noel's favourite armchair, a skinny man with sunken eyes, an oddly-shaped head that a phrenologist might have read for criminality and weak morals, a recessed chin of the type that, were it carved upon a mountain, the vertical from the clavicle to his scraggly underlip goatee wouldn't represent a degree of difficulty more than a high 4 on the Yosemite scale. Plenty of acne-scarred placements on the pitch. Free climbing possible.

A sharp pain shot through the back of Miranda's left eye. The plate tectonics of premonition and common sense ground against each other. Well, she thought. Well, *shit*.

Her hand instinctively went to her pocket. Loose change and tissue-grommets, but no phone. Her lifeline to rescue sat on the kitchen bench, less than ten paces away. It might have been Timbuktu for all the distance she'd need to cover. Between her and the phone, DeDe stood like an unlikely Cerberus in clingy rayon and underarm stains. A cigarette drooped from her fingers, dotting the carpet with ashes.

Unusually, DeDe remained silent. It was the friend that spoke. "Hello Miranda."

Affronted that the strange man should even know her name, Miranda glared at DeDe. Noel's no-good sister remained as impassive as a background extra in a television movie.

The man kept talking. "Find much on your walks?" he asked. "Y'know, buried treasure and stuff?"

"I don't have time for this."

She made a sharp turn towards her bedroom, only to have DeDe's friend leap at her, snarl her ponytail in his fist and yank her to the floor. A punch in the face was deflected enough so that his knuckles caught her cheekbone instead, but the flash of white light in her left eye put all the fight out of her.

He was yelling.

He wanted to know where she got it.

"The money," he shouted. "You tell me where's the goddamn old money."

• • •

The grass, Miranda thought. That's what she hated the most of all the things she could name and hate. Its profusion and fecundity. The dark glossiness of those dark-green blades as they rose up at the corners of the yard, fellating the quarter-acre of rear yard with buffalo creepers and razors. Slutty grass, as grass went, not willing to confine itself to the concrete edging she was sure she'd seen on the sale day.

The civilised architecture of the concrete was now a geological layer somewhere between the reactive clay and a tonne of composting greenwaste. After her first few abortive attempts at getting the mess under control, the epic weekend of snapped brushcutter wires, disturbed snakes and lawnmowered stones peppering her shins like sniper fire, Miranda called defeat and vowed never to set foot in the yard again.

Even still, she had made an enemy. Sometimes she imagined it was waiting for her, in that watchful way of predators who have not the speed for a chase, but with endless reserves of patience. She would see it outside the kitchen window, a magnet for gnats and mosquitoes, taunting her. She dreamt of glycophosphate and stealthy watering with poison.

Then there was the house, but she didn't hate it so much as despair of it, buyer's remorse coupled with a desire not to flee a situation without making some kind of defensive effort. The house had been kind of run down when they'd bought it, languishing at the bottom of a real estate agent's kill-list after cannier couples had opted for the housing developments a street over. The neat-as-a-pin first-home-buyer's bargain turned out to be a too-small panelboard cottage with the roof slumping at the end corner, down where the termites had been found but were not there because *here's the certificate of inspection and pest control, bit outta date but it'll be alright.* The floor listed like a ship taking on water in horse-latitude doldrums. In cold weather the nails worked themselves out of the wood, their iron heads catching unwary feet, tearing divots of skin. Over the course of a week Noel came home with armloads of carpet offcuts, not a matching metre of pile among them.

In the heat the wood swelled and shrank, made doors fly open or refuse to close. As the night temperatures fell, the timbers would shrink incrementally through each floor joist, sending a thrumming along the main corridor like scattered footsteps.

They shouldn't have bought so suddenly. But they were eager to get out of their rental apartment, on account of the feud they were having with the housebound guy next door who, while waiting for his workplace injury payout, funnelled his indoor life into creepy obsessions, spent his days with his ear pressed up hard against the wall, listening for each toilet flush or too-loud breath. The guy would go through their recyclables, call up the body corporate upon finding a non-renewable biscuit wrapper among the milk cartons. His obsession bordered on cruelty. Miranda worried that one day he would front up to their door with a shotgun, told Noel so, demanded they move. Noel was a bit of a softie. He said, yeah, okay.

Then there was Noel's sister. Plastic DeDe who smoked all through the place even though Miranda told her to *fuckin' quit doing that, go outside, the landlord will kick us out* and DeDe was all, *you're not the boss of me bitch* and left butts in all the coffee cups and the body corporate planter-pots, and Noel wouldn't do a thing because, *DeDe's got a condition, Miranda, c'mon.*

So on account of DeDe's condition, on account of Noel's last words to his dead mother to look after the younger sister through her unspecified disorder, questionable friendships and defaulted loans, on account of the guy next door who thumped on the walls every time a tap turned on and yelled at them to *shut it or I'll come round and kill you*, on account of the cops who looked at him in the wheelchair he only used on occasion and laughed and said *I doubt you'll have a problem Ma'am just ignore it and keep the noise down*, for all those little irritations mounting and compounding, they moved.

Moved too far out, one of those satellite country towns swallowed by urban sprawl, about as part of the city as the far side of the moon. A deceased estate, the house was pretty beat up. Miranda, a little more worldly-wise than Noel, smelt marijuana and bong-water leavings in the mouldy carpet. The yard—huge— was on first inspection, a mess. By their second visit the real estate agent, on the behest of an overworked legal executor, hired someone to do a mow of the lawn before sale. A desultory clearing had appeared in the centre of the grass and brambles a day before their final inspection, but the edges still rode up about the fence, like the bow wave at the prow of an absent boat. A week before handover, you wouldn't have thought a gardener had looked sideways at the place.

"We'll bulldoze the lot next year," Noel had said, "or perhaps the year after that, as soon as we get some equity in the place. Soon as we reduce DeDe's debt and get her back on her feet. Like I promised Mum, before she died. Just do what you can."

Miranda had seen the monthly repayments DeDe's credit card debt was costing them. More than the mortgage, and growing. No wonder they couldn't afford anywhere better than this to live.

Unable to find an equitably paying job nearby, Noel took up commuting to the office, two hours each way. Miranda hardly saw her husband any more. She worked from home. Day after day she would digitally construct the layout of pedantic council websites and supermarket leaflets with the gnawing resentment of an indentured worker paying off a distant relative's political prison sentence.

Occasionally something interesting would come in the deluge, like the playbill to an amateur production of the Turandot opera in the local hall, a bouldering guidebook or a game hunter's magazine article. Page mock-ups of husky, stout men standing next to gutted animals strung up on welded frames. Sometimes she imagined DeDe hanging there, the men grinning, winking eyes saying: *darlin' we fixed your problem for ya.*

Her life wasn't supposed to be this way. She had walked into the wrong theatre production, an operatic tragedy, when she should have been a character in a fluffy rom-com. Once, while punching mountain climbing ratings into a table, Miranda imagined configuring her situation a difficulty, the hump she would need to get over. Yosemite Class 5.12, she thought. ABO, *Abominablement difficile.* Equipment failure likely. Nothing on the pitch will hold a fall.

• • •

Days after the last of the moving boxes were unpacked, DeDe Barker had appeared one morning on the doorstep, lugging a leopard-print trolley case and a make-up bag big enough to hold a human head.

"Took ya long enough to answer the doorbell," she had said accusingly.

"Why are you here?" Miranda blurted, then regretted, because dealing with Noel's sister required the kind of mewling diplomacy reserved for tin-pot despots and hermit kingdoms. DeDe was the kind of person to dwell on verbal slights, take a pun the wrong way, feel as if the merest criticism was an affront and a challenge.

On that awful, dream-ending day, DeDe's face had been as flat and featureless as a supermarket model hawking the latest pleather sofa. On top of the Botox, she'd had one of those multi-shaded, frosted haircuts with glued-in extensions that couldn't cost any less than five hundred bucks at a salon. Miranda's thoughts spun like a vulture over the rising sum of money Noel's parents had paid the credit card company so DeDe wouldn't go bankrupt, the bulk of their will that went towards DeDe's in-home care once they were gone and she could no longer mooch, slotted it in the list of shitty things like the length of time it had taken Noel and her to save a housing deposit, the senior Barkers refusing to give a loan or go guarantor for Noel, but willing to pay off a fucking credit card for his no-good sister, that made Miranda lie awake some nights.

"Got no cash. My condition got me kicked out of a job las' week."

With a sinking horror, Miranda saw the taxi that had deposited her nemesis still parked in the driveway, the driver's arm lolling out of the window as if panhandling for alms.

"What's he waiting for?"

DeDe breezed through. "Just fucking pay him, all right? I don't want to hear your bullshit."

Something broke in Miranda then, and she took hold of DeDe's hair, the extensions separating in her hands, threw her out, yelling and yelling, not making much sense, locked the door, her heart hammering as if she'd been a character in one of those horror films Noel so adored. And DeDe pounded on it, screaming, and then pounded on the window until it broke, and the screams became higher pitched and hysterical, punctuated with *I'm bleeding I'm bleeding.*

Miranda tossed DeDe a tea-towel through the broken window and called for an ambulance, an affront to DeDe far greater than the gash in her forearm.

The ambulance turned up with the police eleven indeterminably long minutes later. The taxi driver had called in a tale of civil unrest and an unpaid two hundred and eighty-five dollar fare. DeDe screamed blue murder. She went off to hospital in the back of the divvy van on account of the medics refusing to take her while she was raging.

Half an hour later Noel called from work.

"How could you do that to my sister? You know she's got a condition! There's five hundred dollars in the biscuit-tin, you could have just paid it and called me."

Miranda's mind went to the biscuit tin. Fifty dollars a week went into it. Her little habit, one given up on when last year two thousand dollars disappeared over the course of a month and Noel had flat-out lied and said he'd needed it for car repairs.

The lie burned, when the head-gasket blew on the Commodore and Geoff at the auto-shop remarked he'd never seen Noel come in, not once. At least if he'd been having an affair Miranda could have wallowed in self pity, but Noble Noel was protecting his sick sister. DeDe had taken the money. Her new clothes had littered the bathroom floor, worn once, discarded, hundred-dollar lipsticks mashed into the carpet.

DeDe returned a day later, pale and weak from blood loss, but triumphant. Noel fussed over her. Miranda lost the spare room, the one she had set up her painting easel in, the one where the sunlight came through the window so buttery and creamy you could have frosted a cake with it. There was no room in her wardrobe office. All her paints went into the cellar under the house, with the easel, with her untouched canvases.

Unable to take out her anger on the smirking, narcissistic thing waiting in the sunshiny room, Miranda attacked her other enemy. Slaughtered the grass with the petrol brush cutter until the green chaos snarled up in the blade, and whipping debris flew up, slicing her arms with a hundred paper cuts.

She returned to the shower that afternoon, already littered with DeDe's makeup and cheap chemist-store perfume, rank with alcohol and fake-civet, more animal secretion than scent. Miranda wept from the pain of the water on her grass-bites, her own self pity.

Fucking grass, she thought. *Fucking grass.*

Tomorrow I'll make plans to leave, she decided. *I'll transfer some cash into my savings account and I'll leave.*

But the next morning a wave of nausea gut-punched her. She clung to the toilet as if enduring a storm. And when she checked the little-used app on her phone, the pink one that checked periods, she was nearly two weeks late.

• • •

She didn't tell him.

Miranda knew she should have; but all of a sudden she was pregnant and had the harsh crystal clarity, even when the rest of her mind seemed to have caught a weird brain-flu, that she could not support a child on her own. A little part of her hoped that the malign tide that had washed DeDe up on their shores would one day soon wash her back out again. There was only so much daytime TV Miranda could stand.

The pee-on-a-stick test turned blue.

For three months she tried not to think about it. Maybe she wasn't pregnant. Stress made periods stop, right? Could cause false positives. And she was stressed.

But one day Miranda woke and the lingering nausea was gone, and it might have been three months or maybe four, and she hadn't shown, or got a belly yet (and had been waiting until that time to face up to it herself).

DeDe was out of the house. Miranda's nemesis had taken to long benders in the city with new friends, had not come home the night before. The miscarriage was so painless, a spot of blood, and a gush, and the bathroom floor was smeared with blood as if someone had clubbed a seal to death on the tile floors.

A twist of muscle, an expulsion as subtle as clearing her throat. Wrapped up in a gob of dark blood and mucus, Miranda knew that it was the baby, or the foetus, really, not much bigger than her thumb.

And it was over. The three-month diversion was over. She knew she should have been sad about losing the baby, but deep in her secret heart she could only feel a whirling, blessed relief.

• • •

Miranda didn't know how to dispose of it. Didn't want to flush it down the toilet or throw it out in the garbage. Burial was too personal. She tossed her body's issue into the back yard, into the grassy pile. Let nature consume it the way nature did, she thought.

Noel didn't come home that night. The company's contract meetings were being held up by an international firm's reluctance to concede on a few points. Something.

DeDe had developed a habit of partying into bad hours. Miranda heard a man's voice out in the livingroom tonight, nasally, whiny. A druggie sort of voice. DeDe had returned late, with him in tow. Miranda sat up with her back to the bedroom door and fretted over the nicer pieces in the display cabinet. A car pulled up after midnight, then left, twelve cylinders growling down the street, waking the neighbours.

Even in the silence Miranda couldn't sleep. Thought of her baby, tangled up in the grass, consumed.

In the dawn's first light she had a notion that maybe she should go outside and see if she could find the little corpse, do something proper. No sooner had her bare foot stepped onto the back porch than the instep of her foot drove directly into a thick, bladed hunk of metal.

• • •

"Well," the doctor said, "You shouldn't be leaving your mother's jewellery outside."

Miranda gave a grimacing kind of smile. "Not my mother's. Picked up some things from the op shop. Cleaned a few pieces yesterday. Forgot I left it on the patio."

He put in the last stitch, wrapped Miranda's foot in gauze, gave her a tetanus shot and firm instructions. But all Miranda could think about was the brooch in the kidney dish. A cursory wash in the doctor's office revealed an ugly gold thing covered in pearls and paste-diamonds. It was too big to be anything other than costume jewellery.

"Where'd you get it again?"

"Op shop."

"You must have paid a lot. Real gold? They look like real dimonds to me. Know a bit about mid-century cuts. My wife's a gemologist."

Flustered, Miranda mumbled she didn't know, but her next stop took her to a pawnbroker in town. He offered her a weird amount with such gimlet-eyed insouciance, two hundred dollars for something that surely wouldn't fetch five bucks at a Salvos. At his affectation of casual disinterest, the distant panic at her refusal and a price higher by a hundred dollars, she began to suspect she wasn't in the possession of any old tat.

A trip into the city then, and the jeweller who had made her wedding ring.

"Wow, nice find. A handmade *memento mori*, gotta be nineteenth century. For a child, I think. The photograph of the deceased goes here. If there was one, it's gone. These are bluebirds. The gems are significant. It's old. Do you know anything of its provenance?"

"Provenance?"

"Where the brooch is from. It's an odd design."

A funny thought made her want to blurt out, *my backyard bought it. The grass brought it to me after I gave it my dead baby, like a cat will bring you a dead bird if you feed it.*

She declined his offer to sell the brooch. Even by diamondweight and gold alone the brooch was pushing upwards of ten grand.

She stopped by the supermarket on the way back, hobbled home with their shopping. In two days Noel didn't once comment on her funny walk. He had turned into a zombie-husband throwback from the nineteen-fifties, food in one end, money out the other, a ghost in between.

"What's for dinner?" he would ask, as if making an afterthought comment about the game show on telly.

"Steaks," Miranda said.

• • •

Half a kilo for them, the rest for the yard. The steaks brought a coin. So at least there was some transactional weight attributed to whatever you fed the yard, she thought. It was a nice coin, something that might have been recovered off a sunken ship. She quickly discovered that the grassy knoll had no time for bone and cooked leftovers. The fresher the meat, the more it gave up.

Soon Miranda collected a small trove of gold coins from different eras, and once, a particularly expensive slice of veal brought a Roman denarius with a worn-down bust of some wreath-headed Caesar. Occasionally she would entertain the thought that she was going mad, a housewife on Quaaludes madness, but it was a pleasant kind of insanity. She was feeding her tame grass-monster. It gave her something else other than DeDe to think about.

Miranda kept her booty in an empty container of Gumption in the cleaning cupboard, somewhere DeDe would never go, on account of the caustics that would ruin her acrylic nails, and the general requirement to do physical labour.

The knoll and Miranda forged an agreement. She let the yard grow wild and soon the backyard was covered in a veritable forest of rampaging lawn.

Which earned a visit from the council.

• • •

"Your grass is rather long," the council man said. He was as bowed and nuggety as the guy who had restumped the south end last week, courtesy of their new wealth. His polo-shirt had the council logo on the left pocket. "It presents a fire hazard."

Miranda feigned ignorance, even though she knew full well these semi-rural outposts had caveats you'd never see in the suburbs, things like maintaining your paddock and not letting your stock wander across the road.

"And we've received a couple of complaints," the council man sighed, as if the complaints were something both he and Miranda shared, an onerous burden he confided to her alone. "The noise. You know."

The council would never have come in the first place if the neighbours hadn't complained. Not if it hadn't been for DeDe's friends, the ones who sat on the back landing, hollering and pissing on the boards so that the urine sunk into the dry wood and gave the porch an ammoniac stink. They'd taken to lobbing their beer cans into the back yard, and oftentimes the debris would clear the rear fence to clatter on an adjoining roof. The grass didn't like them. It never gave Miranda gold presents on a night they were around.

"So yes, if you could get the backyard under control and limit the noise to daylight hours . . . "

He handed her some leaflets for a gardening service, left with a cheerful wave.

She ignored him as a daylight ghost, and returned back to her work. The rock-climbing magazine had commissioned her for more layouts. She'd sold some of her coins recently, had bought a very nice upgraded computer. What else was she supposed to do? It was not as if there were any instructional guidelines in dealing with the flora of carnivorous suburban landholdings. She was free climbing out into the unknown now. Aid-category climbing on uncharted routes. Tenuous placement of bodyweight-only holds. Complex and time consuming.

• • •

Only much later, when Miranda pondered over What Happened Next, did she realise she should have factored DeDe in to the problem that the yard presented her. Despite her clever hiding place, DeDe had probably discovered the Gumption container during a careful reconnaissance of everything that might hold money. DeDe had developed hunter's patience since the biscuit tin incident, had watched the container's value increase. Like a climber who knows they cannot top-out alone, DeDe needed a belay-holder to make the last ascent into some ill-gotten wealth. Called her druggie friend, who came over to wait for Miranda to come home.

Now Miranda was lying on the ground, him standing over her, the ringing in her boxed ears like a Puccini opera. The friend's thin druggie face had paled down to a bloodless pudding-bag of rage that made his face look like a mangled, chinless ghost over his shabby black shirt.

He grabbed Miranda by her hair.

Panic is a funny thing, has its own anaesthetic qualities. The room spun. Her graphic-design brain kicked in, saw everything from a camera-view. DeDe leant against the Dutch-angled doorway, saying, "Just tell him where you're finding the money, Miranda. He'll kill you otherwise." She dropped the cigarette butt on the carpet, stubbed it out with kitten heels.

"I'll call the cops," Miranda blurted.

"You fucking call the cops you'll be dead before they find me. And your brother."

"Hey, Ronnie, you goose," DeDe shouted, "Leave Noel out of this."

"Shut up," Ronnie said to DeDe. "You's the one owes me the money."

Miranda sagged against the grip of her hair. He let her go, a man who knew surrender.

"In the back yard," Miranda said. The words came out cold.

"All of it! All of it!"

The cold night stung her freshly cut face. The bunker-light above the porch didn't illuminate the yard, only set the rotting wood apart from the rest of their property, now awash in soft darkness. Her cheek throbbed. She tasted her own blood.

"Go on then. Go get it." DeDe's friend shone a flashlight into her face.

She didn't fear Ronnie so much as she feared the beast she had been feeding for the past twelve months. Perhaps it would see her as the ultimate meal. She hesitated, earning her a shove. Not hard, only disrespectful, making her wince from the sheer embarrassment of it. Ronnie was a man used to hitting women.

She stepped off the landing and into the grass. She could feel it move beneath her feet, an undulating carpet, rippling like the back of a large animal when a fly lands on its hide. It tasted her blood. The flashlight at her back didn't help. She didn't quite want to see what was coming.

Condemned, Miranda walked into the centre of the yard, her feet feeling the emplacement of bones throughout the warp and weft of the grass. Bigger bones than the lamb shanks and spare ribs she had ever thrown it, and with all the surrender of a drowning man she bent over, waiting to be seized.

And yet. And yet.

"Why are you taking so fucking long?"

"Box is heavy," she called back. "Can't lift it on my own."

"Jesus," he cursed, "Jesus, bitch, whore."

Funny enough, that in the end DeDe wasn't so dumb. Only she said, "Ronnie, careful, there's something moving out there."

Too late really. Half a dozen paces, then the yard ate him.

• • •

Perhaps he didn't really get eaten by grass. Perhaps metaphor, mnemonic, memory-fault. Whatever it was, DeDe fled inside before Miranda returned to the porch. Didn't see Miranda weeping in exultation, as if she'd topped out on a killer peak, arms raised in weary triumph: *Vincero! Vincero!*

Didn't call the cops either. Didn't do much more than collect her belongings and Ronnie's car-keys, her mouth pursed in a resentful cat's-arse. The script had played out wrong. Wasn't supposed to be this way, DeDe's gangster moll fantasy ending disrupted by a projectionist's error, like when you're halfway through a gangster heist movie and the reel skips over into the B-movie sci-fi title.

DeDe called Noel three hours later, hysterical over the phone. Noel couldn't get a word in edgeways. She refused to come back, ever, ever, oh my god!

"DeDe, please, please."

His sister hung up. The tide had washed her out.

Miranda comforted Noel after.

"It's for the best, darling," she said. "It's for the best that she's gone."

The recriminations were personal, self-pitying. *If Mum was still alive, she would never forgive me! DeDe has a condition! She can't look after herself!*

Now that was so much bullshit, but Miranda only pressed her battered cheek into the indentation between Noel's sob-heaving shoulder-blades. Later, she would blame her cheekbone bruise on a door, that old, old excuse.

And Ronnie? Well, bone and gristle he was, and meth-bitter to boot. Maybe you weren't supposed to taunt the yard with a diet that might not be repeatable. But he had a transactional value, and had once been living meat. Worth more than a coin, definitely. Perhaps even an entire fifty-k credit card debt. Tomorrow morning, before Noel was up, she would see what the backyard's learned opinion amounted to, and collect her side of the bargain.

•••••••••••

THE LOVE LETTERS OF SWANS

TANSY RAYNER ROBERTS

The papyrus was warm between my fingers as I sat on the wall above the port of Sparta, feet swinging in the sunshine. "She imports this from Egypt," I said aloud. "My mistress loves the Phoenicians and their magics. I believe she would gild the whole Palace if the king would let her."

Chloris, sitting beside me, reached out a hand as if longing to touch the letter for herself, then let it fall. "Your mistress is a slut, Hymnia," she said. "Everyone knows it."

No, not that, never that. I shook my head at her. "She's never done this before. Never made eyes at a single dignitary, or flashed her breasts at a passing prince. She chose the king good and proper, and she seemed to like him well enough."

"And look at her now, making eyes at a Trojan," said Chloris. Her eyes gleamed in the sunshine. "Can I read this one?"

"Only if you know the secrets of the Nile," I scoffed. "My mistress is not going to let her words out into the world without enchantments on them, is she?"

"I know a few secrets," said Chloris, reaching her hand out for the letter.

I held back, not wanting to let her try. "There's a word that unlocks it. She gave it to me. But I mustn't tell you, it's only for his ears."

The boat was not yet here, still bobbing out at the horizon.

"Tell me the word," begged Chloris. She was so pretty, and so bold. I would never catch the eye as she did, nor command others to my will. Gods pity me, but I craved her friendship. She was a slave, every bit as I was, and yet I wanted her to like me.

"Eggshell," I said in a whisper, and the papyrus shimmered before us. My mistress' words danced across the rough brown surface, burning like the sun.

Paris, Prince of Troy
Your words are attractive, and your poetry extremely elegant. I am impressed that you take so many words to convey a simple message: 'Fuck me, lady, I have earned you.'

Believe me when I tell you that nothing you or your goddess of love have ever done has earned a night in my bed, much less the disruption of my rather comfortable life.

You are a beautiful, shameless man, and you dishonour us both with your passions and your promises. Our poets run wild with tales of wives who lost everything because they believed a lovely, wicked tongue.

Do not write again, baby prince. You are out of your league.
Helen, Queen of Sparta.

"See?" I said, delighted. "She's not a slut. She's sending him back where he came from, good and proper."

"She's not virtuous neither, not with words like that," said Chloris, much impressed with 'fuck me, lady' sprawling across the page in gilded ink.

"He's hardly acting like a gentleman himself," I sniffed. "Begging her to run away with him, just because she smiled once or twice in his direction at her husband's banquet. Not a brain in his head, that one."

"I'd give him a tumble in a heartbeat," said Chloris with a throaty laugh. "Half a heartbeat, all painted and oiled as he was that night, ready for action. He wore sapphires in his own ears. Imagine what he'd give to a wench he liked." She shivered in delight at the thought of it.

I rolled my eyes and risked a friendly elbow in her direction. "He had no eyes for any but my mistress. You think he'd want you? He believes the goddess of love has Queen Helen marked out for him, that she is a grand reward for his mighty deeds. He's not going to take a wine pourer instead."

Chloris gave me a dirty look. "There's more than wine pouring in my future. You just watch me."

• • •

Queen Helen was bathing when I returned to her, the papyrus all but on fire between my guilty fingers. She reclined in a shallow bath as two house slaves scraped at her skin with oil and strigils. Another combed and trimmed her hair close to her head, so that it would be comfortable beneath her many golden wigs.

Helen had learned many tricks from Egypt in her youth, when she and King Menelaos were first married and the world loved them for it.

She had secrets too, my mistress. Two long, fine scars ran down her back, between the shoulder blades and all the way to her waist, where the wings had been severed only days after her birth. My mother was midwife to Queen Leda, and always scoffed at the idea that Helen and her sister were born from eggs.

"That lady worked as hard as any other mother, to bring her screaming scraps into the world," she insisted when anyone got a cup of wine into her.

No one wanted to know that, though. They wanted to know if it was true that the Queen had lain with Zeus in the form of a swan. If you've ever wondered how stories like that get started, you need look no further than the slaves after dark, drinking and telling tales of their masters.

"I'll say nothing more," my mother would insist, and then if a cup or three were forthcoming, she would tell the tale of the baby princess who was born with white wings, and had to have them removed by a doctor's knife.

I always thought she was exaggerating, until I came to the Queen's household myself and saw those scars of hers. Occasional fine white feathers grew back along the scars from time to time, and discreet slaves plucked them out before they became too obvious.

Those scars weren't the only mark of the swan upon Queen Helen. White downy feathers grew thickly at her pubis, instead of curly hair, but she refused to let the slaves do anything about that. Menelaos, the king her husband, liked to be reminded that she was divine.

In bed, he called her 'my goddess' and 'queen of the heavens'. Hard to imagine she would look elsewhere, with a husband who saw the stars every time he gazed upon her.

Today, though, I was not sure her thoughts were on her husband at all. The queen tipped her head back, allowing Eurynia to massage her scalp with oils.

"What did the ridiculous prince think of my letter, Hymnia?" she asked in a lazy voice.

I hesitated. I had never spoken anything but the truth to my mistress, but today the truth might earn me a beating. "He laughed, my lady," I confessed.

"Did he indeed?" Helen sounded intrigued rather than angry. "Did he scribble anything in return? A grovelling apology for his cheek?"

"He wrote you a message," I murmured, trying not to think about how Chloris and I had already pored over his reply before returning to the palace. I was worried she would see it in my eyes, that I had betrayed her confidence to impress a friend. "I have the papyrus here. The release word is 'sea-foam'."

Helen, Queen of My Heart
Your crudeness wounds me, though it makes you no less lovely in my eyes. Indeed, I have earned you. Indeed, I will fuck you. I offer you my father's city across the wide waters, and myself—a husband young enough to keep you wet with pleasure for the rest of your life.

The goddess Aphrodite has spoken, that you shall be mine. I would bow down and worship you in her name. Helen will be wife of Paris, and princess of Troy. There is no other possible future for us.

You were made for our goddess, born of the lusts of Zeus and his concubine Leda. Your mother may have thought herself a queen in her own land, but she learned quickly that it is wise to kneel down in submission when offered a mightier phallus.

Submit to me, Helen. Let me love you. The seas will burn with the flame of our lusts, and the goddess shall be sated at last when you cry my name to the winds.

Paris, Servant of Desire.

"Gods above," Queen Helen whispered as the papyrus grew taut in her hands. "This man is dangerous. There shall be no more letters, Hymnia."

"As you say, my queen," I said in relief.

Helen stood up, allowing the water and oil to cascade off her as she strode carelessly across the room, dripping on the mosaic tiles. "No, wait. I shall write once more. I must convince him that I am an impossible mark for this quest of his."

My heart sank. A bold young man like Prince Paris would surely respond to words like 'impossible' as nothing more than a challenge. "As you say, my queen."

Paris, Prince of Fools

Queens and wives have been ruined for far less than these letters between us. We shall not speak, nor write again. You have nothing to offer me, younger son of a lesser land. I am the queen of the city that birthed me. I chose my husband to rule at my side. You will not break me nor tempt me to leave Sparta, and you shall never possess me.

Sail back to Troy and be grateful that you escaped the flames that would set the world alight if Menelaus, King of Sparta, thought himself cuckolded by a whelp like you.

Favourite of Aphrodite, never forget that I am a daughter of swan-shaped Zeus. Approach me again, and I shall peck your eyes out.

Helen, always of Sparta.

• • •

We sat on the sun-kissed wall, Chloris and I, reading the letter that Helen had dictated, crossed out, and re-written more than a dozen times before she was satisfied with it.

"That's that, then," I said, wanting to believe it. "We'll never see him again."

"Are you blind?" said Chloris. "She's practically begging him to snatch her out from under her husband's nose. That's a call to arms, that is, not a farewell."

"She wouldn't," I insisted. Above all things, I believed in my mistress's fidelity.

"You'd better hope he sees it as a love challenge and not a rejection," said Chloris.

My confusion must have shown on my face.

"Well, if he takes it as an insult, he'll lash out at you, won't he?" she pressed. "Whip you, I wouldn't be surprised. Got no reason to be kind, if the lady he wants is having none of him."

I had been whipped before, but not since coming into service for her mistress. Queen Helen had always been gentle in her admonishments when a mistake was made. "He wouldn't dare, not the Queen's messenger," I whispered.

"You won't be the Queen's messenger any more, not if he don't need you to send no more messages," taunted Chloris. "And she can't defend you, can she? Not and risk him telling the king what the letters were all about. Best to drop the papyrus into the ocean, never let him see it."

I drew my knees up to my chin and hugged them close. "Can't do that. She'd expect the papyrus back." One way or another, I could be in for a beating today.

"Tell you what," said Chloris, with a smile as bright as day. "I'll take it for you. I'm not afraid of the prince. And he won't know me, so can't risk offending my master, can he?"

I felt a shameful flood of relief. She was my friend after all. Maybe all this had been worth it. "Really? You'd do that for me?"

"Why not? I fancy another glimpse of the pretty prince." Chloris hopped off the wall. "I'll bring the papyrus back after."

• • •

I waited on the wall as long as I could, but Chloris did not return. Finally, I ran back to the palace to perform my various duties. There was a fancy dinner on this evening and it was easy to keep out of the queen's way, with all the dressing and primping and tasting to be done.

I didn't see Chloris later, not anywhere around, even after the dinner started and most of the palace slaves gathered around the kitchen to share gossip about our guests.

Prince Paris had not made an appearance at the dinner, and King Menelaos took this as a grave insult, though Queen Helen did her best to smooth things over with him with her usual deference and humour.

I was sick with fear that the Queen would call me over to whisper privately about the return of the papyrus, and ask if there was some final missive from the bold, foolish prince.

So I busied herself at the feast, making sure there were others around me at all times so there was no chance the Queen could summon me. Not without making it far too obvious that she had a secret.

Later, as the feast settled in, I ran to the door slaves to ask if Chloris had returned to the palace. Both claimed to have seen her, which worried me. Why would she hide from me unless something had gone wrong? I hurried off to my nook in the chattel quarters and relief exploded in my chest when I saw the papyrus tucked into my sleeping roll.

If I was quick, I would be able to take it to the queen's rooms and leave it near her bed, so it would appear to her as if it had been there all evening. The previous word, 'honey pears', did not release any words. Either the magical papyrus was blank now, or the Prince had added his own lock upon the page. In any case, it should be safe from prying eyes.

I hurried along the brightly painted corridor that led to the queen's quarters, so engaged in my task that I barely heard the pot that broke, moments before I burst through the doorway.

And there, oh. A sight I wish I had never seen.

Queen Helen of Troy lay on her back in bed, sprawled beneath the flexing, sweaty muscles of a man who should not be here. Paris of the painted eyebrows and jewelled ears. Tangled together, they groaned and gasped with something that sounded more like laughter than passion.

Shocked beyond all reason, I pressed myself into the side of the door, hoping not to be seen.

Too late. Paris arched his back and looked at me over his shoulder, poised to thrust again into my mistress. "Like what you see, little one?" he snorted.

Helen gave him a shove so that he fell, wet from her and still hard of phallus, back on to the bed. "She's no use," she protested, swinging a long leg over to straddle him like he was one of those horse gods the Trojans favoured, taking him deep inside her. "Little Hymnia is good as gold, and would never summon anyone to see her mistress's terrible secret. Break another pot."

There was something in the way she said those words, a mocking tone that I had never heard in the mouth of the Queen. Still, it was familiar. My embarrassment overwhelmed me, red and hot, and yet I let my eyes fall downwards to the place where flesh met flesh. Coarse hair curled around her mound, hair that ought to be feathers. The creature fucking Prince Paris in the bed of my mistress was not, and never could be, Queen Helen of Sparta.

I ran away, though I could not possibly run fast enough. A familiar laugh trailed after me as I scampered back down the corridor. Not the queen's laugh. That sound was Chloris, through and through. Was it really the prince grunting beneath her, or had she wiped the prince's face over that of a bath slave as easily as Helen and Paris had wiped letters on and off the Phoenician papyrus?

I know a few secrets, Chloris had said. She was Phoenician herself, so she had always claimed. What other magics did she have?

I hurried my step, but her words caught up to my mind finally. *Break another pot.*

They wanted to be caught. Whether he was the real Paris or not, they were doing it in the name of that horrid prince. He was the only one who would benefit from Queen Helen's reputation being sullied in her husband's house. Did he expect her to seek refuge in his ships when King Menelaos lost faith in her?

Chloris, Chloris, what have you done?

Queen Helen was not in the main hall. I stared in horror at the Queen's empty seat. If only she had remained here, under her husband's eye, no man could ever accuse her. Perhaps there was still time . . .

But no, there was already a shouting from above, and I could see the king noting the commotion.

I turned and ran again, cursing the palace for its maze-like corridors. I fled to the east wing where the children slept and there, emerging from her daughter's bed chamber, was Queen Helen at last.

"My queen," I gasped. "Danger. You are accused . . . "

"Why," said Helen with a half-smile across her beautiful face. "Who accuses me? Have I committed some offence?"

"One of your servants—wears your face—in your bed, my queen. With Prince Paris . . . "

Helen's face went very still. Her smile faded into nothing. "There is still hope, Hymnia," she said after a moment's thought. "Catch up the babies—no, wait. Let them sleep for now. I shall find my husband and show him my innocence."

She took my hand, walking steadily, though I could see she was afraid of the outcry and bustle we could hear coming from the main part of the palace. Footsteps came running towards us, and

Helen raised her voice to call the guards, only to realise that these armoured men were not hers to command.

Trojans wearing the false colours of Sparta advanced upon us, weapons at the ready.

"Come quietly, madam," said one of them. "We would hate to ruin that pretty face of yours."

Helen shoved me suddenly towards them and I fell willingly, grasping at their blades in the hopes of taking them inside me, of saving my queen. Pain blurred through my body, and the last thing I saw was red and black and feathers.

• • •

Not dead.

I was not dead, for I awoke again in the knowledge that I had failed. The ground swayed beneath me, back and forth, and bile rose in my mouth at the unnatural motion. I rolled over in the narrow bunk and opened my eyes.

A ship, then. I knew this ship. It was the same cabin I had visited so many times, to deliver those wretched messages back and forth on the magic papyrus. If only we had it now, perhaps we could summon help.

But who would listen to us, the captured queen and her slave?

Helen sat on a packing crate, barely glancing in my direction as I made my state known to her. "All is lost," she said softly. "By now, my husband thinks me a madwoman and a slut, run away to sea in my lust for a Trojan sword." She said those last few words with great distaste. Whatever she had once thought of Paris as they exchanged flirtation and banter, he was not beautiful to her now. "I will never see my children again."

She wept then, and I did not dare to comfort her. There was nothing I could say.

A Trojan sailor brought oils and fresh water to Helen, commanding her to make herself presentable for Prince Paris. My queen all but spat at him.

The sailor smirked at her, darting out of range with a nimbleness hardly suited to one who pulls ropes all day. "A fine obedient bride my master has bought himself," he chided her.

I knew then who this was. No sailor at all, not with that prissy manner and the secret smile he hid behind the insults. "Chloris. Are you so ashamed of your real face now?"

The sailor gave me an arch look. "My master thought it a sensible precaution if I was to live among his soldiers and sailors for a time. Women are unlucky at sea, you know. At the first sign of a storm, they'll be demanding he throw one or both of you overboard."

"You're the one, then," said Queen Helen in a low voice. "The traitor who sold me to the Trojans."

The sailor passed a hand over his face and became Chloris, as snub-nosed and freckled as I remembered her. "I never served you, lady. I betrayed no one."

"You betrayed me!" I said, outraged. "You used me to get close to Prince Paris, and to wreck our lives."

Chloris scoffed. "How can I have betrayed you, Hymnia? You're not a real person. You're property, just as I was property. We don't have feelings, or loyalties. We are just owned." She sneered at my queen. "And now she is going to know exactly how that feels."

Queen Helen leaped to her feet, striding towards the girl. Her golden hair tufted up like the feathers of an angry bird. "You little snake," she breathed. "You have started a war, and orphaned my children, and for what? A prince who will never remember your name?"

"He knows my name," Chloris growled at her. She passed her hand over her face again and became Helen, that Helen I had seen in my mistress's bed, the slightly too-perfect version of the golden queen. "He calls me Helen, and Wife, and Queen, and Mine. He calls me Ohhh and Harder and Do That and Bend Over." She preened at the queen whose face she had stolen. "He's already had you, in every way possible, without ever laying a hand on your precious skin. You really should have listened when he said you belonged to him."

The real Queen Helen hissed between her teeth. "He still wants me, though, doesn't he? He wants the woman who said no, not the one who says 'yes master'. He wants my ambrosia wrapped around his cock, not a pale imitation."

Chloris frowned at that. "I may be an imitation, lady, but if you don't submit to him fast enough, I'll be the one he carries home to Troy as a trophy. He told the whole city he was going to marry Helen of Sparta, and one way or another, it's going to be true."

Helen's face became very calm, which always happened when she was dealing with someone very annoying, or very dull. "Well, then," she said. "I had better hurry up and submit to my new husband, hadn't I? If nothing else, it will put you out of a job."

• • •

So he came to her, Prince Paris of Troy, the doom of queens. To summon him, Helen slapped Chloris across the face and scrawled the words 'I submit' across the girl's face in fiery words as magic as the ones that had once appeared and disappeared on the enchanted papyrus. Then she threw the girl out of the cabin, to be her messenger.

The prince arrived, stinking of oils and scent, delighted with himself. Chloris came too, clutching at her master's back, probably half-hoping that Helen had served the invitation in order to reject the prince.

But no, Helen was the Queen of Sparta and had been a wife for many years. She knew what to do with a man. She placed herself on the narrow bunk, the picture of docility, with her gown artfully arranged so that he would look at nothing but her breasts.

"Your highness," she said in a voice that was neutral with only a hint of frost. "I hear that we are to be wed."

"Oh, my Helen," breathed the lying prince. "I would not take you against your will."

She showed not even a flicker of distaste. "If this is our destiny, then indeed we must be married. You have given me little choice but to obey."

"Obey me in my arms, not with your mouth," said Paris, flinging himself at her. "Though I will have your mouth too."

They sank back on to the bed, his mouth lapping at hers.

Chloris stood as a statue, leaning on the closed cabin door as the sea gently rocked us, and Paris groped beneath the gown of his new wife.

"You made this marriage," I said in a low voice, gripping her wrist with my fingers, nails digging into her skin. "The least you could do is witness it."

There were cries coming from the bunk now, cries and groans, and I wanted to shut my ears to it, but I wanted more for Chloris to see what she had done.

Her face changed, though, and I saw fear on her face. Then I, too, looked towards the couple.

Paris struggled in the arms of Helen, and it was not pleasure that came out of his mouth now in those cries and groans. Her arms wound hard around his neck, and trails of white feathers burst from her skin from wrist to elbow, wet and spiky.

She rolled him over and straddled him effortlessly, letting her gown fall away as she did so and feathers, there were more white feathers everywhere, sliding from her shoulder blades in the long dipping shapes of wings.

Paris shuddered beneath her as her hands lengthened into golden claws and sank into his white, oily flesh.

"You have burned my life," she told him, tipping back her head and letting her scalp burst into bright white feathers, streaked with blood. "But I will eat yours."

Chloris cried out, turning her face into my shoulder so as not to see Helen's face transformed into a streak of whiteness with a bright golden beak instead of a mouth.

Swift and bright as the sun, she pecked again and again, tearing at his skin, his flesh. Then she caught him up, divine creature that she was, and burst through the side of the ship. We rocked back and forth, water pouring in the damaged side, and Helen of Sparta flew free of us, still biting at the ruined body of the prince. Finally, high above the water and far enough from the ship that no one would ever rescue him, she dropped the creature like a stone.

We heard running and thumping from the sailors above us fighting to keep the craft afloat. My feet were wet. Helen was flying and flying, barely a dot on the horizon now. She was free, and she had left us long behind.

There was a pounding on the door behind us. Paris had barred it when he thought this was his wedding night, but now it was only a few splinters between us and a crew of sailors we did not know.

"Highness, Prince Paris!" cried out his men. "We must leap to one of the other ships, we are sinking!"

Chloris and I, equally abandoned by our queen, stared at each other.

"They will tear us apart," I whispered.

Chloris shook her head, and changed herself into the false Helen, the sprite she had worn for Prince Paris' benefit. "Not me. I will be brought safely to Troy."

"You fool," I hissed. "Do you think Menelaos won't start a war over this?"

"He will rescue me, then. I don't care. I just want to live. Not one of them ever thought I was worth keeping alive, not even your precious queen." She pouted at me. "If Paris is alive, Helen will be safe."

"Paris is feeding the fishes now."

"I know," she said softly as the door shuddered behind us, again and again. They were trying to kick it in. "I need another Paris, to keep me safe. To keep us both safe. I won't be a slave again."

I closed my eyes, and felt Chloris' hand brush over me, transforming me with her Egyptian spells. "It won't work, we can't be them," I tried to convince her.

"We can be them more easily than they could ever be us," she replied.

It was painless and drugging, the illusion she wrought upon me. When I looked into the polished bronze, though, I could not deny that it was convincing. The sight of myself made me tremble down to my toes.

When the sailors knocked down the door, they found Prince Paris of Troy and his new queen, Helen, waiting for rescue. Not once, as they pulled us along to alight from one ship and row to another in the fleet, not once did even a single sailor remember that Helen had been accompanied by a slave girl.

Hymnia had disappeared entirely.

I could not imagine my future, as we sailed onwards to Troy. This trick was not of my making, and yet I had agreed to it.

I was a Prince, and Chloris was a Queen. If there was a war now, we would be at the heart of it.

My heart broke for Helen, the real Helen, flying across the ocean in that monstrous form of beak and feathers. A mother without children, a wife without a husband, a Queen without a city.

And yet, as long as I had known her, she had never been more magnificent as when she caught up that wretched, sorry excuse for a prince and let him sink into the waters.

Whatever songs they sing of Helen—once of Sparta, now of Troy—whatever lies they tell, I shall always remember her as a swan, and flying, and free.

●●●●●●●●●●

BRIDGE OF SIGHS

KAARON WARREN

10 am/Client: Mr P/ Subject: His son (16) Overdose

Terry needed a fresh ghost, so he dressed warmly and headed out, camera around his neck, syringes safely packed into the bag over his shoulder.

There were many places to look. People committed suicide in surprising places sometimes, such as a change room in a large department store, or the car park at a primary school, or under the pier at the beach, but more often they jumped from the tops of buildings, from bridges, from dams.

They jumped from the hospital roof too, staff as well as patients. But security could be tight, and once he'd been locked on a roof overnight and didn't want to repeat that experience.

He drove to Culver's Dam instead. Some nights he had a feeling for where the ghosts would be; other times it was research and asking questions.

He loved the hunt. He loved that there was a purpose to it but more than that, it proved time and time again that there was something BEYOND. That his mother did not blink out into nothingness.

Terry parked his car near the entrance to the dam bridge, water noise nearly deafening him. There was one car already parked there; a purple sedan. The bonnet was damp with water spray and cold to the touch so it had been there for some time. It could belong to a hydro engineer, manning switches, checking equipment, or to a sightseer (although in this cold no one would stay so long), or the car was abandoned, its driver over and into the hydrodam.

Feeling the cold, he gathered his camera and syringe bag and trekked to the bridge where he climbed the many stairs, feeling the tension in his thighs. A thick mist settled over the dam and in his hair and on his face. His hands felt frozen so he stuffed them into his pockets but found little warmth there.

Reaching the bridge, he could barely see three steps in front of him. Here, the water roar was so loud he could scream and no one would hear.

He set up his camera and looked through the view finder, seeking features amongst the water droplets.

He didn't think much of those who killed themselves here. Poisoning the water supply, hurting others. Like those who threw themselves in front of a train, or over a wall at a shopping mall, or onto a busy street, it caused trauma to strangers that surely eased no passing and perhaps led to further suicides among those who saw or who felt responsible.

He saw nothing, so walked further along, gazing through his viewfinder until he saw a middle-aged man, soaked to the bone, shivering with cold. Bare feet. Once their shoes were off it was too late to do anything.

"It's an amazing view, isn't it?" Terry said.

"Yeah, nice view," the man said, glancing out as if seeing it for the first time. "Peaceful."

"It's like the end of the world, isn't it? As if all life ends here," Terry said. "As if nothing matters, no one cares." His voice was gentle but it carried.

The man closed his eyes, gripping the railing. Terry hoped he wouldn't have to get close to the edge. There was a chest-high fence, but he still felt vertigo at the thought.

"You like taking photos?" the man said. He squeezed his eyes shut, as if instantly realising the stupidity of the question.

"Yeah. It's the one thing that keeps me going some days."

The man leaned forward, looking over the edge. "I don't really have anything like that. Are you a drinker?"

"Depends on what it is."

"Whisky my dad left me. Last drops. He was an alcoholic."

"Mine shot himself in front of me."

They exchanged glances; both shrugged. "Go grab it for us? You've got shoes on."

The man threw him the car keys.

Terry took a warm winter coat that was lying on the back seat of the purple car but could find no flask. The car was dirty, uncared for, and it smelt of pizza. Nothing in the glove box beyond official papers. No music, no letters, no photos, no devices.

When he returned to the top of the dam the man was over, so he had wanted privacy in his last moments and had gained it by sending Terry to look for the flask. The mist was thicker, more dank.

There. There it was. His flash was powerful and froze the ghost in place so he could suck up the mist into his syringe.

He stowed his equipment in the backseat, a sense of wellbeing overtaking him. It was always this way. Taking the spirits filled him with grace and kept him from going over himself, some days.

Terry didn't want the man's car, but was glad to have the coat.

• • •

His Aunt Beryl called up the studio stairs. "Are you decent?" She'd caught him once, shirt off, and she'd never forgotten it. "Come on up," he said.

She appeared behind a bunch of purple hydrangeas, holding them out like an offering.

"This'll bring a glow to your cheeks, you beautiful man. Although look at you! Picture of health!"

"You know I want pink or red flowers," he said. He said it most times. "Purple gives off the wrong colour."

She was a stupid woman. She understood him though, accepted him, and she had been his mother's best friend. Her bright red fingernails were so long they curled down over the tips of her tanned, crooked, wrinkled fingers. She wore a lot of rings (including an ostentatious engagement ring, although her fiancé died decades before), smelled of cigarette smoke and used Tabu perfume that made his studio reek. Her toenails were brightly painted as well and she wore sandals too small for her. Her cracked heels hung over the back and her toes stuck out the sides.

She owned the florist shop in the nearby mall. She wore a floral coat that she never washed, over a miniskirt far too short for her. Tabu perfume and old, old sweat. She collected unused flowers from the hospital and turned them into bouquets, charging full price, sometimes selling them to people who would take them back to the hospital.

He liked lots of flowers for his photos. They gave the impression of warmth and life and they provided a focus, a discussion point.

The funeral director texted >>We're heading up now<<.

Terry had Aunt Beryl hide behind the black curtain and climb into the Mama Suit, black gloves stitched into the black curtain, so that she could hold the dead boy up without being seen. She hated it, she said. Hated it when they were cold, hated it when they got warm. But he needed her there, to hold the chin up, keep the shoulders back.

Teenagers often needed help sitting up.

• • •

It was good to meet clients at the entrance, not leave them waiting in the hallway with the dead loved one. Terry stood in front of the magnificent trompe l'oeil of The Bridge of Sighs, the concealed doorway leading not to a Venetian prison but to his studio.

"Here we are," the funeral director said. Terry modelled the timbre of his own voice on this man's; it was so perfectly kind, honest, and masculine. The funeral director's judgement was excellent in deciding the level of service to be provided, but the final decision was Terry's. "This is Mr P. The father." They never shared full names. "I've told him of the comfort you can bring him, in the fullest terms."

"The mother?" Terry asked quietly.

"At home. Inconsolable."

Terry's mother would have been the same. She would not have functioned again, if he'd died before her.

"Come on, then," Terry said. He led the man by the elbow, leaving the funeral director to roll in the trolley with the dead boy.

He gently lifted the boy into the chair in front of the black curtain, then nodded to the funeral director, who whispered, "You're doing a good thing," to the father and left.

Aunt Beryl took grip on the boy.

The father stood close, nervous, hesitant.

"You hold his hand while I set up," Terry said. "Strong boy, wasn't he? What did he like most? Was he a burger lover? Or a vegetarian? A lot of kids are these days." Putting the client at ease was part of the job.

Terry pulled on some gloves, opened the fridge. There was champagne, cold, but not for this shoot or any like it. He took out the recently-filled syringe. The ghosts leaked out of the needle if he left them in the fridge too long, forming yellow, viscous puddles on the shelf, like spilled egg yolk.

The father noticed nothing.

Terry bent over the boy and injected the syringe into the corner of his eye.

The boy twitched, and his cheeks reddened, chasing away the blue tones the overdose had given him.

Terry stepped behind his camera and took a quick dozen shots. "Hold him if you like. Take him in your arms."

Hesitantly, Mr P stepped forward. "He's warm. He feels warm."

"It won't last long. Make the most of it."

Mr P held his son close. Beryl knew to let go at that point, take her arms away.

"Say your goodbyes, then. Make him sigh."

Mr P whispered in his son's ear until the coldness began to creep back. Terry took the boy and settled him into the chair.

"There."

Mr P was pale. "God. I don't know if his mother would have wanted that or not."

"But you got to say goodbye."

"But it almost feels like . . . .that empty feeling of fullness you get from eating a packet of potato chips."

"The photos will make it worth it. You'll see."

"But he's still dead, isn't he?" Mr P said.

Terry, a professional, kept his emotions in check. He would have given anything to have that moment with his mother, yet this man didn't seem to appreciate what he'd been given.

It helped that he felt as if his mother was beside him, whispering in his ear. "Oh, you angel. Oh, such a good man." This was what he worked for, beyond all the other benefits. This sense of benefaction.

• • •

Terry had been sixteen the first time he saw a ghost in the mist. His mother and Aunt Beryl ran the florist together then, and he helped with deliveries. This one was a rooftop memorial to a suicide. Terry's father was long dead by then; "I love you son," and then a deep sigh, then the gunshot, with Terry sitting beside him. Terry couldn't remember a mist forming, but later, it was there. He knew that.

"Be careful near the edge," his mother said. "Even an accident might be considered suicide if you deliberately put yourself in harm's way."

It was misty on the roof, rendering his vision unclear, and he rubbed at his eyes, the bouquet wedged under one arm. He squeezed his eyes tight, opened them, but the mist seemed even thicker. He saw a slumped figure, dejected, so very sad, and reached out to it, thinking to comfort this loner, this apparent outcast.

As he touched it, it seemed to snarl, to reach for him, and he jumped back, landing on the feet of the mourners behind him. Like many in grief, they were disconnected to their bodies and didn't react.

Later, he managed to get hold of some CCTV footage of this suicide, and he watched it over and over again. The moment he looked for, beyond what the others saw (the death of a woman with post-natal depression) was the mist forming, like a small cloud rising from the ground and hovering on the rooftop. As he told his mother, "If I stare for long enough without blinking, I see a face or a figure."

She was arranging flowers in a cut glass vase, her taste impeccable. She was like a delicate flower herself, Terry thought, pink and easily damaged. His father had been like a stick insect, attached to her, always wanting to draw her nectar. She said, "Oh, that poor woman, stuck in limbo. No heaven, no hell." She was a great believer in such things. She liked to remain in a state of grace at all times, just in case she was taken suddenly.

"What about Dad? Is that where he is?"

"He didn't die that way," she said, in denial, always in denial, but Terry still had the tiny blood spattered t-shirt he'd been wearing that day.

No one else could see what he saw. He read about a group of people who lived by diving and fishing, who trained their eyes to see better underwater, and he took up swimming, long laps along the bottom of the pool, eyes open. His mother on the side, holding a towel, terrified of not seeing his head bob up again.

Eventually he trained his eyes to look through the water and thus the mist, to see clarity beyond it.

He would use this skill to prove to himself that his mother's death was accidental.

She and Beryl had always wanted to travel, especially once they were both widowed. They saved for years, then hired someone to take over the shop when they flew to Europe with their hair done, their lipstick on, their matching suitcases packed neatly, their promises to write often. He didn't see them off. He was deep in a world of buying sex and selling drugs, where stories of his childhood meant nothing. He sold dreams to people, sold calm, sold respite, and lived well off the proceeds.

Two weeks later, Beryl called him, hysterical, the line bad, voices behind her that she tried to shush. His mother had drowned in a Venice lagoon, off the Ponte dell Liberta. Beryl said, "Come get us, Terry. Come bring us home," but he was in no state to fly. In the end Beryl did it on her own. He'd sobered up by the time she landed.

It wasn't until he saw his mother's body he believed she was gone, and even then, he couldn't reconcile what lay in the coffin with the woman he knew.

"It was an accident, wasn't it?" he asked Beryl. "Tell me she didn't want it."

Because otherwise she'd be stuck there in the mist, graceless. She'd said to him, "Always resuscitate. Even if I'm a vegetable. I don't ever want to be one of those people you see." She was the only one he'd told about the mist.

"No, no, she didn't want it! We were walking with all the other tourists. One minute we were talking, next minute she was over. She did not want it, Terry. All she talked about was the future, and you, and wanting to see how you fared. She wanted better for you."

He drew a line then, under the man he was and the man he would be.

• • •

Beryl sat with him and held his hands at the funeral. There were so many flowers people sneezed uncontrollably, but Beryl said, "This is what she would have wanted."

She handed him a camera. "Your mother took lots of photos, Terry. I know she'd want you to have this. Next up was the Bridge of Sighs. There's proof she didn't want it. She was so keen to see that place, and we never made it." Beryl cried then, great snuffling sobs, and he left others to comfort her.

• • •

He had the photos developed and he saw what his mother had given him.

Photos of mist, in many of the places they travelled in Europe. "Here there are ghosts," she was saying to him. "And here, and here."

Would he find her there, in the mist? He had to know.

He travelled to Venice, to the Ponte dell Liberta where to his great relief there was no mist, no matter how much he squeezed his eyes and squinted. So he travelled to the Bridge of Sighs, because he wanted to finish her voyage for her. He would look out as those long-ago condemned did, and he would listen for their sighs echoed in the walls.

He heard nothing, but he did see the mist, and flying in the mist, ghosts.

He knew about the belief that suicides did not pass over, that they were confined to the earthly plane. Terry thought it was the embodiment of the sigh that stayed behind. The last sigh so many made before jumping.

The window was like a slice of pizza. He could see the canal, buildings on either side. In the distance, another bridge, laden with tourists and beyond that; more buildings, so much water. He thought, "They're out there."

He began to follow the trail of suicides: the tallest buildings, the bridges, and he found the mist each time.

It was on the Nusle Bridge, in Prague, where he stood transfixed but somehow lost, that he understood what he could do. A young woman, shoes held by the straps, her lips red, her blond hair wild and wispy around her head, said, "I feel as if he's here. Don't you? Stuck there, in the mist."

He squinted and did see a face.

"Your husband?" he said.

She nodded. "If only you could capture him. Give him to me." The woman ran her hand through the mist and shivered. "You might give him a second chance. Them."

He took a photo, wanting to capture her grief, the moment she reached for the husband she thought waited there. The flash froze the mist and, within the mist, a face. He reached out to touch it, thinking it would disperse, but he could run his fingers through it and feel it, wet.

If only he could capture it.

The widow watched him, her cheeks flushed, and soon they were sharing wine, she was laughing with her head thrown back and he knew that she was using him but that made it even better.

• • •

Back home, he established his photography studio above the funeral parlour. Beryl and his mother had long supplied flowers to the parlour, and Beryl was the one who made the suggestion. "You have such an affinity with the grieving. An understanding. You'll be wonderful," she said, and the funeral director agreed.

It took experimentation to discover that syringes worked best to capture the ghosts, but it was not time wasted. Every capture gave him strength. Among the first was his father, trapped in a small wet mist in the backyard over the swing chair. Terry flashed the photo, froze him, syringed him. It was a gift he didn't think his father deserved, but he wanted the mist gone.

His father became one of the yellow stains. Terry soaked it up in a napkin and he kept that with his mother's water-stained Italian silk scarf and his own tiny t-shirt.

He wasted many this way until he remembered the words of his lover in Venice (You could give him a second chance), but what led him to make that first injection? He liked to think it was his mother, helping him as he pressed the needle, unseen, into a deceased elderly woman and watched her cheeks colour.

He didn't know what happened to the spirits next. His studio was always cold and sometimes, he thought, misty. But flash revealed no ghosts there. He liked to think he freed them, but truly he didn't care.

12pm/ Client: Mr S/ Subject: His Fiancée (29) Car Crash

Terry walked into the forest; it was a favourite hunting ground, when he was in the mood for a hike and the fresh air. He loved the smell of pine, and the crunch underfoot of growth and of insect bodies.

The mist was thick at the base of a massive tree, and he took his photos, gathered his spirit, before pausing for a quick sandwich and coffee from his thermos.

The funeral director came out with him once and while the man saw the mist, he did not see the faces within, although he did feel chilled to the bone and a sense of the "Heeb Jeebs," he said.

• • •

Terry turned on soft lighting and played romantic music. He threw a satin sheet over the couch and added Erotica to the oil burner.

Mr S was in his mid 30s. His hair was a mess and his clothes dishevelled and there was a furtiveness about him. The dead woman lay on a trolley, covered by a soft blanket.

"Slight rush on this one. Her parents hate him," the funeral director said in Terry's ear as he passed the trolley over. "Apparently a restraining order on him, hush hush."

"No worries, we're good to go."

"Enjoy," the funeral director said.

"It's a sad name for a photography studio," Mr S said. The light from the stained glass windows in the foyer bathed him in a deep, colourful glow.

"Kind of," said Terry, "But I also think of the last sigh as both a release and an acceptance. It tells you your loved one was ready to move on. That they are okay." He loved this metaphor, having once read a description of Franz Mesmer's studio as being 'filled with the sighs of sweet music and soft female voices'.

He settled the dead girl onto the couch, arranging her so she appeared to be resting. Aunt Beryl was at the florist; he didn't need her for this one.

As Terry worked, he asked, "How long had you been together?"

"Two years. But I dumped her. It wasn't working out, so I dumped her. She went out and got blind drunk. This is my fault, I shouldn't have dumped her." The body was severely damaged; broken limbs, deep bruising. Her flesh was spongy in places.

"It's not your fault. You loved her dearly. I can see that. She was a lucky woman." Terry's sleeves were rolled up high around his triceps. He knew he shone under the lights and that the life in him, the brightness, contrasted starkly. He was a handsome man and he knew it, square-jawed, wild-haired, and he was always flicking it out of his eyes. Women shifted it for him sometimes, tucking it behind his ears. He knew he had them when they did that.

"God, look at her," Mr S said. "Can't you cover that up so she looks normal?"

The whole back of her head was dented. The funeral director had done his best cosmetically, and they nestled her head in cushions, hiding the damage.

Terry pulled on gloves, walked to his bar fridge and removed a syringe.

He'd scratched himself before, raising blisters which were filled with tiny growths, so he always wore gloves now.

"What the fuck is that?"

"It's going to help us make her look better in the photo. Trust me. It's an element of the universal fluid that runs through us all, even your beautiful girl. Her flow has been interrupted, but I can get it going again very, very briefly."

Terry emptied the syringe into the corner of her eye. Stepped back. Waited for the moment. That sudden flare of colour in the cheeks, as if the flesh was infused with dye. This he needed to capture.

A twitch. The glow. "There it is!"

"Is she alive?"

"Just for a moment."

He heard a soft sighing and it was so sweet it made all else seem empty. The smell was ammoniac, though. It made his eyes water.

He took some shots. "Touch her. Go on. She's warm."

There was no personality in the revival. It was the physical body alone that reanimated. No conversation, no thought process.

Still, Terry said, "Say goodbye. *I love you* always feels good. She might hear you. Think of her as in a coma. Your voice might pass through to her. And hold her while she's warm. She'll feel good."

"I'm sorry," Mr S said to her. "I'm sorry I made you die. If you hadn't left it wouldn't have happened."

Mr S touched her.

"Go for it," Terry said. "Most people do."

"Really?"

Terry showed him some photos. "Really. Look. I can take a record if you want. Just for your private viewing. You have to be quick, though."

Grief sold. Grief-struck fucking even more so.

The woman blinked. Her mouth opened.

Terry took the photos then printed them out while Mr S went to the bathroom. He added his special touch to them, here and there, the colours he loved. Split lip red, Vagina pink. All shoots excited him, but these ones in particular. He didn't relieve himself though; he had a date that evening and looked forward to it. The only dead one he'd ever been tempted by was an actress. The funeral director alerted him, describing her wild bush, her protuberant labia, her large and obvious clitoris. There were no loved ones but that didn't matter.

Terry took photos anyway.

They say a photographer (pornographer) should never star in his own work and Terry agreed. He took plenty of photos, though. She was a beautiful woman.

• • •

He presented to Mr S, now waiting in the viewing room, flicking through magazines. Terry liked his clients to sit with him at the large desk on the comfortable chairs. He made coffee or cocoa or he poured wine and he had chocolate truffles to eat.

"You're a magician. How do you do it?" Mr S said, surprised even though he had seen the body, felt the warmth.

"I colourise here and here. It's an art."

"You're a genius."

Another high-paying happy customer. Terry loved to help.

He sprayed air freshener around the studio to absorb the odours. His nose was sensitive to the smell of decay, although he was far more used to it today than he once was. He burned incense by the handful and people liked it. It made some of them think of church, which was a comfort for most.

2pm/Client: Ms T/Subject: her daughter (stillborn)

He didn't take bookings too far in advance. He needed to be ready to move, ready to snap on an hour's notice or less. The funeral director kept him updated with lists and he watched the papers, so he could vaguely estimate his day if he wanted to. There was never a dull day, never a quiet one. He sold dreams in a different way now, but he still sold calm, respite and comfort.

• • •

Aunt Beryl took a call from the hospital. "Can you go? There's a lady there who needs your help."

"It's better to do it here." She knew that.

He'd never tell the truth of it.

The mother arrived, supported by her sisters. Hair drawn back into a loose, messy pony tail, done by someone else, he thought. Her face washed clean—the sisters again, he thought, and the clothes were her pregnancy ones, as if by wearing them she could pretend she hadn't had the baby yet.

"Come in," he said. He asked the sisters to wait downstairs. Before Aunt Beryl went back to her shop she filled the place with yellow roses and they brought a deep warmth. He took the dead baby gently. "So beautiful, so pure," he said. He nestled her sideways on the soft cushions.

He syringed the mist into her small, clouded eye.

Her cheeks flushed.

"Oh!" Ms T said. "Look! She's alive, she is! I told them. Those doctors." She picked her baby up, held her close. Shucked off her shirt, engorged breasts leaking colostrum.

He snapped, filmed, clicked, close up of her stretched skin, the bluish nipple moist and dripping.

The baby didn't suckle.

"She's warm. She feels warm. Why doesn't she drink?"

He took photos of the baby before the warm flush faded.

"She doesn't have the strength, poor darling."

The baby lost her warm colour. The spirit had departed. She looked greyer than before, like marble, and so cold his fingers chilled touching her. He placed her in a basket and covered her head.

He laid roses around her. "Such a beautiful girl."

He called for the funeral director to collect her. Ms T sat slumped in the corner, her shirt still unbuttoned.

"That was amazing," she said. "I don't know what you did."

He showed her the photos on his camera.

"She looks alive. She really does. Doesn't she? I'm not imagining it."

He didn't show her the shots of her tits. He'd cut her head off for those, no need for permission.

She stood up shakily. He took her arm, held her steady. "It's okay. This is difficult for you. It's the worst thing you'll ever have to go through. No one else can imagine it."

Mothers were so grateful they often wanted to do him right there, by the cash register, as if he could make them another baby.

This one didn't have sex with him and he didn't want it, anyway. She'd be all messed up down there after giving birth, he knew that, but he wouldn't mind sucking on those milky tits.

"Do it again, what you did," she said, her voice throaty with grief.

"I can't do it again. I only do it once. I'm sorry."

"Oh, God, please. Please. I'll give you all I've got. Have you got a girlfriend? A wife? One day you'll have a baby and you'll know what it's like."

He had girlfriends, but not the kind she meant.

She fell to her knees, her arms around his shins, begging, weeping. He was glad his mother had died first because he'd hate her to suffer like this.

He wasn't sure how it well it would work a second time. Oddly, no one had ever asked him before.

"This has to be the last time. We'll take one last photo so that you'll never forget your beautiful girl."

5pm/Client: Ms T/ Subject: Her daughter (stillborn)

Terry dressed in a pale blue t-shirt, some lightweight pants. He didn't have time to enjoy this hunt, so drove to the city's tallest building where he climbed to the roof and took out his camera.

He thought of the woman in his studio with her milky, firm tits, and her needy lips, and her gratitude. And he thought of the baby and how much he loved to see them revived, how god-like he felt when that movement came to them.

He patrolled the roof until he found it, a small patch of mist. One two three ghosts there, a family, perhaps.

• • •

His studio was always cold.

Ms T waited, sleeping on the couch. He took a few photos, wondering if she'd notice if he moved her around, shifted her arms and legs.

She stirred. She could almost be one of his subjects, he thought.

"Come on," Ms T said. She sat rocking her baby; it had a glossy sheen to it now. He couldn't call it a girl anymore; it had moved beyond anything very human.

He bent over the child. Ms T saw him this time and gasped to see what he was doing, but then the child stirred, sighed, and the mother cooed and sang.

Ms T danced around with her baby but then started to sob as the body cooled again. Held her up in the air, hoping to revive her. Her daughter's mouth fell open.

"You killed her! What did you do! What did you do?"

"This beautiful soul has left now. Didn't her hear her sigh? She's done. She was ready." He walked to the door, looking for the funeral director.

"Yes," she said. She rolled her shoulders. He'd heard that breast-feeding woman were easily sexually stimulated and he wondered if that was happening here. He gave her his charming smile, the one women liked and thought was only for them.

"Let me help, then," she said. "Let me be part of it."

2pm/Client: Mrs J/ Subject: Her husband (heart attack)

Ms T (he called her Mama T. She loved that) proved adept at wearing the Mama Suit, happy to sit sheathed in the black curtain for hours. Sometimes he forgot she was there as he went through his routines, but always they shared a glass of champagne afterward.

She never went with him on a ghost hunt; in fact to him she seemed only to exist in his studio.

He captured this ghost at the hospital, locked roof or not, after hearing a report of the suicide on the radio. On the way back to the studio he'd stopped by Auntie Beryl's shop and bought some roses for his Mama T.

She cooed. "From the hospital?" she said. "Did you collect my baby? Is that who you've got in that syringe?"

"No. It couldn't be," and her mouth formed a sweet moue that made him want to touch his fingers to her lips.

"Sit with me," she said, and he sat beside her. She lifted his chin, kissed his neck. He wouldn't say no, never did, birth-mess or not.

"Close your eyes," she said, and she kissed him on the side of the mouth. His tongue flicked out, catching her lip, and she kissed him harder.

"Wait there," she said. He liked surprises. "Eyes closed," she said.

She opened his fridge and scrabbled in there. "Champagne," she said. "We need champagne."

"After the client," he said.

"Now. I can't wait."

She popped the cork. Sat on his lap and swallowed some from the bottle, then poured some into his mouth.

She held his eyelid open. "Such beautiful eyes," she said. It was gentle, aggressive, made him itch to get at her. It felt as if she was looking deep inside him.

"Here's my baby," she said, purring like a mother cat, but she didn't mean him. She meant the syringe she held. "Here she is," she said, as she injected his eyeball. "Here she is. I've been watching you. I've figured it out."

But she hadn't. Of course she hadn't. When had he ever injected into a living person?

He was instantly filled with despair and a sense of . . . the opposite of vertigo. He wanted to fall, to fly then fall and land and he wanted oblivion desperately.

His skin formed large, pus-filled blisters like spiders under the skin, and moving hurt. The blisters leaked clear fluid and he wondered; is that him leaving me? That poor sad suicide who had nowhere to die but the hospital? He reached for his phone to call Aunt Beryl; she'd save him. Instead, he slumped to the ground. As the blisters opened, the heat of him and the cold of the studio formed a subtle mist, but he could not see anyone in it. He heard the funeral's director's deep and comforting voice as he ushered the client in, felt Mama T rocking him like a baby, cooing, and he thought he remembered his mother singing to him that way.

His skin was so puckered, so painful, each time she rocked him he wanted to scream but there was no sound beyond her sweet whispering comfort.

• • •

' . . . filled with the sighs of sweet music and soft female voices' from *Harper's Weekly* February 1873, "Delusions of medicine. Charms, talismans, amulets, astrology, and mesmerism" By Henry Draper

• • • • • • • • • • •

KNEADED

S. G. LARNER

My Mama loved to knead. Her flesh jiggled and her breasts swayed as she pushed and wrapped and pushed again. She smelled of sweat and flour and the earthy-sour of the Mother-starter.

I stood beside her in the humid kitchen and watched her, breathing in the heady scent and tracing patterns in the fine white dust that settled like snow on the bench. "I'm meeting Daniel soon," I said.

Mama wiped her forehead with the back of her hand. It left a white smear against her brown skin. She looked at me, from my feet to my head.

"Oh, my lovely Berry, you're growing up, and I hadn't noticed." She leaned over and kissed my nose then frowned. "I'm not ready for you to fly the nest."

"Are you mad with me?" I asked.

She resumed her work and said what she always said. "No, my sweetling, but be back before sundown. And stay out of the old forest. It's dangerous in there."

I watched a little longer as her strong brown hands wrestled the dough into submission, then put on my coat and left.

• • •

Daniel waited by the cobbler's shop. A few autumn leaves danced through the air, one settling on his dark curly hair. He brushed it off and grinned, then looked away. A ruddy glow stained his pale cheeks.

"Well met, Berry," he said as he offered me his arm. I took hold and we walked, oblivious to the clatter and bluster of the town's goings-on. He steered me to the old bridge. I glanced up—he'd grown in the short space of time since I saw him last. He reddened again when he noticed my gaze.

"Why are you blushing like a maid, Daniel Sweeney?" I asked, flipping my skirt against his leg. He mumbled something.

"I didn't catch that."

He stopped in the middle of the bridge, and leaned against the rail, staring out over the water. "I'd like to kiss you, Berry."

My heart did a little jig. I draped myself next to him, following his gaze to the deep river below. A kingfisher dive-bombed, surfacing with a silver streak in its claws as it flew off. Heat spread through me.

"I'd like that." I turned and studied his profile: his lips were full and inviting. He smiled and glanced at me out of the corner of his eye. Then he moved swiftly and we were pressed together. His olive green eyes twinkled.

We kissed, and it was awkward and wet and fumbling. I giggled when we separated, but Daniel had one eyebrow raised.

"Were you eating your mama's jam buns?"

I blinked, swishing my skirt. "No. Why would you ask that?"

He shook his head, his eyes unfocused, and said, "You taste sugary."

"Well," I said, catching his hand and placing it on my chest. "Aren't you lucky I'm so sweet?"

His eyes refocused and he grinned. "Yes, I am."

• • •

He walked me home, planting one last graceless kiss on my cheek. Mama called from the kitchen when I opened the door. A waft of cinnamon tickled my nose as I waved to Daniel and went inside.

I hugged Mama from behind, peering around her generous form to watch her shape the doughy lump.

"Is it a gingerbread man?" I asked.

She shook her head, body shuddering with the movement. With a satisfied grunt she poked raisins into the 'head'.

"What is it, then?"

"It's something for me, sweetling," she said, and I let go of her waist, stepping back so she could put it on a tray. I considered the little loaf.

"It looks like a baby."

"Mmm." She smiled at me. "Harold Croft visited while you were walking with Daniel. Annie's in early labour. I said I'd go around when it was time."

"Exciting," I said. "So that's not for her?"

"No, nor for you."

I pouted, then asked, "Mama, why don't other people taste like me?"

She tipped her head to the side and looked at me. Heat crept up my cheeks.

"I mean, when I kiss your forehead, you're salty. But I'm not. And Daniel . . . "

Mama's eyebrows shot up.

I bit my lip. "No one smells the same as me. Not even you. Is there no one like me?"

She wiped her hands on her apron, took it off and hung it on a hook. "You're just special." She kissed my cheek. "You're my sweetling."

I glanced at the dough baby. "Mama, am I a real girl?"

Her face paled, and her mouth flapped wordlessly before she finally said, "Of course you are. What a strange thing to say!" But her gaze shifted from mine and she hurried off before I could ask anything else.

• • •

The next morning the air was frigid and my tummy growled. Why was the house so cold?

Then I remembered Mama bustling into my room in the middle of the night with the news that it was Annie's time. She'd said *I'll be back when the babe is safely delivered,* and then she'd mumbled something about how Annie had best enjoy it while she could, because it would grow up and leave her soon enough. Then I'd dreamed that Annie's baby had been made of gingerbread. I screwed up my face. "I never want to have a baby," I muttered as I kicked my legs out from under the quilt. In the kitchen I stoked the embers and looked around for the cob Mama usually prepared for breakfast.

But there was nothing, just the special dough proofing under a kitchen towel. I opened the pantry: a jumble of smells wafted out but nothing appealed to me. My mouth watered as I inhaled the enticing scent of the yeasty little manikin—musky cinnamon and cloves dusted in brown sugar.

Not for you, Mama had said.

"Well, why not? She can make another," I said to the silent room. Then I put Mama's concoction in the oven.

I sat on a stool and watched the dough transform. When the top was golden I yanked it out, searing myself on the tray. My skin burned brown, not pink.

"No matter," I said and inspected the steaming bun. The raisins had sunk into the head. I tore a leg off and shoved it into my mouth.

My tastebuds sang with pleasure at the caramelised spices. It was soft and moist and I soon devoured it all, licking sugar off my fingertips.

After my tummy settled I left the house, the shock of the sudden chill outside goose-pimpling my skin. Gripped by an urge to visit my father, I took the left branch where the path forked. Frost crackled underfoot and the late autumn trees shed coppery leaves around me.

"Berry!"

Daniel hurried toward me.

"I knocked on your door but no one was home. What are you doing out here?"

"Walking," I said, and offered him my arm. The graveyard huddled in the new forest, so-called because it had been logged so heavily it scarcely resembled the old forest. Groves of evergreen conifers displaced the deciduous oaks, beeches and maples. Father slept beneath a mound thick with pine needles, slightly off-centre in the clearing. I dropped to my knees and traced the words on his headstone. I couldn't read. Daniel leaned over my shoulder.

"William Baker," he said. "Beloved Husband, taken too soon."

"I don't think about him, really," I said. Daniel kissed my palm. I grabbed his hand and tugged him away. We meandered in silence, straying off the path.

Daniel glanced around, his eyebrows creased with worry. "I think we're in the old forest. Look how different the trees are, and there's more undergrowth. We should go back."

I ignored him. Under an ancient oak I stopped and spied a sliver of rock obscured by a layer of leaves. I hunkered down and picked it up. The stone was icy but I dragged the sharp edge across my skin. Red liquid welled from the wound.

"Berry," he gasped. "What are you doing?"

I raised my arm to my lips and touched my tongue to the cut. Syrupy, it hinted of raspberries and sugar. "Try it," I said.

He frowned and shook his head. I sighed, grabbed his wrist and with a quick movement cut him. He cried out and flinched away from me. "Have you gone mad?"

"Quite mad," I agreed and lunged forward to lick the crimson line that oozed down his skin. The metallic drop burned my tongue.

Daniel looked as though he might throw up. "Is this what everyone's blood is like?" I asked.

He grimaced. "Well, I don't make a habit of drinking it, but yes, I suppose so."

I thrust my bleeding arm under his nose. He recoiled but I snapped, "Smell it. Taste it. Do it!" I backed him against the oak tree, and he raised his hands to ward me off. "Just do it, you coward," I said.

He slumped and leaned in to sniff like a dainty cat inspecting its food. A wave of confusion washed over his face, and he touched a finger to the sticky fluid. "Berry?"

"Go on," I said.

He stuck the tip in his mouth, then shook his head. "It's not possible," he said.

"I know, and yet, it is."

"What does it mean?"

I sighed and sagged, suddenly weak. "It means my Mama lied to me, and I think I ate a baby. But not a real one. One like me."

Daniel scratched his head, his eyes wary. "I still don't understand."

"Neither do I, Daniel." I patted his shoulder. "I'm probably just a little bit crazy. You should go home."

He gazed down at me, emotions running over his face as fast as a hunted rabbit, too fast to catch. "Let's go back," he said.

I shrugged and followed him through the trees to the path, where he hesitated before saying, "I think you're a bit wild for me." He had the grace to hang his head as he hurried off.

• • •

The house was cold for the second morning in a row, which meant Mama was still seeing to Annie. Dawning sun softened the hard angles of the room. I got up and stoked the fire, shivering while I waited for the warmth to penetrate my bones. Did I even have bones? I tapped my fingers on the floor and concluded that yes, I must have.

Then I remembered what I'd done.

"Mama will be angry," I said, opening the door and searching for her round form. A few leaves skittered across the ground but the path remained empty.

I rushed into the kitchen and began throwing ingredients together to make a replacement. My technique was not refined: all I managed was a lop-sided effigy. I poked and pushed at it but couldn't create an exact replica of the one I'd eaten.

I frowned, stepped back and contemplated it from every angle. I deflated. This wouldn't work. The kitchen towel settled over the sub-standard thing, hiding it from view as I retreated to the living room to brood.

I heard heavy footfalls outside and jumped up. Sweat gathered under my breasts. The door swung inwards and Mama followed it, beaming at me even through her haggard mask of exhaustion.

"A hard birth?" I asked, moving forward to help her sit.

"Long and hard, but the wee lad and Annie are fine." Mama's eyes misted over. "Such a bonny lad. I would have loved a son, you know."

"I'll get you some tea," I said, "stay there."

I bustled around the kitchen, brewing chamomile tea. A shadow at the corner of my eye made me turn; Mama stood staring at the towel-covered tray.

"Mama," I began but she strode forward and pulled the towel off. Her gasp pricked at my heart, and my hand shook as I reached out to her.

"What have you done?" she said, mouth trembling, gaze cold.

The lie, unlooked for, fell from my lips. "I'm sorry, Mama, a racoon got inside and ate it. I tried to make another, but I'm not as good at it as you. I tried." I bit the inside of my cheek and stood still and straight as a beech.

Mama looked around, for evidence, perhaps. "But, it was . . . " She rounded on me. "You stupid girl! How could you let this happen?" Her eyes narrowed and she loomed over me. "You're going to leave me soon, aren't you? You'll leave me to my tears and my loneliness!"

"Mama, please . . . just make another?"

"It's not that simple," she said, shaking her head. "The Mother-starter needs to be fed, the spices have to be just right . . . all I ever wanted were babies, lots of babies, and while breeding sows like Annie Croft pop them out every year I must suffer this burden alone." Mama sagged against the bench. I touched her arm and she glared up at me. "You stand there, blossoming like a fertile flower, taunting me, on the cusp of abandoning me. Get out. Get out of my sight."

I got out.

• • •

Twilight spread dark shadows through the woods and I realised I was lost. Fingers of dread brushed my spine as nightfall loomed in the old forest. Trees twisted into menacing forms. I hugged my shivering body and pushed through the undergrowth, the path lost to me some time ago.

Smoke drifted on a faint breeze. Buoyed, I followed the acrid scent. I tripped over roots but stumbled on as the smell of smoke and baking bread grew stronger.

In the dimness I saw a thicket of brambles that almost entirely covered a small A-frame cottage. Thorns trailed down the wooden planks, grey with age, but I stepped up and knocked carefully to avoid the spikes.

The door opened and an old woman looked out. Her grey hair draped like spider web across her shoulders, and written in the wrinkles of her face was the wisdom of a lifetime. She raised her eyebrows but still ushered me into the warmth.

"Well, what do you want?" she said, popping a kettle on the stove. "What's your name, girl?" She peered at me. "Why can I smell jam buns?"

Flustered, I replied, "My name is Berry," and skirted some rather odd-looking sculptures of men with giant protuberances. "My mama—"

"Yes, yes," she said and brushed a bony hand against the red smear on my arm. With a nail she scraped at the dried crust and then stuck the fingertip in her mouth. "Ah. I think I know who your mama is. She didn't quite follow orders, did she?"

I stared. "I don't understand."

The kettle whistled and she poured a tea. Spearmint steam curled from the surface as she handed it over.

"Sit," she said, waving at a small chair covered in crocheted blankets. I perched gingerly, afraid of spilling the boiling liquid on myself.

She sat opposite me and sighed. "Do you know what you are?"

"What I am?" My lip trembled. "Are you a witch?"

Her laugh was the crackling of autumn leaves: dry and papery. "Not every old woman in the woods is a witch."

My cheeks warmed. "Sorry."

She waved away my apology. "Why are you here, girl?"

I shrugged, sipping at the hot minty liquid. "My mama got mad, and now I'm lost."

She squinted at me for long moments. "Let me tell you a story.

"Once upon a time there was a woman who wanted to have a baby, but no matter how much she and her husband tried, no baby would grow inside her. She went to a herb woman, a midwife, and begged for help.

"The herb woman was troubled but gave the younger woman a special Mother-starter, one that had been handed down for hundreds of years. She told the young woman to make a little unbaked bread-baby, and tend it carefully for a month. At the end of the month she would be able to conceive." The old woman paused, staring at me with a frown. "Here is where my knowledge ends. The fertility charm was changed, somehow."

"So you are a witch."

The old woman blushed. "It's such a negative word," she replied.

"So what happened? Why am I what I am?"

She put her tea down and picked up her crochet needle. "Is it just you and your mother, dear?"

I nodded. "Papa was killed . . . " my mouth dropped open. "Oh. Before I was born, she told me."

The old woman leaned back and pursed her lips. "The charm was designed to enhance her fertility. Without her husband . . . " She glanced at me speculatively for a moment. "Strange things can happen, when hope and desire and death change the course of magic. She must have tended you even after his death, and her love was eventually rewarded by a cry as you took breath."

I pondered her words. A slow sickness spread through me. "Then, if you are telling me true, I ate my sibling."

She smiled. "It was just bread, girl. You ate a delicious bun, that's all. Without the blood magic to transform the fertility charm, it was just food." As she spoke her eyebrows furrowed and she tapped her chin. "When you think about it, it's an interesting proposition: a pregnancy stimulant eating one like itself. Who knows what might come of your actions?"

I made a dismissive gesture. "I did not lie with Daniel. What would have . . . happened to me had she gotten pregnant?" I bit my lip.

"I'm not sure you want to know," the old woman replied. At my silence, she sighed. "At the first sign of pregnancy your mother was to bake and eat the manikin that became you."

I struggled to breathe.

"I'm sorry," said the old woman. "But be comforted that your mother chose to love you, and in doing so, gave you life."

"My blood tastes like jam," I said. "My sweat is sugary. Daniel is scared of me. What will I tell people?"

"Tell them nothing. People are afraid of things they don't understand."

I finished my tea, swirling the dregs around the bottom of the cup. My mouth was fresh from the spearmint. "I need to think."

I stood and held the cup awkwardly. She took it from me and gazed into my eyes. My heart fluttered, a moth trapped in a bone cage.

"I'm sorry, Berry, that I had a hand in this," she said. "If you need my help, seek me here." Then I was out of the cottage and into the crisp air. The bramble thicket was an impenetrable mass at my back in the dark forest.

It seemed the birds sang nervously as I tried to retrace my steps. My hands trembled and I hummed a lullaby to calm myself. My feet crunched the brittle brown leaves that carpeted the ground. Shadows flitted through the trees; each time I saw movement I froze, then forced myself forward.

Stars glimmered in the sky when I at last pushed the door open. Mama cried and ran to me, gathering me up in her arms.

"I'm sorry, sweetling," she said. "Forgive me."

"It was careless to leave the shutters open." The lie sat bitter on my tongue. "I'm sorry, too."

"All is well," she said, and beamed at me. "I made another.

That Mother-starter is very old, but I had enough left to make a new one without feeding it."

My cheek twitched. She clucked and sat me in a chair, draping a blanket around me and getting me some bread. I nibbled at it and licked butter off my lips.

"I found the herb woman in the old forest," I told her hesitantly. "I know what you did. I know what I am.

"She thinks my father's death changed the magic, and gave me life. Without that sacrifice, the dough baby won't come to life." I took a deep breath. "You must needs be content with me."

Mama looked away. She looked at the ceiling, at the walls, at the window. Then down to her hands where they clutched each other, and back up to my face.

"You don't know what it's like," she said in a whisper.

I raised an eyebrow. "What?"

"I want a baby. With every part of my being. You're growing up, will marry and leave me. I *need* another baby."

"I'm sorry," I said, putting my hand on her warm knee. "I wish you could."

Her expression changed. One moment her face was open and sad, the next it was closed and sly. She stood. "What I love about dough is that I can re-use it for almost anything, as long as it's not baked." She took a step forward. "I never baked you."

Mama lunged for me. I shrieked and kicked her in the knees, jumped out of the chair. She fell hard onto her side, her head hitting the ground. I paused, worried, but her hand snaked out for my leg. The hunger was still plain to see on her face. With a bitter sob I fled the house.

• • •

A little dough baby was proofing inside me.

"Get rid of it," I begged Granny, as I'd come to call her since the night I'd returned to rap frantically on her thorny door. Her face darkened.

"I dare not meddle. You're a fertility charm impregnated with a fertility charm. I cannot know what effect the herbs might have."

When my belly began to swell, I'd asked, "Will I ever be safe?"

And she'd sighed and answered, "From me, yes. My tastes are simple, and I have no hunger I cannot satisfy on my own."

Which was little comfort.

I could feel the babe squirming. I imagined it devoured me as it grew, as I had eaten it. I was torn between two urges: give it to Mama and cure her of the madness, or abandon it in the forest for the wild creatures to feast on.

"It might just nibble its way out," I said with a glum sigh. Granny rolled her eyes.

"I highly doubt that," she said.

The baby was born in a gush of raspberry cordial. When I held her to my chest and breathed in, her cinnamon-clove scent filled my heart with joy.

"We're the same," I said, beaming up at Granny. "I'm not alone anymore."

Granny smiled back, but worry tinged her eyes. "I'm glad for you, Berry, but there must be no more."

My mind was already filled with thoughts of babies made from gingerbread, but I replied, "Of course, Granny," and stared down at my sweet baby girl.

Cinnamon turned her head to my breast and began to suckle. I closed my eyes and dreamed of a horde of sugary children to slip unnoticed among the salty ones.

•••••••••••

OF THE COLOUR TURMERIC, CLIMBING ON FINGERTIPS

GERRY HUNTMAN

Ball's Pyramid was the ultimate climb for the three friends. It was a massive, ancient volcanic plug that projected over five hundred and fifty metres above sea level like a giant shark's fin cutting through the Pacific Ocean. It had been scaled only a handful of times, and always by the easiest routes. It took three years for Jason to get permission for them to even set foot on the declared nature reserve. His fiancée, Becky, and best friend, Dave, were as eager as Jason to climb the monolithic rock from the hardest, sheerest route. No 'beta', as their craft described it—without the taint of any foreknowledge or advice.

The ocean wind swept across Jason, causing his hair to dance and his coat to flutter like a thousand butterfly wings. He was standing on a narrow ledge and had set several anchors in the rock to secure the group from being blown off the island. He glanced up the sheer face, rising four hundred and fifty metres, and then down the slightly off-vertical cliff one hundred metres to the sea. A large rubber dingy was moored to a rock outcrop, bobbing incessantly and maniacally in random directions, while much further out to sea was the *Osprey*, the charter boat from Lord Howe Island that brought the rock climbers to their Holy Grail. The boat would wait three days while they attempted the climb. The waves didn't cause too much trouble when they transferred from the twin-engine dingy through the pungent sea-spray to the slimy rocks at the base of the volcanic plug. The winds were too strong to attempt the summit this day, especially when they were climbing it the hard way.

With the noise of the sea and the frequent winds, there was little point in working with walkie-talkies. Jason was given a small flare gun to signal if the party was in trouble, and the captain of *The Osprey* had instructed the rock climbers to abandon their efforts and return to their dingy as quickly as possible if a similar flare emanated from the boat.

Jason noticed Dave, still scaling the easy lower cliff formation to join him at the narrow ledge, which was going to be their base camp. He was puffing, carrying most of the tent equipment, including porta-ledge devices enabling the three to sleep in their tents in safety. Jason laughed, as Dave—strong as an ox and nearly as large—always ended up with Sherpa duties. Dave wasn't overweight—far from it. The tall, ginger-cropped South Australian was stout and didn't have an ounce of fat on him. He would have made a great AFL ruckman. They usually climbed together during the warmer months, and 'fitness freak' Dave would supplement his winter training with some serious rowing on the River Torrens.

Becky was thirty metres behind Dave, taking it easy and enjoying the warm-up climb. She was very capable, probably the most technically skilled climber of the three, and fastidious with safety procedures. When climbing, she always had an intense, professional look about her, with her long dark hair tied back in a ponytail, popping from under her helmet, and brows creased in concentration above her expressive, brown eyes.

Dave finally pulled himself onto the ledge and carefully placed his large bundle on the widest possible location.

Jason swung his arm around, grasping Dave's hand with his own. "Thanks, mate. That was a big haul."

Dave wiped sweat from his forehead, despite the cooling winds. "Someone had to do it." He took a small swig of water from his Nalgene flask, and his countenance turned serious. "Mate. While Bec's still climbing—haven't had a single moment alone with you, 'specially with you two moving to Sydney—I wanted to tell you there's no hard feelings. I know I said it over the phone a few months back, but I want you to really, really *know how I feel.* When Bec broke up with me I was gutted, especially since—you know, my best friend and all."

Jason grasped Dave's shoulder with his right hand. "Hey, I didn't—"

"You don't need to say it. It took a while, but I realized that it wasn't meant to be." A small tear formed in one of his eyes, and a gust of wind sent it streaking along his cheekbone into nothingness. "Jeez, I look at you two and all I can see is joy. Someone out there will do it for me, but Bec and I didn't have that chemistry."

They hugged, as they had always done since primary school when something important had been resolved or achieved.

"Whoa, am I meant to see this?" Becky asked over the whining wind.

"Just a tender moment," Jason said. "You can join us, if you want."

"Pass. Maybe we should get these portas set up. Haven't used one for years."

Dave moved toward his pack when out of a crevice a fat, black chitinous creature scuttled near his foot.

"Shit!" he yelped, and without thinking, crushed the creature under his climbing boot. It was an insect, larger than a human hand, with six legs and a bulbous, pitch-black exoskeleton. Yellowy-grey liquid oozed from the mangled body, which even with the wind smelled acrid, like vomit.

"Christ!" Becky cried. "Do you know what you just did?"

"Ah. Not exactly."

"One of the reasons why this lump of vertical rock is a protected environment is because there might be twenty or so of these stick insects living here. And that's it. They used to crawl all over Lord Howe Island, but they were wiped out by rats introduced by a shipwreck. These are the most endangered insects in the world. You probably wiped out five percent of the existing population in the wild, dickhead!"

"Shit, I forgot. I just hate insects and spiders. What are we going to do?"

Jason crouched near the insect's corpse and squeamishly nudged it. "It's sure big. If a scientist or another climber finds the remains, they might ask questions. It was an accident, but I don't want trouble. I say hide it in the crevices—if we try to fling it out to sea, the wind might blow it back onto the rocks."

Dave was visibly relieved. "Thanks. It was an accident."

"Dumbfuck," Becky said, and slapped him playfully on the back. "But it was a mistake."

Jason used his boot to slide the creature into a small crack in the cliff wall. Some dirt and mould had accumulated in a small natural recess a metre above it. He scraped the material onto the ledge. Dave and Becky helped.

"What's this?" Jason asked, staring at his palms.

A layer of fine orange-yellow powder caked both his gloves. The others had the same, and they could see its source—a small area where the powder was thickly clinging to the wall of the recess.

Becky wiped her hands on her front shirt. "It looks almost like turmeric powder. You know, for curries."

"And as clingy," Jason replied. He sniffed it carefully. "Almost smells like turmeric too." He kept rubbing his hands together, but little of the material was loosened from his Cordex gloves, nor the exposed areas of his lower arms. "I could be wrong, but I think it's a mould, or some kind of spore. Never seen anything like it."

Becky nodded. "Yeah, but that's weird. I read pretty much everything I could find about Ball's Pyramid, and I didn't get any reference to this. There's precious little that grows here, and these ugly buggers only survive because of a few solitary bushes near a tiny water source. I reckon this mould, or whatever it is, should have been in the literature."

"No one's climbed this rock at this time of year," Jason replied. "Maybe this stuff only comes out for a few days a year, set around some special time."

"Solstice," Dave stated, trying to wipe off the powder onto his trousers, and managing to get a smear on his face and onto his helmet. "I remember reading in the paper this morning that today is the Winter Solstice. Just saying."

"Could be," Becky said. She suddenly cried and jumped back, too close to the hundred metres precipice for comfort.

The insect, half covered in the material that was scraped from above, moved.

The three climbers stepped further away, unable to speak. Dave lightly whimpered, barely audible over the swirling winds.

The insect made a few loud scraping sounds, and walked off. Nearly walked. One leg was missing, several others were broken. Its body still had glistening flesh and yellow pus hanging out of its thorax. And yet it managed to crawl on its assembly of uneven legs. It grew in confidence and managed to actually scuttle along the ridge. Becky screamed and leapt over the creature as it waddled by.

"It was dead," Jason stated with urgency. "It was as dead as you can fuckin' get!"

• • •

The next day was perfect for climbing. The wind had died down to almost a sigh and it was mild, a few degrees above the average for the year. The insect episode had been a topic of interest into the early night, but the climbers had chores to do and needed a good night's sleep for the day's long, tough climb. The collective view was that the insect was hardy and had successfully scampered elsewhere, ultimately to die. If there was time, they agreed to look for the body after their climb, to make sure it could not be found by anyone else.

They set off early in the morning with Jason at lead. It was, as expected, slow going as he took minimum risks and spent much of his time setting bolts and anchors for clipping in belay ropes. This was a high-grade climb, and it didn't take long for the three climbers to have their skills stretched to the limits and for the pleasure of the challenge to seep in.

At one of the belay points they took a break, hanging from their ropes, drawing in the view of the ocean, from over three hundred metres above sea level.

"Sublime," Dave said.

"Completely," Becky agreed.

"By the way, guys," Jason said, inspecting his hands and arms. "That turmeric stuff hasn't come off yet. It's gone through my gloves onto my hands, and it's also stained my lower arms."

"Tell me about it," Becky replied, with a tone of annoyance. "It went through my shirt and I've now got yellow boobs."

The two men exploded into laughter, and Becky couldn't help but join in.

"Got stuff on my hands and legs," Dave said. "I tried a bit of water to wash it off, and eventually it does clean up, but we can't waste our water."

They soon set off again, climbing the rock face of the island. At times they scaled small, protruding outcrops, but much of the climb was up sheer cliffs, dependent on fixing pitons, bolts, and other anchors into narrow cracks and gaps, none of which were ever climbed before.

Dave was in last position along the route, one he was happy to have. Jason knew his friend was a good, reliable climber, but he was the weakest with respect to technique.

"I thought The Totem Pole was a tough climb," Dave said, approaching the next belay point for clipping. He was referring to a nearly two hundred foot high rectangular rock in Tasmania that looked more like Cleopatra's Needle than a sea- and wind-eroded rock, and was considered one of the hardest graded climbs there was.

"Yeah," Jason shouted back. "It's like this face has five or six of them."

"More like—" Dave's feet slipped and there wasn't sufficient hold with his hands. He didn't cry out. He was experienced. Instead, he focused on bracing himself for the jarring of the fall when his rope extended to its length from the last belay point. As if the gods had frowned on the group, Dave's rope hooked over a small pimple of rock close to his descent path. When the climber reached the full length of his fall, stopping relatively gently due to the elastic nature of the rope, the portion that was hugging the rock formation pinged back to its straight position, catching Dave by surprise. Dave started twisting and swinging several metres to his right, failing to control himself as he was unable to catch hold of any part of the cliff.

"Rope!" cried Becky, which signified a problem with Dave's safety line.

He grabbed hold of a narrow crack in the cliff face with both hands, forming fists and jamming them in. He glanced up and saw that his belay rope had shredded when it ground over the rock it had hooked onto. He heard the rope snap as it was severed, and gritted his teeth when the full weight of his body concentrated on one of his fists. He separated his left hand from the gap, hoping to find another purchase to grab onto, while his legs raced about, also seeking the sanctuary of a hold.

"Christ!" Dave breathed in and out quickly to build up his oxygen levels for the struggle ahead. "Not sure if I can do this myself, guys! Would sure like some help!"

Becky was the logical rescuer. She was thirty metres diagonally above, while Jason was much higher.

Becky quickly readjusted her equipment, and carefully rappelled down until she got to the belay point where Dave fell prior to clipping. In seconds, she connected a figure-eight device and repelled from her new anchor point.

Dave started to lose it, screaming, "Shit! Shit! Shit! I can't get any holds! I can't keep this up for much longer!" His face had turned a bright red and Jason could see, despite the distance, a look of mortal terror in Dave's eyes.

"I'm coming!" Becky cried, stopping her descent several metres above Dave's altitude, but five metres to his left. She quickly scanned the vertical terrain and shook her head, having made the sober assessment. "I can't dyno across, Dave. The same kind of crazy rock that cut your rope will do the same with mine. I've got to set up a new anchor point."

"Quickly!" Dave grunted, hardly able to muster the strength to speak.

Becky expertly constructed an anchor by inserting a hex into a narrow space, attaching two cams. She completed the device with a sling and carabiner, and a spare, short belay rope. She unhooked herself from her original belay rope and grabbed hold of her new protection.

Inexplicably, the upper rock formation that held the hex disintegrated.

With the instinct of a seasoned climber, Becky grabbed for purchase with both her hands, but it wasn't good enough. There was a quick intake of breath as reality coldly encompassed her. She silently slipped down the sheer rock face.

"Becky!" Jason cried, stunned that another accident could have happened so suddenly, and then horrified when he saw that she had no protection.

Becky managed twice to slam her hands onto outcrops, hoping against hope to stop her fall. Instead, it barely slowed her descent, and it caused her body to tumble.

With tears flowing down his cheeks, and despair screeching from his mouth, Jason saw his fiancée smash into a large outcrop one hundred and fifty metres below, followed by Dave falling, screaming, and trailing a useless umbilical cord.

Amazingly, she didn't bounce off the rock and careen into the ocean. She was dead, unmistakably. The moment her head hit the rock, there was a six foot red wash glistening on the surface. Her body and limbs were misshapen, at odd angles, like a discarded marionette. Her helmet was nowhere to be seen.

Dave fell almost the entire distance to sea level, and with dignity totally ignored, shattered on the sea-washed rocks. The only saving grace was that it was too far to see the details. But it was hard for Jason to take his eyes away from Becky.

Jason hung there, not even remembering to secure himself, crying, swaying, and cursing God.

• • •

His eyes kept returning to Becky's body. He wasn't looking for something, nor hoping for the impossible. He just had to see her. It wouldn't be long before he would never see her again.

His gaze turned to the *Osprey*, wondering if they noticed the catastrophe, and saw no signs of activity. His eyes tracked back to the outcrop.

She wasn't there. Just a fan-shaped smear of drying blood and gore.

Where . . . ?

There was a shadowy movement slightly to the right of the outcrop.

He shifted his body and focused.

It was a climber. *Another climber*, his brain kept hammering at him. He swallowed and realized how dry his throat was. It was Becky. She had landed with her body in a sideways position, shattering her head. Her face—what was left of it—was distorted but unmistakably hers. A single eye stared upward as she climbed by grasping onto the smallest of ridges and gaps with her fingertips. Sometimes her boots would fail to find a ledge, but her fingertips— becoming ragged as she progressed—held her weight.

He was washed with a fleeting moment of insanity when he welcomed the idea of being with his Becky, but as she got closer he saw her state in more detail. The sheer horror of the thought of being close to such fresh ruin was overwhelming. He panicked. He unhooked his belay rope and climbed. For his sanity, for his life.

• • •

The adrenaline had worn off. His body was aching, bleeding, after several desperate lunges to get away from Becky. And yet she closed the gap, easily. She was very close now, only ten metres below him, and that single brown eye, which was fixed on her climbing, was now targeting him. She was dead, *she had to be dead*, but her eye was alive. As she knowingly gazed on him, a ragged, bloody smile formed on her tattered face.

"Jase, why are you leaving me?" Her voice was distorted, hollow like the grave.

He couldn't climb anymore. He was spent, and the universe collapsed around him, his sanity imploded into a singularity of hell. "Y—you're dead," he whimpered.

"No, you're wrong," said the fractured voice. She hadn't slowed her movement at all. In fact, she had picked up her pace.

"Y—your face, your body . . . broken."

"My heart beats, Jason. I want to hold you, to make the nightmare go away."

The thought of her being so close, to be centimetres away from her gaping skull and fragmented bones, caused him to almost faint with overwhelming horror. To kiss her lips, blue and cold . . .

Becky was only a few metres away, her blood-crusted, shattered smile inviting doom. "Embrace me. Stay with me forever."

Jason fumbled in his jacket pocket and pulled out the single shot plastic flare gun, something that had escaped his thoughts in his despair. He pointed it at the gap between Becky's chest and the cliff wall, firing at point blank range. He closed his eyes as the intense heat of the burning magnesium enveloped her breast, flinging her off the cliff.

To his dismay, while Becky fell, lighting up like a bonfire, her hands whipped out and finally, successfully grabbed hold of a protruding rock. The rest of her body slammed into the cliff, breaking more bones, and yet she held on. While grasping onto the cliff with one hand, she expertly fastened her body by rope to an anchor. She flapped incessantly at the fire encompassing her, trying to put it out, not once crying out in pain.

Jason thought she would come for him again, but she slowed down. The flapping became a few feeble swipes, and as the acrid smell of burnt flesh and hair rose up to him, she collapsed, hanging limply on her belay rope, still burning.

Jason set up a harness and sat in it, trying to recover. He ignored the smell of the smouldering corpse. It was now, it seemed, a real corpse.

Another movement came from below.

Oh no, sweet Jesus, no!

Dave's corpse was climbing the cliff face. He was some distance down, but he was a worse mess than Becky had been. His limbs and body were so broken he climbed in fits and starts, bones grinding against each other each time he moved. There was an odd whooshing sound that seemed to emanate from the body, and when it got closer it became apparent why—Dave's head had been completely shattered, and while remnants of both it and his helmet girdled his neck and shoulders, the sound was coming from his exposed windpipe.

Jason prepared himself for oblivion. He hadn't the strength left to climb, and he was certain his sanity was going to give way completely. Either way, or both, there was total darkness.

Dave moved—he had no eyes. He could not see. As the corpse was climbing higher, it also made wide horizontal detours, almost as if it needed to fully cover the area of the cliff face, to make sure it wouldn't miss anything. His ragged hands would reach out and feel for whatever it might find.

Me.

Jason was certain that this blind corpse would find him, and God knows what would happen next.

Dave reached the level of the cliff where the still- smouldering corpse of Becky hung. It moved first one direction, and then scampered like a crab toward her. His hand touched her blackened body. It moved quickly, urgently, over her torso, and found what remained of her face, which curiously was untouched by the flames. Gently, like a mother caressing a baby, the hand touched and followed the contours of Becky's face. The shoulders of the corpse slumped, and then a louder whooshing sound came from the gaping neck. It was almost emotional, a voiceless keen.

With supernatural strength, Dave's corpse pushed himself a dozen or more metres away from the cliff and fell, limply, into the sea far below.

You lied, my friend. You still loved her.

• • •

Jason climbed to the summit of Ball's Pyramid because it seemed the right thing to do. He wasn't in a fit mental state, but he risked it. Death wasn't so poor a prospect as he once thought. The wind had picked up a little but he was able to sit at the top of the geologic wonder with some comfort, and observe his surroundings.

He saw another dingy being lowered from the charter boat into the sea. *They have binoculars. They know something is wrong.*

He looked to the northwest and saw Lord Howe Island, twelve miles distant. *People live there. And tourists visit regularly. Eight hundred at any one time.*

Jason knew that the turmeric-coloured spores caused the re-animation of Becky and Dave. And the stick insect. How, he had no idea, but he guessed that Ball's Pyramid's isolated position, and the very narrow window in each year when the spores appeared on this most desolate of islands, had dramatically curbed its propagation. The three rock climbers were the first in thousands, if not millions, of years, to give it a chance to move on. He guessed that the reanimation of Becky stopped when the spores were all destroyed by the fire and heat.

He stared at his hands and arms, noting the yellow stains. He looked down at the distant corpse hanging from the cliff, where sea gulls were fighting over Becky's flesh. The crew of the charter boat would arrive soon, and regardless of how difficult it was, would do what they could to retrieve Becky's body. They might even be surprised by what they found floating in the ocean.

Jason checked his climbing gear and mentally charted a route back down that would make use of the anchor points already set in the cliff.

Jumping from the summit still seemed a sweet and strangely relieving idea, but the thought of reanimating chilled him like nothing on this earth.

He started the climb down, forgetting how exhausted he was.

He had a job to do.

• • • • • • • • • • •

NEW CHRONICLES OF ANDRAS THORN

CAT SPARKS

Andras Thorn was a famous traveller and the uncle for whom I was named. By the year of my birth, three times he'd voyaged all the way up to Carpenter's Gulf. By my tenth summer his attentions turned inland: beyond the Sand Road and The Verge's scattered outposts. Beyond Grimpiper and the farthest stone.

He chronicled his journeys in a book with toughened leather bindings. Not just any leather, mind you; leather cut and cured from a monster's hide. A thunder lizard, bred for battle. The one he'd killed had been the last of its kind. Or so he said. Uncle Andras's outrageous boasts were the stuff of local legend, such as the time that chronicle stopped a bullet from piercing his heart.

Outlandish tales of Uncle Andras peppered my childhood years. All but my mother worshipped the ground he walked on.

"Don't you take after him," she warned, already regretting the name she'd saddled me with. But by then it was far too late. My uncle's laughter shook the rafters of our family home. Wine flowed and tales grew wilder with the telling. By fifteen I was itching for a chronicle of my own, dismissing the future laid out by my mother's emporium. I craved relics from the Dead Red Heart, not to mention the pulse-racing exploits that went with them.

Uncle Andras claimed to have stood upon the walls of Axa, lived amongst the Knartooth clans, crewed a whaler out of Fallow Heel. But *those* were not the tales that made my own hairs stand on end. My mother's caravan had often veered near Axa and other of the ancient fortress cities. Each one a still, unchanging monolith: blast-proof ceramic ringed by unexploded mines. Perhaps people lived in them and perhaps they did not. Phantom inhabitants who never showed their faces.

Only one name stirred the fire in my blood: *Ankahmada*. A city so lost, no-one knew where to look for it. Not even my uncle, for all his rugged talk. Ankahmada: ancient like Axa, without window, door or gate. Some whispered it to be a living thing. Ankahmada: relic of the days before the Ruin. The lure of it set hardened men to fighting. Was Ankahmada the city or the name of the God-King that dwelled within its walls? Both, it was claimed by many travellers.

I had to find out. I would be the one. My destiny—And it might have been had the blighted storm not cut across my path. Boiling up from nowhere like a jinny from the sands. Stripping me of everything, save for that thunder-lizard-hide-bound chronicle— my illustrious uncle's parting gift. Something he surely *would* have wanted me to have, had he chanced to wake when I'd stolen the best of his camels.

I'd tucked that chronicle inside my shirt as the sand rasped and stung and scratched my face. Cocooned within my traveling cloak and dug in deep beside my camel's carcass, that chronicle pressed firm against my heart as I waited for death, whispering prayers to Kashah the Dog-Headed Warrior, patron saint of explorers and lost causes.

But death did not come. The storm blew over, revealing wind-whipped crests that stretched forever. I was lost as any man has ever been, with sun-ravaged skin, lips blistered in the land of my uncle's stories and surrounded by dunes that sang and shifted: the home of serpentes the length of sailing vessels. Creatures that— according to uncle's chronicle—would coil and strike to protect their territories.

The nest of the serpente must be given the widest berth, underlined in heavy ink upon the page. Far more use than the elaborate, garish maps inset between each colourful adventure. Each one laboriously lettered, yet conforming to no familiar geography. Where, precisely, lay Drifted Gully, the Fallen Towers of Cambera or Broken Arch?

Not a single serpente had crossed my path since I snuck from Evenslough. Setting out in the mist of dawn, my passage was marked by sandskate shells, each one belly-up and empty, picked clean by the rot-black carrion birds that took a curious interest in my journey.

Such tiny details I had jotted for posterity—my own entries beginning where uncle Andras's left off—while sheltering in squat, box-like bunkers barely interesting enough to bother sketching. Bunkers dating back before the Ruin, each cobwebbed corner marked with ashen campfire dregs and the bones of explorers who had died beside their dogs. I wondered if the poor fools had been trapped by serpentes, storms or other, *stranger things*?

Uncle's tales were amply laced with the savagery of misborn beasts: unimaginable horrors that called the Dead Red Heartland home. Monstrosities of discreditable birthright: part animal, part human, part machine. Merchant Queen Kamalini was always one for the grotesque and I'd half-presumed he invented them for her pleasure (and her not insignificant coin). His most celebrated exploit, *Kalyca by Land and Sea,* had been hand-lettered on kid vellum by a brace of fat, expensive monks. The masterpiece, complete with gold leaf and lurid illustration, hung in the dining chamber of Evenslough Palace—so they said. Not that I had never dined there. My uncle was drunk when they cut the ribbon. He'd been drunk every single night since.

I encountered no such creatures, except for once—that clutch of fossilized eggs. Unidentifiable shrieks past the midnight hour and markings in the shifting sands that might, perhaps, have been the tracks of beasts.

And then the storm in which I rightly should have perished—yet the winds had blown themselves apart, allowing me to crawl from my dead camel's side. I was lost, with only faithful Kashah to guide me—should I survive till nightfall and should that night be amply spread with stars.

And so I walked each step on borrowed time. Three days beyond my last meal; half a day since my battered waterskin extruded its last pathetic dribbles. Ankahmada still no closer than a dream. Soon my mind would cloud with cursed mirages. What I hadn't counted on was *smelling* them.

By the elongated shadows of afternoon, the scent of roasting meat was overpowering. It filled my senses and I could think of nothing else. A dream, of course. A waking dream. There was nothing to see but russet dunes, glazed and shapeless in the sun's relentless glare.

The wind intensified as I trudged. A blast of spiced aroma hit me squarely in the face. I might have drowned in my own salivations, as gritty with dust, sand and longing as they were.

Up ahead through the shimmering haze, blobs of colour began to coalesce. And something else. Something towering and dark that seemed to my fevered eyes like a human face. Onwards I strode, foot after foot, breath after laboured breath, each lungful drinking in the tang of spice, acrid thornbush, burning bricks of dung. Strangers. Fellow travellers lost. I would throw myself upon their—and Kashah's—mercy. Either they would feed me or they'd kill me. My fate, it seemed, was entirely in their hands.

The closer to their camp I staggered, the more the scent of roasting flesh intensified, forcing me to gag and swallow. Forcing me to my knees. The giant face came into focus: a stone-hewn, flame-blackened godhead towering over a group of men and women gathered around a fire. Their facial expressions—and that of the god—made fierce by the flickering light.

"By Oshana's grace, it's a youth!" said one of the men, his words slurred casually with drink.

The weight of their eyes felt heavy upon my skin. The cooking smells were too delicious, the fire too comforting.

A row of skewers roasted over coals, each one affixed with chunks of glistening meat. My aching throat flooded with saliva.

"Is he pretty?" asked a second man. "Bet he's hungry. Where can he have come from?"

"You're a desperate dog, Narat," interjected a female voice. The others laughed.

"Come and join us," said the woman, stepping forward. "We've had a good day of it out in the dunes. Come share with us the fortunes of Oshana."

I blinked sandy grit from my eyes. The thick-set woman wore traveling robes, embroidered and in very fine condition. Hair cascaded around her shoulders, unbraided and relatively clean.

Hesitantly, I went to her, empty waterskin dangling flaccidly at my side. The woman gestured to a space upon the blanket. She sat and I obediently sat beside her.

"Following the pilgrim trail?" she asked.

I nodded weakly, although I'm not sure why. There had been no pilgrims. No trail but occasional, crumbling bunkers scattered with red sand, ash and bone.

"We've been here a day and a night. I am Getta." She gestured at the others. "That one is my husband, those our sons and their wives. We've come all the way from Blessed Silence. Sold everything we owned to get this far."

Blessed Silence? I had never heard of it. I nodded. "My uncle . . . " I'd been intending to explain the whys and wherefores of my condition but the words dried up before they hit the air.

Getta nodded sympathetically. "The pilgrim trail is not an easy road." Her words did not seem solely for my ears, but also for the night-shrouded dunes and the sprinkling of stars above our heads.

Her sympathy was useless. I needed food and drink. I hung my head, lest the spectacle of pathetic longing fill them with uncharitable disgust.

"Looks like the poor lad could do with a sup of wine," a male voice boomed from the darkness. The one who had called me pretty. Somebody else laughed, another of the sons. I closed my eyes, knowing that whatever they asked, I would oblige, so desperate was my need for sustenance.

A dull thud sounded on the sand before me. I opened my eyes to a plump waterskin and Getta's equally plump fingers poking at it. "Drink!"

I snatched the 'skin, unstoppered it and gulped. Sweet, sweet water blended with unfamiliar herbs.

One of the sons pulled a skewer from the flames. I tried not to gawk as he hacked the meat into portions. Each piece landed, wet and glistening, on a tray.

"You must be starving," said Getta. "We were almost out of food ourselves. Fortunately Oshana was watching over us."

A man speared a hunk of meat as a plate was placed in my hands. "Get that into you, lad. Looks like you could do with it."

Another man made a comment I didn't quite catch. Getta laughed in response. "There was no luck about it! My husband wore an amulet of Oshana while hunting, which I had prepared for him according to the rites of Kharakhan. We are not lucky, son, we are blessed and favoured. Blessed and favoured of the great Oshana."

"A whole nest? I call that lucky, blessed or not," he replied. "Fat ones, too. Fattest things I've seen since Blessed Silence."

A whole nest.

My gorge rose in desperation, but I wrestled it back down. "What kind of nest?" I asked, my voice weak and watery. At first I thought no one had heard me.

"Ten plump, succulent serpente babies," said Getta proudly. "We shall feast well for a week at least!"

"You violated a serpente nest? You killed the mother serpente?"

Getta smiled, triumphant. "There was no mother. They were unguarded. The amulet of Oshana—"

Giddy with loss, I let my plate drop to the rug. "The mother will be back for them," I whispered. "If you've eaten the flesh of her young, she will know it. She will smell her babies on your breath, the scent of them oozing from your pores." I pushed the plate away from me. The hardest thing I've had ever had to do.

Getta smiled condescendingly. "Ordinarily, perhaps that would be so. But Oshana protects her faithful children. None who wear her amulet will come to harm." She paused suddenly, considering me closely in the firelight. Her face was large and round and soft. "You are not a follower? No wonder you're so frightened!" She put her own plate down and clapped her hands. "Maja! This young man is without protection! Bring one of the sacred relics from my jewel chest."

Pleased that an alarming situation was in the process of being rectified, Getta resumed her eating. Thick lips smacked in delight as she devoured bite after bite. "'Twas the divining of Oshana led us this far into the Red, you know." She chewed with her mouth open. "We stumbled upon the pilgrim trail by accident—or so we thought." She nodded at the fire-blackened face towering above. "They say this is the likeness of a famed king in these parts. Ankahmada. Perhaps you've heard of him?"

Ankahmada. My heart skipped.

"We are simple boneshell traders seeking a new supply for buttons," Getta continued. "Barely any gets traded south these days, you know. Supply was choked, so we came to dig it up ourselves. This stretch of sand is thick with ancient bones."

Simple was right. I tried to clamber to my feet but a wave of nausea held me to the rug. Nothing had ever smelled so delicious as the roasting serpente flesh. Getta's extended family shovelled fingerfulls into their mouths. Thick juice dripped and dribbled through beards and over chins.

Uncle said... Uncle Andras wasn't here. Uncle Andras—that fat old fraud—had probably never been so hungry he couldn't think straight. If Uncle Andras was so smart, how come he never got rich like Kamalini? His stories were all camel dung, made up to fool the elderly, young and stupid.

I lunged at my plate, shoving meat into my mouth, afraid it might crawl back upon its bones.

"That's the spirit," said Getta, washing her mouthful down with a hearty swig. Drying her lips on the back of her hand as one of the wives passed her something wrapped in cloth.

She handed it to me. "You must wear this amulet at all times, even when you think you shouldn't need it. Oshana will protect you like she protects us all."

Accepting the trinket, I slipped it onto my wrist, then swallowed the last morsel on my plate. After all, I had not *seen* any serpents, save that one small clutch of fossilized eggs—which were likely older than the dunes themselves.

One of Getta's smiling sons speared me another dripping chunk. I nodded as he carved it into segments, ate until my bulging stomach ached. Nestled back on the comfortable rugs, I studied my companions by firelight. Who were these people? Wealthy, or at least they once had been, that much was clear from the clothing on their backs. But boneshell was an armorers' commodity, far too valuable to waste on the frivolity of buttons. Getta chattered at great length, her stories embellished with sweeping movements of her arms. How had the lot of them made it this far without being robbed and murdered?

"I have never heard of Oshana," I admitted eventually, my hand resting across my stuffed-full belly.

"Really?" said Getta, pausing her conversation. 'Wherever do you come from? I find that almost impossible to believe.'

"Born and raised in Makasa," I replied, a story that was only half a lie. I'd been hoping to impress, but she'd clearly never even heard of it.

"Your family are merchants? Wine or cloth, perhaps?"

I nodded. "My uncle is a famous traveller. Andras Thorn— perhaps you've heard his name?"

Getta smiled kindly and shook her head. I noted the subtle upturn of the corner of her lips as she evaluated my social caste and found it, thankfully, beneath her own.

• • •

The sound of men and women shrieking jolted me from slumber. I sat up, confused, at first believing myself back in that wretched old Grimpiper boarding house.

A fresh scream sent me scrambling to a wary crouch. The leaden weight of half-digested meat brought memories flooding to the fore. The fire had shrunk to little more than embers. Constellations and a sliver moon splashed light across the sand.

The family of Oshana worshippers ran screaming in all directions, tripping over cooking pots, their own feet and discarded weaponry.

A foul stench hung upon the cool night air. As my eyes adjusted, something large and pale flickered from side to side. Unmistakably, a mighty serpente's tail. The mother, searching for her stolen young.

There would be no escaping her fury and retribution.

All who had eaten of her babies' flesh would die. Instinct and terror held me still as others were smashed to messy pulp or else bitten clean in half, all the while screaming prayers, beseeching their useless, foreign god.

I was going to die for my stupidity and my greed. Die without ever clapping eyes upon my uncle's fabled city. Not even my gnawed-on bones would be recovered.

One of the wives stumbled into the open. She had been standing with her back pressed to the enormous blackened godhead. She should have stayed there, frozen in its shadow. The serpente spat out whatever it was chewing. It lunged, body sliding at angles across the roughened sand. Her screams lingered longer than I hoped.

The full extent of the serpente's form was now evident. Head to tail, it stretched almost as long as a Sand Road caravan.

Sweat dried upon my shivering skin. The creature was taking its time with its vengeance. It was in no hurry. So long as I had sweat, it would sniff me out.

My bent legs ached with cramp as I fixed my eyes upon the serpente's jaw. Perhaps it would gorge itself to sleep? But serpentes did not sleep out in the open. According to my Uncle's chronicle, they made their nests in pits or caves, emerging to feed whenever a chance was offered.

I slid my knife from its boot-sheath, gripped it tightly and waited. The creature's snapping jaw resounded with the crunch of bone and gurgle of blood. When it finally tired of the wife's remains, it tilted its head and rose to sniff the breeze. It had caught the scent of something fresh.

Me.

The creature swung its head around, muscles of its underbelly rippling, one by one. A stab in the eye. My only chance. Half-blind, it might not have the will to strike.

The mighty serpente swung its head, rekindled embers illuminating its full magnificence. Its gaping maw revealed twin rows of jagged, bloodied teeth. I leapt, knife raised as the beast bore down on me.

But the beast had no eyes to stab, just dark ovals where they should have been. No vulnerable place in which to plunge my blade. I swung wildly, slashing air as its head jerked out of reach. I fell, the knife slipping from my trembling hand. Scrabbling for it blindly in the sand, my fingers curled around something else. Something solid. My uncle's chronicle.

It must have tumbled from my shirt. Without a thought, I clutched it to my heart.

The serpente backed up, poised and ready to strike. It did strike, enveloping me in rancid stench. I closed my eyes and waited for the end. Clinging to my final breath. Hoping desperately against hope.

The serpent sniffed: first my throat, then the chronicle. Sniffed again, its nostrils flaring in disgust. And then, in an instant, it coiled and fled, knocking me to the ground with a lash of its tail. Impact forced the wind from my lungs. I pushed myself to my knees while drawing deep, frantic breaths. My chest and shoulder pained me, but I was otherwise unharmed. By Kashah, why had the serpente let me live? I had eaten its babies' flesh, like all the others. Why should *my* life not be forfeit too?

Hours passed before I was able to search the ruined campsite for survivors. There were none. I fed the fire with trampled scraps until it roared at full ferocity. Tomorrow I would bury them. Tonight I needed flame and stars to comfort me through solitude and darkness.

On my back beside the fire, I watched Kashah the Dog-Headed Warrior as many believed Kashah watched over them. When I'd been lost in that desert storm, the warrior had been my only friend. One bloody campsite massacre later and it was still just the two of us. Kashah striding his way across the heavens with me below, making my way on foot.

And that was when it dawned upon me. The chronicle, with its thunder-lizard bindings. Hide my uncle swore had stopped a bullet. Had the serpente smelled its ancient nemesis? Was that why it coiled its tail and fled? Beasts were driven by primal instinct. This one had been dumb enough to let me be. No point in guessing at its reasons.

When morning came I buried what remained of Getta's family. There wasn't much. Gnawed bones covered with bloodstained carpets.

I took as much of their water as I could carry, avoiding the remains of the serpente babies lying trampled in the fire's ashes.

That blackened godhead watched me leave, its features dull in daylight. As the sun climbed higher into the pink-streaked sky, distance grew between me and the carnage. But my bearings had become completely addled. In which direction lay Evenslough, the Sand Road or my poor camel's bones?

Those waterskins clung damp against my back. Not enough to get me far, but maybe. . . just maybe. . . Getta and her tribe had heard of Ankahmada. That fabled city was now my only hope. Maybe fortune would grant her favour. Had Kashah been guiding me all along?

Eventually, respite from the monotony of the dunes. A cathedral of jagged ivory: the jutting ribcage of an impossibly large, long-perished beast. The petrified bones of a thunder lizard, source of the buttons poor Getta and her family had been seeking.

Two carrion birds materialised, small specks against the faded blue. I watched them enviously, safe upon high, surveying the length and breadth of their domain.

As I stood between towering ribs, admiring the dead thing's symmetry, the surrounding sand began to boil and churn.

I froze, praying for a cruel trick of the wind, my vision, or the bright, persistent sun.

No such luck. The serpente mother. Following close. I fled for the nearest dune, its blade-thin edge carved to a crescent by sculpting winds.

Could serpentes climb? I crawled on clumsy hands and knees, soft grains clinging to my sweaty skin.

My stomach clenched as the serpente raised her head, then lunged playfully at my rough, scuffed trail. I kept still as a stone carved idol as she sniffed the breeze to gauge my whereabouts.

As shadows lengthened into afternoon, that serpente mother circumnavigated the dune's base, making no effort to shimmy up its crescent. That big dumb animal could take me any time she wanted. It might be several weeks till she was hungry.

Those carrion birds were not indifferent to my predicament. Both perched upon the jutting bones, confident the long wait would be worth it. Perhaps they had seen what I could not: Ankahmada, blue jewel glinting in the sun. Fabled home to a god-king and his treasure.

Andras Thorn was a famous traveller and the uncle for whom I was named—but the last words in this chronicle are mine. Should you find this book, return it to Evenslough. My mother will pay good coin for it. My uncle too—if he's not off adventuring in the taverns of Grimpiper or Fallow Heel.

The chronicles of the younger Andras Thorn took place as I have written them. My water is gone, my skin burnt raw from sun. Paper brittle and my ink run dry but at last I can see it: Ankahmada: blue-jewelled city—even if I will never reach its gates. I cradle a useless amulet in my palms while faithful Kashah watches over me.

••••••••••

A PRAYER FOR LAZARUS

ANDREW J. McKIERNAN

Daddy keeps Momma chained up in the barn out back. Far enough away that visitors wont hear her moanin and screamin. Close enough so we can check on her a coupla times a day. Take her some food. Empty her bucket. Sing her a song if she aint in a mood. Emma tries to sing her hymns but she dont like those no more. She likes Neil Diamond and Don McLean, specially that one about the starry, starry night. Sometimes I just leave the radio on in there for her to listen to.

Out in the barn theres less chance Momma will hurt someone, thats what Daddy says. Less chance she'll try do somethin to herself. Cause when Momma's in a mood you dont never know what she's gonna get up to. Not one of us want to do our chores on those days. We're all supposed to take turns but Emma's too young and upsets easy, and Jimmy's too lazy, even though he's oldern me. He says its a girls job anyways, which means its up to me most days.

Theres a bucket by the backdoor and Daddy always keeps it filled with slops. The sort of thing we used to feed the pig. When we had a pig. We fed that to Momma. Raw, which is the only way she'd eat it. Just a little bit each day chopped in with the vegetable peelins and apple cores and eggs shells. That pig's all gone now and Momma's gotta make do with possum when Daddy can catch one. We know that aint enough. We know she wants more. You can tell just by the way she looks at you.

Once our supper's done we all put our scraps into that bucket. If there are any scraps. Daddy and Jimmy hardly ever leave nothin on their plates. Sometimes I try and sneak in a chicken bone with meat still on it if theres nobody watchin, and when thats all done someones got to take the bucket out to Momma.

Winters are worse than summers. In summer, the heat brings out the old smells of the barn. Animals and straw and the smell of warm grain. Strong smells. Memory smells. In summer, its still light enough that the sun shines through gaps in the walls and the inside lights up all golden like a church with stained glass windows. In winter, its just cold and dark. Colder than a witch's tits, as Daddy would say, and darker than the hole between her legs. Theres a lightbulb inside, but its weak and yellow and the switch is still ten paces away from the barn door. Ten paces through the darkness, knowin Momma can see me but I cant see her. I can hear her though, snufflin and growlin. Without those warm summer smells of straw and livestock I can smell her too. Smell her so bad all I want to do is hold my breath and run outside.

On good days Momma will be just sittin in the corner. Maybe starin at the floor or maybe chewin on a mouse. Sometimes she just stares at the plaster Jesus Daddy hung up. She wont be no trouble though. I can open the stall gate and go right in and change her bucket without even worryin. If I feel darin I might turn my back as I walk out. Daddy says we're supposed to walk out backwards. Keep our eyes on her at all times. Sometimes though, she dont even notice I'm there. Thats the times I might stay behind and sing her a song or tell her about my day. I know she aint listenin but thats okay. I just like havin someone to talk to.

On the bad days, Momma's impossible. You can hear her long before you get to the barn, even if the doors are closed. Momma'll be screamin and moanin and most none of it will be words. When there are words, its all cussin. Theres a sound she makes like a dog barkin too. And then theres the rattle, rattle, rattle of her chain as she tests its strength. None of us like those noises but I think they bother Daddy worst. He just rides off on a tractor for an hour or two, leaves things for us kids to look after. At night? He drinks beers until he falls asleep on the couch.

Inside the barn the sound is even worse. I just want to put my hands over my ears but the bucket is heavy. Heavy for me anyways. I always need both hands to carry it and my winter earmuffs dont even keep out the cold let alone the sounds. You just have to try get used to it. Put up with it I mean, cause you cant never really get used to it.

Momma will be in her stall, maybe tearin at her chain or bangin her head against a wall. So far she's smashed five of Daddy's plaster Jesuses with her head. There'll be food everywhere and the bucket busted. Lettuce and tater peels and bits of plastic and plaster litterin the floor. There'll be piss and shit all over the place and blood too cause Momma's taken some of that plastic and cut herself with it. Just scratches really. Arms and legs and boobs and stomach. Her face sometimes too. There aint nothin to do but take down the hose. Clean out the stalls and give Momma a good wash too. Neither of us like it, but she tends to settle down after that.

Those are the worst days of all, summer or winter.

At least she's stopped tryin to kill herself I guess.

• • •

I remember the first time the Lazarenes came to our door. It wasnt long after we all realised Momma was sick. Someone in town must a told them cause I know Daddy never would. I'm guessin it was Doctor Roberts.

Momma was upstairs in her bedroom. She werent so bad back then. Most days she was fine and we'd just lock the bedroom door. Only sometimes would Daddy have to tie her to the bedposts. He did this with the leather belts for his pants, the only ones he had, and on the days Momma was in a mood he'd get around havin to hitch his britches back up round his waist. Momma was okay that day though and Daddy didnt have to worry about his pants fallin down. Lucky for him, with guests at the door and all.

We dont get many visitors, livin so far out of the way. Even Mr Wallace the postman only drops by once a week, and thats only if theres mail to deliver, which Daddy says there never is except bills. So when we heard the knock we all wanted to be first to answer it. It was like someone had fired one of those starter pistols and everyone came runnin. Everyone except Emma, who was still just a baby. And Momma, who was still in her bedroom with the door locked tight.

Werent much of a race in the end. First Jimmy pushed past me and by the time either of us got close Daddy was already standin there. He waved us away. Neither of us moved. Not me, not Jimmy. We stood there and waited and Daddy did too. He didnt open the door neither. Just glared at us. The knock came again, loud and echoey in the long hallway. It made me jump and that made Jimmy jump and we both ran back into the kitchen out of sight.

I heard Daddy open the door, then the voice of a man I didnt know. His words came out soft and slow like he didnt have quite enough breath. He didnt sound happy or sad or nothin, just sort of empty, and I didnt understand the words he said neither. Not what they meant. Daddy must of though.

Would you like to offer a prayer to Lazarus? Thats what the man said, and when he said it Daddy went wild. Started cussin worse than Momma ever did. I never heard the man say nothin back though.

I tried to squeeze past Jimmy to get a look but he was takin up most the doorway. By the time I'd got through, Daddy was slammin the door shut so hard the photos on the walls shook and settled again all crooked. I ran into the front room and looked out through the big bay windows.

There were two of them shufflin away down our path. They both wore white, not fancy suits and not robes but somethin in between. Their heads were shaved too, the skin thin and bluish and scarred.

Just as they got to the gate, one of them turned and I will never forget it. His face was all bluish too, specially his tight thin lips. He had sunken hollow cheeks and temples, and dark holes for eye sockets. And the eyes in those sockets? They were cloudy and dead and I wasnt sure if they were lookin up at Momma's bedroom window or if they were starin right at me.

Demons! my Daddy screamed and I nearly jumped out my skin. He held the Bible tight to his chest, Momma's Bible, and he was tremblin. Stay away from my wife, he shouted, this is a House of the Lord and you cant have her, and his spit flew and gathered and on the window glass.

Whether the Lazarene heard him or not I dont know. He turned away and they both continued on up the road and didnt look back again.

• • •

We couldnt take Momma to church no more on a Sunday so Daddy brought the Reverend Stevens home to her.

At first this worked out well. The Reverend would come every Sunday right after Mornin Service. He'd spend an hour alone with

Momma. Always insisted she never be tied down while he was there. He prayed for her, talked to her, retold his sermon. Always finish up right about when Daddy had dinner fixed too. I reckon the smells must a wafted upstairs like some sort of timer. Smells good, sermon's over.

Back then Momma was mostly calm when Reverend Stevens was there. If she wasnt before she would be soon as she heard his deep voice comin up the stairs singin Amazing Grace or The Lord Is My Shepherd or And Let This Feeble Body Fail. Hymns always settled her back then. Well except that last time. The Sunday after the Lazarenes came, that is.

All week since their visit Momma had been playin up a treat. Twice she had to be tied down for tryin to get out the window. First time was just for bangin on it so hard she broke the glass. Second time she almost got out on the ledge before Jimmy saw her and we dragged her back in. All the time she was cussin too, mainly at Daddy. By the time the Reverend arrived though she was untied and quiet as a mouse.

We all except Emma followed The Reverend up the stairs. He was singin I Know Not The Hour as he went and he stopped singin at the top and opened Momma's bedroom door and went in and closed the door behind him. You could hear him greetin Momma and offerin her up a prayer. I dont think the door was locked while he was in there cause that could only be done from the outside and Daddy had the key. He hadnt turned no lock that I could see. Just sat on a chair opposite, his head down in his hands like he was prayin too.

Jimmy and I retreated to the bottom of the staircase. Tryin to listen but tryin to keep an eye on Emma in her playpen too cause that was our job. We couldnt see much from where we were. Just the top of Daddy's head pokin up over the last stair. We could hear the Reverend clear enough though. His prayers and his borin old sermon too.

I have no idea how it all started. Nobody does except Momma and The Reverend. I dont even remember who started screamin first. It might a been Momma, but the Reverend's got a pretty high pitched holler too. Either way, the bedroom door burst open and the Reverend come rushin out. His black shirt and white collar were near torn through and there was blood all over his face.

That woman has the Devil in her, the Reverend shouted and slammed the door behind him. Daddy got up from his chair. First thing he did was lock the bedroom door with his key. By the time he was done the Reverend was almost at the bottom of the stairs. Jimmy rushed past to be with Emma but I held my ground.

Is Momma gonna be alright? I asked the Reverend and he stopped and looked at me. Half his nose was just a big red flap of skin hangin down over his lips. There were scratches and bite marks all along his arms and neck. Blood dripped from the left side of his head and I think he might have been missin an ear.

No she is not going to be alright, the Reverend told me in a voice that sounded strange cause of his nose and all the blood. Your mother is Satan's whore, he said. She will get older. She will get sicker. She will die and die and die until she's rotted away, and that is God's punishment. I'll pray no more for her peaceful end.

Then he just walked away and out the front door.

Daddy was still comin down the stairs but he stopped when he saw me cryin. He put his arm round me. Sat me down on the bottom step.

What did he say to you? Daddy asked but I couldnt speak.

Its okay, he said and held me tight. His heart was beatin real fast. Its okay, he said again and I looked up to see he was cryin too. He was starin out the still open front door and we could hear the Reverend's crappy old car drivin away real fast into the distance.

That was the last we ever saw of the Reverend, though I think Daddy received a letter from his lawyer once. It was also the last time Daddy ever let Momma hurt anyone. Now Daddy makes us all listen to the Reverend's Sunday Night Miracle Revival hour on the radio instead. He plays it real loud when the hymns come on and I know he's just doin it to punish Momma.

• • •

So anyway, thats why Momma got moved out to the barn. Daddy says what happened with the Reverend is the reason, but I dont believe him. I reckon its in case the Lazarenes come knockin again. So they wont see Momma and Momma wont see them. Daddy says that would be best for everyone.

Daddy always keeps the bedroom door locked now. Aint nobody allowed in there but I hear him late at night when he thinks we're all asleep. He creeps in and sits in there but I dont hear no cryin or nothin. I know it used to be his bedroom too, before Momma got sick. I dont know why he dont take the room back for himself but he dont. Every night he's sleepin on the spare bed in the sewin room.

I think its a shame, all Momma's nice things locked up in that bedroom. Like Daddy's the only one allowed to remember her that way. Every day I go out the barn and every day my memories of her are replaced with somethin horrible. Am I supposed to forget she was beautiful? Thats why I sneaked the key last night while Daddy was asleep in front of the TV. I crept upstairs and unlocked the door. Didnt open it though. Not at first. Just stood there with my hand on the cool brass doorknob. Hopin that when I opened the door Momma would be sittin at her dresser, brushin her hair and lookin at herself in the mirror.

When I went in she wasnt there. The room was empty. There were dark stains all over the bed and the carpet. It was blood. I have no idea if it was Momma's or the Reverend's. It made me think of the Reverend's face with his nose hangin off. It made me feel sick. I took a deep breath like the air was poison and rushed in and took a photo from the dresser. It was Momma when her and Daddy first met. Her hair was up, showin off her long neck. She had makeup on and her lips were red and her cheeks pink. She was smilin. I cant remember ever seein her smile.

I ran out of the room with the photo still in my hands. Ran before my breath ran out. Before I had to breathe in the poison.

In the hall I sat down and cried, Momma's photo clutched tight to my chest. Maybe I fell asleep then cause when I woke up I was in bed. Daddy mustve carried me there. Momma's photo was propped on the bedside table. It looked like she was smilin at me.

• • •

Momma dont look like her photo no more. Thats part of the sickness and some say millions of people caught it. Daddy and the Reverend say only sinners caught it, but now even the unrighteous are safe cause the government gave us all shots. Came too late for Momma though and Daddy wont even tell me how she sinned. I cant ever remember her bein no such thing as a sinner. All I know is she'll get older and she'll get sicker and she'll die and die and die. The Reverend once said a sermon about Resurrection and Eternal Life. Bet he never imagined it would look like Momma.

First of all she got thinner and none of us really noticed. I think Daddy must of noticed cause at first he was holdin and kissin Momma more than before. He bought her a new dress that was short and tight and black. Momma didnt feel like wearin it though. Told Daddy she was too tired for those sort of games. She stopped eatin then and got thinner still. Started sleepin most the day. When she was up she was always bumpin into things and she bruised somethin terrible. Purple and blue and yellow all over her arms and legs and face. Eyes goin all filmy. She started talkin to herself. Cussin under her breath. Sometimes she got angry. Threw things. Smashed things.

All this happened and none of us really noticed til she fell down the stairs chasin the cat. Broke her leg and the bone was stickin out and that didnt stop her nohow. Momma dived onto that cat before it was halfway out the catflap in the kitchen door. Cant blame Emma and Jimmy and me too much. We werent much more than babies. How would we know what a person should be like? Daddy should of realised sooner though. He knows Momma better than anyone. He shouldnt of left Jimmy and me at home with Emma when he took Momma to see Doctor Roberts either, and he shouldnt of told me to clean up the mess in the kitchen.

Who is it asks a seven year old to mop up their dead cat?

• • •

Its cold outside and Momma's been wailin all day. I dont want to go outside but thats the way it is. Daddy and Jimmy have gone into town and wont be back til late, and Emma's asleep on the couch.

Its not just the cold nor Momma's wailin why I dont want to go outside. Reason is, the Lazarenes were here again.

I didnt open the door. Just stood quiet in the hall and waited for them to go away. I could see their thin shapes through the frosted glass. Their long necks and bald heads. I had to wait ages. I'm sure they knew I was there.

• • •

Nine times my Momma's died, least that I know of. Twice from infection, once from heart failure, and another time she had a stroke. Once Daddy made her have a shower and she fell down and broke her neck. Her head was wobbly for weeks. We think that time was an accident. All the times other than those? Momma done it to herself on purpose.

First time she died was after chasin the cat. Daddy didnt bring her home that night. Doctor Roberts rushed her straight to hospital and she stayed in there for ages cause her leg wouldnt get better. Just when the doctor was thinkin of choppin it off, she died. Next day? Guess what? She woke up again.

Her leg was mended, but not proper. Its still bent at a funny angle and leaks blood and pus. Thats the way it is with the sickness. Momma'll never get better, no matter how hard she tries. Daddy says this means she might not ever get to Heaven. Maybe not til Judgement Day, cause no one knows how long her body can keep goin. We all just have to be patient, Daddy says.

I dont think Momma believes him, or maybe she doesnt want to wait that long, cause she keeps tryin to get to Heaven anyways. First she hanged herself in the attic with a scarf and swung there two days before Daddy found her. Then she drowned herself in the bathtub. Another time she tried to cut her wrists with a butter knife and it took me all day to clean up the blood. Once, she drunk drain cleaner and that wasnt nice for anyone.

Jimmy, who is two years oldern me, says there are other times too. Times I dont know about. He says he saw Daddy, back when Momma was still in her bedroom, and Daddy was holdin a pillow over Momma's face. And when I was at camp for two weeks? Jimmy says Daddy didnt feed her nothin at all. I dont know if Jimmy's tellin the truth or if he's just bein mean. Boys can be mean, but I dont think Jimmy would lie about Momma.

• • •

Momma's wailin stops real sudden and that gets me worryin if maybe she's gone done somethin to herself again. It makes me forget all about the Lazarenes.

When I go out the backdoor I almost forget her bucket too, but I go back. Its late and Momma will be hungry. The bucket aint very full though, what with Daddy and Jimmy still in town and only me and Emma home. Daddy says us girls eat like birds and how Momma's the one gonna suffer for that. Momma's always the one gets to suffer, seems to me.

I remember to take a torch, but I dont need it. The night is clear and the moon near full like a big old chicken's egg in the sky. I can already see that the barn door is open and theres a light on inside. This is where I stop cause I know Daddy's not home and I wonder if maybe I left the light on last night or if maybe Emma was out singin songs to Momma? I dont know. I dont think so. And all the time that I'm wonderin I dont even realise I've started movin forward again. Just small slow steps, but before I know it I'm standin real quiet at the barn door and lookin in.

The door to Momma's stall is open and she's just sittin on the dirt and straw, all calm. Theres a Lazarene kneelin and it looks like he's talkin to her. I cant hear what he's sayin, but I can see his lips movin.

I'm just about to step in and say somethin, cause I know Daddy wouldnt like it, when I feel a hand on my shoulder. Its firm but gentle and colder than the night. I shiver at its touch and turn just my head, as if my body has been frozen, and I'm lookin up into the face of the other Lazarene.

His skin is thin as Bible paper. Eyes all milky. Lips so tight they couldve been stitched together. But they arent cause next thing the Lazarene opens his mouth and speaks to me.

This sickness will not end in death, he says. No, it is for God's glory so that God's Son may be glorified through it.

His voice sounds desert dry. Rough and rattlin in his throat and lungs. I have no idea what he is talkin about. His words sound like somethin the Reverend would say. The Lazarene looks towards Momma's stall and nods his head as if he's pointin at somethin with his nose. I look and see its at Momma's plaster Jesus hangin on the barn wall.

Those were the words of your Saviour, the Lazarene says. Is it right that your mother should suffer so? That she should suffer for the glorification of another?

I'm not sure what he's askin but I shake my head. No, I say, Momma shouldnt have to suffer.

His long fingers are still grippin my shoulder and he leads me into the barn. Theres some sort of strange incense makin things foggy and all smellin like flowers. I can see Momma and the other Lazarene still sittin. The Lazarene is sayin somethin, maybe prayin. Looks to me like Momma's actually listenin.

You'd best leave, I say and my whole body is tremblin. Daddy will be home soon and he dont like you much. He says you're devils who wanna stop Momma from goin to Heaven.

Theres a change in the dry rattle of his breathin and I wonder if he is laughin.

We'd rather release her from hell, he says and we stop at Momma's stall and just stand there sayin nothin else. The other Lazarene has taken a little box from out his robes. He opens it and takes out a little paper cup and what looks like one of Daddy's vitamin pills, but red. The Lazarene peels the lid from the cup and leans forward. He's offerin the cup and the pill to Momma, one in each hand, like he's the Reverend offerin up the Lord's Supper at Communion.

He better not get too close, I say. Momma bites.

They crave the flesh and blood of their Saviour, the Lazarene says. But they cannot have it. And why? Because their Lord Jesus Christ is dead. Surely you must know this. When was the last time he answered your prayers? When was the last time he answered your mother's or father's prayers?

I dont know what to say. I'm thinkin of an answer when Momma reaches out and takes the pill. She stuffs it in her mouth like its some juicy treat. Grabs the cup and tips it between her lips. The lump of her throat moves up and down when she swallows. She looks at the Lazarene before her and smiles. My Momma actually smiles.

When was the last time my prayers were answered? Right then, thats when! Right that very moment with Momma sittin calm and serene and smilin. Not just her teeth either, which are brown and rotted away, but the smile is in her sharp boned cheeks and hollow clouded eyes. It is a smile I've only ever seen in the photograph. Never in real life.

I turn to thank the Lazarene for whatever it is they done for Momma. He's lookin right at me and looks sad. This Communion is not permanent, he says, it is just her first.

And thats when I see the truck headlights comin down the long drive to the house.

You have to leave, I say. My heart is racin all of a sudden but the Lazarene just looks and doesnt even blink. Lazarenes never seem to blink. You have to go, I say again more urgent. You have to go, Daddy's got a gun.

The Lazarene seems to smile and inside his mouth is all wet grey gums. He has no teeth at all. I pull away from his bony hand

and realise I'm still carryin Momma's bucket. Its so late and she hasnt even eaten. Daddy will be furious.

I'm shakin as I enter Momma's stall and the other Lazarene is standin up now, his hand restin gently on Momma's head. I cant see his little box, so he must of put it back inside his robes. He looks at me as I enter and I tell him he's got to leave too. I can hear Daddy's truck pullin up outside the house. If I'm not inside and Daddy sees the lights on out here, he'll come outside for a look or send Jimmy to do it maybe. Either way would be bad.

I step between the Lazarene and my Momma and put the bucket down. She down looks at it and then up at me and then over my shoulder.

Thank you, Momma says, and I'm too stunned by her words to know if she's thankin me or the Lazarene. When I look around, the Lazarenes are gone and the barn is empty of everythin except me and Momma and the smell of incense.

• • •

Daddy didnt find out about the Lazarenes visitin, least not that night he didnt. I was back inside before him and Jimmy had even finished unpackin the truck. It wasnt til the mornin when he went out to check on Momma that he knew somethin had happened.

I went with him, followin close behind cause I was scared of what he might find. Thought maybe I could distract him if I had to. There was no way of distractin him from what we saw when we come out the backdoor though.

The barn doors had been painted over with a giant green cross. Like four arrowheads all aimin for the middle. As soon as Daddy saw it he went batshit. Started screamin real loud for the effin demons to leave his wife alone. He was runnin before he'd even finished sayin the words and I had trouble keepin up. Daddy has such longer legs than me. He got to the barn doors first and pressed his fingers to the cross. They came back green and sticky with paint and the color looked strange against the red rage of his skin. He reached out and grabbed the handle to slide open the doors and the handle became green too.

Inside the barn, Momma was sittin quiet in her stall. Her chain was piled up in her lap and she was fingerin it like a Rosary. She stopped when Daddy opened the stall gate. No longer beautiful.

No longer the woman in my photograph. Over time her hair had fallen out in sympathy with her teeth. Skin pulled thin across her skull. Her cloudy eyes starin right at Daddy.

Lord behold, she said, he whom thou lovest is sick.

Her voice was dry as sand. I hadnt noticed til then just how much she looked and sounded like one of the Lazarenes, but she did. Their bodies were healed and scarred where Momma's still ran red and yellow with infection and rot. Their heads were smooth where Momma's flaked skin and hair. What she was sayin sounded like somethin the Lazarene would have said too. I didnt recognize it but Daddy did.

Did you let them in here? he asked me and there was thunder in his voice and in his eyes and in the beat of blood at his temples. What did they do to your Momma? he shouted. Tell me what those demons did to her or I'll get my belt.

For me, tellin a lie is like holdin your breath, except the air you are holdin in is the truth. You can only do it for so long before you burst. Thats what happened while Daddy was screamin and threatenin the belt. I couldnt hold that truth in no more and it all just come rushin out.

The Lazarenes were here, I said. But I didnt let them in. I came out to feed Momma and they were in here and I asked them to leave but they wouldnt. I think they were tryin to help Momma, Daddy. They said Jesus couldnt help her cause he's dead. Is that true? Is Jesus dead?

I'm sure Daddy was goin to hit me then cause he raised one hand up over his head and his palm was open wide for a slap. He didnt do it though cause next thing Momma spoke again.

He shall rise again in the resurrection at the Last Day, Momma said. He shall rise again at the Last Day like Lazarus.

Thats when Daddy turned on Momma and forgot all about me. His hand came down and grabbed Momma's chain. He took it up and coiled it round her neck. He pulled it tight and I thought he was goin to lift Momma right up off the floor but she grabbed at the chain with her hands and scrambled to her feet. Her eyes were all bulged. I could see she couldnt breath. One of her hands was caught up in the chain, the tips of her fingers pokin out and bendin all wrong and turnin purple. Momma lashed out with her other hand and her dirty nails raked Daddy's face. Daddy pushed her hard back to the ground and started draggin her across the stall and I just knew he was goin to hoist that chain over a rafter and hang her.

He remembered me then. Get out, he shouted, just get out!

And I did. I ran all the way out the barn and to the house and up the stairs to my bedroom. From way outside in the barn Daddy was still shoutin scripture and Momma was screamin and I was thinkin that Jesus must be dead cause if he wasnt how could he be lettin this happen?

· · ·

Daddy came to my room later that night. The shoutin and screamin from the barn had stopped and when he came sat on my bed he smelled of sweat and beer. He didnt talk for a while and it looked like he had been cryin. There were four long red scratches down his cheek. I didnt have no sympathy for him.

I hate whats happenin to your Momma, he told me. I hate that she's sick but thats the hand the Lord has dealt. It hurts us all to do what I have to do, but the Lazarene are demons. Satan sent them, just as he sent your Momma's sickness, to stop people gettin to Heaven. We cant let that happen to your Momma can we? Do you want her to become an agent of Satan? Do you want her to leave us?

I shook my head and said, no Daddy. I didnt know nothin about Agents of Satan. I didnt know nothin about demons. I didnt want Momma to leave us neither, but didnt she leave us years ago? When she got sick? Left us bit by bit?

Daddy held me and we both cried, though I think for different reasons. Daddy just didnt want to let Momma go. I wanted her back. I'd do anythin to have her back, but I didnt tell Daddy that.

· · ·

First thing this mornin I sneaked out to the barn and looked at Momma. She was just layin in her stall, the chain still round her neck. Her face was blue and bruised. Her eyes wide open and already a fly settled there.

I closed her eyelids and untangled the chain. Once I got to the leather collar at her neck I took it off. Underneath, the skin was calloused in places, rubbed raw in others. There was nothin I could do about it without goin back to the house for the iodine. Did it matter? Would Momma feel it when she woke up in a few hours?

I thought she would. She'd be weak and tired and probably in a mood. She'd be hungry and she'd want to eat.

When I went back, everyone was still sleepin. I took the iodine and some bandages from the bathroom cabinet and two apples from the kitchen. On my way out I spotted Momma's Bible layin on the kitchen table and I took that too.

Momma still werent awake when I got back so I dressed her wounds and waited. I sat on an old musty straw bale and ate one of those apples. It was sweet and fresh and the juices ran down my chin and onto the Bible as I turned its thin pages. I read about Lazarus and how Jesus knew his friend was sick but let him die anyways. So that God's Son may be glorified, thats what John wrote. I didnt like the way Jesus used his friend to make himself look good in front of people. I felt sorry for Lazarus.

When I looked up I found the sun was full up and I had eaten both the apples. I felt bad about that. I looked at their teeth-stripped cores and knew Momma would be needin more than that anyways. I thought on what I could fix her to eat and all that readin about Jesus and Lazarus made me think.

• • •

I'm sittin in my bedroom lookin out the window. Waitin for Daddy to go out and see what all the ruckus is about. It hasnt started yet but it will soon and I have to be ready when it does.

Daddy went out watchin Sunday football and gettin drunk with his mates but now he's snorin on the couch. I'm sure the noise will wake him though.

Momma woke up a coupla hours ago, but I aint fed her yet. Only time I went out there was to put the radio on for her real loud and close the barn doors. I've got my own little radio set up next to me. I hear the end of the news and then the weather and through the window I can see the big green cross still painted on the barn doors. My heart is beatin real hard. When the weather stops playin my heart skips the beat of dead air. Starts again with a rush at the sound of the next program.

Prayers and blessings listeners, a familiar voice says. You are tuned to Reverend Steve Stevens Miracle Revival Hour. We'll take some talkback soon, but lets start the evening with some music.

The Reverend plays Abide With Us, The Day is Waning and then Rise From Your Graves, Ye Dead. I can hear it not just from my radio but comin from the barn too, I've turned the radio up that loud. I hate to do it cause its really botherin Momma. I can hear her screamin and shoutin like a banshee.

Half way through There's A Light In The Valley, Daddy comes rushin out the back door. Its good that he's drunk cause he's stumblin and not fast, which gives me time.

I get up and rush down the stairs and out the back door too. I catch up just when Daddy's gettin to the barn doors. He's got his shotgun with him and he puts it down to open the doors. It doesnt take much for me to keep runnin, my arms out in front, and I push Daddy into the striped lights and shadows of the barn. I dont even think. I just slam the doors and pick up the shotgun and jam it barrel first through the handles to lock them shut.

I can hear Daddy shoutin at me and bangin and I can hear Momma makin that sound like a dog barkin. The Reverend is on air for just enough time to introduce the next song, and then the screamin starts. For the first time ever its Daddy not Momma makin the noise.

I walk back to the house and In Our Day Of Thanksgiving starts playin. I know the words and I sing along. When I get inside I'm goin to make a phone call. When they answer I'll say, hello I'd like to offer a prayer for Lazarus. I'd like to have my Momma back.

···········

SOUL PARTNER

IMOGEN CASSIDY

I didn't get a lot of opportunities to go east in my job—for some reason the beach wasn't a hotspot of supernatural activity. I guess it could have been all that sun and sand, or maybe it was the combination of wealth and youth that stopped people from being upset about things like ghosts and spirits and the occult . Or perhaps in some cases they took it too seriously and didn't want an actual practitioner like me mucking up their idea of how it should work—even after the magic came back there were still a lot of people out there who wanted to make their own interpretation of spirituality. The real occult avoided that sort of thing.

I parked the Echo right outside the address my potential client had given me, grateful for small mercies. It was the middle of summer—logically I should have had to park kilometres away and walked up and down the whole of east Sydney searching, but miracle of miracles, there was a small spot just outside the place, looking out over the water. I paused for a minute after getting out of the car and rested my elbows on its roof, gazing out across the green park and strip of yellow sand before the water.

"Ms Foster?"

The voice was warm and rich, hitting a lot of buttons that I didn't necessarily want hit right now, and coming from somewhere behind and above me. I turned and looked up.

My client—I assumed that was who it was—was standing on a glass fronted balcony with a slightly better view than the one I had until a moment before been contemplating. She was dressed in a pair of cut-off denim shorts that exposed a long length of brown leg, and a loose white shirt over an equally white bikini top. Sunglasses covered her eyes and most of her face, and she held a martini glass in one hand.

"Oh, come on," I said.

She looked puzzled. "Ms Foster?" she said again. I shook my head and grinned.

"Don't mind me," I said. "Ms Paine, I presume?"

She smiled, showing perfect white teeth, and motioned with her free hand. "Come in and up, Ms Foster. The door is open."

"Of course it is," I muttered, and locked the Echo, walking across the street and up to the lavish double doors. I debated touching up my hair in the brief moment I would be out of my client's gaze, but decided it wasn't really worth the effort of a glamour spell. Sometimes you just can't look good next to someone—the best you can hope for is that you find someone who doesn't care if you don't.

The thought of Gloria made me square my shoulders and smile a little as I walked up the open plan staircase towards the balcony where Ms Paine was standing. Just because I wasn't tall, dark and mysterious didn't mean I wasn't loved.

She was sitting when I got there. White marble and glass created a lot of glare and I was glad I had my own sunglasses as I sat on the chair she offered to me. I tried not to sprawl in its unexpected comfort and put on my best professional face, while she set her martini glass down on the glass table with a delicate clink and rested her (perfectly manicured) hand next to it.

"You wouldn't go into any detail on the phone," I said. "Which is fine. But you said you needed the services of a wizard."

"I do."

I spread my hands. "I know I'm not exactly Gandalf, but you did look me up before you rang? At least I'm presuming you did."

"The occult and I aren't exactly strangers," she said, "but this is a delicate matter."

I tried my best reassuring smile. "If you weren't looking for discretion you would have gone to the police, Ms Paine," I said. "I'm good at discreet."

She took a sip of the martini, seeming to consider again. This was no skin off my nose—if she didn't want to hire me, she was still obliged to pay my call-out fee, that was very clear in my telephone spiel. I lost nothing but a nice afternoon drive and the company of a pretty woman for a short conversation if she decided I wasn't good enough for her troubles.

Mentally, I prepared myself to take my kit and go home.

Then she spoke. "I'm afraid someone is attempting to steal my soul."

"Ah."

"I need you to find out who."

"Oh."

"And stop them."

"Uh huh."

"Can you do that?"

I rubbed a hand through my hair. "Well, there are a few options with soul stealing. Most of the time the demon in question can't get through a simple magic circle. I can teach you a basic household protection spell that will keep you safe at home, and make you a charm to carry around with you to stop them from . . . "

Ms Paine was watching me with a small smile. It was the kind of smile that made you stumble and forget words.

"What is it?" I asked.

"I think you've misunderstood me, Ms Foster," she said, then reached up and took off her glasses. "The soul that they're trying to steal is not a human soul. As such the kinds of protections you talk about will not work."

I blinked, looking for the first time at her naked eyes.

Yellow.

Slit like a cat's.

"Ah."

• • •

Magic isn't a simple thing, it never has been. It's always been there—at least that's what the foremost wizardly minds were saying these days—but it's never been taken that seriously. Practitioners who are any good at it are pretty rare, and when something magical happens most people are happy enough to convince themselves that it didn't. Or at least, they were, until late 1945, when a hole opened in the universe and more magic than we'd ever been exposed to poured back into the world and set up residence, a bit like an elderly relative who doesn't know what time it's suitable to turn off the lights when he's staying at your house.

You can't explain away something that big. You can't say you don't believe in magic when six people on your street start being able to light fires with their brains. Or you can, but you better have good insurance.

It settled down a bit after that. There were a rash of magical talents, but most faded back into simple sensitivity and everyday life continued on. A percentage of them, though, developed into full blown adepts—like me and like my uncle—and it became pretty obvious that it was genetic in some way. It skipped my mother and my brother. But I got the full kit and kaboodle, as they say. Not much chop, having a wizard for a daughter, especially one who likes fire, so my parents sent me to live with my uncle at a pretty young age. He taught me what I knew about magic and a lot more besides, and passed on his wizarding business to me when he got on the wrong side of an ice demon.

I still missed him. But I wouldn't deny that it was nice being my own boss.

• • •

Ms Paine was obviously a demon, and Uncle Tim had been pretty firm on what we did with demons. I stood up, and stepped back, managing not to look totally incompetent, and started to sketch a banishing sigil in the air.

Ms Paine held up a hand. "Ms Foster, don't." She stood as well, and as she did she touched a finger to her cheek. Her eyes changed— moving from yellow to deep brown, and she smiled—a completely different smile to the one she had been giving me before. This was younger. More uncertain.

I frowned. "Lady, you have a demon inside you, I need to exorcise it."

She shook her head. "No. Please. This is why I called you and not the police. I don't want it exorcised. That's the whole problem."

"Wha . . . ?"

"Sit down and let me explain, if you would. It's a complicated story, and I really do need your help." She paused. "We both do."

She wasn't following the regular formula for demons, I had to give her that. The last time I'd faced down with one it had flattened a warehouse before I'd managed to banish it back through the rift. At least this one was pretty and didn't try to eat me.

I sat.

"Okay, Ms Paine. You've caught my interest, I won't lie. But forgive me if I'm not going to take this case with no questions asked."

"I would not hire you if you did." I lowered my hands, but not my guard. Ms Paine smiled wryly, then nodded. "It's true, I do have a demon . . . ah . . . inhabiting me. But it was a mutual decision. A . . . partnership, if you will. The demon—Fiducia—had something I needed, and I had something it needed." She spread her hands. "Simple really. No-one was hurt by the deal, and no-one will be, of that I can be absolutely certain."

I cocked an eyebrow. She'd named it. She'd named it *trust*. Obvious demon was obvious.

"Look, Ms Paine, I don't want to be a downer here, but demons are good at making you think everything's going to be okay. It's kind of a thing with them."

She shook her head and looked down. When she looked up again her eyes were yellow. "You're an adept, Ms Foster, and I am familiar with some of your work."

I swallowed. It wasn't necessarily a good thing to be known of by a demon. "Oh?"

"Your uncle made many enemies among my kind."

"He was good at that, yeah."

"I was saddened to hear of his death, however. And I believe that humans . . . overreact to us. We do harm because we are used to having limited access to your world." She spread her hands. "We are long lived, and change is anathema to us."

"Hey we're short-lived and not so keen on it either," I said. "But I hope you're not suggesting that we all sign up for demon passengers in order to better human/demon relations because I don't think there's many that are going to be keen the way Ms Paine was. Or seems to have been."

"You do not believe this was voluntary."

I sighed. "It's possible. But I'm betting there's no way she would have known the full consequences of agreeing to the deal, and if I'm going to help you and not . . . you know . . . exorcise you. You're going to have to convince me that she hasn't changed her mind."

"I haven't." Paine's voice changed at the same time as her eyes, but there was a steel to it that hadn't been there before. "It's . . .

not exactly what I anticipated, I won't lie; I wanted this. I searched for a compatible demon. She helps me."

"How?"

Paine's eyes narrowed. "I don't need to go into the advantages of possession, surely, Ms Foster? Or are you not as knowledgeable as your resume would suggest?"

Demonic possession granted the body inhabited by the spirit certain advantages. Strength, speed, better concentration, the ability to wield magic if the host had even a slight talent. Most possessions didn't last very long, however. "How long have you been in there?"

"Four years," Paine said, smiling slightly.

I took a breath. "Okay, so you make a deal with a demon, you get certain advantages, the demon gets to touchy feely in the real world and now someone is trying to forcibly evict it. Who knows about your deal?"

"My family. Some of my colleagues. A few of my friends."

"You're awfully open about this, Ms Paine."

"They're all people that I trust."

"It's possible someone is attempting to make a similar deal to the one you already have, in which case they would simply be calling your demon by name. No connection to you whatsoever."

Paine nodded. "We have considered that, and are confident that you could track someone who was attempting to unseat our hold on this body."

"I could . . . probably wrangle something, yeah."

"It would be appreciated. My dream wards are working when Arietta is her most vulnerable, but you would know that they're not—"

"—A good idea to keep up forever. Yes." There was gear I would need to do this ritual, another thing I probably didn't need to explain to the demon duo, and really, not very much else to discuss. Aside from one important thing.

I took a breath. "If I find out this was done without consent I will exorcise you. And Arietta, if you need help—"

She smiled. "I believe you are the right person for this job, Ms Foster," she said. "And it pleases me that you have Arietta's safety as your primary concern. I do assure you it is also mine."

"Yeah. Well. Your idea of safe and my idea of safe are probably a little bit different."

"Good luck, Ms Foster."

• • •

I drove home. Gloria was there when I let myself in, but she was in the shower, so I limited myself to poking my head around the curtain and giving her a kiss before I started assembling my kit. A few ritual objects, a focusing crystal, nothing too bulky. Soul stealing wasn't a subtle art and I doubted I'd need a lot of magical muscle to get a psychic imprint of whoever was bothering the demon duo. The problems would start after I'd identified them.

That would be the interesting thing. There weren't many magic users in Sydney I didn't know, and most of them weren't the type to try to steal demonic souls from people who had willingly agreed to take them on. There were plenty of demons out there if that was all they wanted, so why not get a different one when Arietta's decided to be stubborn?

There were a lot of strange things about this case.

Gloria came out of the bathroom just as I snapped shut my goody bag. "Client turned out to be a winner then?" she said.

"Not sure yet," I said. "But whatever this is it's worth investigating."

"Gumshoe Jill."

"Something like that.' She kissed the top of my head and started pulling work clothes out of the wardrobe.

"I'll be out late tonight, I think," I said. "Ritual."

"Mmm. Should be home after you any way—we've got a few late tables."

I tilted my head, watching her dress. She smiled at me over her shoulder. "Love you," I said.

"Love you too, magic girl."

• • •

Magic rituals are all about focus—you need to get yourself in the right frame of mind to access your power and you need to prepare your body as well. Normal spells are easy enough—most of us can manage to focus on a task long enough to get it finished—so I can blast a bit of fire or do a banishing sigil or a soul gaze without any preparation at all. An apprentice (something I desperately needed at the moment) would have a little more trouble than an adept, and a sensitive (someone with magic talent who hasn't been trained at all) only manages to work magic when they're extremely stressed or motivated.

I'd been a pretty stressed and motivated child, which was why my parents had sent me to my uncle just after I'd hit puberty.

I didn't hold it against them. At least I'd had a relative who didn't blink an eye at me when I started bringing girls home instead of boys—he was way more concerned that I'd blow up his kitchen the night before the grand final. We'd gotten on, my uncle and I.

This wasn't the sort of job it was a good idea to do on your own for any length of time. He'd warned me about it, and there were reasons why we took apprentices that weren't just because we wanted someone to do the filing. Mine always tended to leave after a few months. I told myself it was because I couldn't afford to pay them much, because the job was thankless, because I was a bad teacher, but maybe it was just because the one person I wanted by my side wasn't there any longer. I wanted them to be him, and that was just something they could never manage.

I missed him like fire.

• • •

The sun was setting as I made it back to Bronte, and it was stupidly beautiful in that way that only Sydney can manage. Warm, salt-scented air blew off the water and messed up my already messy hair . . . it wasn't as though I was trying to impress a demon or anything.

Arietta opened the door. She'd changed her clothes—now she was wearing a t-shirt and sweatpants, looking a bit like she'd just come from the gym, but without the sweat and disarray that I always seemed to bring back from abortive attempts at exercise.

She glowed.

"Ms Foster, thank you for being so prompt."

I tried for a charming grin. "You're my only client right now," I said. "Don't feel too special."

"I'll endeavour not to." She motioned me through into the living area I had passed through briefly that morning. It was awash in steel and glass. I wondered if the demon just liked looking at itself in its new body—there were enough reflective surfaces in this place for a fun park maze.

Mirrors were supposed to be windows to the soul. I wondered how true that was when your body had two of them.

"I'm going to make a magic circle, you'll need to be in the centre with me, and then I'm going to have to . . . link to you. Spiritually." I swallowed. I wasn't the best of liars but I did okay on holding back certain bits of information that clients didn't need to hear— like the spirit of your dead wife is actually all in your head, or once the magic circle closes I'll have the ability to evict the demon from you, or that once I've joined with you spiritually I'd be able to tell straight away if this deal has been coerced.

Arietta didn't flinch when I told her where to stand and as I drew the circle (some people use fancy pink salt, but the SAXA stuff is just as good and it's cheap and comes in a handy easy-to-pour shaker) I felt the familiar tingle on my skin that told me I was stepping closer to the rift. The place where magic comes from. The place that had torn open 50 years ago and changed the world forever.

It sealed with a slight change in pressure—I felt my ears pop as I worked my jaw to let it equalise, then nodded at Arietta.

She stood directly opposite me and I raised my hands, placing them on either side of her face. Her skin was warm and smooth and full of vitality. I could sense life under it, and the subtle extra energy that the demon was giving her.

I closed my eyes and let my consciousness seep into hers.

• • •

Looking into someone's head is a bit like looking into a teenagers' bedroom. It's usually messy, and it's full of stuff that means absolutely nothing to you. Like said teenager's room, there will be indications of strong emotions and important events—like posters of rock stars and old toys—objects that have meaning to them.

Arietta's mind was almost frighteningly neat. Hers was the bedroom that had been meticulously ordered. Had I wished, I could probably have read Arietta's entire childhood from the perfect display of memories that was laid out. But I didn't need to do that, and quite frankly, it would have been weird.

Underneath the perfect order of Arietta's memories I could feel the presence of the demon. If a human mind was like a teenager's bedroom, a demon's was like a galaxy of stars—each individual memory was a giant ball of flaming gas and absolutely nothing that I wanted to get anywhere near. I had no doubt they would burn.

Yet the two minds existed happily in the same space. I could sense no coercion—none of the telltale signs that magic had been used to subvert her will. Arietta's 'neat' mental state could be attributed to the demon sorting her memories while she slept—a more efficient way of dreaming than we clumsy humans managed. While they communicated freely, there was no merging. Instead it was a mutually beneficial arrangement. Arietta was more successful and physically beautiful (not that she hadn't been to begin with, but the demon had enhanced her base sex appeal simply by imbuing her with so much more vitality) and the demon experienced the human world their kind so lusted after.

I had to admit, I envied them a little.

If you wish, Ms Foster, I could contact one of my associates and you could enter into a similar arrangement.

Of course, the demon was aware I was there, in ways that Arietta was not.

"No thanks, sport," I said. "I don't think even one of your kind could clean up the mess in my head. And anyway, I kind of like it."

Humans are illogical.

"We're not the ones going around burning down . . . " I stopped before the demon's wry mental chuckle started and rolled my metaphorical eyes. "Oh never mind."

Conversations with demons in other people's heads. And these are just some of the things I do in a day's work.

We are close to the time the attacks usually begin. Arietta is for all intents and purposes asleep. I have been able to repel the intruder, but they are becoming more canny.

There was a slight hesitation before the demon continued.

I must tell you, Ms Foster, now that we are alone, that I believe the adept attempting to dislodge me is known to Arietta, and myself. She has not allowed herself to consider him as a suspect, but I believe she is being foolishly naive.

Interesting.

"So who is it?"

The man who originally conceived of the idea of making a deal with a demon in the first place. They were in a relationship. To be married, I do believe. He left shortly after we made our . . . arrangement. She lost touch with him.

So I couldn't just ask for his address and finish the ritual.

"Well if it is him and he shows up, I'll be able to follow him back to where he's hiding. You're . . . exceptional for a demon, you know that don't you? Most of them aren't one for reasonable discussions, or deals."

That is because you do not see us at our best, Ms Foster. The transition to your world is taxing. And it enrages us. Should you choose to contact us in our element we are far more reasonable.

"Funny how it doesn't always seem that way," I said.

• • •

When the intrusion came it was obvious. Arietta's ordered world had no place for the shove of pure energy and emotion that accompanied the working. Amateurish. The practitioner had very little natural talent, which made my job harder rather than easier. I stood, holding out my hands to Arietta and the demon, who took them without hesitation. Fiducia's hand felt smooth and synthetic in mine, while Arietta's was warm and rough. It was symbolic, but it gave us strength. Not enough to stop them from coming, but more than enough to stop them from being successful.

As Arietta and the demon had found out though, you could only stop them for one night. If he kept coming back, eventually he would get through and Fiducia would be pulled away.

That's why I had to follow him back to the source.

He was puzzled by the strength of the defences this time around, but went ahead with the spell in any case. Another sign of an amateur at work. He had no chance against us. I did my best to make it look like Arietta and the demon had just been better prepared, rather than calling for extra help. I could be subtle, at least when it came to magic.

When I felt him start to withdraw, I loosened my grip on the hands and consciousnesses of my clients and followed him out of the initial breach he'd made in Arietta's subconscious, and back out into the world.

I kept a pretty detailed map of Sydney in my head. My uncle's doing—he trained as a PI before he took up full-time wizardry. We're the detectives of the supernatural—there's even a wizard branch of the police these days (most young wizards end up working for the government in some capacity, something that I was happy to have sidestepped).

There are just too many ways magic can go wrong. Part of the reason most people just didn't bother.

But there were always a few people who thought magic was the answer to all their problems. People like this guy. His mental signature lead me to a house in South Granville—bit of a hike from there to Bronte physically, and a nice place to disappear if you weren't keen on being spotted by your Eastern-suburbs ex.

He didn't know I'd followed him. I was pretty good at this.

• • •

I opened my eyes and dropped my hands from Arietta's face. She blinked a few times, obviously disoriented, then nodded at me.

"You were successful?"

"I think so. He's holed up out west, I can go there tonight and sort this out."

"I want to come with you."

I eyed her. "Could be dangerous. He doesn't seem to have a lot of training but he does have power. There could be sparks."

"Fiducia will protect me. She might even be able to help."

I'd figured.

"Okay." I stood up and dispelled the circle. "Do you have a handyvac or something? For the salt? I've got one in the car."

She chuckled. "Don't worry about it," she said. "The cleaners come tomorrow."

I made a face. One day I'd have enough money for cleaners. "It's a bit of a drive, but he won't be going anywhere tonight, not after expending that much magical energy."

"Are you not tired also?"

I shrugged. "Pretty sure I've been doing this a lot longer than he has. He hasn't got the muscle you get from training either. I think he's an amateur. Should make this pretty straightforward even if he does decide he's not going to come quietly."

"Come quietly?"

I stopped and looked at her. "He invaded your consciousness without your consent. That's a grade four offence. I'm your witness. Your guy's a criminal, Ms Paine."

SOUL PARTNER • IMOGEN CASSIDY

"But he was trying to exorcise me," she said.

I tilted my head, beginning to think that the demon had been wrong—she'd known all along who was the most likely perpetrator behind these attacks.

"So he should have called the authorities or a professional to deal with this. You don't go poking around in someone else's head without training. That's how things like Merrylands happens."

She shuddered. The Merrylands incident was burnt on the consciousness of everyone—a perfect example of how magic could be misused. The poor bloke who'd done most of the killing couldn't even remember his own name anymore.

We walked to the car. Paine hesitated before she got in. "You won't hurt him, will you?"

I looked at her. "I'll try not to," I said.

• • •

The drive out to Granville was silent and quick. Traffic was light for a change. I hastily turned the radio off after starting the engine. Somehow I didn't think Paine would be a Prodigy fan.

We didn't talk. The silence wasn't comfortable.

• • •

The house was pretty typical for the area. A medium-sized block with a single storey fibro shack perched on it. The grass in front was overgrown and the cement path cracked and full of weeds.

There was a light on near the back of the house, but I suspected our man was asleep. Magical workings took it out of you, especially when you were just starting out.

I touched the gate and felt the tingling of a weak ward. If I opened it he'd be alerted, but it was a simple enough thing to dispel. I made a gesture and said a few words under my breath, absorbing the power that would have awakened him. It gave me a little jolt of energy that I wasn't going to admit to Paine that I needed badly. I was tired from the workings I'd done earlier . . .

. . . I was just good at hiding it.

I motioned to Paine to get behind me and be quiet (at least I hope that's what I communicated to her) then tried the door. It was locked, but that was no great problem. A quick glance along the street revealed we weren't likely to be noticed—the street lamps were paced pretty far apart and the house was set back a good way from the path. I pulled out my set of lock picks and got started.

"Can't you use magic for that?" Paine asked.

"Clumsy and likely to be felt by our friend," I whispered back.

"We could just knock."

"Don't spoil my fun."

Picking locks was easy enough if you had the correct equipment and pretty much impossible if you don't. At least that's what I told myself. My uncle had bought me a set of lock picks (I didn't ask from where) when he found me trying to break into his cabinet of magic supplies.

He said if I could make it into the cabinet with nothing but a bent safety pin he didn't need to teach me any magic.

Funny bugger.

There was a click under my fingers and the door swung open. No fancy deadlocks on this house. I guess the people who built it didn't really think they had anything worth stealing.

It was a depressing place, smelling of instant noodles and garbage. The carpet was an undistinguished brown colour and worn with the tread of many feet; the rooms were dark and dingy. A single corridor lead to the back of the house where I'd seen the light. I moved carefully, my shoes were pretty good on carpet, but I wasn't the sneakiest of people.

That was why I jumped when we heard the voice.

"I know you're there. You disabled the ward very professionally, but you didn't think that I'd be quite so diligent about checking them, did you?"

I didn't.

Paine had grabbed my arm when the voice sounded, her fingers cold and strong where they pressed into my skin.

"Robert?"

Suspicions. Confirmed.

"Arietta?"

We stepped into the light of the kitchen.

• • •

He might have been handsome, once. He certainly had the whole 'rough and ready' thing going for him now. Slender, dark hair, beard. If he trimmed up the beard and washed his clothes maybe someone like Arietta would give him the time of day. But I couldn't help but think, as her elegant heels clicked on the torn lino, walking towards him, that there had been an unbalance in this relationship before she got herself a co-inhabitant.

"Robert what are you doing?"

He rocked back, as though she had hit him. "What do you mean?"

"What are you doing? I hired this woman to find out who was assaulting me and . . . "

"Assaulting? Ari you have a demon inside you!"

"I put it there! You were with me when . . . "

"You didn't want it, it forced itself . . . "

"When did I say that? When did I say anything even approaching that?"

Chests were heaving. Cheeks were flushed. If I didn't know better I would have thought I was watching an episode of Game of Thrones.

"Hey. Guys?"

Robert turned on me. "You're a wizard, right. Did she tell you what she did?"

"She did, actually."

He looked at me as though I was crazy. "So?"

"So what, mate?"

"Why didn't you take it out?"

I tilted my head and looked at him. "From where I'm standing there's only one dangerous person in this room and it's the one invading someone's head without permission."

"I've been studying. I'm nearly there. I can get it out of her. You're just interfering."

I frowned. "Have you been listened to anything she said?"' . . . ever, I added silently. "She doesn't want you to take it out. If she wanted it out she would contact the relevant authorities to do it. Me, for example. She certainly wouldn't rely on someone who doesn't know a summoning sigil from a pentagram."

"They're the same thing!"

They were.

"Not the point. You need to butt out."

I felt the power gathering before he even lifted his hand, but there was a reason I was a professional and he wasn't.

Behind my lips, there was a tingling as I spoke the word that would focus kinetic energy at him, and he was thrown backwards against the wall with a decent amount of force. Not as much as I could muster first thing in the morning (after a coffee, of course) but enough that he was shocked and dazed. He lay there, shaking his head to clear it, and blinking up at us.

I glanced at Arietta, who was looking back at me with an amused smile on her face. I didn't need to check her eyes to know it was the demon speaking. "Did you just use the word *arse* as a magical focus, Ms Foster?"

I shrugged a little sheepishly. "You gotta go with what works."

She shook her head, then moved to where Robert was lying. He scrambled to get back away from her, but her progress was inexorable.

"S . . . stay away from me. Demon."

"Robert you're being irrational." Her voice was calm, and she reached out one hand to touch him. He tried to flinch away, but that demonic presence gave her strength that was otherworldly. He let out a low wail. "And dangerous. To yourself and others. You need to rest now."

"Bitch!" he screamed. "You took it and it was meant for ME!"

I tilted my head, several pieces slotting into place. "Ah. Now we come to the crux of the matter."

Arietta looked back at me. "He was a completely unsuitable host."

"You're telling me." I fished my phone out and started dialling the local police station. They usually had at least one wizard on staff at all times, especially since most crimes like this happened late at night.

"Granville Police."

"Jill Foster here; I'll be in your files. I've got a suspect in custody . . . "

Arietta moved more quickly than I thought was possible, the phone was in her hand and she was shaking her head at me. "No," she said. "This is over. We don't need to involve the police."

"Ms Paine, he's dangerous. He's untrained. He's stupid. Not a combination you want anywhere near any kind of magic."

"I'll take care of him."

I frowned. Then I took a deep breath. "And what do you think, Fiducia?"

The demon managed to sound completely sincere yet entirely unenthusiastic. It really was like a marriage, I guessed. "She wants this. I promise to make sure she does not regret it."

I cocked an eyebrow, then shook my head. "Fine. Find your own way home, and my bill will be in the mail." I held out my hand. "Phone, please."

Arietta placed it gently in my hand. "I promise you'll be generously compensated, Ms Foster."

I nodded. "Good. But don't think I'm not going to keep my eye on you." I looked hard at the now slumped figure of Robert. "All of you. If there's any suspicious demon activity or inexplicably bad spells getting thrown about by dangerous amateurs with no training and less sense you're the first people I'm blaming."

Arietta's lip twitched. "You will have no cause for complaint, I give you my word."

"I think I've mentioned how much I trust the word of demons before." I sighed, looking at them both, then shrugged. "Can you find your own way back or do you need a lift?"

"You may go, Ms Foster."

I left.

• • •

Two weeks later I was going through the final shortlist of apprentice applicants (there were three—who was I kidding? There had only been three in the first place) when the office buzzer went off. Walk in clients were rare, but not unheard of, so I answered.

"Ms Foster?"

I recognised her voice. It was, after all, a very nice voice. "Come up, Ms Paine."

She was wearing a business suit and heels. I hadn't really been looking at the time (Gloria was giving a barista course in Melbourne this weekend, so I tended to forget about things like dinner and the fact I had a bed) but it was pretty late for any kind of visitor, and I wondered if it was just what she wore all the time or if she actually had business at this time of the night.

I'd never actually asked her what her job was.

"Ms Foster. I thought I'd bring you your payment in person." She handed me an envelope. I was professional enough not to open it, or look too surprised. I had specified I wanted to be paid by direct deposit. Cheques went missing too often on my desk.

"That's kind of you," I said. "How's your guest . . . how are your guests, I should say?"

"Fiducia is as she always is. Robert is steadily improving. I suspect in time he will become a competent adept."

I doubted that but held my tongue. "He's not giving you any more trouble?"

"No. And he will not." A small smile played on her lips. I wasn't going to ask.

"Anything else I can help you with?"

"Fiducia has an offer," she said.

I swallowed, putting the envelope down. "I'm guessing it's not one that I'm going to like."

She smiled, then stood, smoothing her hands over her skirt. "That's for you to decide. At any point. We are very patient."

Ms Paine walked out. I opened the envelope. There was cash— quite a lot more of it than I'd charged—I'd have to buy Gloria some flowers. And a small card, like the recipe cards my mother had used, back before we had iPad apps for that sort of thing.

A summoning. A demon name. A short, beautifully handwritten note at the bottom. *One of my colleagues would like to discuss terms.*

It would have been very easy to call forth a small fire spell and watch it burn, but instead I put it in the top drawer of my desk and got back to work.

I still needed an apprentice, after all.

• • • • • • • • • •

1884

MICHAEL GREY

It was all Tesla's fault. Or his kindness, depending on your discretion.

Nikola Tesla was the most dangerous man on Earth, but only those few who had read the most deeply of all could have known. Desperate to prove the safety of his alternating current, he undertook increasingly drastic public demonstrations. The grandest of all was the floating battery-barge *The Future*. It was an unfortunately apt name.

The world's press and assorted dignitaries gathered at Liverpool docks to listen to the genius describe his latest creation. The boat was to harvest the potential energy of an entire storm front, hold its captured electricity for a while in its locomotive-sized cells, and then harmlessly discharge all that unfathomable power into the ocean.

The demonstration was an incredible success, according to an attending reporter who wired his editor from the boat. An hour later though, *The Future* was gone, sunk in calm seas, cause unknown. With it went Tesla and fifty-six journalists, industrialists, and crewmen.

In the aftermath an odd spree of coastal abductions and impersonations barely caused a stir. A few days later, Her Imperial Majesty the Queen Victoria announced subtle amendments to her titles and honours—and, it was noted, to her voice and manner. *The Future*, such as it had been, was quietly forgotten.

· · ·

Martin Fisher was thinking about the girl again. The little match-seller had worked at the junction of Dockins Row and Fletcher Street. She could not have been older than nine, and had done nothing more unlawful than stand on the wrong street on the wrong day.

It had been his first arrest for Dissent, under one of a slew of new laws brought in since Her Most Ancient and Imperial Majesty had assumed that title. What was to have been a quiet affair turned into a brawl when the man he tried to arrest bolted into the streets. Fisher gave chase, finally tripping him on the corner of Dockins Row, just yards from the match-stick girl, and held him there until the wagon arrived.

Those wagons were another sign of change, painted matt black, windowless and devoid of ornamentation—bar the Queen's new coiled seal, done in silver on the door. The Agency's men, the Black Hoods, jumped wordlessly from their ride. They took custody of the dissenter, pulling him from Fisher's embrace on the ground and forcing him towards the wagon. He fought them and screamed wild accusations the whole way. What he shrieked, Fisher could not remember. His attention had been on the girl, drawn by the force of some cruel prescience.

The Hoods waited until the man was by the wagon, already shivering from its cold miasma, before they opened the door. The sunlight couldn't touch the utter darkness of its interior, yet the girl stared into it, fixated. The man was thrown in, and the door slammed. The carriage rocked in time with his muted shouts once, twice, then it fell still and silent.

That was when the girl started screaming.

Fisher had watched the colour seep from her face as she looked into the carriage. Her utter terror had kept her silent, denied her dread a voice. Why could she not have held on?

If she'd lasted thirty seconds more, the carriage, the Black Hoods, and their unfortunate passenger would all have gone. But . . . she'd failed. The Hoods turned, first staring at the girl, then looking at each other. Body language gave away their uncertainty, and for a moment, Fisher thought he might be able to save her. Pick her up, and carry her away. Then the man climbed down from the driver's bench.

Fisher didn't know his name. It was the first time he had seen him, but even so he knew one of *Them* when he saw one.

The man moved oddly, walking as if unused to just two legs. While the others all wore those black hoods, he was undisguised, his face bare. It was all the more chilling that this fellow, so otherwise undistinguished, would allow everyone to see his face and know what he did, whom he served. What he was.

He walked to the girl, still screaming, still staring, and reached down to take her hand.

"What are you doing?" asked Fisher, somehow finding his voice.

The man looked at him. His expression was enigmatic, but gave the faint impression of confusion—as if at dinner a bowl of stew had quietly asked not to be eaten.

"The gi-rl saw." His voice was like his gait, staggered and ungainly.

"She has done nothing," Fisher said. He forced himself to step between them and the wagon.

"The gi-rl saw," he said again. "She will come."

"No." Fisher shook his head. The girl had fallen silent, but she still stared at the ominously still wagon.

"She will come. Or you will come, Officer Fi-sher."

It was the way the bare-faced man had said his name, rather than the fact that he knew it at all. God help him, but he'd stepped aside and let the man go. Let her go.

He'd visited that corner every week since, and every week he stood there alone for an hour before wandering home. The rest of his free time, he attempted to remain in drunken oblivion.

"Officer Fi-sher."

Fisher flinched and looked up from the table. Silence had replaced the regular hubbub of the inn around him. The bare-faced man stood above him, towering over the table and its empty gin bottles. He didn't know how the man had found him, and didn't ask. They'd have found him wherever he was. "What?" He laid his head back down on his arms to ease the painful thumping.

"Officer Martin Fi-sher. You are wanted."

The memory was still too raw for him to summon much concern. "Yes? And what am I wanted for?"

"You are wanted at the Pa-lace, Officer Fi-sher."

His eyes snapped open. "Why?"

"You are wanted at the Pa-lace, Officer Fi-sher. Tomorrow. Nine o'clock." The man turned and walked away.

The noise of the inn returned by degrees, reassuring him that the man had gone.

He's not truly gone, Fisher thought. *They never will be.*

• • •

France was mobilising, according to the *Times*. 'The rest of Europe watches the second rise of the British Empire with jealousy,' it declared. With fear seemed the more likely truth. Britain truly ruled the waves, and continental fleets had been sunk, or just gone missing. So France prepared to defend her shores with her old war machines. The tractor-pulled *basilics* with their flame throwing cannon, the repeating rifles of the *Grande Armée*, even the almost legendary *Earthmovers*.

"My great-grandad fought against the Earthmovers," Fisher overheard one old man say to another as he walked by St James's Park.

"He never did. He'd be dead, and you'd not be here."

"He did too. He were at Waterloo. Said there were four of 'em, and had his Generalship not had his agents fix 'em before, the battle would've gone the other way. Like moving castles he said they were, with cannons the size of barges."

They won't help, Fisher wanted to say. *The biggest guns in the world can't help you when it only takes one in an army, just a single one of them to reach one of your officers, and then it's all over.*

He kept his mouth shut. Either one of them could have been an informer or a Black Hood. The Hoods were everywhere, with and without their black hoods, becoming the everyday people of the street. The man behind you at the pie stall, a woman in the crowd at the playhouse . . . or one of a pair of old men, leaning against a wall swapping tales, listening to what they heard around them and remembering every name and face.

He found it hard to despise the Hoods. They were just people, like him, caught in times where you did what you had to do if you wanted to survive. But even if he couldn't find hate for them, he still guarded his words and his actions. It was madness not to.

So he went on his way, leaving the two old men to their stories.

The frightening thing about Buckingham Palace, the most insidious arrogance, was how much it had not changed. The Scots Guard arrayed themselves around the gates, but it was otherwise the same. It told London that *They* were not frightened of the people—'*We* do not have to defend ourselves from *you*.'

The only notable difference to the Palace was the state of the telegraph towers. Steepling wooden poles, they had connected the Queen to the airdock towers at Greenwich. The telegraphs had fallen into disrepair now, the wires dangling useless and the poles split with rot. The palace had no use for them, not since the continental governments cut communications. As for the airdocks themselves, *They* hated anything which took them further away from water.

He presented himself to the gate. The guard there snapped his heels and asked Fisher to follow, marching off to a side door. Fisher did so, and was led through ante-chambers and narrow halls, into a book-lined study and out, and finally to a gallery with high ceilings and windows, and an unlit hearth at its centre.

The guard left, after instructing him to wait. And wait he did, standing in the spot he'd been left, fearing that being discovered out of place would earn a punishment rooted him to the spot.

But minutes passed, and then tens of minutes, until boredom more than bravery sent him over to look at the paintings along the wall. There were so many, and so large. The first was a seascape, featuring a battle of a hundred ships. He recognised *HMS Victory* in the fray, and surmised that the artist had depicted Trafalgar. He admired the bold strokes and fine detail. Everything was captured through the smoke and movement of battle.

He moved onto the next, and found himself at a loss. It showed a land battle, although he couldn't identify the regiments, or even the armies. Two sides fought in a barren landscape, under a red sky. Not the red of sunset, either. Fisher got the impression of a sky deliberately and perpetually crimson, with black clouds sailing over the ruined scenery. The men who fought did so not with an appearance of determination or pride, but with the wild delight of zealots. Even those caught in the blasts of cannon or pierced with bayonets seemed to have no regrets, no sadness. It was as if they would gleefully die or kill for their cause, and welcomed either with equal relish.

"Magnificent, are they not?"

He caught himself, suppressed the urge to spin, and managed to turn calmly. A man walked towards him, slim and unassuming, dressed well but sombrely. He was pale, too. What Fisher had first taken for a powdered wig of the old style was in fact a shock of grey hair, and the man's cheeks weren't rouged, but bore the redness found under the rimmed eyes of someone who had not slept well in a long time.

"They are," he said, keeping his voice agreeable.

"These," the man pointed to the Trafalgar painting and its neighbours, "were originally hanging in the National Gallery." He waved past the last painting Fisher had looked at. "These others were . . . Well, I'm not exactly sure where they came from, but her Majesty desired them hung."

Fisher's glance followed the man's gesture. He saw more of the paintings of the latter sort. The next in line was dominated by the livid greens of rainforest. Vines and grass crept up a statue which hurt his eyes when he tried to focus. He blinked, and looked back at the man. "Sorry sir, I am at a disadvantage," he said.

"Of course, my apologies. My name is Benjamin Disraeli. I have the good fortune to be the Prime Minister for Her Most Ancient and Imperial Highness, may she live forever."

Fisher recognised the man then—what he had become, anyway. Disraeli had been Prime Minister before Tesla's demonstration, and had remained so. There was never a question of elections being held. But the man bore little resemblance to the illustrations in newspapers and posters. It occurred to him that Disraeli's portrayal in the newssheets had not altered with time. The fellow you could see in the papers today was years past his date, and bore little resemblance to the withered, hunted man before him.

"May she live forever," Fisher echoed.

Disraeli smiled, as if he were pleased to hear him repeat the phrase. "And you would be Officer Martin Fisher. I am glad you could make it at such short notice. Your reputation precedes you. Not many individuals have worked to make the Empire safe as you have."

"I do my duty as best I can, sir."

"Quite, quite." Disraeli turned and began to walk down the gallery, arms crossed behind his back, shoulders a little slumped. Fisher accompanied him. "I presume you were told nothing about why you were called?"

Fisher shook his head, careful not to look at any of the paintings on either side.

"Such are the ways of some of our, hm, people. We require a service of you, Mister Fisher. Something beyond your usual remit. Tell me, do you know much about your great-grandmother?"

That gave him pause. "Do you mean Joanna Fisher?"

"The very same."

"She caused some stir in her day. She hunted ghosts and spirits, sir, and advocated suffrage for women."

"She did that, yes. But I'm referring to her marriage."

"She was married?" Fisher was surprised enough to stop.

Disraeli paused. "Why, yes. It was very hush-hush. I believe she thought it would damage her public image as a strong, independent woman, or some such. That it was not common knowledge in your family surprises me, though." He nodded that they should continue. "Your grandfather was born inside wedlock, Mister Fisher, and that is why we need you."

They reached the gallery's end, and stood before an arched double door. Disraeli twisted the handle one half turn, then paused. "You have not been in the presence of royalty, have you, Mister Fisher? Please try and remain calm." He twisted, pushed and stepped through.

The room seemed cramped after the scale of the gallery. Tall windows on the right-hand wall allowed anaemic light to fall in, highlighting the shadows rather than illuminating the room. A hearth, set but unlit, dominated the far wall. A rug of complex patterns and hunting animals covered most of the floor, and in its centre, on a stick-thin chair, sat the Queen.

She wore her customary black, and faced the windows, showing them her profile. Her head tilted slightly back, mouth and eyes open and unmoving. Fisher wondered if she had heard their entrance. If she had, there was no sign, but even so Disraeli placed his palms together and gave a short bow.

"Your Supreme Majesty, may I present Officer Fisher?"

There was no response.

Stuttering, Fisher said, "It is an honour, your Majesty."

"You are welcome here, Martin Fisher." The words were cold and layered, and seemed to enter his head without touching his ears.

He blinked, but her Majesty had not moved, offering only the same still profile. "I . . . Thank you, Ma'am."

"You are confused. That is to be expected. Come stand before us, where we can see you in the light."

He looked at Disraeli, who nodded, and edged around towards the windows.

Halfway through his circuit he stopped, took a quick breath, and swallowed the scream clawing up his throat.

He stood obliquely to her, enough to see that she sat as one would expect any other person to sit—straight-backed, hands crossed on her lap. But he could not take another step, save at his sanity's risk.

Mottled grey tentacles fingered through the Queen' hair. One tip protruded from her bun, waving as if it were a snake's tongue tasting the air. Another was plastered across her forehead, curling around her face, framing it. The narrow end was feeling around inside her open mouth. Within that insane vision, he spotted a pallid inflation at the other side of her head, something slick, which rose and fell like a breathing sack. Nothing on Earth could have compelled him to move even one inch further, but he forced himself to stand his ground.

"Do not be alarmed, Martin Fisher. We are aware of how we appear, but we are in no discomfort."

"I am—" he glanced at Disraeli, who nodded "—gladdened to hear so, Ma'am."

"You are a good subject, Martin Fisher. You do much which promotes the stability of our Empire. We ask of you another task."

"Of course, your Majesty."

"Benjamin Disraeli?"

"Your Majesty." Disraeli walked over with another bow. "What Her Most Ancient and Imperial Majesty requires, Mister Fisher, is an envoy to France. Since the misunderstanding with our last ambassador, France has refused to meet with anyone of royal blood. Their reactions to our attempts at contact range from the hostile to the downright violent. However, we believe they would accept you as a messenger for the crown."

"Me, sir?"

"Indeed. You see, your great-grandfather was French, a gentleman by the name of Michele Doriole, the younger son of a landowner from Anjou. The marriage was performed and consummated in France. However, your great-grandmother returned to England pregnant with your grandfather while Monsieur Doriole, for reasons unknown, remained in France and slipped beyond our records."

"This would allow me entry to the country?"

"Yes. Your heritage gives you a favourable light in the eyes of the Directorate. We have already made enquiries in that regard."

Fisher's eye's flicked between Disraeli and the Queen. Did he dare entertain the thoughts threatening to creep into his mind? Would they be able to hear them? His gaze shifted to the thing attached to Victoria's face. He could not think of it and her as a single being the way Disraeli apparently could. He could almost feet it extending those tentacles towards him, invisible and knowing, reaching into his mind.

He closed off the thought before it could take root. "I would be honoured, your Majesty."

"We are pleased to hear so, Martin Fisher." The layered voice was all around him. He fought an urge to look behind himself.

"Excellent." Disraeli clapped his hands together. "Travel arrangements are already in place, Mister Fisher. You will depart tonight. An airship has been refurbished for this purpose. The speed is beneficial, and it will show to our neighbours that we are more willing to be adaptable than they give us credit for."

An airship! Fisher suppressed a smile. He would be out of the country in a day. He could run, vanish, never be heard of again.

The door he'd entered through opened up. In came a servant in the royal livery, holding a silver tray. "We have a range of proposals we wish you to deliver to the French Directorate," the Prime Minister said. The servant approached. The tray bore a bulging folder tied with a red ribbon, and a small, wooden box. "You won't be negotiating, simply delivering the package to their hands. You will find a top sheet with a brief description of the salient points, so you can converse over the main topics if need be, but you are not to promise anything beyond what is laid out in the documents. And there is this." Disraeli took the box, holding it at the corners by his fingertips, and, almost reverentially, lifted it up to the light.

An inch and a half square, it resembled a thruppenny snuff box. It looked a little odd, however. The wood was dark brown, almost black, with a smoothness which suggested age rather than polish. There were no discernible grooves to hint at a lid.

"What is it?"

"You will be staying in the Paris Residence with Monsieur Eugène Spuller, the minister for foreign affairs. At some point in your stay, you must deposit this in his chamber."

Fisher looked closer at the box. "Why?"

"That is something you do not need to know," Disraeli said, and offered it to him.

"And what do I do afterwards?" As he took it he felt its weight shifting, as if it held liquid.

"Nothing whatsoever. Just place it in the room, preferably somewhere unnoticeable. Mention it to no-one, complete your task, and return home."

He lifted it to the light, holding it as the Prime Minister had.

"You need not be so delicate, Mister Fisher," Disraeli said.

"Martin Fisher is observing the reverence owed," the Queen's voice said, inside his head. "Complete this task, Martin Fisher, and you will be rewarded. We will not forget your service. We never forget."

• • •

It was the first time Fisher had been on an airship. It was more turbulent than he anticipated, the gondola swung heavily below the balloon as the winds buffeted the ship across the Channel.

At first, he had been disappointed to be travelling at night. It would have been nice to see England from the air. From up here, he could have pretended it was still the country he grew up in. Instead he screwed his eyes closed and forced an image of the match seller into his mind. This was no longer his home, and he would be damned if he would have a part in its future. He kept his eyes closed, only opening them as the sun dawned, when the pilot finally announced their descent.

Where London sprawled, Paris seemed to have grown organically out from a central point, like tree roots. Where London was smothered in perpetual fog, the air here was clear, showing every building and every person walking its streets in fine contrast. As his ship slipped towards the airdocks at Montmatre, the strength of the French army stood to attention, arranged in regimented blocks, ready to greet his delegation of one.

The airship was directed to dock at the lowest port in the tower, and he felt sure this was to give him more time to gaze over the France's might. At the lift's exit, he was met with a corridor of bayonets. Entire regiments bordered a red carpet at the dock's entrance, leading him to his host. The walk took several minutes, past row after row of stone-faced soldiers resplendent in sky blue.

But he kept his gaze on the end of the carpet. At first, he thought they were two small fortresses, strangely rounded against the angular architecture of the city, lined with crenulations and spiked with long-barrelled rifles. It was not until he saw the immense cannons that he realised what he was looking at.

"Earthmovers," he whispered. The silent threat France had held against Britain for nearly a century, there for him to see. *Two* of them. He wished he had time to look more closely, to see how they had negotiated the winding streets of Paris, but he was at the carpet's end, facing a smiling man with an outstretched hand.

"Monsieur Fisher?"

"I am, sir." He took the hand, shaking firmly. "And you would be Monsieur Spuller."

"Just so. Welcome to France." Spuller opened his arms—in essence a welcome, but with a sweep which took in the armed forces surrounding them. Fisher took heart at the power of the country he intended to call on for asylum.

• • •

Fisher allowed the rest of the morning to unfold as it would, and Spuller seemed to take pleasure in acting the guide. The minister showed him each regiment on the airdock grounds, one after the other, and then took him on a walking tour of the streets.

It was disconcerting at first, seeing so many people out and about, smiling and talking openly. He heard unrestrained laughter for the first time in a year, and struggled to keep the tears from his eyes.

"Are you enjoying yourself, Monsieur?" It was not the first time Spuller had asked.

"Very much so, sir. There is something I would like to know, however. Were those Earthmovers I saw before?"

Spuller looked blank for a moment, then laughed. "*Les Trembleterres*? Indeed, you are quite correct. They have been brought out of retirement. There has been much advancement in weaponry since they were last used. You understand, Monsieur Fisher, your Empress has not shown the best of faith in her dealings with Europe, and we must move to defend ourselves."

"Very understandable, sir. However, I would suggest that perhaps attacks from the air would be more effective." He stopped and looked into his host's eyes. His words were treason. Aiding a foreign power, even through intelligence, was a capital crime. Spuller could not have missed his intent, and Fisher was elated to see a twinkle in the man's eye.

"We had thought so too. Have no fear in that regard. The privateers of the Alps have aligned themselves with our cause. Should it come to it, we will dominate the skies as we will the land."

The pirates of the Swiss Alps! Hope flared. If France had truly managed to unite the unruly air captains under a common cause, they would be able to bomb England into submission. Up there, in the sky, *They* had no reach. Fisher felt a smile steal over him.

"Ah, but look at the time, Monsieur. You must be famished! Let us retire to my residence, where we can speak privately."

"I would like that very much, sir."

• • •

Dinner was luxury itself. Beef in a delicate sauce, served with vegetables cooked in way he'd never known was possible, washed down with a heady red wine. Fisher found himself in pleasant company. The group consisted of Monsieur Spuller and his charming wife, along with two Generals—introduced as Henri de Bonne and Laurent de Chaillou—and a Captain Johann Schneider, who did not wear the blue uniform of the Generals.

They sat around the dinner table, behind empty plates and full glasses. Madame Spuller had retired to another room, and Fisher allowed himself to relax in an easy atmosphere he'd forgotten could exist. General de Bonne was finishing the tale of a smuggler band he had once chased, and had everyone belly-laughing at how his troops had marched past the same barn three times without realising the men they hunted were inside.

Spuller seemed particularly taken by the tale, more than once begging the General to stop while he wiped a tear from his eye. "Please, General, you will make me cry!"

Fisher noted that Captain Schneider had not joined in with the laughter. "You did not enjoy the General's story, sir?"

Schneider offered him a brief smile. "I have heard it before, Monsieur."

"Yes, our General is a famous story teller," said Spuller. He collected himself. "I am afraid we must speak of more sober things, Monsieurs." He placed his hand on the file Fisher had presented earlier. "I have yet to read your proposals, Monsieur Fisher. However, I believe I can guess with some accuracy what they will be, and I am afraid we will not be able to accept them."

Fisher had come to the same realisation during the day, and welcomed it. He had made up his mind. All that was left was finding the correct way in which to make his request. "The Queen will be saddened to hear that, sir."

"And will it be you who delivers this sad news?" asked Captain Schneider.

Fisher found himself disliking the way Schneider had leaned in as he spoke. The Captain had remained distant through the evening, up 'til now. "Perhaps," he said. "What will your role be, Captain?"

"Oh, nothing grand. I am a delegate for the other captains in Switzerland."

"Captain Schneider is here as spokesman for the allied Swiss air captains, Monsieur Fisher," said Spuller.

Fisher felt a sudden warmth towards the Swiss man. "Then I must express my honour at meeting you, sir. You head a formidable force. And perhaps this is an opportune time to ask you something, monsieur Spuller. You see . . . "

Without conscious awareness of reason, he turned to back Schneider, as all the other eyes around the table were on him. The Swiss Captain opened his mouth. There, in the darkness, he saw something move, too thin, too grey to be a tongue. It darted forward quickly, barely protruding from his lips, and flapped briefly in the air as if to taste it. Captain Schneider's mouth closed, and it was gone—taking with it Fisher's moment, his body heat, and all the hope he had left in the world.

"Oui, monsieur?" said Spuller.

"Er." Fisher could not take his eyes from Schneider, who smiled in a way that made him shiver. "Er, where . . . Where is your toilet, sir?"

• • •

Fisher rolled the box over in his hands, feeling the cold emanate from it in clammy waves. He still did not see what it could be, but he understood that it would tip the balance of history. He closed his eyes, and sighed. He had been a fool to think he could run. He knew now with absolute certainty that his kind were no longer masters of their own destiny. One man could not hope to stand in *Their* way. God help him—any god left—he dared not face them as an enemy.

He realised that he'd been standing outside Spuller's bed chamber for too long. The others would come and look for him soon. He twisted the handle, both relieved and revolted that it wasn't locked, and walked in. He purposefully avoided looking at the hints of female occupancy—the scarves hanging from the hat stand, the tiny perfume bottles on the dresser—and walked to the bed. As carefully as he dared, placed the box on the floor and pushed it beneath.

Disgusted with himself, he turned and left, pausing at the door as he heard something hollow, something *wooden*, tip onto floorboards. He did not want to look. He wanted nothing more than to close the door, go home, and slip into a sleep from which, if there was any mercy left in the world, he would never wake up. But something beyond his control, some base human urge to know, turned him. Beneath the bed the box lay in two halves. The hollow sides were open to the world. A viscous slick led away into the shadows beneath the bed.

• • •

The alliance with France was greeted with cheers across London. Street parties were allowed as France reopened its embassy in Knightsbridge. Whitehall took the opportunity to announce the joint Anglo-French war on Spain and Prussia, while Austria-Hungary ended its policy of neutrality to join the alliance, after a visit from a French delegation.

Martin Fisher rested his head on the inn's faithful table, gently rattling the empty bottles surrounding him. The Queen had been true to her word. She had offered him anything he wanted, and he had asked to be free. He walked from the Palace no longer an Officer of the Agency. He bore no delusions. His liberty was nothing more than a thinly-draped disguise. It was less than a day before he saw the bare-faced man in the street, standing within a flag-waving crowd, watching him with an awful patience.

They would come for him, and he found that he no longer cared.

•••••••••••

ESCAPEMENT

STEPHANIE GUNN

In the darkness, three things are constant:

The ticking of my clockwork Heart.

The twenty-two scars that encircle my right forearm.

The one hundred and four small, straight scars on my legs.

Each one of these scars, circle and line alike, was made by a Mother, her crescent knife cold as she made the practiced cut, her fingers colder as she rubbed ash into the new wound to ensure a keloid scar.

The scars on my arm mark the number of sun cycles I have survived. The scars on my legs, the moon cycles I have failed.

I sit here in the darkness, run my fingers over my arms, my legs, counting the scars that mark off my life. Listen to the ticking of my Heart.

I wait.

• • •

I was born with smooth planes of bone where my eyes should have been. I should have died, the way so many other babes born in the outer City die at birth. I did not. Even at a day old, the Mothers said, I appeared to see, my not-eyes following them as they moved around the room. Later, when I learned to walk, I never stumbled, even when they deliberately placed obstacles in my path.

I "see" the world as shadows. People are what I think of as light and colour. Each one is a unique shape, and in all, there are shadows within the light. In my sister, Eight, there is a shadow where her right leg should be, more shadows clustered within the cage of her ribs. In the seeing world, these shadows are a twisted leg and stunted lungs that make her wheeze when she walks.

If I could see myself, I know there would be shadows where my eyes should be. Perhaps there are more hidden inside where I cannot see, missing pieces that I do yet know.

We are all made of missing pieces, outside the Wall. None of us is whole.

• • •

All Sisters have a flat metal plate set flush against the skin between our breasts, anchored to the bone with screws. They are fixed there when we first bleed, our clockwork Hearts slotted onto the plate. From then on, the Heart will tick away every moment of our moon cycles.

Each morning, the Mothers make the rounds of the Dormitories, wind our Hearts with the heavy key they wear chained around their waist. There are ticking things beneath the Mothers' robes; I do not know their name or function.

The Mothers remind us, as they wind our Hearts, that if the clockwork winds down, our flesh hearts will fail.

The ticking of my Heart is so loud sometimes in the darkness of the Dormitory that often I forget that those gears and cogs don't actually drive the flow of blood around my body. That I have another heart at all.

• • •

I wore thirteen scars on my arm the first time the Fathers visited me.

Eight and I had begun our moon cycles at the same time, and we linked hands as we joined the Sisters moving towards the Moon House. She leaned heavily on me to compensate for her twisted leg, and by the time we entered the long hall, her breath came hard. We chose adjacent beds, lay down.

The only sounds I could hear were the ticking of our Hearts and the shuffling of the Mothers' soft-soled boots as they moved down the rows of beds, checking Hearts, checking flesh.

Some Sisters were proclaimed ripe, and given a key from the pouch at the Mother's waist. More were bade to leave the Moon House; some wept as they scuttled out, while others were silent.

I turned my head as a Mother reached Eight's bed. I looked towards the City. The Angel and the Towers were denser shadows in my internal darkness. It was a comfort to me, even then, the fact that I could always "see" the Angel and the Towers, no matter how great the distance or how many physical walls stood between us.

The ticking from beneath the Mother's robe grew louder as she finished with Eight, and moved to my bed. The sound grew louder again when she folded the skirt of my dress up to my waist. It was cold in the Moon House, and goose pimples rose in waves on my skin. The Mother's hands were like ice as she parted my thighs, slid her fingers inside me.

She kept her hand there a moment, the ticking beneath her robe growing louder still. I kept my not-eyes on the Angel and the Towers. And, as I lay there, the Mother's fingers pressing hard into me, I saw a light flaring high on one of the Towers, a light brighter than anything else I had ever seen in the darkness. I started, half sitting up. The Mother pushed me back down, muttering sounds that she probably thought were placating. She removed her fingers, folded my skirt back down.

I kept my eyes on that light, trying to assign a name to it, a colour. It flared brighter, and I felt something warm gathering deep inside of me.

The Mother pressed a key into my hand, and the light vanished; only the deep dark of the Tower there again.

I curled my fingers around the key. It was larger and heavier than the ones the Mothers used to wind our Hearts, the metal warming quickly against my skin.

Eight reached out to me, drawing my attention away from the Tower. She also had a key in her hand.

•   •   •

The Fathers came to us.

The one who was assigned to my bed was what I thought of as blue, shadows crowding deep in his belly. He was gentle enough, and there was little pain, a thing I was grateful for. Eight was not so lucky; her Father was rougher, and she made small, twisted sounds with every thrust.

After, we laid still until the Mothers bade us rise. We unhooked our Hearts from our chest plates, slotted them into the clocks on the wall. As one, we used the keys we had been given to wind the clocks. As one, we lay back down.

We Sisters spent three moon cycles in the Moon House, rising from our beds in the mornings only to use the latrines and wind our clocks. The Mothers brought us nutrient wafers. The bars had a strange, earthen taste that lingered in my mouth long after I had swallowed the last bite.

If, with three moon cycles, we did not bleed, we progressed to the Sun House.

As the clocks ticked, other Sisters bled, and left. Soon, only Eight and I remained.

The night before we were moved to the Sun House, Eight slipped out of her bed and into mine, pressed something flat into my hand.

"It's a photograph," she said. "I know you can't see it, Nine, not the way you see everything else." She took my fingers in hers, traced them on the cool, smooth paper. "There is a man here. He's tall, with dark hair and eyes. Next to him is a woman. She's sitting up in bed, and she's dressed in white. Her hair is bright yellow, and she has something on her ears that glitters like water in the sun. She looks exhausted, but she's smiling. I've never seen someone with teeth so white. She's holding a baby in her arms, a beautiful, perfect thing wrapped up in a blue blanket. You can't see if all three are whole, but I think they must be. The baby, at least. Otherwise, why would she be smiling? The man is holding a tiny white thing. I don't know if it's food or a decoration, but on top of it is a flame."

"Flame? What is that?"

I heard her wave a hand through the air, as though searching for a description. "When you burn something, like in the recycling centre, you can feel the heat?"

I nodded.

"There's light that goes with that. Bright, gold and red, with blue at the very bottom. Sometimes it burns your eyes, too, so you keep seeing the flame, even after you've looked away." Eight turned the paper over, guided my hands over the rougher side. I could feel lines and swirls impressed there. "One of the workers told me what it was called, said that there were names written on the back."

"Names?"

"He said it's what people had, before the numbers." Eight traced her hand over the numbers embedded in the soft skin inside my left forearm. Mine are 120509, hers 120508, our nicknames arising from the last numbers. We are as close as Sisters can be. "He also said that there was another word he recognised. 'Family'."

"Family?" I asked. "What does that mean?"

"I'm not certain. When I went back to ask him, he was gone. Recycled, I suppose. He was old. Maybe family means happiness."

She let me hold the photograph a while longer before she fell asleep in my arms. She moved in her sleep, dreaming of the baby she would bear. I stared up at the shadow of the ceiling and thought of the strange words. Of *family*, of *flame*.

Of the light I had seen in the Tower. The brightest thing I had ever "seen".

From that moment on, I thought of it as the flame.

• • •

Our pains began on the same day, a fact that surprised neither Eight nor I.

The Mother who was tending us in the Sun House scuttled from bed to bed, bringing the scent of Eight's blood to me. We made no sound. This was not true pain; this was duty. This was how we served the City.

My child was born first. A daughter: her wailing loud in the Sun House. In my mind she was what I thought of as green, her colouring bright apart from slim shadows on the sides of her hands. When she curled her fingers around my thumb, I could feel the extra digit there, slender and wiry. I felt something warm spread behind my Heart. My daughter was as close to whole as anyone I had known. She would certainly be Chosen.

As Sisters, we were allowed only one chance to hold any viable children, to feed them with the rich birth milk. I held my daughter close, luxuriating in her warmth as she fed easily. I thought of the *photograph* that Eight had described, thought of that strange word, *family*.

I was so focused on my daughter that it took me long moments to realise that silence had fallen over the Sun House. I turned my head, saw the bundle of shadows that the Mother held. Eight's child was born twisted, dead.

That night, Eight burned the photograph. She never spoke of it again.

• • •

This is the world:

In the centre of everything, the Angel.

She stands in the centre of the inner City, watching over us all. Surrounding the Angel are the four Towers, the homes of the Chosen. They are the ones born whole and pure, the ones the outer City serves.

Around the inner City is the Wall. It is tall, broken only by four gates, one at each point of the compass. Outside the Wall, the outer City. Our buildings crowd close to the Wall. Many, I do not know the function of. I do not need to know. A Sister's life revolves around three only: the Dormitory, the Moon and Sun Houses.

Around the outer City, there is no wall. There is no need for one. Beyond us, there is only emptiness.

The Mothers describe the City as a machine, a great conglomeration of gears and cogs that circle around and around, everything centred on the Angel.

She watches over us, and she waits for the day when all of our sons and daughters will be born pure and whole, will be Chosen.

• • •

Eight told me once, before the first time we were visited by the Fathers, that the Angel was gold, the tall column she stands on black. In the morning light, Eight had said, the Angel gleams brighter than the sun. It was the only time that I had envied Eight's true sight.

The morning after my daughter's birth, I was roused early by a Mother. The Mother led me to the Wall, where together we waited for the gate to open. The baby mewled, pawed at my aching breasts. I wrapped her tighter, knowing that her hunger would not last long. In the Towers, she would be given food far superior to my thin milk.

The sound of grinding gears and cogs came from inside the Wall, and the gate rolled open. The air that moved over us was warm and scented with metal and oil, smothering the flesh and earth scent of the outer City. The Mother bent to bless the child, a ritual murmur, and then stood back to let me enter the inner City.

The tall shadows of the Towers rose before me as I approached the centre of the inner City. There were other buildings between them, low and long. I had never heard them spoken of. Knowing the Mother was watching me, I dared only a few quick glances at the buildings. No lights to be seen. No flame.

Then, as now, there is only a short span of time in which the gates were allowed to open, a cool sliver in between night and day. I hurried, knowing that I had to be back outside the Wall before the gate closed again. To be caught within was forbidden. The inner City was no place for the likes of me.

It *was* a place for my daughter. I approached the Angel, stepping around so I was on the opposite side to the gate I had entered. My daughter writhed, her arms working free again and reaching for my breasts.

"Reach out to the Angel," I whispered to her. "Not to me."

I looked up at the Angel. To my not-eyes she was a shadow, a suggestion of outstretched wings. Something twisted behind my Heart, and I realised that I had been hoping for some miracle, that I would be able to truly see the Angel.

My daughter's wailing increased in volume when I laid her down at the base of the column. I held out my hand, and she grasped at my finger, drew it into her mouth and sucked. In my darkness, her fingers were pale green, but for the shadow of the extra sixth.

"They'll fix your hands," I said. "The Mothers said it would be simple in the Towers. You will be Chosen."

The baby sucked harder, pulling half of my finger into her warm mouth. Around me, the inner City was silent and still.

I knelt down, pulled back a fold of the swaddling, laid my ear on my daughter's chest, listened the beating of her flesh heart.

A moment only I allowed myself, and then I left her there beneath the Angel. As I walked back to the gate I was aware of the ticking of my Heart beginning to slow, its winding overdue.

I left her behind, but ever after, I held the memory of her heart close. Regular and strong was its beat, a clock that would never need to be wound.

• • •

Twelve sun cycles passed.

When ripe, I would go to the Moon House and lie beneath a Father.

Most cycles, I conceived. But after that first time, I never progressed to the Sun House. Always, before three moon cycles, I bled.

In this time, Eight bore a half dozen babies. All were born early. All were born dead.

After the first time, we never held hands on the way to the Moon House again.

• • •

The Father shuddered as he spilled his seed in me. He kept his face turned away from my not-eyes as he lifted away.

When all of the Fathers had left, we lay still. Our Hearts fell into synchronisation with each other, then out again. There were only six of us this time, the smallest group of Sisters I had ever entered the Moon House with.

When the Mothers bade us, we rose, unhooked our Hearts and placed them in the clocks, wound them up. Mechanisms groaned as Hearts and clocks meshed and began to tick as one.

I pressed my fingers against the clock, feeling the vibrations of the mechanism moving through my skin. I had grown familiar with the Moon House clocks over the sun cycles. As my Heart ticks off my moon cycle, the larger clock ticks off a cycle of weeks. With each revolution of the clock's hands, one week passes, and one crescent-shaped marker emerges from the edge of the clock.

As always, without my Heart, I felt strange. Unanchored, unreal. The Mothers assure us that the Moon and Sun Houses can sustain us without our Hearts. So long as we stay within their walls, we are safe, and our flesh hearts will continue to beat.

• • •

The weeks passed. Each morning, we wound our clocks, used the latrines, consumed our nutrient wafers.

One by one, the other Sisters began to bleed. I smelled the copper of their blood, listened to them remove their Hearts from the clocks. The clocks, unwound, slowed and slowed, and finally stopped.

Finally, only I remained.

For the first time since my daughter, I progressed to the Sun House.

• • •

Only one bed in the Sun House creaked beneath the weight of a Sister. I chose the neighbouring bed, pressed my Heart into the clock above. The clocks were larger here, with two dials. The smaller one ticks away the weeks, the larger moves with the moon cycles. The crescents around the edge mark off the latter. As I wound the clock, a crescent clicked out, some arcane machinery inside recognising the revolutions made in the Moon House.

I lay back down, aware of the Sister in the other bed watching me.

"Nine," she said, her voice breathless from the baby crowding her lungs.

"Eight?"

She nodded, the shadows coiling in her skull shifting with the movement. It had been over a sun cycle since I had seen her up close, our cycles out of sync. In that time, shadow had eaten at the long bones of her arms and legs, curved like a cupped hand beneath her left breast.

I pulled my blanket over my legs, forced a smile. "How long do you have?"

She touched the sheet stretched taut over her belly, skin moving against cotton with a ragged whisper. "Only one moon cycle. The Mothers think that he could be whole. The first whole child born outside the City since the War." The shadows in her face twisted as she smiled. "I think it's happening. We're all becoming Chosen."

"He? You think it's a boy?"

"A feeling. A mother's knowledge."

I thought of my own daughter, given to the Angel. She would be almost a woman now. If mothers had some esoteric sense of their children, then I should know where she was, what she was doing. When I searched my world for her, I saw nothing but darkness.

Turning over, I curled my legs up. I could see nothing within myself. I pressed my fingers to my stomach, the flesh softening now from the rich nutrient bars, and wondered what was growing there.

• • •

The day the second crescent appeared at the edge of my clock, Eight's pains began.

Mothers came and went. Day turned to night, and then day again. The black, clotted stench of old blood filled the room.

After the second night, they brought the knife.

There was no light, no colour to the thing sliced from Eight's womb. Just dense, fisted shadow.

• • •

The Mother who came the next morning told me that Eight had volunteered for recycling. The nutrient wafers she brought me tasted like blood, like bone.

• • •

A moon cycle later, I woke in the dead of night to find my sheets heavy with blood.

I stood, wrapped my blanket around me. I did not bother to staunch the flow of blood. The floor of the Sun House had seen enough blood in its time, what would a few more drops matter?

On the threshold, I paused. Behind me, I heard a click as another crescent emerged from the clock above my bed. My Heart was still connected to the clock, the plate on my chest empty.

And then I saw it: the flame. High on the same Tower again, burning more brightly than I had remembered.

I stepped outside without conscious thought, focused only on the flame. My flesh heartbeat was erratic, but my heart was still beating. Without my clockwork Heart, I was still alive.

I watched the flame until a Mother found me kneeling on blood-soaked earth. She led me into the chapel, sponged the blood from my thighs. Sliced with her crescent knife, rubbed ash into the wound. Watched as I removed my Heart from the clock, returned it to my chest.

I had been lucky, the Mother said. Another few minutes outside without my Heart, and my flesh heart would have failed. Lucky I had stayed so close to the Sun House.

When I went outside again, the flame was gone. I rubbed at my bandaged thigh, knowing that there was little space left for more scars.

• • •

For two moon cycles, I waited. Twice, my own blood puddled useless and thin between my thighs. Then, finally, I was allowed to join the other ripe Sisters in the Moon House.

If I could have, I would have closed my eyes against both light and shadows. And if I had possessed true eyes, they would have flown open as the last Father entered the hall. For he shone with bright, perfect light, a flame walking in the shape of a man.

He burned so bright that he dimmed the other Fathers almost entirely. And I realised, as he walked down the beds, why it was that he was so bright.

He was whole.

He affected a limp, and I could tell by the shape of his light that he had one arm bound close to his body. Despite the binding, there were no shadows there, no missing pieces.

He paused at the foot of my bed, but a Mother came up, the ticking loud beneath her robe, and ushered him on to another Sister.

I wanted to push away the Father who came to me. Wanted to tell him to stop, even as his movements became more frantic, his seed spilling.

For the first time in my life, I willed my blood to come early.

• • •

I hurried along, shivering lightly in my thin robe. I worried my thumb against the newest scar on my thigh, worrying at the edges of it until the skin opened, began to bleed again.

All of the other Sisters and Mothers had been sleeping deeply when I had slipped out of the Dormitory. None of them had seen me go.

I didn't even know where I was going, not really. I just knew that I'd needed to get out of there.

Was I looking for the flaming man? I didn't know. I did know that I shouldn't have been surprised to find myself at the Wall. I leaned against the cool stone, listened to the machinery within click and groan. The gate nearby opened, warm air moving like breath against my skin.

And then I heard something else. Hidden beneath the sound of mechanics was the unmistakable sound of a weeping child.

"Hello?" I asked.

The weeping broke off abruptly.

"They will not speak back," a voice said from behind me.

I turned. Standing there was the flaming man. I stiffened, then fell quickly into a posture of obedience: head bowed, hands clasped. "The Mothers sent me on an errand, Father," I lied.

"You're a Sister. You don't get sent anywhere but to the Moon and Sun Houses." He pronounced the words strangely, as though they fit ill in his mouth.

I groped for another lie. "I . . . "

"It's okay. I'm not going to report you." His flames flickered, narrowed. "You can see me somehow, can't you? Even though you don't have any eyes."

"I can hear well."

He laughed. "What's your name?"

"Name?" The almost unfamiliar word brought with it a memory of Eight's photograph: ashes, now, as she was.

His light tightened, curled in upon itself. "I forgot. They don't give you names, just numbers."

I looked up at him then. His arm was bound again, but he was still undoubtedly whole. And I knew, then, that he shouldn't be there either, that he was hiding something more than just his wholeness. "There was someone who called me Nine. For the last number." I held out my arm, displaying my numbers.

"Other people wore numbers once," he said, his voice quiet. "That ended, too." He cleared his throat. "My name is Nataneal."

"Nataneal." I repeated the name slowly, its syllables like broken stone in my mouth. "You don't have a number?"

He paused, then slid his bound arm free. He grasped my hand, pressed my fingers against the inside of his left arm. There were numbers there, but they were warm, not cool as mine were.

"They're false," I said. "Who *are* you?"

"Who are *you*, Nine?" He slid his arm back into its binding. "How do I know that you're not going to run back and report me?"

I pressed my hands together. My skin was warm from contact with his numbers.

"If you are going to report me, do it now," Nataneal said. "Otherwise, I will be here again this time tomorrow."

In the Wall behind me, the gate machinery groaned, the gate sliding closed with a thud.

"If you come tomorrow, I'll tell you about the weeping child."

He left me alone there, his flame vanishing into the shadows hanging low over the outer City.

After a time, the child began to weep again.

• • •

That night, I dreamed of two heartbeats. They threaded together, falling into synchronisation, then moving in counterpoint, creating a strange and beautiful music.

• • •

The next morning, Nataneal was waiting for me at the Wall.

"You didn't report me," he said as I approached him.

"Is it that good?" I asked. "Your deception? A limp and a bound arm?"

His flame swirled, moving into almost geometric shapes. "No one looks closely. Out here, people barely look at each other at all. You're the only one who's looked at me directly. You saw me." He slid his arm out of its binding, straightened his spine. "How did you know?"

I pulled my shawl tighter around my shoulders. "You said you would tell me about the weeping child. Is it some trick of the machinery making that sound?"

"It is no trick."

We walked slowly along the Wall. The air grew warmer as we moved, and I knew that the gate was open.

Nataneal's light swirled for a moment, and then he turned to the Wall. I heard the grinding of stone against stone, then the sound of something heavy meeting the ground. Nataneal's hand pressed against mine. I felt the beat of his heart beneath his skin before he moved his fingers down to my wrist, lifted my hand towards the Wall.

I expected cold stone, and it took me a moment to realise that he was moving my hand further than it should have gone, that my hand was moving into the Wall itself. He kept his thumb pressed against my wrist for a moment, then his hand slid away.

"Be silent and still," he whispered. "Wait."

My Heart ticked a dozen times, and then I felt something brush my fingers. I stiffened, thinking of the machinery, but realised quickly that what I touched wasn't cold metal, but warm and soft. Fingers, small and crusted, but alive. They curled around mine, probed into the cup of my palm, then fell away. The soft sound of weeping rose. I breathed in, tasted thick, fetid air.

"There's a child in there," I said. "There's a child in the Wall."

Nataneal pulled my hand back. When I lifted my fingers, I smelled old blood, unwashed skin, darker things.

"A girl child," Nataneal said. "Perhaps five or six sun cycles, small for her age."

"We have to let her out!" I grasped at the edge of the hole, my nails scratching at the mortar. "Where is the door?"

"There is no door."

I ran my hands across the Wall, searching. "There has to be! How else did she get in there?"

Nataneal withdrew a nutrient wafer from his pocket. By its scent, it was one of the richer ones from the Sun House. He handed it through the hole, then slid the stone back into place.

"They lower the child in through a small trap at the top of the Wall" he said, his voice flat. "It's done as soon as the child is old enough to understand the process of operating the gate. It's quite simple, just the pressing of a few levers, turning a wheel. Most are lowered in when they are three sun cycles or so. Once a week, someone comes to supply them with nutrient wafers, take away their wastes. When they remember, of course. Sometimes it takes weeks before someone notices that the gates haven't opened. The gates are not a priority for the City." He smoothed a hand over the loose stone. "It took us many moon cycles to loosen this stone. It was the first one, back when the Walled children were just rumours."

"Children? There's more than one?"

"Two per gate, one at each side. Four gates, eight children. None of them last long, of course. Some go mad, scratch at their own throats and wrists until they bleed out. Some try to climb back up to the trap, not realising it cannot be opened from within. I heard of one who reached eight sun cycles before he grew too large for the space in the Wall and slowly suffocated. It doesn't matter to the City, of course. There's always new children, and it's a simple matter to reach in with long tools, slice the dead child into parts and draw them out one by one."

My flesh heart was thudding against the plate between my breasts, hard enough that I thought I should hear it. I didn't want to ask the question, knew that I had to. "Where do the children come from?"

"You and your Sisters breed them for the City. You leave them in the shadow of the Angel."

I bent over and retched. The thin bile that came up tasted like copper, like ash.

When I was done, I sank to my knees, pressed my forehead against the Wall. After a moment, Nataneal sat next to me, close enough that I could hear the thudding of his heart even over the ticking of my clockwork Heart.

"This is how the City runs," Nataneal said. "Once, before all this, they harnessed sparks in a different, forgotten fashion to run the machines, to illuminate, to pump water, to raise the gates. Now, Walled children control the gates, and belowground, children pump the bellows running the engines to move wastes along the pipes. There are steam engines on the Towers, but even there, children must climb to maintain them."

I looked up at the Towers, tried to gauge their height. Tried to imagine being that high. Vertigo clutched at me.

"There are no ropes, nothing to keep the children safe," Nataneal continued. "The children climb the cage holding the pipes and pumps. Many fall."

"I gave a child to the Angel," I said. "Twelve sun cycles ago. She was as close to whole as I have seen. They said that she would be Chosen, she would enter the Towers."

"They lied. No one has ever entered the Towers from outside."

I looked at his wholeness anew. "And has anyone come out?"

His light swirled, moved into that geometric pattern again. "I was one of the Chosen," he said. I smelled salt on the air. "They lie to us, too, Nine. They tell us that no one remains outside the Towers, that the world was blasted away by the War. They tell us that we are waiting until the world is safe enough for us to go outside again. They tell us nothing, except in the vaguest terms, and no one thinks to ask."

"Why are you telling me this?"

"Because you looked. Because you saw. Because we need you."

"We?"

"The revolution." He pressed his hand to mine briefly; I felt the fluttering of his pulse. "We should get back before anyone notices we're missing."

I pressed my hand against the Wall once more, let him lead me back.

• • •

This is the true world, as Nataneal told me:

The Angel stands in the centre of the inner City, the four Towers around her. The tall, black buildings are caged with brass, surrounded by pumps and pipes to bring water to those who live within, to remove wastes. Steam engines power these networks; larger engines at the base of each Tower provide power for everything else. All of these networks and engines are maintained by children who live in the low, grey Dormitories which squat between the Towers.

Over time, the children are affected by what Nataneal calls radiation. When they are too sick to work aboveground, they are sent below, to pump the bellows driving the pumps of the waste systems. The bellows are pumped around the clock, and once a child is sent belowground, they never see the sun again.

There are the Walled children, too, and probably others running systems that Nataneal didn't know about.

Within the radiation-shielded Towers, selective breeding maintains genetic purity. All are subjected to regular screening to ensure their own Chosen state.

All of the children of the Towers are educated, but none are told the truth.

Most do not question. But there are those who have, and they are working together inside to bring the truth to light, to free those born to slavery both within and without the Towers. Nataneal is one of the first to discover a way outside, but he will not be the last.

• • •

The Mother's fingers tore into me. I clenched against her, wanting to force her out.

She leaned over to check my Heart, her fingers still inside me, pushing harder. The ticking beneath her robes jarred and skipped. "There is no room for any more scars, Sister. This cycle will be your last."

She pulled her fingers out roughly, pressed a key into my hand. The metal was cold, and did not warm against my skin.

• • •

That night I lay awake in the Moon House, listening to the ticking of Hearts in the hall. I laid my fingers next to the plate set over my sternum, felt the beating of my flesh heart.

My fingers moved across the plate, found the empty socket where it intersected with my Heart. The Mothers told us that if we removed our Hearts outside the Moon or Sun Houses, we would die.

The Mothers said my daughter would be Chosen.

The Mothers said.

Nataneal was lied to. How much of what the Mothers said to us was a lie?

I slid my feet out of bed, the stone floor cold beneath my soles. The room smelled like sour sweat, like seed. There was a hint of a darker thing, too, a scent that put me in mind of the Walled child. *Death.*

It was death that I smelled. Their death, and mine.

I pushed the door open, and, Heartless, I stepped outside.

One step, two, and my own flesh heart continued to beat. Faster now, but steady, my blood pounding in my ears.

Three steps, four and I was running, *flying*, searching the houses and halls for Nataneal's flame.

• • •

In the end, he found me, his flame appearing from out of a small building leaning against the back of one of the men's halls.

His hands closed over my arms. "Nine, what is it? Are you well?" His fingers touched my empty Heart plate. "Did they . . . ?"

I shook my head. "They lied to us. They said that we'd die, but it does nothing. It doesn't keep us alive. It *controls* us." I paused. "How much else have they lied about?"

I saw his frown as a swirling in his flame. "You should come inside. It is safe in here."

He drew me into the building, and the world went away. I stumbled, and was glad for his hands on mine. Without that touch, I would have thought myself suspended in nothing. Even his flame was gone.

"You can see it, can't you?" he asked. "It's something like what they use to shield the Towers. It blocks most electromagnetic radiation, most sound as well."

He guided my hand to the wall. It felt smooth and slightly warm, like skin with no pores or hairs. I realised, too, that there was a steady ticking in the room. The sound of clockwork.

"It requires energy to pass through it constantly," he continued. "It's a simple engine, made by a member of the resistance."

"It's strange, not being able to see you," I said. I hesitated, then reached up, pressed my hand to his face, tracing the curve of his jaw and cheek. I encountered dampness; I touched my fingers to my lips and tasted salt. "The Mother said this cycle was my last chance. If I do not produce a child, I will be recycled."

"Recycled?"

I touched his face again, felt the shape of his frown. "They recycle our bodies when we are no longer useful to the City in any other way. And make us useful again, as much as they can." He was still frowning. "The nutrient wafers."

He swallowed hard. "And I always though the filtered water in the Towers was bad. Oh, Nine, what you have all lived."

His arms came around me then, pulling me close. I laid my cheek against his sternum, listened to his heartbeat, aware of my own synchronising with it.

"We have been doing testing, as much as we can out here," he said, his voice resonating within his chest. "Few, if any, of the Fathers possess fertile seed. There has been too much contamination, too much radiation." He swallowed again. "But I . . . "

I pulled back, just enough to be able to touch his face again. His eyes were closed, his lashes damp. "You have been kept shielded for most of your life," I said. "Your seed should be strong. If my fault in bearing lies with the Fathers . . . " I trailed off, unable to finish the thought.

"I wouldn't . . . I couldn't . . . " His eyes opened, and I knew he was looking directly at where my own eyes should be. "You have been forced enough."

It was my turn to swallow. "In the Towers, if people want to, how do they start?"

He smiled. "They kiss."

"Kiss? What is that?"

His smile widened, and I realised how young he was. At least a half dozen sun cycles less than me, probably more. "I'll show you."

And he did.

• • •

Afterwards, I knew that I carried a daughter.

I felt her flame within me, and though I could not see her, I knew also that she bore two shadows where her eyes should be. She would see the world as I did, my gift to her.

I was the only Sister moved to the Sun House. Inside, everything smelled like blood and death, and the rich nutrient wafers they brought reminded me of the Walled child. I pressed my fingers into my belly, thought of my daughters.

Nataneal was always nearby, his flame visible to me through the walls. I watched him talking to others, watched other bright flames join his, knew they were putting their plans into motion. And I began to hear words from outside the hall, repeated often, like a prayer: *When the Angel flies, we will all be free.*

When I could slip out in the early mornings, I met him at the Wall, brought nutrient wafers to the children.

One morning he met me with a bundle of cloth in his hand. He unfolded it, moved my hand to trace the shape of what lay there. Two small clockwork mechanisms, a meshwork of cogs and gears that vibrated at my touch.

Nataneal lifted one of the mechanisms and pressed it to my not-eye. The gears shivered, and I felt the teeth of cogs pressing into my skin, seeking purchase. Small points of pain flared, and for a moment, I saw Nataneal's face. He was beautiful, his eyes a bright, clear colour that I could not name.

The gears shivered again, and the mechanism fell away, leaving me in my darkness again.

Nataneal caught it neatly. "These are only a prototype. They can be modified."

I pressed my hand over his. The metal was warm between us. "I've seen all I need to. And you have beautiful eyes." I rose up on my toes to kiss him, then pressed our joined hands to my stomach. The clockwork eye shivered again. "I think our daughter will need them more, if she is to walk in two worlds."

"She will change everything." Nataneal pulled me close. "Things are moving quickly. Seeds are growing in the outer and inner Cities."

"'When the Angel flies, you will all be free'?" I asked. "I hear them chanting it outside the Sun House."

"We're painting it, too, anywhere we can. They remove the words, but we simply paint them again." He kissed the top of my head. "Before, things would have been so different. We would live together in a house, raise our children together. Sleep in the same bed every night. There would be no Mothers, no Towers. Just us."

"Maybe it can be that way again."

He was silent for a long time. "Maybe."

• • •

• • •

When my pains began, I was alone. It was night, and none of the Mothers would be due to enter the Sun House until morning. I thanked the Angel for that small mercy.

Beneath my mattress were the clockwork eyes. Their vibrations had comforted me through many sleepless nights, my daughter always turning in my womb, hands pressing out, reaching for them. I slid the eyes out now, cupped them in my palm.

I went to Nat21neal's hidden place. He was awake, and waiting for me.

There, hidden from the City, our daughter was born.

She slipped into the world easily, and she did not cry. Nat21neal slid the clockwork eyes into her empty eye pits. A sound like blinking, and then I heard the gears tighten.

I felt her smile, felt her clockwork eyes move from her mother to her father. And we were a family.

Nat21neal produced a small curved knife. Not quite one of the Mothers' crescent knives, but not an ordinary knife, either. We cut her first arm scar ourselves, marking her birth.

• • •

Nat21neal called her Lucia. He said that it meant "light".

We remained in the hidden place as long as we could, curled in each other's arms as Lucia fed and slept and fed. If we could have, we would have stayed there forever. But nothing remains forever. Even the Angel, Nat21neal said, would fall to dust one day.

All I knew is that I wanted Lucia's life to be different to mine. I didn't want her to know the Moon and Sun Houses. I didn't want her to be Chosen. I wanted her to know a different world. One, that, perhaps, Nat21neal's revolution could begin.

So when someone knocked at the outside of our shelter and summoned Nat21neal, I was glad to let him go.

"The angel will fly," he said, kissing me, kissing Lucia. "The angel will fly, and we will all be free. Stay here. I will return."

• • •

It was an accident that undid us.

I'm not certain, even now, what it was that did it. Lucia's flailing hand as she fumbled for my breast, my own knee as I crouched to change her. But I know that the clockwork mechanism that sustained the warm skin that hid us from the City was broken. It ticked once, twice, sighed and was silent.

The light and shadow of the City flared into life in my inner vision. And for the first time, I "saw" my daughter. Brighter even than Nataneal, and flickering in an ever-changing spectrum of colours.

I held Lucia tight, unsure of what to do. There were other rebels hiding in the outer City, but I had no idea where they were. So I froze, and waited, and hoped that Nataneal would return.

It was the Mothers who came, the ticking beneath their robes filling the small space. Lucia began to cry.

They reached for us both, their hands like stone.

• • •

Even the Mothers, cruel as they were, could not bear to waste a living, almost whole human.

They gave me a choice. Lucia could have numbers set into her arm, could serve the City as I did. Or she could be given over to the Angel, a place found for her in the inner City.

I heard the things they did not say, and I chose the Angel. If they had given her numbers, they would have torn out her clockwork eyes, perhaps found some way to scar her inner sight, as well. No Father would ever want to look upon clockwork as they lay with her.

In the Angel's shadow, perhaps someone would take pity, let her keep her eyes.

And soon enough, the Angel was going to fly. And we would all be free and none of this would matter at all.

• • •

And so I entered the inner City again, passed through the gate opened by a Walled child. I called out softly as I passed, but there was no answer from within the Wall.

When I stepped into the square between the Towers and Dormitories, I stopped, my arms tightening around Lucia. For unlike last time, when the City had been still and dark, there was light and movement. A flash up in one of the Towers, bright as Nataneal's flame. And outside one of the Dormitories, a girl, her light shining green and blue and red. Almost whole, but for shadows wreathing her hands.

I smiled at her, allowing myself one moment only of thinking that she could be my older daughter. I wanted to go to her, see if the beating of her heart matched the one in my memory, but there was no time.

I crossed to the Angel, laid Lucia down in the shadow. Making certain that the Mother waiting at the gate could see me, I leant down, pressed my cheek to my daughter's chest, memorised her heartbeat.

• • •

They kept me alive afterwards. As punishment, perhaps, or as an example to others.

I was sent to haul water, to scrub floors, perform any menial task the Mothers could think of. I did whatever they said.

And I waited, the memories of three heartbeats dancing through my mind.

• • •

And so, sun cycles passed.

There were whispers, and occasionally I caught a glimpse of flame—of a whole person, a Chosen—flitting amongst the shadows of the outer City. I did not see Nataneal, but I heard his heartbeat always in my mind, and I knew that he lived. That he was working with the rebellion, seeking to free us all.

Then, one morning I awoke and saw his flame waiting at the Wall.

I slid from my bed, from the hall. No one stirred.

Nataneal's light was dull, eaten by shadows at the edges. When I wrapped my arms around him, I felt his bones pressing out against his skin.

I started to tell him about Lucia, but he pressed his fingers to my lips. "I know. It's the safest place for her. And I'm going to get her back." He kissed me quickly. "It's today, Nine. The Angel is going to fly today. We uncovered a cache of weapons, and we're going to use them to make her fly. And everyone will see, and they will know to rise up. And we will all be free, and we will be a family. You and me, and both of your daughters." He kissed me again, more gently this time. "Wait here, Nine. I will return."

I sat down, my back to the Wall. The cool brick warmed as the sun rose, then began to cool again.

I heard Nataneal's voice, amplified somehow: "When the Angel flies, we will all be free!"

The explosion, when it came, was quieter than I had expected it to be. Like something falling hard against soft sand, like the world inhaling. A moment later, a wave of heat prickled across my skin, and then, in the darkness behind my not-eyes, light flared. Pure white, it was brighter than anything I had ever seen, making even the flames of the Chosen seem dim. In the wake of the light came darkness, deep and thick and absolute.

I waited for my sense of the world to return, to be able to "see" the Wall, the Towers. There would be lights and colours, soon, too, as people saw the Angel fly and began to rise up.

Everything was black.

There were other sounds, short sharp barks that I could not identify. And then, only silence.

• • •

And so, I wait.

I run my fingers over the scars on my arms, on my legs, count them over and over. I listen to the ticking of my clockwork Heart. The night passes, and it begins to slow, the silence between ticks expanding.

Everything stays black. Everything stays silent.

Nataneal will return soon, and he will bring my daughters, and we will be a family, and we will be free.

I just have to wait.

• • • • • • • • • • •

THE BULLET AND THE FLESH

DAVID CONYERS AND DAVID KERNOT

Camouflaged in military issue fatigues overlaid with body armor, Harrison Peel sprinted with stealth along the savanna rise. Ahead, a Zimbabwean farmstead burned like a pagan bonfire in the reds and oranges of a pre-morning light. Dark columns of smoke twisted and contorted skywards. Flames licked like mad tongues from square holes where there had once been windows.

Up close, Peel crouched, gazed along the scope of the cocked M4A1 assault rifle on full automatic fire. He could smell blood, the aftermath of a killing almost unbearable in it obviousness. The scent of scorched petroleum was stronger.

Advancing, Peel discovered the first body. The well-dressed man in civilian clothes had been cut down by a volley of bullets, but the empty gun holster highlighted the victim was experienced in violence. The wounds in his chest were close together suggesting the work of professional soldiers.

Peel marched on, suspecting an ambush at any moment. Instead, he counted further bodies, two, three, four . . . all put down by precision gunplay. He identified a shiny shard of glass clutched in the hand of the fourth dead man, recognized it as a diamond of significant size. Not sure what to do with it, Peel pocketed it. Diamonds were the currency of a war-torn Africa, and this one had to be worth a hundred thousand US dollars or more.

Frantic movement, thrashing from under a pile of corrugated iron sheets startled him, unnatural sounds as if something wet and long shaped flipped on the earth under it. He imagined a survivor rolling in their own blood but the noise was all wrong.

Cautiously, terrified, Peel stepped toward the discarded metal.

In a bizarre circle around the shaking iron were more corpses. Unlike the other bodies there were no bullet wounds, rather death had been by dismemberment, flesh ripped from their bodies and scattered near and far. An arm here, a leg there, Peel identified a Zimbabwean National Army corporal chewed from the waist down, the lower part of him missing. It was as if he had been eaten.

None of the body parts moved as they should. The only sound came from a under the corrugated iron sheet. Whatever it was, it was rattled its cover and tried to remain hidden. It was too small to be a man. Perhaps a young child?

Peel raised his rifle when he heard another man run toward him from behind. He turned quickly, weapon leveled, and relaxed when he spied his field partner, Emerson Ash, who had approached the carnage from the opposite direction to Peel.

"All clear," Ash stated for the record. "I count three down, two ZNA soldiers and Abdul Farzi."

"Shit!" Peel nodded. The man they had come to extract was now a corpse. "Farzi you say?"

Ash nodded. "'fraid so."

This was bad news but in this moment Peel focused on securing their position. He trained his weapon back in the general direction of the iron that continued to rattle.

"Something still alive?" Ash pointed his M4A1 assault rifle on the iron and took a cautious step forward. He too was decked in dapple-green camouflage fatigues and body armor. Both men were former Australian Army soldiers—they knew how to run military ops by the books and could plan the basics of any tactical military operation in their sleep—but their roles in the current geopolitical environment were as covert operatives, field agents employed by global intelligence organizations. Different sides of the same coin, thought Peel.

The flopping wet shape wouldn't let up thrashing. It sounded increasingly to Peel like the death-throes of a snake with its head cut off, and tapped randomly against the curved iron shell covering it. It was too big to be a snake, too small to be a man. He didn't want to go near it, but he had to.

"Cover me," Peel said to Ash and edged forward cautiously, weapon raised and his eyes fixed on the view through the weapon's advanced combat optical gunsight. The sweat on his shaved head was almost unbearable as it rolled along his face and hung precariously off his nose and chin in an irritating way.

"Roger that," said Ash.

At the sheet, Peel kicked it over.

The shape *was* like a headless snake, but it was no snake. The thrashing thing became violent and aggressive now it had been exposed. It resembled a branch or a vine, a moss covered tentacle tapered at one end, shredded by bullets at the other, and lined with a dozen snapping, salivating mouths in place of branches. It thrashed like a whip at Peel, narrowly missing him, unable to gain purchase because whatever it had been attached to was long gone, but still very much alive and threatening.

Peel and Ash didn't hesitate, they released volley after volley of 5.56mm rounds into the mass until it was cut to pieces. Now it thrashed as smaller, less effective parts.

Yet the mouths still snapped and salivated.

Ash took a thermite grenade from his webbing and looked to Peel. "Fire in the hole?"

Peel nodded and they both moved backward from the threat. Ash lobbed the grenade and the two men sprinted. The galvanized iron and the creature detonated in a flash of heat, flames and debris, incinerating whatever it was they had discovered until it was no more.

"Did you smell petroleum?" Ash asked after the flames had died down.

Peel nodded and reloaded his weapon.

"I reckon the ZNA took out that farmstead with man-portable flamethrowers," said Ash. "I reckon that's what the petroleum smell is from."

"Maybe they used flamethrowers to put down the rest of this creature."

"Maybe."

They strode from the destroyed remnants of the farmstead and Peel admired the striking contrast as the sun rose above the distant rolling hills dappling the African savanna, the granite kopjes, and the wooded landscape in vibrant earthy colors. The landscape was pristine and unspoiled in comparison to what they had just witnessed.

Peel stopped at the top of the hill. "We were too late," he said, voice a low, barely audible growl. "I wanted Abdul Farzi in custody . . . before he gave up whatever weapon his was selling to the ZNA."

"We will have to find another way, Major," said Ash.

"I'm no longer a Major," said Peel.

"And I'm no longer *Sergeant* Ash, and yet here we are, sir."

Peel nodded, recognizing Ash's desire to revert to military protocol. This was a military field op and how things were done. "The weapon, did you see it?"

The former sergeant shrugged. "Nothing I recognized."

Peel paced, his frustration grew with each second they did nothing. "Intel said Farzi was selling a weapon of the ESB kind, an Extra-terrestrial Sentient Being. In other words, an alien horror like we just saw."

"Yes," Ash's eyes lit catching Peel's meaning. "You think we just found part of it?"

"Seems likely. So the buyer, Colonel Nambutu, has it? The rest of it?"

"I'm guessing so."

"And the blood is fresh."

"Also correct, sir."

Peel took in another quick scan of their surroundings. The landscape of undulating savanna woodlands, and low rolling hills and granite outcrops would be perfect for an ambush, and yet . . . Peel had an idea.

"Ready the Jeep, I'll be back in a minute."

"Roger that." Ash took off in a double march down the hill to where they had hidden their vehicle. Peel didn't wait and sprinted up a granite rise. He clambered onto the suspended layered boulders that were like pinnacles, and scared away the baboons who used the rocks for the same purpose he wanted, as a look out.

High on a rock, Peel scanned the savanna. It didn't take long to spot the dust trail of three Zimbabwean National Army troop trucks. He took their position and general direction, and scrambled back down to where Ash gunned their vehicle.

Peel clambered into the passenger seat and set his assault rifle down. "I've got him." He gave Ash the coordinates of Colonel Nambutu and the trucks, and they took off at breakneck speed along a dirt road.

Peel wiped the sweat from his head and remembered why they were here. It had started with an unexpected telephone conversation in London, then a National Security Agency briefing in Cyprus where Peel had met up with Ash, followed by a military flight direct to Francistown Airport in Botswana. After that the two had crossed into Zimbabwe illegally, because surprise was required, time was against them and their presence had to be deniable.

"Ash, tell me. The Cambodians develop a covert biological weapons program involving extracted alien matter from hell knows where. The Saudis buy it. They sell it to the Zimbabweans via Abdul Farzi. But why the ZNA, they have no money?"

Ash shrugged. Pell knew he concentrated on the road because they were driving fast and the deep potholes threatened to flip the vehicle.

Peel massaged his forehead. He didn't need a headache today. "I'm sick to death of fucking governments playing with alien horrors they can never control."

"Perhaps it's not what the Zimbabwean's have now, but what they might have to offer in the future. This is a potential diamond producing region, right?"

Peel nodded. He touched the stone in his pocket, and liked how Ash could put incomplete puzzle pieces together and see a discernible picture anyway. "This region is rife with resistance fighters, backed by Botswana diamond mining companies."

"And Colonel Nambutu wants to eliminate them," said Ash. "So the Zimbabwean State mining companies can come in and set up instead—"

"—and so Nambutu decides he'll finish off the resistance the easy way . . . with Farzi's weapon." Peel completed his field partner's sentence.

Ash grinned. "There are two RPG-7s in the back. You might want to prep one, sir."

Peel grinned with Ash, and they sped on. Peel had a lot of time for the sergeant, finding the man quick to assess any situation, and he always had Peel's back. More importantly, they shared a similar sense of humor.

Not far in the distance, dust trails from the three trucks ahead swirled skyward. Despite the gunned down ZNA soldiers at the farmstead who'd been a part of this group, Peel and Ash could still expect at least a couple of dozen more ZNA soldiers to contend with. Not great odds, but the end results if they didn't at least try to stop Nambutu were too hideous to consider. Nambutu might think an ESB weapon could solve his problems, but reality was he would soon create a bigger mess than anyone could conceivably control, anywhere. Peel had an inkling of what kind of weapon the Cambodian's had placed on the market, xenobiological because Peel had stolen samples of something similar from that country long ago. He'd thought he'd put that threat down, but maybe not.

The former Major turned NSA consultant reached in the back for a rocket launcher, loaded a HEAT, or high explosive anti-tank warhead and then stood precariously in the roof top hatch, balancing the seven kilogram weapon on his shoulder while they bounced along the rickety road to catch the convey.

Until now Nambutu and his men had failed to spot them, but Peel soon realized he had thought this too soon. Automatic gunfire peppered the front of the vehicle, the windscreen fractured, headlight glass shattered, and lead penetrated the radiator, but Ash maintained speed and course.

With the last truck in the convoy in his sights, Peel fired the weapon. The rocket launched and light grey-blue smoke erupted around him. He felt no recoil as was often expected by novices who used the weapon, and watched the HEAT warhead accelerate away at three hundred meters per second.

Whoomp!

The missile struck the last truck low. It shattered with a sound that hurt Peel's ears, and the truck spun in the air, sending ZNA troops into the sky with it as flapping body pieces.

Then the truck thudded onto the earth, rolled, and kept rolling toward Peel and Ash at an alarming speed.

Ash overcompensated, hit an obstacle, a pothole maybe, or perhaps he panicked in response to the fiery, gutted hull of a heavy military truck bowling toward them.

In that instant the Jeep rolled, and Peel was thrown from the vehicle. He instinctively curled into a ball before thick scrub broke his fall, and hundreds of the African bush thorns cut his skin.

Peel sat, momentarily stunned, and pain nodules erupted all over his body from the thorny cuts and bruising. He forced himself onto his feet and checked for broken bones. Thankfully nothing was.

He half ran, half limped to the wreckage of the Jeep, finding his M4A1 in the dirt nearby. He smiled, something had to go right today.

The Jeep had rolled, doing a complete flip but ending up righted when it had come to a rest. Emerson Ash was still buckled into his seat, bloody and bruised when Peel reached him. His wounds didn't seem too serious, but one could never tell just by looking.

"What happened?" Ash asked groggily.

"Stupid private mistake, I fired too close. Are you okay?"

Ash checked himself over. "I'm good, Major."

"Then let's get to work."

Ash climbed from the wreckage of the Jeep, readied his M4A1 and grabbed a case of thermite grenades. He divided them between him and Peel. "I think we are going to have to be generous in giving today."

"I think you're right." Peel smiled.

"I'm also thinking about that tentacle, Peel."

"Roger that. We can't assume it was the only one."

They took to the road, covering each other in turns as they advanced upon the wreckage of the decimated ZNA truck. The other two trucks had stopped a hundred meters or so down the road and soldiers were disembarking, ready for gun battle. What at first appeared to be men, were smaller, lighter people. They readied Uzi submachine guns and AK-47 assault rifles.

"Child soldiers." Peel hissed through his teeth like it hurt to join those two words together. "Nambutu's more of an asshole than I thought."

"I'll let you kill him then, sir, if we get that choice," Ash responded sarcastically, which made Peel chuckle. "I don't care what Nambutu's bought, I'm not killing children."

"Well then, we're agreed," said Peel through gritted teeth. They had likely already murdered children when they destroyed the first truck. That was enough innocent blood on his hands for one day. Peel didn't want any more.

One child fired his assault rifle wildly, more to scare than to do any real damage. In response Peel and Ash ducked behind the wrecked truck. It was instinctive to return fire, but they couldn't, not if they were to keep their words.

"Fucking, fucked up Zimbabwe," Ash exclaimed.

"You can blame President Mugabe for this country falling behind the rest of Africa," Peel countered as he glanced toward their advancing foes. The young boys had covered half the distance already between Nambutu's forces and the wrecked truck. Their only option was to disappear into the scrub and run for it. But that left Nambutu with his ESB weapon. That would be a whole lot worse.

More gunfire, shots that sounded concentrated on a specific target that wasn't them. Peel snuck a look when the bursts silenced momentarily. Between the children and the truck wreckage was an oil drum he had not noticed earlier. It had rolled from the truck wreckage, metal coils encased it with a strapped-on battery. It looked to be generating a magnetic field.

The tallest boy in the group was close to the drum now, and fired his Uzi. He didn't miss and the drum split open. Peel half expected it to explode as the oil inside ignited, but that wasn't what the drum contained.

A tentacle, moss covered and overrun with snapping mouths tore out of the split drum casing, then another, and another until dozens of the slimy, vegetative limbs thrashed widely. The pseudopods were too large to have fitted inside the drum, and Peel wondered if it was some kind of dimensional folding contraption that had contained the creature. He had witnessed similar abominations in Pakistan not that long ago.

The monster finally broke free and the drum exploded around it, sending metal shards flying in all directions as blast shrapnel. Peel crouched low and hit the dirt, as did Ash.

Thud!

A sheet of the drum embedded into the truck right next to them, saving Peel from instance decapitation. It reminded Peel of the corrugated iron at the farmstead.

The gunfire had ceased and Peel looked up again. Child soldiers were running everywhere, probably terrified of the creature from their darkest nightmares they had released. It was fully free now, standing more than fifteen meters high upon three legs that resembled fern stems but ended in hooves. At the top of its body were branches of tentacles, some thirty or forty meters in length above its central mass, which was covered in snapping mouths. It had no eyes that Peel could see, and probably didn't need them.

Several of the children were already dead, crushed or swiped by the angry creature. Peel watched as another boy was stomped underfoot by the monster, and there was nothing he could do to save him. The surviving children had dropped their weapons in fear and fled into the thick savanna woodlands.

"Oh fuck!" exclaimed Ash when he took in the enormity of the alien horror before them. He fired his weapon at it, emptying the clip. It did nothing.

What they had seen before in the homestead was tiny in comparison. It had not been allowed to grow as this one had.

"What the fuck is that?" Ash exclaimed again, looking pale and shaken.

"I don't know, but the classified Code 89 files that cross my desk suggest it might be referred to as a Dark Young of Shub-Niggurath."

"And what the fuck is that?"

"Something fucking scary, not of this Earth, and probably the weapon Nambutu just bought himself."

"He's got more?"

Peel shrugged. "He needed three trucks."

Ash nodded, but he seemed wary of Peel. Although he and Peel were friends and colleagues, they worked for different masters. Ash was an Intel cyber-analyst with the Australian Defence Force while Peel was an Intelligence consultant with the US National Security Agency. Both worked to put down Extraterrestrial Sentient Beings wherever they appeared across the globe, but with different databases to draw their knowledge from. There was no knowing what each other knew outside of their shared bilateral arrangements.

"I encountered something similar in Cambodia a long time ago," Peel said and wondered what they should do now.

A tentacle thrashed toward them, it collided with the truck and sent it rolling away. Peel and Ash stood exposed.

"Run!" Peel yelled and bolted, following the path of the child soldiers. He didn't have time to look back to see if Ash followed.

Under the cover of the scrub Peel kept sprinting, but he could hear the creature behind them, crushing trees and foliage as it ploughed through the semi-tropical forest.

He saw a boy in front of him, no more than ten and dressed in camouflage and terrified. Peel lifted the boy under one arm without a second thought and kept sprinting.

"Let me go, Mabono!"

The boy struggled but Peel ignored him. He then bit Peel, forcing the Australian soldier to drop his human cargo. Peel trip on a root, fell with boy.

"Musudhu! Pamhata! Dambe!" He leapt onto Peel, punched and kicked him.

"Stop it!" Peel yelled, and protected himself with counter blocks, yet reluctant to hit or restrain the boy into submission, even though it would have been simple enough to do.

The boy stopped, pale and looked up over Peel's shoulder.

Peel turned. He realized he had dropped his weapon somewhere. But he wasn't really looking for the M4A1, but staring up, struck dumb by the huge, hideous monster that had followed them, with blood and sap-like goo dribbling from its many mouths. Its tentacles still thrashed wildly, while fifty or more nostrils huffed and snorted, smelling the air. He could smell it too, an odor like a fern forest gone moldy.

Peel knew he was a dead man.

Then it moved off, crashed through the undergrowth on its huge, fern-like legs, and Peel couldn't understand why.

The boy tried to run and Peel had just enough sense of mind to grab him, hold him in a lock until the boy gave up the will to resist. When his captive's breathing slowed, Peel talked to him in calm tones. "I'm not here to hurt you. I'm here to save you, from that monster, and Colonel Nambutu. He took you from your family, right?"

The boy gave up fighting Peel's grip, so Peel released him. The boy stood alone and Peel half expected him to run, but he didn't.

Peel scanned the bush for any signs of the sergeant, but there were none, and he resisted calling out while the monster was so close. He'd tried Ash through their radio mic to no avail, but he hoped Emerson Ash was alive, he was a smart individual and his friend could take care of himself.

"Nambutu sent you to release that monster, knowing you'd die when you did."

"How do you know that, Mabono?"

Peel tensed. He instincts screamed at him to flee this place before the monster returned, but he also wanted to save this boy, and as many of the boy's friends as he could. "I know what men like Nambutu are like."

"You wear a uniform like the Colonel. You are no different."

"I am different. There is a UNHCR refugee camp in Botswana, just across the border where you can be processed, and hopefully, reunited with your parents. I can take you and your friends there."

The boy hesitated, wanting to believe Peel, but afraid.

Peel noticed his M4A1 lying in the dirt. He desperately wanted to pick it up, to give him some level of comfort that he could protect himself, but he knew if he did he'd scare the boy.

"My name is Harrison. I'm from Australia. You heard of Australia?"

The boy shook his head. Chances were he'd never seen the Internet, or a computer, or any form of technology that could put him in contact with the rest of the world, or understand what he did not have in his dictatorship destroyed country.

"My name is General Velempni!" the boy exclaimed proudly.

"Velempni?" Peel asked. "That's a fine name." He didn't want to image what tortures the boy had been subjected too. A favored trick of despot warlords like Nambutu was to have children practice firing assault weapons while blindfolded, not realizing that they were killing bound and blindfold men, women and children in the target range. The shock of what they did numbed them, terrified them, and so they became indoctrinated through the allocation of powerful names that made them feel like powerful soldiers. That was likely where the title 'General' came from.

Peel would not use that title.

He heard screaming, more gunfire and in the distance, the monster flung a body far and high across the sky.

Peel lifted his assault rifle, readied it, and he took Velempni's hand. "We have to find your friends. Get us all out of here."

Velempni didn't resist as they took off in a brisk pace. Peel found a trail where a dozen light-footed individuals had trampled through the undergrowth ahead of them. No doubt more young boys forced into soldiering.

They passed acacia, ziziphus and mopane trees. When they crossed over bare granite rock tiny lizards with rainbow colored reflective skins darted for cover. The trail was simple enough to follow, with bare footprint and boot prints in the dirt to lead the way, and occasional drips of blood. All the time they could hear the monster never far away, tearing through the undergrowth searching for more victims to trample and consume. They heard stampedes, kudu antelope or zebra most likely, fleeing the creature.

Ahead, Peel could see the trail led to a rise of domed granite and balancing rock formations. Someone in the group ahead was smart enough to realize they might find cover there. Peel wondered again what had happened to Ash and tried the radio with no luck. The sergeant still wasn't responding.

At a corner in the thick scrub, a volley of bullet ripped the air above Peel. He ducked instinctively, readied his weapon and crept forward to find a dozen boys ranging from ten to maybe sixteen huddled together. The eldest was the only one with a weapon, an AK-47 and he had just depleted the clip. When he saw Peel with Velempni, his eyes grew wide with surprise.

"Sizabantu!" Velempni yelled loudly calling his friend's name. "The Mabono helped me."

"I can help you all," Peel spoke loudly taking the opportunity to win their 'heats and minds' as the Americans liked to phrase it. "I can get you away from here, all of you." He pointed at the eldest boy. "You, Sizabantu your name?" Despite almost being shot, Peel kept his voice calm and authoritative. "Are you in charge?"

The eldest boy nodded. Although he was trying to be brave, he let his guard down for a moment and expressed relief that an individual other than himself was taking charge. Peel didn't doubt for a moment that in the back of all their minds, all these children expected him to transform into a tyrant at any moment, like every other corrupt soldier in this destitute land. He had to treat them with respect and caution. He was also thankful he was the only one with a weapon that worked.

"Any of you hurt?"

Sizabantu pointed to one of the smallest boys, who had a deep wound on his leg, the source of the blood they had been following. "Ngqobile got cut by the exploding drum."

Peel moved forward and checked the laceration. It was deep and bleeding fast. He took his first aid kit, wiped down the cut with iodine and used strip bandages to hold the wound in place. Peel took a tube of skin glue he always carried for emergencies, and sealed the wound.

"Can you walk, Ngqobile?"

The boy shook his head.

"I'm going to carry you, okay?"

He nodded, so Peel lifted him. The boy was lighter than he expected, malnourished most likely. That would make his work easier and his hatred for Nambutu stronger.

"We head for that granite dome. We should find cover there."

They took off at a brisk pace, and Peel was relieved to see everyone kept up. He counted their number at eleven. If he could save these eleven children, then he would have done some good this day.

Peel heard the Mil Mi-24 helicopter gunship before he saw it, flying low from the northeast, from Bulawayo. He could just make out the Air Force of Zimbabwe insignia. It cut through the air fast in their general direction.

Up on the rise now, scrambling through the granite rocks, Peel could see down into the valley from where they had fled. The creature was also easily visible, rising above the tree line with its head of thrashing tentacles about a kilometer from them now. It moved with alarming speed, faster than their Jeep could drive, and the undergrowth did nothing to slow it. It still hunted.

The gunship flew low in the direction of the monster. It fired a high explosive anti-tank missile—not at the creature as Peel had hoped—but near it sending the scrub into a torrent of energetic flames. The creature moved away from the heat, toward Peel's direction.

Colonel Nambutu was herding it toward them.

Peel readjusted his grip on the uncomplaining Ngqobile, and picked up the pace. The rise they headed to was sharp and wide. If they could get over the rocks, perhaps the creature would be too cumbersome to follow them, and they could escape.

Meanwhile the gunship fired another missile, closer this time to inform the creature they meant business. It had the desired effect, forcing the Dark Young to move toward Peel and his group.

What the gunship didn't expect was the range of its tentacles, and one whipped out faster than Peel could register. It smashed the Mi-24 with enough force to crumble the cabin.

The gunship fell like a rock out of the sky. The overhead blades, still spinning, sliced at the offending tentacle, severing it and the monster screamed with many mouths in unison. Peel had never heard a sound so chilling.

Neither the crew nor the gunship would survive the incineration on impact with the savanna forest. The creature, however, did.

Peel's gut went cold; a wall of fire and a monster on one side, a high rise rocky peak on the other. Then the creature trotted toward them. It had nowhere else to go, and the scent of their flesh had caught its attention.

"Run!" Peel bellowed with all the volume he could muster.

The group split, scrambled up the rounded granite rocks. The closer they reached the peak, the steeper the track climbed. Peel lost his M4A1 without remembering when, and Ngqobile seemed heavier with each step. He checked his holster, finding the 9mm Glock handgun ready should he need it. He checked for thermite grenades, found three.

Then Peel had an idea.

"Run!" he yelled again to the last of the boys he could see, who were ahead of him now. "Get over the rise, head southeast and I'll come after you."

He sat Ngqobile on a rock and caught his breath. His chest hurt with the exhaustion of constant, rapid breathing to oxygenate his complaining muscles, and he wondered again where the hell Ash was right now.

Peel turned to the small boy. They were alone now. "You should follow your friends."

The young boy shook his head. "I can't."

"You're leg still hurt?"

He nodded.

Peel nodded too. "Okay, we'll go together."

The sounds of sizable trees being crushed underfoot grew loud as the monster advanced upon them. It could probably smell them, human flesh. Peel appreciated the fear that grazing antelopes faced upon the African savanna; the horror of knowing that in the end their death would be one of being eaten alive. He didn't want to go out like that.

Peel took the three grenades, primed them and threw them one by one in a fan pattern. Each detonation created a wall of flames, deterrent enough—he hoped—to send the creature in a different direction.

"You ready to go again?"

Ngqobile nodded. He even managed the slightest of smiles.

"Thank you," he said quietly, "for saving us."

Overcome with emotion, Peel didn't know what to say. So he lifted the boy with both hands now, and strode up the steep path. If they could just get over the hill, he kept telling himself, they would survive this.

All too soon the flames behind them burned out, and the creature advanced again to hunt them.

Peel wanted to demand that the boy run, but he couldn't ask that of him. So he pushed harder, until all the muscles in his legs and back screamed for him to rest, and he ignored them.

He couldn't find an easy path that led upward, and soon Peel found he was cornered, in a granite ravine where the walls were too steep and too smooth to climb.

"Fuck!"

He was going to die. They were both going to die.

He put Ngqobile down.

"Are you okay?" the boy asked.

"We'll be fine," Peel lied. "The monster didn't see us head this way."

Then they saw the tentacles, rising above the forest, no more than fifty meters from them. There was a boulder in its way, several dozen meters wide. The creature rolled it out of the way with a single pseudopod as if it was nothing more than a silk curtain blocking its path.

Peel's whole body felt like jelly. Normally he had some kind of plan, even a crazy plan, but right now he had nothing, and only seconds to find one if he were to see this day through to its end.

He had nothing.

Ngqobile wrapped himself tight around Peel, gripped for life that wasn't there. "I don't want to die like this, taken by the devil."

The Dark Young advanced. Its hundred nostrils snorting as it sensed them, moved in slowly for a precision kill. The rest of the creature was stationary while the head of tentacles thrashed with the same madness when it was first released.

Ngqobile helped Peel take his handgun from the holster, until Peel held the muzzle directly over the young boy's heart.

Peel hesitated. He had always promised himself, if he had a choice he would rather take his own life than let an abomination like this one claim him. But never had he expected to have to make this decision for another, and a child at that.

"DO IT!" the boy screamed, and tore Peel from his melancholy to the horrors about to transpire. The monster was close now, only a dozen meters separated them. Peel felt the creature's hot breath on him, like the stench of a lion after a feast.

The boy grabbed Peel's trigger finger and the weapon went off. Ngqobile fell lifeless at Peel's feet as a mist of red sprayed him.

Shocked, the Australian spy turned toward the monster, placed the hot muzzle against his forehead, and willed himself to pull the trigger.

But he couldn't do it.

He closed his eyes and tried again. There had to be a way out, and suicide was a path open to him.

And he still couldn't pull the trigger.

A blast of heat from an explosion shocked Peel. He opened his eyes and saw the Dark Young on fire, burning from its central mass outwards. The tentacles above still thrashed, but with anger and pain now, and a dozen mouths poured out that horrific scream. In that instance, Peel was sure his ear bones shattered.

He watched Emerson Ash stand from the undergrowth. He dropped the shell of a second RPG-7 and lobbed several grenades into the central, burning mass of the creature. He was killing it, slowly, when no one else had been able or willing to do so.

In a state that felt like slow motion, Peel lifted his Glock 9mm and fired, every last bullet landed into the creature. He didn't know if he did any good, but he didn't want any bullets left over. The bullet and the flesh. He still might do it, kill himself, after the atrocities he had caused. With his weapon depleted the choice would not be his to make.

The creature fell, burning like a pyre and twitched now rather than thrashed. Ash walked up beside Peel and handed him the M4A1 he had dropped earlier. "You'll need this mate."

Peel nodded, went through the motions of checking then loading a round into the chamber. He couldn't talk. He couldn't respond. He was going into shock, and even though this realization was clear to him, he couldn't stop himself from embracing that dark place.

"Major!" Ash exclaimed. The cyber-analyst looked to the dead boy, then back to Peel again. "You did what you had to do Major, now let's get out of here."

Peel couldn't move. His legs wouldn't respond.

And then he was sick, dry retching only because he hadn't eaten in over twelve hours. Being sick was all he could do to remind himself he was human, so he took his time.

• • •

Peel and Ash returned to the trucks and discovered a savanna littered with the fleshy remains of human and animal corpses, Zimbabwe National Army soldiers and zebra being the highest amongst the body count. The Dark Young of Shub-Nigguarath had been thorough, hunting down all that moved on two or four legs. The ZNA soldiers left protecting the two surviving trucks had not stood a chance, and the monster had decimated them quickly and cleanly.

Peel had never seen so much blood.

More uncanny, perhaps, were the two trucks themselves. They had not been touched, not even a scratch.

They advanced with their assault rifles ready, unsure what to expect. Then Ash raised a hand and indicated that Peel should slow. He pointed under the closer of the two trucks, to where a man hid.

"Come out or I'll shoot," Ash commanded.

"The m-monster?" the man exclaimed.

"Gone," Ash answered sharply. "Now move."

When the soldier refused to comply Peel fired a bullet into the chassis of the truck, just above the enemy soldier. The man moved quickly then, clambered to his feet with his hands raised high. He was as scuffed, bruised and bloody as Peel and Ash, and just as terrified.

Peel noticed the insignia on the man's shoulders. "Colonel Nambutu?" he asked.

The despot nodded.

Peel didn't hesitate and put three bullets into the man's chest, dropping Nambutu into a rapidly expanding pool of his own blood.

Ash faced Peel and raised an eyebrow. "That was unexpected?"

"Do you have a problem with it?" Peel asked in all seriousness.

"I promised you could have him," said Ash.

Peel stepped forward over the twitching corpse. Just to make sure, he put three bullets into the man's head and shattered the skull and the brains inside until it became a pulped mess of meat.

He had hoped to feel better, killing Colonel Nambutu, but he felt nothing. He couldn't remove the image of Ngqobile's last pained expression as he pulled Peel's finger on the trigger. He couldn't stop analyzing that he was more willing to let one of those monsters take his life than take his own. Killing the Colonel had done nothing to silence the darkness within him. Revenge was a hollow promise.

"Major, we should check the trucks," said Ash quietly. "Find out why they were untouched."

The former Australian Army officer nodded and the two men peered cautiously into the back of the first, and then second of the trucks. There were six oil drums in each, each coupled with magnetic field generating batteries.

"We should destroy these," said Ash.

Peel nodded through the dark fog that clouded his mind.

"I guessed that creature sensed more of its own, either afraid to hurt them or wary of more predators taking over its patch."

Unsure how to respond, Peel searched the trucks' inventories and the corpses, gathering grenades and explosives, enough to set up a large detonation in each truck. In the vehicle they had toppled earlier, they discovered an additional four barrels. Together he and Ash packed the explosives into three clumps around each truck's fuel tank.

Hours passed before they completed their work, and they stood far back, ready to run should they need to. The goal was to destroy, not release the creatures, but they would only know when they executed their plan.

"Ready?" Ash asked.

Peel nodded.

Ash lifted his weapon, stared down the sights and shot the first petrol tank. The explosion was loud, hot and intense, and it sent the second nearby truck into an all-consuming fireball. Ash fired one more shot, incinerating the first truck they had toppled earlier that morning.

Peel and Ash stared down their scopes, ready for more of the horrors to materialize from the flames, but none did, they had caught them early.

They marched from the scene of carnage. Their work was done.

• • •

After consuming some rations, rehydrating, pulling forgotten thorns from their flesh, and cleaning their wounds, Peel and Ash marched again. They picked up the trail of the former child soldiers, followed them across the granite dome rise, and headed southwest toward Botswana.

Upon the peak, with the sun setting ahead of them, the two Australian's stared down at the carnage they had been party too. Peel couldn't believe they had survived, and wondered if he had deserved too.

He shook his head at the thought, hating it. He couldn't let negative chatter get the better of him, because that was the path of madness. But he needed an action to undertake to appease his soul because revenge was not the answer. Otherwise he wasn't certain he would survive this day with any mental fortitude left in him.

"Africa's beautiful." Ash stated it as if it were a matter of official record. "If you don't count those corpses over there, and those flames, and that blast site . . . oh and the corpse of creature . . . and . . . "

Peel could see Ash tried hard not to laugh, and the man was right, because all they could see before them was the carnage and aftermath of battle. Nothing majestic about it at all.

"Mate, shut the fuck up," Peel quipped.

"Is that an order, sir?" Ash almost chuckled.

Peel sensed the man was relieved Peel was finally talking again.

Peel wanted to laugh too. He really did. He wanted the world to go back to the way it was before today, when he didn't have the blood of children on his hands.

"Damn straight it's an order."

He felt a sharp object rub against his leg, and he remembered the diamond he'd recovered earlier. He'd forgotten that he had a hundred thousand dollars in his pocket.

"Sergeant?"

"Yes Major?"

"You think we can catch those boys before the border?"

Ash grinned. "Sure."

Peel smiled, an action he thought he'd never be capable of again, but he was wrong. Redemption came not from spilled blood, but offering possibility to deserving others.

"Let's go then. I have something very important I need to give those boys, to help them on their way."

●●●●●●●●●●●

NECROMANCY

KYLA LEE WARD

Did you think to escape me by this ploy?
To escape *me*? Did you think you could hide
so I would not in season find you out?
And dig yourself so deep into this grave
that I could not exhume you, should I choose?
I must call this a poor and common plot
for such as you, and an unworthy death.
I see it now, and scarce can bear the thought!
To break yourself upon the mundane wheel,
to suffocate so slowly, day by day
beneath the weight of earth, who gleamed so bright,
who saw so clear and far! And did you think
that as all darkened, so you would forget?
By subtle transfer, I too would forget?

A common grave, and yet it has some charm;
An avenue of solemn, shading trees,
now lit by lamps as darkness claims the sky.
Such quiet neighbours, such a spread of grass.
White roses at your head, brick at your feet.
But false the name engraved upon the post;
I know the truth, and now I see that here
you swelled, engendered small and squirming things;
To share your bed with such profligacy!
But yes, I understand your real intent,
to gain annihilation through decay.

But we were strong, my friend, who taught me love.
The magic that we wrought was stronger yet.
Those sigils in your skin protect you still:
your form is whole, your eyes, they are aware.

You knew full well that I would not forget.
Not in a thousand years; such is the price
of this my Art, the sweet, forbidden Art
that once we shared. I bring dreams into light,
distil desire. On summoned wings, I fly —
oh, how we flew! How sang, how wonderful
were you and I! And even in your sleep
that memory struck, and so your rising gas
became blue flame. And so it was that on
this late Midsummer's Eve, I found you out.
You stirred to feel my tread upon the grass.
Then heard my voice command your corpse to rise,
by your true name. Remembered then, too late,
the dead no longer have recourse to flight.

But now, my slave, you must recall my touch.
The coldness of your skin gives me no pause.
As my hands play your nerves awake, my breath
shall resurrect your lungs, my kiss your heart.
Of greater value than black pearls in wine,
this kiss, and of more potency. And now,
as muscles twitch and tongue begins to stir,
I conjure you to speak, and not to lie.
This sovereign Art interrogates the dead
and such you are: your choice was made long since.
You abdicated wand and word, and fled,
left me upon the crossroads, crimson-stained.
Did you think that would weaken me? Destroy
the tang of my sharp will? Not for one day.
Else you would not have taken such long steps.

I cherished deep those stains upon my hands,
inscribing sign and sigil in that ink.
So vast our sanctum seemed, but I kept faith.

Through cobwebbed noon and midnight's blackened vault,
the lonely hours saw me attend the flame.
I starved and stole; performed such sacrifice
as made the one you saw seem but a game.
And now you claim that was the way you died!
That mine own blade had entered in your heart.
Whatever you believe, the fear was all:
your fear of what I dared. Had I not laughed —
but how may I say now that you were wrong?
How may I swear that you alone were safe?
How may I even wish that you had stayed?
And there it is. The knowledge that I craved,
Not from your tongue at all, but from my own.

Left in the shell of our vast sanctum, there
I tended well the flame, annealed my will,
so grew in solitude, in power and time
to fill it. Now my name elicits awe.
My slightest work commands a fitting price.
I have attained all once we dreamed, and more;
such wisdom as could only come with time.
The truth that at the crossroads was unguessed.
And not one part of this may I regret.
Perhaps, if you had stayed, we would have done
the like, but not the same in part or whole.
So do I owe you thanks? Nor payment, no.
To leave was your own choice. This one is mine.

So on your brow I lay my final kiss,
complete the work that neither could alone.
Return you to your bed and at each step
let first the borrowed fire vacate your eyes —
Dark gods, your eyes! I'd keep them so for aye,
as mirror or preserved within a ring.
But I am done, so let them cloud once more,
and let your hair grow thin and grey, and fall,
your sinews slacken and your belly burst,
and even those ink vows beneath your skin
must drain away, must drain into the dark

where all things coalesce, save you and I.
Peace shall return to this sepulchral green.
And yet I think that you will not rest well.
The silence once resumed, will not rest well.
I think at each All Hallows, you will stir.

•••••••••••

SHADOWS OF THE LONELY DEAD

ALAN BAXTER

His eyes are tight with pain as he turns away from me, buries his frustration in the pillow.

"Something I said?" I ask nervously. "Or did?"

He shakes his head, rustling against the duvet pulled up tight under his chin. "I'm sorry. It's not you . . . I can't . . . This has happened before, I . . . I don't know why."

"It's okay. We don't have to. No pressure, you know."

He sniffs, turns it into a humourless laugh. "Sorry. I'm damaged goods."

I put a hand on his shoulder, remove it quickly as he stiffens. "Oh, Jake, don't say that, it's okay. It happens to loads of guys, but no one ever admits it. Stay here, just sleep, you know."

He nods. "Maybe in the morning?"

"Sure."

· · ·

I don't push for anything in the morning. Something difficult is happening and I like him too much to scare him off. I make coffee and bring it to the bedroom. He's beautiful, a wave of dark hair half obscuring his face, cheeks dusted with two day's growth. He smiles softly as I creep up to the bed.

"I'm awake."

"Hi there."

We stare at each other for a moment, still getting used to how the other looks, everything so new.

"Sorry about last night," he says. "First time I stay and I can't . . . "

I hold up one hand, pass the coffee with the other. "Doesn't matter. We've got plenty of time, right?"

His smile comes back. There's an edge of melancholy that seems to live behind his eyes, but that smile pushes it away like a breeze behind clouds. "I guess so. Thanks."

"Take your time getting up, have a shower and stuff if you want. I need to get ready for work. I start at ten."

• • •

The hospice is quiet as I enter. Mary offers me a subtle nod from the reception desk and I push through double doors into the smell of carpets, disinfectant and death. Claire Moyer catches my attention, coming the other way.

"Mr Peters last night," she says. "About three."

I nod. "Thought so. His family there?"

"No. No one."

I shrug and walk on, drop my coat and bag in the nurse's station. Poor old Mr Peters, his daughters stopped visiting about two weeks ago, when he started to spend more time asleep than awake. It doesn't really matter. We all die alone.

Even people surrounded by loved ones are utterly alone as they slip away, the sea of grief around them unnoticed. Death is the only truly personal thing there is. No one can ever understand it, even someone like me. I've seen death take people hundreds of times, held their skeletal hands as the darkness closes in and their breaths stretch further and further apart until they don't breathe again. But I have no idea what it's like.

I check the roster, see who needs medication, bathing, feeding, simple company. I knew Peters was leaving last night. I hope he didn't realise his daughters had stopped coming, but it's surprising what gets through the haze of terminal illness. Even as their minds go and they forget the faces of people they've known their whole lives, moments of clarity spike through the deterioration like lighthouses sweeping the night and they ask, "Where's my wife?" "Where's my son?" And they know they're alone whether those people are there or not and the last of their resolve crumbles as they slide into that stygian unknown.

Edie Sutton is on my list. She needs a wash, and a feed if she's up for it. Doubtful she'll eat, she hasn't managed more than a couple of teaspoons of jelly a day for almost a week now.

I'm surprised to see her awake as I enter, eyes wet and frightened in the glare of spring through thin cotton drapes. I take a sponge lollipop, dip it in the glass of water beside her bed and gently press moisture to her cracked lips. Her chin quivers as the liquid rolls over her desiccated tongue. "That taste good?" I ask quietly.

Her eyebrows rise, the almost translucent skin stretched tight across her skull wrinkling like tissue paper. "Tired." Her voice is barely audible, but you get used to listening for their words, every syllable a struggle.

"Had enough, huh?"

Tears breach her red, sagging eyelids and she nods ever so slightly.

"You can go whenever you like, love," I whisper.

A moment of softening around her eyes. "Can I?"

"Of course you can. You've seen everyone you were waiting to see."

"My Damon?"

"He'll be here at lunchtime." Her son. Visits regularly as he works nearby, sits with her every evening for hours. "Another couple of hours."

She closes her eyes and her exhalation is slow and weak, like heat escaping a long summer day. She'll be gone soon, I'll have to keep a close check. I lift her hand, a collection of brittle sticks loosely attached to an arm like old bamboo wrapped in papyrus, check her radial pulse. Barely there and so slow. I let my mind pass through my touch, search out the decay and failing organs, take the shadows of her dying softly into myself. I can't cure her, but I can collect the scourge, its malice.

A dark stain spreads into me and I store it away.

• • •

The day goes slowly and quietly. It's usually quiet here, except those moments when someone cries out, sudden terror giving voice to weakened lungs as they momentarily face their mortality without the softening armour of fatigue or drugs. Or the howls of grief, sometimes from friends and family, sometimes from the sick themselves. Sometimes both.

I clean up Kathy Parsons, who's been uncontrollably shitting viscous blood onto plastic sheets for more than a week now, check her meds. She exudes the sickly sweet, cloying odour of death. She's terrified. Only forty eight years old, eyes always wide in child-like fear, but she's got a little while to go yet. A little while to reach some kind of acceptance, though not all of them do. Some are gasping in disbelieving horror, even with their last breath. Almost everyone dies scared, especially the young ones. Some people are calm and accepting, content as they drift away, but they're rare, usually very old. Everyone has time to think as they lie here, suspended in the last darkening hours of their life. It's good that some find peace in that mortal dusk.

I reassure Kathy as much as possible, sit with her as a sedative soaks through her struggling veins.

Edie's pulse is almost gone when I check her again an hour later, breaths so far apart every one seems certain to be her last. I call her son to tell him he needs to get here, but his phone goes to voicemail. I leave a message imploring him to hurry if he can.

I pull the chair up beside her bed and take her fingers in my palms, rest my forehead against the back of her hand. Her frailty wafts into me and I soak it up, gather that insipid, creeping death into my cells. It can't hurt me. I don't know why, but it can't. So I collect it. I don't know why I do that either. Because I can. It doesn't heal them or ease their suffering, but at some level I like to think they know I share their pain and that offers some subconscious solace.

Edie's pulse weakens until I can't feel it any more. Her breaths are tiny, sharp intakes, almost imperceptible, more than ten seconds apart. Her exhalations are silent, air leaking from lungs little more than deflated sacks of inert offal.

Fifteen seconds apart. She's going.

Her life leaks into the air and the shadow of her sickness, her fear and loneliness, washes through me and she's gone. I shudder with the gift she's given me. My hands tremble as I stand and move away to mark her chart, dimness swimming behind my eyes.

Her son is hurrying along the hallway to her room as I emerge and his face falls when he sees me.

"I missed her?"

"I'm sorry. Only just. She passed moments ago. But she didn't wake again since this morning."

He barks an uncontrollable sob and tears tumble over his cheeks. We're all five years old when our mothers die. "I can see her?"

"Of course."

I'll send the counsellor down with the relevant pamphlets after he's had some time alone with her.

• • •

Not much else happens through the day, which pleases me. It's terrible when more than one patient dies in a day, as the first one feels somehow cheated of their time in my mind.

Jake is parked outside when I get home, an embarrassed smile twitching his lips. "Hi."

I'm so pleased he's there. "Hi." I had wondered if I might not see him again. Our few faltering dates that led to our first night together had been cautious but full of hope. When something got in his way last night, I worried it would frighten him off.

"Try again?" he says, holding up a bottle of red.

"I'd really like that. I have some steaks in the fridge and wait til you try my potato rosti."

• • •

We gently fumble at each other's clothes, clumsy with nerves and the dull edge of the wine. Edie's death still floats around me, within me, but that helps. I embrace it. Nothing makes me hornier than death. Something about mortality reminds us at a level beyond thought of the importance of contact, of touch, of the life within lovemaking.

I'm not too proud to admit I usually masturbate a lot in the privacy of my home after we lose someone. It's unavoidable, the desperation to feel alive—to feel *life*—especially when I've absorbed the death into my marrow like I do. I hope Jake can see it through this time.

I'm as gentle as I can be, as caring as I know how. He shivers and stiffens with nerves as I run my hands across his shoulders. He looks into my eyes, a nervous smile. "It's okay, I'm sorry. I want to." He reaches back and unclips my bra, lets it drop beside the bed.

"You are so lovely," he whispers.

There's tension, fear, but he keeps assuring me I should continue and so I do and he eventually performs. It's soft and urgent, but electric. Afterwards he grabs hold of me and hugs me against his chest so hard I have to gently force a breath into my constricted lungs.

"That was wonderful," he whispers, his hot breath tickling my ear.

"It was," I say. "I'm glad."

He holds me tight and his breathing changes. He turns his face away. I push away to look at him and tears stand in his eyes.

"I'm sorry," he whispers.

"Are you okay?"

"Yes, really. It's hard to . . . this is difficult for me. But please, don't feel bad. I just can't help it."

"Anything I can do?"

He smiles, leans down to kiss me. "Just keep being so nice to me."

"That's easy."

I settle beside him and turn to let him spoon me, push myself back into the curve of his body. He's so warm and strong and vibrant—the opposite of poor Edie's hard, cool, frailty, all jutting bones and oxygen tubes.

"Was someone less than nice to you?" I ask, biting my lip the moment it's out. Probably not the thing to say.

"Something like that."

I stroke his hand, not game to risk saying anything else, ask for any more of his secrets.

"I'll tell you one day," he says, voice thin with pain.

He holds me tight until we fall asleep. It's good to have someone so alive to hold on to, a beacon against the shadow of all the death in me.

• • •

The days at work pass slowly and my hours rotate to nights. I prefer the solitude and peace of the night shift, and most deaths happen then. It's strange how people who have been unconscious for days or weeks almost always seem to slip away in the depths of the night, like they know somehow that leaving while the sun shines is unusual. I remember Edie dying in the middle of the morning; her shadow still drifts through me, the echo of her disease. It's all that's left behind, her life and body far away now.

We haven't lost anyone for nearly a week. The orderlies are taking bets on how much longer it'll be. Sam's aiming high, reckoning another few days. Marek is less confident, thinking Mr Patel will die tomorrow. They're both wrong. Jack Oswald will die tonight, maybe in the next two hours, three at the most. I can *feel* it. I've always been drawn to death, always offended by the hopeless indignity of it. And I've always sought to care for the dying, take into myself something of their pain, a memory of their suffering. I was destined for this career.

I pad into Oswald's room, put a hand against his cheek. It's very cool, his eyes flickering gently behind thin, pale lids. I was wrong, it's happening already. No one to ring for old Jack, he has no one to come. "Last of a line and good riddance," he said to me when he arrived three weeks ago.

"You can't be all bad," I'd said, and he laughed.

"Not bad, really. Just not much good either. Never had kids, wife died twelve year ago. Worked fifty years for fuck all and here I am being tucked away in a corner to die alone."

"We all die alone, Jack," I said, an attempt to soften his hurt.

"Yeah, but there's alone and alone, ent there."

Darkness swells up in him. He hasn't woken in five days. He had a drip in his arm feeding him a bare minimum of hydration, anti-nausea medication and painkillers—a poor simulation of normal life while he dies—but we took that out a few days ago. He's a skeleton under linen stamped with the name of the hospice.

He'd asked me the week before to speed it up for him. "Can't you jab me wiv somefing, make it happen? What's the fucking point in hanging on?"

I'd told him I wished I could, and I meant it.

We wouldn't let our dogs and cats suffer like this but we'll happily put our own parents away to wither and waste into ignominy and despair. They deteriorate to frightened babes again as everything they've ever been deserts them, and we think it's the humane, moral thing to do, to let that happen. To watch it happen while we tell them everything will be okay. Which is the worst line of bullshit we ever try to sell in a world powered by lies and deception.

Jack's eyes pop open, a flood of panic blanching his already ivory face. After a moment he focuses on me and nods, a tiny movement of understanding and he's gone. His darkness swells into me, the entropy of his illness drawn up through my hands where I hold his. It adds itself to the blackness I carry inside, that I've carried for so long. Will I fill up one day, no room for any more, and then what?

With trembling fingers I close Jack's eyes and fill out the paperwork. Marek will win the bet. His guess was closer even though they were both wrong.

• • •

"I want to tell you why sex is so difficult for me." Jake's face is creased with what looks to me like grief.

"You don't have to."

"I know, but I want to. We've been together a couple of months now and it feels serious. It is, isn't it?"

I nod vigorously. "Oh, I hope so." I really do hope so.

Jake draws a deep breath that shudders on the way down. "I never knew my real dad. He left when I was too little to remember."

I open my mouth to say something, I'm not really sure what, and Jake holds up a hand.

"Let me get this out in one, or I may not make it."

I nod and he smiles, squeezes my hand across the table.

"I don't mind not knowing him. My mum was young and irresponsible. She's always been fucking useless, so I can hardly blame my dad for leaving. It's what I did, first chance I got. She should have protected me, but she couldn't even protect herself." He draws another breath, sips wine. "My mum shacked up with Vic when I was about six years old. She'd knocked around with guys before then but never for long. She did her best by me, even though her best was bloody rubbish. But when Vic came along, everything changed.

"He drank heaps, was always on the edge of violence. Mum told me how much she loved him, but it was clear she was terrified of him too. She said how we needed him to pay the bills and he wasn't such a bad guy. Even with two black eyes and a split lip she'd tell me how he wasn't such a bad guy."

Rage flares in me and Jake can see it in my face.

"Let me finish." He reaches out, strokes my cheek. "You're such a good and decent person, the way you care for the dying, you're so good to me. You couldn't be less like Vic *fucking* Creswell." He drinks more wine, his hand shaking. "Anyway, it wasn't long before Vic started . . . touching me."

I let out a soft sound, part growl, part moan of dismay.

A tear breaches Jake's lashes. "I'm sorry, I need you to know this."

My knuckles creak as my fists clench in my lap. "I want to hear. You shouldn't carry this alone."

Jake nods, sips. "Anyway, he went from fondling and making me do things to him to raping me in very little time."

"You were six?"

"I was probably eight by the time he started that."

He says it like that makes it somehow better than if he were six. "What a fucking . . . "

"He ruled my mum and me, did what he liked to us. My mum should have protected me, but she was trapped too. He would beat her if she tried to intervene. Beat me if I threatened to tell. We lived in terror. When I was fourteen I told mum we had to go, we had to run away. She said we had no money, where would we go?"

"There are shelters," I start to say and Jake nods again.

"Of course, but that wasn't the point. You know what she said to me, after years of beatings and sexual assaults?"

I sigh and shake my head. "She told you she loved him."

"Yep. So I ran away. I have no idea what they're doing now. He could have killed her for all I know. I haven't spoken a word to her since I left. I was on the street at first, then in shelters and care. A foster home took me in when I was sixteen and I was a bastard, doing all the things my mum did and worse, acting like her boyfriends, thinking I was different."

"You're nothing like that," I say. "You're amazing."

He smiles, but it's not enough to chase away the melancholy this time. "My foster mother is a lady called Glenda Armstrong and she fixed me up. Wouldn't take my shit, made me finish school. I was lucky. She gave me direction, I got a job, turned myself around. Twenty five now, finally feeling like I've got it somewhere near together. And then I met you. For the first time I feel something real, instead of just angry fucking because I thought that's all I deserved." His tears have stopped and there's anger in his eyes.

"You should be so proud of where you've come, given where you started," I tell him.

"But I'm scared and you mean a lot to me and that's why it's so hard for me to be intimate, emotional. It's always been an act before, an act of defiance more than anything else, a show of power. But with you, I have no guard and it's terrifying."

I stand, move around to hug him and kiss his hair. "I'm honoured," I whisper. "I'll never hurt you."

"I know."

The shadows of all the people who have died with me mask my vision, make Jake a distant blur. "So many wonderful people die every day, struck down by disease or age," I say. "And yet fuckers like that Vic get to live."

Jake nods against my chest. "There's no justice in the world. We have to hang on to our luck when we find it, because that's all there is."

. . .

After nearly a week of no deaths we get two in a day. The darkness wells inside me, that delicious blackness I can't help but gather. Sometimes I think it's going to overwhelm me, but there's always room for more. The journey home is muffled by the circling presence of their passing.

Jake comes around not long after I get home, bag of shopping in hand. "I'm going to make us a great dinner tonight. Special recipe! Something Glenda taught me."

"Great! I'm glad we're having a good dinner. I have to go away for a couple of days."

"That's sudden." His brow is creased in concern and it breaks my heart a little.

"There's a two-day course Claire Moyer was supposed to go on, but she's come down with something. Someone needs to go, it's about a new drug administration practice, and they asked if I'd step in. I head off early in the morning to Newcastle. I'll be away overnight, back by dinnertime the next day. Sorry."

He smiles. "Don't apologise. Work is work. Let's enjoy tonight then, eh? Maybe you can lend me your key when you leave and I can get my own cut? Then I can have something ready for when you get back on Thursday?"

I raise my eyebrows, give him a crooked smile. "Your own key?"

"If you think . . . "

I sweep him into a hug. "Of course I think. I'd love that."

. . .

It took a lot of searching to find this place, but hours of free time in a palliative care hospice can be put to good use with a search engine and access to hospital records. Hints from Jake about where he grew up and a keen eye. Plus friends in social services to join the dots. The idea, the realisation, hit me like lightning when Jake told me his story.

There's a broken down car on the front lawn, leaking oil across the dirt like black blood. The house is peeling, the paint reminds me of the skin of a dying woman's lips. I knock on the door, heart hammering against my ribs.

A large figure shimmers through the frosted glass panel and the door swings open. A man stands there in shorts and a stained shirt. He's a tall bastard, muscular, but a beer gut mars anything close to a good physique. He has muddled tattoos on his arms and legs, grey and black stubble across his face like a TV tuned to static. His eyes are dark and mean. "Well, hello, darlin'."

"Victor Cresswell?" I ask.

His eyes narrow. "What?" He glances to my hands, probably checking for a summons.

"*Vic* Cresswell," I ask.

"Yeah."

I hold out my hand. "It's nice to meet you."

His lip curls in a sneer and he takes my hand, squeezing too hard to assert his dominance as he puffs his chest out. "Nice to meet you too, sweetheart. What the fuck is this?"

And I let my darkness out. It rushes through my palm, desperate to escape, and races into him. I feel it gust up his arm, into his chest to nestle in his lungs. It wraps shadowy arms around his liver and coats his gallbladder in an inky embrace. It snakes through his intestines, finds his prostate and slips down into his balls.

A shudder ripples through him as I break our grip and smile, turn away.

"What the fuck was that all about?" he yells as I make my way back to the waiting taxi, a tremor in his voice.

As I tell the taxi to head back to the station he stands in the doorway, one hand rubbing absently at his throat. There's a patina of fear across his face. How much does he suspect? I give him a month at most before the decay begins to set in. Before the tumours start to blossom through his organs. Black, flowering death.

I'm empty inside, somehow hollow but with whiteness swelling into the places where I've collected all that dark over the years. Perhaps I shouldn't have let it all go, should make it last. It's disconcerting, I'm a little lost without the shadows of the lonely dead inside me. I'll have to start collecting again. No matter, at least three at work have less than a week left.

I knew I gathered it for a reason. A shame it took me this long to realise what my purpose is. I have a mission now, giving this unfair blackness to bastards truly deserving of it.

I'm going to be busy.

• • •

Jake is watching television and looks up in surprise as I enter the house. I'm glad he decided to stay at my place, not his. When the moment's right I'm going to ask him to move in.

"I thought you weren't back until tomorrow," he says, smiling. It's genuine happiness on his face and that warms me.

"We got through the training in one day and finished up in time for me to get the last train back. So here I am." I had taken into account that Vic might be harder to find, maybe not home. It had all been much easier than I anticipated.

"Well, that's a lovely surprise," Jake says, gathering me into a hug.

I breathe deeply of the clean smell of his skin. "Yeah," I say. "Maybe there is some justice in this world, after all."

••••••••••

THE WALKING-STICK FOREST

ANNA TAMBOUR

It started like this. When the blackthorn trees were bare, Athol Farquar would pollard them—sawing them down to their gubbins, pruning them almost to the ground, just low enough so that, once the raw winter passed, a great number of new branches would shoot up quick, in a vertical panic of desperation while the sap ran strong. Come spring, there Athol would be in the thicket that was the forest, tying up (with soft woollen twist) the short young fresh-fleshed pinkies to the rods, and from that moment on they could push up all they liked, but every movement was caught and bent to measure.

Every day Athol would come, his woollen bonds stuffed in a pocket of a vest he'd made from his ancient khaki jacket; a girdle of wires loosely wrapped around his waist, and ready in his left fist, an ingenious set of grips he'd forged to shape the discipliners themselves, be they wire, iron, or his sculptured cages of beaten tin. Often he was bare-chested, his hands and arms hardened from years of smithing, so the thorns that could kill with a scratch were nothing to fear. Or maybe they were, but he didn't pay them any more heed than he did the feisty rapier-sharp branch tips everywhere that he hadn't pruned, which could have flicked his cheeks or eyes open. It was almost as if he enchanted the blackthorn. Thorns were his caressers. Branches bent to his will. And he loved bringing up his creations so much that many a moonlit night he spent bending, moulding, tending, admiring and listening, hearing and smelling the night breath of the forest.

The fact is, the pure air suited him. The sloes that the unpruned branches grew, purple and sour as a preacher's face, suited him too; so every autumn, after the first frost, he'd fill a few sheepskins with the firm fresh plums and eat his fill before their skins lost their face-powder bloom. He macerated the rest of his pickings patiently till his sloe gin was devilishly smooth. He'd start his day with a drop of it in his mug of tarry tea, drunk surrounded by his forest.

The young trunks couldn't help but grow, yet every day their own wills were subjugated more, till they were no longer something you'd think should have thorns and leaves but something leaping, roaring, splashing, slithering, dancing, moaning. Nothing so mundane as a tree, let alone a many-trunked bush. When a blackthorn walking-stick-to-be grew to this stage in life, he cut it. Farquar did almost no finishing after that. Even his seasoning and colouring was done without what he considered cosmetic abhorrences—painting, staining, shellacking, gluing pieces on. The only additions he ever made were: to the tip, he fitted a metal cap, robust but finely made as any goldsmith's ring; and occasionally— to finish snakes, women, that sort of thing—he would inset eyes he made of the whisky-coloured cairngorm stone that only he knew underlaid the walking-stick forest.

Yet for all his ability to propagate treasures more unique than a Fabergé egg (which any master goldsmith can duplicate) he wasn't vain about his gift, but moved, and ever more secretive. On some nights, bent over the blackthorn, his chest hurt like that of a lover's, as he felt something from the forest that he could never explain. Trust? On a fateful day in the hell of 1915, he'd seen a chair made of contorted tree limbs; and in the ruins of a church found a pearl shaped like a sheep, and a shard of an ivory saint, its halo still proud. From them grew his plans to make walking sticks that looked alive, if he survived. He had prodigious skill and ingenuity, but had set out with modest aims, little imagining how the forest that he loved and protected bristled with life in ways he could never fathom. Take two of his masterpieces: a man petting a dog, and two playful lovers. Natural development? Bah! There was something preternatural going on. The blackthorn that grew at his guidance into such impossibilities trembled at his touch like a filly eager to be bridled.

Athol Farquar called no man master, and certainly didn't bow to any god. He made his quietly famous sticks to order—never setting his discipliners on a shoot he didn't know the future master of, and the shape this little innocent would grow up to be. He demanded to be paid first, and what he charged was so outrageous, he was heavily sought after. But he would only accept a client and an order if they met his unpredictable criteria. He made his considerable fortune on a few men and women who had everything, so they couldn't get enough of his sticks.

These were collectors such as Mr. L——, who'd made his boodle in khaki dyes. His baronic front hall bristled with walking sticks, whangees, pikestaffs, shoot sticks that folded out into stools; tippling and sword canes; and though his taste ran to music hall, an opera cane whose head glittered with diamonds.

He was particularly proud of two vicious knot-ended clubs, "A shillelagh and knopkierie," he was fond of explaining. "See this shillelagh with its head, like an Irishman's, filled with lead? The effect of this, like its simple African cousin here: Indistinguishable! Tap a man's head and you can scoop his brains out with a spoon."

His ballroom looked like a museum—rows of glass cases filled with walking sticks made of precious metals, woods, and jewels. One find, he'd moved to his safe because he was not sure of it anymore after some nasty tittering by other collectors. The seller, a drinking buddy on that cruise ship to New York in 1920, had sworn: "It's fair dinkum or strike me dead. Bavarian unicorn horn."

All of Farquar's customers had huge collections. Each begged to see him as soon as they found out about him, as if he had a cure for the incurable. He dealt with their fevers calmly but firmly, just as he did the most willful shoot or thickest trunk in his blackthorn thicket. When collectors yearned for Farquar, they wanted something as *different* as when the engorged gourmet wants, at long last, simply a drink of water.

Athol Farquar's sticks were prized, like the holy grail, for their purity. Made only of the blackthorn, a wood as humble as the Saviour's cup and crown. And no matter how elaborate the design, a Farquar walking stick was never whittled. If it looked as if its head were a ram's horn, or a running dog, or a woman, that was purely a delusion caused by the natural development of the blackthorn when taken into hand by their maker.

There were some sticks Farquar made that he didn't sell. These were working sticks—crooks he gave to the shepherds in the hills surrounding his little forest. For McAlister, he made a double-handed crook so that the old man could lean on it. Athol Farquar bent the length of this stick to complement the bow-shape of McAlister's bandy legs, the result being that if you saw him at work peering out along the slopes, you'd think, *Now, what a fine specimen of a man. They grow them well in these wild parts.* Grayson liked to snag a sheep from the belly so as not to break a leg, so his stick had one great scoop atop, wide as an unshorn ram. Young Stephenson would want something sharp and fancy to twirl in the village on a Saturday night. Athol Farquar didn't ask any of the shepherds first. He just thought he knew and made the sticks without consulting. Then he gave them out—and to each shepherd, something happened once the first touch of hand to wood was made. Somehow it became a part of him, as necessary as his legs.

These weren't sentimental gifts. The shepherds and Farquar had a relationship that each wanted to maintain. Sheep in the blackthorn would be a danger to themselves, even without his disciplining rods and wires making the forest into a nest of traps. And sheep eating the tender shoots of blackthorn would cut each walking stick in the bud. So he maintained a fence against the sheep, a combination of hedge and sharp banks, so that they'd stay on the grassy slopes and not venture into the forest. The triangle of the forest formed a V, the broad part at the top rising up to the rounded mound where McAlister tramped in every weather. The two sides of the V were valleys. Stephenson roamed the slope on the other side of the valley to the right, and over that hill. Grayson's land was on the left, his rise levelling out to become the closest thing to a plain in these contoured hills. The nearest village wasn't much to talk about. A day's drive by ass-cart, a brisk morning's tramp for Farquar. There was also a scatter of haughty houses within view of the slopes, not that the shepherds nor Farquar had anything to do with the foreigners who tended to rent them, Londoners and such, the villagers said. Neither the shepherds nor Farquar nor anyone in the village had one of those motorized contraptions, though it was already 1924. Young Stephenson wanted one with all his heart but the only way he'd get out of being a shepherd was if he wanted to 'herd' wild cattle. Some Laird out Auchencruive way who thought to turn rubbish into gold was offering mad amounts of money to skilled shepherds to civilise them, for the cattle were not only stupidly ferocious but used their horns like bayonets. He fancied his looks, but no matter how hard he scrubbed himself, he smelled of sheep, and therefore, failure—whereas a man with engine muck under his fingernails wafted the City, adventure, romance, escape.

"The daevil is ut made that," McAlister would say, laying on the brogue whenever he saw a vehicle, though there were precious few that made their way up to these parts, the roads being what they were, and the reasons, fewer. It wasn't the contraptions he objected to. They'd not bothered him in the War. More, the people who swanned around in the beasts. And everyone here agreed.

Not one of the people who craved Farquar's canes put a thought to where he lived, nor imagined his precious forest any more than a one of them had ever put a thought to, say, some tree that provided ebony, or the men who cut it. All correspondence was through the postmaster at Blair Atholl, a man who might as well have been a priest when it came to confidences. Farquar was so strict about meeting his clients in various remote inns and waysides he designated, that one tin-can magnate broke a leg leaping from a train and a moving-picture actress came down with quite useless hysteria.

Farquar's wealth grew as great and discreetly as his fame. He had, however, the habit of thrift. So in every hole he made by pulling up a lump of cairngorm stone from his hidden warren of mines under the blackthorn roots, he stuck a dumpling of soil filled with the old-fashioned dosh he demanded: pre-1917 gold sovereigns.

No one local thought of him as anything more than a poverty-stricken craftsman, actually someone even poorer—because he had not even one rough Highland sheep—than the crofters who spent their winters weaving hoary lichen-dyed tweeds that were prized by Lairds, Lords, and those who with war fortunes, were paving their way to obtaining a Title. The crofter-weavers never knew what power they had, if only they'd learned worth, but the middlemen-buyers who made the rounds of cottages were fierce as wolves, and always bought with their lips curled.

So there Athol Farquar was—as there and unnoticeable as his thicket—and as uninteresting, anyone would have told you. What did he look like? A necessary face. His body? It wasn't ailing. Otherwise, what decent person looked at a body?

• • •

She watched him from the point just below the forest, the point of the V, that deep watercressy place where the spring came out to run down between the two long-sided hills. She'd found and followed that spring, up past its calmness, up where it narrowed and rounded over rocks, up, her feet numb from the frigid waters where its banks were too steep to walk beside it, up towards its secret heart; into a region that half-comforted her with its secrecy, its terror. All around, the forest loomed—a tangled blackness that if rendered by an artist, must be something from a madhouse where the food might be rationed but not the ink, black accented with brilliant, dancing white. The moon was a searchlight. A light breeze made the forest sound like mice in a box of chocolates.

She had left home at the first call of the owls when the moon was already full, and now had been crouching, her ballet slipper-shod feet perched precariously in the stream. She was taking a drink of water from her dish of hands when she heard come, a man. He stopped just far enough away that she could see his khaki vest and his bare muscular arms.

She watched him bend forward toward a branch, and just then, a cloud shifted. Moonlight cut them sharply into silhouettes. Her heart jumped. That branch looked like the reared-up head of a dying horse. The man held its neck while he reached down and . . . what? Was he pulling something up? He straightened out partly and kicked the ground in the area his hand must have been. Was he kicking something out or pushing something in? She couldn't see. Then he turned away and disappeared into the messy blackness. She could hear him—creak, crackle, snap. He was tightening a wire here, stroking a green shoot there and nipping a leaf between his fingernails, not that she could see. As carefully as when she'd crept down the creaking stairs, she crept up the slippery bank . . . and was caught.

The more she struggled, the more thorns found a purchase. First it was her skirt, then the silly flounces in her jacket. Its uselessness annoyed her so much that she'd hated to take it, but as with all her clothes, she had no choice. And now her hair had shaken loose, pins scattering into the branches like so many other spiky shoots. Her unfashionable, wild, waist-length tangle was caught, spreading with each movement to be an ever-larger web.

"Farquar," she called. "Mr. Farquar!" You *idiot*, she thought. It had to be him. Why did I wait?

She tossed her head and barely missed a thorn in the eye, and now her hair was so trapped that she couldn't move. He was too far away now, the forest too dense. She couldn't hear him at all, only frightening noises in the depths of night. The moonlight and small sounds only made everything look leering. There might be wolves here! Are there any wolves anymore, or are they just in stories? Tears flooded her eyes. Her cheeks mottled like a child's. She wrenched as hard as she could, which only served to tear some hair from its roots. "You *ninny*!" she yelled, which helped a bit.

Suddenly he was there, in front of her, tsking. "What a muckle you've made." His voice was deep but rough, his fingers gentle but skilled, and soon she was free. "Put up your blasted hair," he said, handing her some twists of worsted. She hesitated and he turned her like a top, grabbed the great soft mass, wrapped it and bound it as expertly as some Roman maid.

But that was just craftsman's luck. Since the War, he'd not been this close to another woman—to trouble.

His confusion soothed her, emboldened her. "You're Mr. Farquar?"

"That I am," he said without thinking. His instant reflex was always the honest response. And after that, he rarely said anything, not that he knew what to say now, with this—this girl up here, in the secret place—in the middle of the night. If 'twr a man . . . Farquar being the ex-blacksmith he was, one reason he kept to himself was his temper. In war, it had helped being able to beat a man's brains in with one blow. In his regiment, they'd bet on him, till he stopped their fun and took, instead, to poetry and keeping by himself. Now this girl here.

"My father," she said, ignoring his scowl, "will be up here tomorrow morning. . . . This morning."

She was so matter-of-fact, he forgot she was a girl. "How can he?"

"He's hired a detective and I heard them talking."

"What do you want?"

"To warn you." She didn't act like a woman. She spoke simply and her eyes didn't bat at him.

"You don't know who I am."

"I know who my father is. Richard Galveny."

She was so straightforward, yet she bristled with life. He pulled her skirt free of another thorn. Richard Galveny. The name rang no bell.

"My name is Rose, not Cairngorm."

"So what does this have to do with the price of cheese?"

"He wanted you to do the Rape of Cairngorm. You refused . . . Scratching your head won't help you, but will this?"

She posed, with her head turned away.

"Aye." His gut clenched. Richard Galveny. Richard. The man who had signed in a scrawl, and introduced himself as "Mr. Galveny."

They had met at Garnshiel Bridge, that humpbacked thing along the old military road linking the two historic garrisons of Braemar and Corgarff, a place of Galveny's choosing—"for romance," he'd said in his letter. "Do please indulge me," he'd written. "I'm besotted with history." Farquar had believed him.

Farquar was waiting when his client arrived alone, driving himself in a motorcar. Galveny stopped the beast on the top of the hump and invited Farquar into the pines on the wild side of the bridge. The man was impeccably dressed, softly spoken. "Lovely day, don't you know?" he said, and it was his voice that charmed Farquar. A voice made for poetry. The man also respected history. Farquar had been somewhat tense all morning, berating himself for breaking his own rule, indulging a client and putting himself out to meet at a place of the client's choosing, though it wasn't, to be honest, any problem for Farquar, who loved this country and had relished the ramble. "I think you'll appreciate," said Galveny, "the level of verisimilitude I demand. History and romance, don't you know. Can you copy a picture from life?"

Farquar nodded reflexively, a little miffed at the doubt, but he was used to this sort of thing from clients. "You'll think it's alive."

Galveny pulled the picture out of his breast pocket and held it in front of Farquar.

This girl—the one in front of him now—was the one in that disgusting picture.

Even when Farquar had thought the woman in that staged rape photograph a whore, he'd been revolted by the—the decency of the man.

Farquar had refused Galveny in two words, both filthy. Galveny made a gentlemanly threat in return, murmured in the voice of a mellifluous poet. Farquar had said he'd need to think about it. He told the truth. He needed time. He walked over the bridge and stood looking up at the bleak, blank-eyed stone inn. There wasn't a soul around. Galveny's motorcar waited like a patient dog, in the middle of the bridge.

Galveny had found himself a seat in the pines on a low stone cairn. When he saw that Farquar was returning, he rose and primly brushed off the seat of his Highland heather-tweed trousers—cut in that London tailor's presumption of a Scottish baron's kit. As they drew close enough to see each other's eyes, Galveny laughed.

"So it's settled then," he said, and his handsome, politely annoyed, bland, upright-as-a-judge expression changed to one of mischief, like a boy stealing a pie from a ledge. "You're a rogue, you are," he laughed. "How much do you plan to skin me for, you canny Scot?"

"Just this," said Farquar, and caned Galveny's face till he would never look respectable again. Then he took the picture out of Galveny's pocket and walked off while the man was still rolling around on the soft bed of pine needles in pools of his own making.

This was not the only instance of Farquar refusing to satisfy collectors. He'd had to discipline a few, mostly because they got greedy and had to have more of his canes. Or because they asked him to tell them secrets about or in some other way undermine the success of other fanatics who craved his works. Galveny, however, had been unique. The man was a monster, and this girl . . .

She was looking at him, not saying anything. Not being hysterical or making a scene like women do. Yet she was both young and, undoubtedly, a woman—in full bloom. She was, it hit him, the most beautiful woman he'd ever seen.

"Why did you come?" he demanded, suddenly suspicious. Why *would* she come?

"Why wouldn't I?" she spat. "I know what you did. He's coming to *kill* you. He's hired a man called Skulley. D'you know him?"

"Who doesn't in these parts? He's lucky to be alive."

"And Skulley's got a dog."

"Aye, that brute."

"We've got to stop them."

"Why?" Bloody hell, why? "So I caned your old man," he said. "I didn't *save you* from anything. Coming up here, it could have been the death of you." Farquar's voice had gotten louder and rougher by the word. "Why *did you do* this mad thing!" He looked ready to punch her.

"How could I not! " she shot back. "You knew nothing about me. And he's rich as Croesus, and still you . . ." Her eyes, liquidly bright, gazed into his. "And to thank you. And to meet you. And I love you."

It just came out, and as it hung in the air between them, they knew that it was true.

Hie, she'd already bashed what he knew about women to smithereens.

"We've got to kill him first," he said.

"Of course." She took his arm and he didn't flinch. "But what about Skulley? And the dog?"

"Don't take mind o' them gorse-heads. That cur won't come within miles of Stephenson or Grayson. Their sheep could jump in his mouth and he wouldn't gulp. They're the shepherds up here, and that dog's back has met their crooks. And Skulley, he thinks the forest is haunted."

She made a sound like a turtledove. She was *chuckling*. "That wouldn't have anything to do with you scaring the daylights out of a person, would it? That rearing horse!"

An eerie but comforting feeling came over him, of knowing her before, as if she'd been Curlew. Two loners, they'd formed an inseparable bond when they were thrown together in the Second Battle of Ypres, during one of those times in May 1915 when men lost their minds merely from the sound. Just before a push, they read poems to each other, then climbed out and tried not to drown in the holes or get shot while they did their duty. On one relatively good day, at a hellish place named in soldiers' humour "the corner of Joy and Crucifix Streets," where the ground squelched as much with rotting bodies as sucking mud, and bones poked up like stubble, Farquar was in the lead, pulling a horse he planned to shoe. Curlew was pushing from behind. Curlew slipped and fell, spearing himself through the eye on a split arm bone.

This girl was looking at him now, smiling somewhat indulgently. "Get a move on," she said. "I never imagined you as a daydreamer."

• • •

Skulley hadn't lied. He knew these parts and before the quilt of morning fog had lifted, he, with his dog, led Galveny up through the fields of violet harebells, as gorgeous as any spring bluebell but so contrarian here in the kind of cold that chills the bones. Not that Skulley noted, and Galveny walked streaming muttered curses at the ankle-twisting outcrops of limestone and wet grasses, slippery as ice. Up they tramped, passing dead nettle, gorse, stepping on heather and other sharp-scented herbage, till they reached what looked to Galveny to be an impenetrable leafy wall.

"Down," whispered Skulley. "Crawl through."

Galveny was just going to say, "Are you mad?" when he saw the tunnel, little more than rabbit-size. "Crawl," Skulley hissed behind him.

Galveny took his gun off his back and shimmied with it under him, he imagined, just like soldiers had. His jacket back tore and so did one sleeve. He would have liked to demand part of Skulley's pay back when this adventure was over, but he didn't plan for there to be a Skulley capable of listening then.

More than an hour later Galveny, standing in the stream, drank water from his hands, tried to stop them from shaking and failed, and reshouldered his scratched, muddy, new game-shooting rifle. He also held, concealed in his breast pocket, a beautiful palm gun handcrafted in Germany; and in his sock, a knife with a medieval hunting scene of hound and hart.

He was soaked to the bone from first the thick fog, then the drizzle, and increasingly, his own cold sweat. He'd been abandoned and couldn't have turned back if he'd been paid a million quid. He had thought that Skulley would lead him within spitting distance of Farquar's back, for Galveny's armaments were obtained specifically for this event. In fact, his fighting skills were as good as his sense of direction. The man always thought himself quite the navigator, though he could get lost in a steam bath.

His face was a painter's inspiration: the nose as wheezy as a bulldog's, flat-profiled but puffed, textured and coloured at the sides like two bunches of lightly trodden grapes. The cheekbones were off-kilter, and the mouth—with its tattered lips and not enough bone to attach false teeth to—the mouth was a dribbling gape. His voice was no longer that of a thespian but a whisper-loud, hoarse lisp, so many letters unable to be formed in the wreck of a palate that his anger in how they came out only made him a thing unreal, an abomination of a man. Indeed, he'd even frightened the servants in his exclusive little London club. His fellow connoisseurs all cut him off. He was alone. He only had his daughter; for his wife, after that beating, instantly fled to her mother's house, where she divorced him. He looked, she said, like some thing in a War veteran's Home. No one who should expose himself. It enraged her and every one of her friends that he didn't think of their sensibilities.

And his face had only grown uglier and more determined while he hunted for this Farquar. Galveny travelled light, renting through agents, for a season or a few weeks. His possessions: three bags, one trunk, and his daughter. No collector would tell him anything, and only a great deal of money to an Edinburgh detective agency led to him being certain enough to move to the staging house that was luckily free and only ten minutes' walk from his guide, the scoundrel poacher Skulley who'd demanded cash up front. Damn Scots. Can't trust a one of them muckheads. But Galveny had paid up like a lamb. He had no choice.

He rubbed his sleeve against his forehead, only succeeding in scratching his eyelids with grit. Proper daylight would come soon enough, he told himself. Then the forest would be his hunting ground. Ah, you think you're clever, you gorilla—you're an animal living here, with your pretensions. Everything's money. You're no better. And little do you know a Galveny. We remember everything.

He splashed further along the creek, bloodying his knees, chin, elbows on the moss-slick stones, cursing and vowing as he went. His voice had kept him company ever since he'd realised: he'd been deserted by even the dog; and he hadn't the faintest idea where he was, or his path back. Meanwhile, the forest he'd expected to get lighter got even darker—and that sky that wouldn't stop pissing on him didn't help. As he rushed forward, his gun hitting the back of his head at every fall, the scenery closed in around him ever more oppressively, reminding him cruelly of some play he'd had such fun at years ago, some murder mystery that gave him a frisson of fear that lifted when the lights went on.

His eyebrows dripped, blinding him. His ruined lips he could never properly close dripped tears, sweat, dirt, and snot into his mouth. He stumbled up the stream. There didn't seem to be a way into this forest, this intolerably contrarian place that Farquar lived in—"Like a fucking dog!"

Cursing was the only thing keeping Galveny going when at last, in the crotch of the forest, in its deepest darkness, a shaft of light or sound or something alerted him to a way to escape from the stream itself. He grabbed at a tangle of jutting roots and pulled himself up the bank.

On land again, in this bit of clearing, he felt a new man. He was reaching behind to take his gun off his back when his arm stopped in midair, then dropped. He felt four years old again, some *nothingness* grabbing at his back like those nights when his father locked him out on the crumbling window ledge for being naughty.

He ran unseeing, forward into the forest, because suddenly—he had to run. Arms out, eyes screwed shut, he ran straight into the middle of a mob of walking sticks in their adolescence. A rearing horse, a woman brushing her hair, a unicorn, two snakes entwined, and a chipmunk.

Two vinelike ends of some disciplining wires caught him, one by an arm, and another by the back of his neck. Another, unaccountably, looped around his waist. And as he struggled, more wires confoundedly found their way around his torso, ankles, wrists. He wrenched left to free himself, and one very sharp wire slipped, ever so discreetly, into his left ear. Any movement he made only drove it further in.

"Farquar," he screamed. "Farquar!"

Of course he sounded, with no teeth or much of a bottom lip, rather comical, like a ham actor playing a raven.

The screaming only managed to drive the wire deeper down his ear canal.

Then it punctured his eardrum with a burst of purest pain, shoving out the childish fears.

He saw blackness and a brief flash of light, like being in an alley when a kidnapper wags a lantern. His thoughts slipped back to other good times, sights and sounds. A girl crying had squeezed a tear out of his Sir One-Eye. He grew strength from that, and even felt his other senses gaining heightened sensitivity. For after all, his right ear was still sound, and his limbs, though bruised, were sound—*and*, he reminded himself, *with patience comes reward.*

A gusty wind must have settled over this mountain, making the trees thrashing all around take on the oddest character, creating the strangest phantasms of sound—a horse's neigh, just behind his elbow. Assorted chitterings all around.

Indeed, the forest seemed to come alive with sounds, now that he noticed. There were too many to count, but his ear picked out one above all, and strained for it. Low and regular, rough and deep: a woodsman's saw. No. A man's voice—lifting, falling . . . lift, hold, down in a long stroke. Then again and again, in some drawn-out rhythm that threatened to never end, like the bugger was reciting old-fashioned poetry. Interminable. No distinct words, of course. What could make that? Wind shoving two branches back and forth against each other, back and forth . . . till suddenly the air stilled, as if for a moment's silence.

And so close he would have bet his life on it—quiet but deep: "Would you like to hear another?" followed by a soft coo like some bird.

The man's voice had to be Farquar, the primitive bastard! So this was his sense of humour. It *had* to be Farquar. Galveny was thinking fast. Stabbing Farquar in the back now was impossible, and gunning the man down would have needed that poacher to do the work. The only thing for it was to return the next night, alone. Not entering the forest, of course, but by skirting its edges, Galveny reckoned he could set fire to the blighted place, with Farquar trapped in it proper, like an ape in a cage.

Galveny opened his mouth to demand release when something tickled his right ear, and into it poured a warm, moist, low, musical, pitiless chuckle.

His mind, already crazed, shattered. The wire in his left ear drove in further.

Maybe he closed his eyes—he was beyond knowing.

He felt the fetid breath of the forest drip into his every pore.

He heard the swishing hiss of a cobra.

The yipping of a fox.

The love-gurgles of turtledoves.

Strains of a current craze-song for a fox-trot, words and music that bore into you.

A man's conversational syllables, deep as stones dropped in a well.

A ripple of woman's laughter.

But perhaps his last feast of sensations was of smell—that most restoring of all cups—a cup of tea with a kick in it. His nostrils dilated. *Hot with a drop of something ineffable—sweet, rough, strong.*

• • •

Bite and burrow, swell and rot. The flesh is weak, but the rods have never weakened. His skeleton is held bolt upright in that impenetrable tangle.

• • • • • • • • • • •

CHIAROSCURO

CHARLOTTE KIEFT

Chiaroscuro
Melanie Gibbs: second solo exhibition
Opening
Thursday 30th April, 7pm
Venue
Basement, Dougall-MacMillan Building

Sue stared at the invite to her sister's new exhibition, then at the crumbling stairs in front of her. Basement? I guess that meant she had to go down. Not that the staircase looked that safe, with only a flimsy wrought iron bannister for protection from the long descent into darkness. She shivered as she clacked down on her teetering heels, the temperature dropping with each step.

When she was about half way down, Sue heard voices above her.

"It makes sense that Mel would have her opening in a converted toilet," a voice sneered. "I love her dearly, Roger, but we all know that's where her paintings belong."

Sue recognised the round vowels of Fi, Mel's old boss from the Wellington City Gallery, and gritted her teeth. Bloody bitch.

The stairwell took another turn and opened onto a landing where light poured through a doorway. She raised her eyebrows as she peered into the room beyond.

Her sister's new flat-cum-studio-cum-gallery appeared to be a converted bathroom: an ancient porcelain urinal stretched along one wall, followed by three cracked hand basins. The floor was chipped blue and white Moorish tiles, with an elaborate metal grate in the centre. The room's small windows were frosted glass, high up on the walls. Candelabras stood strategically around the room, their dancing flames illuminating where the dim electric bulbs couldn't reach. And all along the walls lurked dark paintings.

A dozen guests were already circling the artworks, the buzz of their talk reaching Sue where she stood. She smiled in surprise and delight. So the paintings were more of a draw card than the wine and snacks this time? It was better than could be said for Mel's first solo opening.

Her sister hurried over. "You said you'd be here early!" She blinked, as if fighting tears.

"Didn't you get my text?" Sue held up her phone. "There was an emergency at work. I had to call in some favours to get here at all."

"I bet if I'd designed a new smartphone, you'd have found a way to be her on time." Her sister's eyes were wide and wounded. "You've never seen the value of art—or supported my dream of being a full time artist. All you care about is that stupid security firm you work for."

"Oh dear. I do hope we're not interrupting something." Fi glided through the doorway, her immaculately groomed husband trailing in her wake like the ultimate accessory.

"Give one of these to everyone as they come through the door." Mel thrust a stack of flyers at Sue. "That's if you can spare me the time away from your 'real work.'" She turned her back to her sister and addressed her guest. "Darling! So good of you and Roger to come."

They exchanged air kisses.

"What an a-mazing place?" Fi waved a slender hand. "Very Morocco meets Warhol."

"It's one of the oldest stone structures still standing in Wellington." Mel gave a brittle laugh. "It's been declared an earthquake-prone building. Officially no one's meant to be here," she added in a conspiratorial whisper, "but, seeing as it's empty, the owner's letting me work—and live—here in exchange for a painting."

Fi raised a plucked eyebrow. "He actually likes your Spring Gelati Collection? You know, my dear, I always thought it sounded more like the name of a teen fashion line than an exhibition."

Mel flushed. "Not those paintings! One of my new ones."

Desperate to defuse the tension, Sue looked at the flyers for inspiration. "You've called this one Chiaroscuro. What does that even mean?"

"It's a Renaissance painting term"—Fi rolled her eyes—"referring to the use of strong contrast between the light and the dark."

"Hmmm." Sue smiled blankly and nodded.

"Like Raphael," Roger prompted.

Sue shrugged. "I thought all paintings were about contrast?"

Fi gave an exaggerated sigh. "Sometimes I find it hard to believe you two are related." She hooked her fingers into the curve of Mel's arm. "Now, why don't we go take a look at these . . . chiaroscuri?"

• • •

Sue examined the last of the paintings, disquiet gnawing at her belly. Her sister's new works were certainly . . . different. Every one of them included the figure of Mel herself, but the backgrounds were dark and shadowed, with her sister's pale skin the only patch of light. Sometimes Mel was pictured alone in subterranean passageways, wandering as though lost. Other times, she was just standing there, head hung low, face pallid. In one, strange shadowy shapes surrounded her. And what could be glimpsed was the stuff of nightmares: misshapen creatures with clawed hands and malevolent eyes that glowered out of the canvas.

"Mel, darling, this is astonishing work." Fi's voice was audible from across the room.

Sue glared at her, suspecting sarcasm, but both she and Roger seemed genuinely entranced. And, for once, she had to agree with her sister's friend. The artworks were beautiful—but the subject matter sent the hairs on the nape of her neck prickling.

"Did you see who just arrived?"

Sue jumped at the voice in her ear, her heart thundering. She hadn't noticed Mel sidle up.

"Beauden Barnett!" Her sister's voice was shrill with excitement.

"What? The rugby player?" Sue stood on her tiptoes and scanned the crowd. "Have you seen him in action? Now there's a work of art!" She snorted. "By the way, I think you'll find his name is Barrett, not Barnett."

"Not the All Black." Mel pouted. "The famous art dealer! His blog 'art:i:face' has a huge worldwide following."

Sue followed the direction of her sister's gaze to a cadaverous man with a shock of silver hair. He was dressed in a T-shirt that declared 'Art is dangerous' and skinny black jeans shot with metallic thread. He stood in front of the paintings, an intense expression on his face as he tapped a fountain pen against his lips.

"Do you think he likes them?" Mel squeaked.

Sue shrugged. "How would you tell? He's so full of Botox I doubt his face can show any expression, approving or otherwise."

Her sister let out a high-pitched giggle, and then turned away. "Oh God. He's coming over."

"Beauden." He tucked the pen behind his ear and held out two skeletal hands to her sister.

"Mel. Melanie." She handed her drink to Sue, and then hesitantly offered her palms.

He grabbed them both and squeezed. "What a marvellous exhibition. Chiaroscuro, but with a definite emphasis on the dark." He gave the shadow of a wink. "A far cry from your previous offering. But tell me." He pulled a notebook and retrieved his Montblanc from behind his ear. "What changed? Why this sudden about turn—from Pretty Pretty to Edgar Allen Poe. Do you have something I can share with my readers?"

Mel swallowed and raised her eyes to the ceiling as if searching for inspiration. "When . . . when I left my job at the Wellington Art Gallery to paint full time, I was so full of optimism. I knew no one thought I'd make it—but I was sure I could prove them wrong. But then I had my first exhibition and it was universally panned." She shook her head, her eyes flicking to Beauden then away again. "It was the lowest point of my life. For ages, I couldn't paint; couldn't even get out of bed."

"So the dark mood of these paintings arose from the initial failure?" Beauden scribbled away in his notebook, his eyes glittering.

Sue scowled. Now she remembered him—this Beauden Barnett had written a scathing review. Her sister had cried for days after reading it.

"It was from the depths of such despair, that all my pretence was stripped away," Mel continued, "and I was finally free to paint at a level I'd always believed I was capable of—even if no one else did."

'Fabulous.' Beauden pulled a business card from his pocket. "How long before you can paint . . . let's see . . . twelve more."

"Wh . . . what?" she squeaked. "You mean me?"

He gestured towards the easel in an unlit corner of the room. "I'll need more paintings like these if I'm to get you 'out there.' There's an opening at the Windmill Gallery in three months time. Let's take your Chiaroscuro out of the darkness and into the light."

Mel raised her hands to her mouth. "An exhibition? At your gallery?"

Sue put her arm around her sister's shoulders, forcing herself to smile. "Looks like that dream of yours is coming true, after all." She tried to keep her tone light, but all the while her eyes roamed across the canvases and her feeling of unease grew. Surely creating such haunting images came at a cost?

• • •

Sue knocked on the door to Mel's basement flat. No response. She glanced at her watch. 11.20am. Her sister couldn't still be asleep, could she?

Two months had passed since the chiaroscuro opening and they'd hardly seen each other since. This last week, Mel hadn't even been responding to her texts or emails. As Sue happened to be in the area for work, she decided it was time to pop in and check on her sister.

"Open up! It's me!"

She tried the handle, grimacing when the door swung inwards. Why had Mel asked her to put that extra lock on if she wasn't even going to use it?

"Who's there?" Her sister moved towards the door, her arm raised to shield her eyes.

"For God sake, put some clothes on!" Sue averted her gaze, but not before she had seen the thin streaks of paint slashed across her sister's naked torso.

"What?" Mel looked down and shrugged. "I had my nightie on when I went to bed." She gestured to the white cotton shift lying on the floor.

Sue flicked on the lights. For all the good it did. "Here. Put this on." She threw a fleecy dressing gown at Mel.

"My body. The paint . . . " Half-clad in the dressing gown, Mel rushed over to the easel and clapped her hands with delight. "It's happened again!"

Sue frowned. "What's the big deal? You're an artist, remember? It's not that surprising to find a painting or two lying around."

Mel moved closer to the easel, her head tilted to one side. "It's beautiful, isn't it?" She traced her own outline with her fingertips, a smile playing across her lips.

"Whatever happened to modesty?" Sue huffed, but then her gaze fell on the painting. "Oh my God." She swallowed convulsively. "How are you going to explain that one to Beauden?"

"He'll love it. I love it. Don't you?" Her sister's voice was brittle.

Sue took a deep breath. Remember. Be encouraging. "It's very . . . " The words caught in her throat and she shook her head. "Jesus, Mel. It's so like gazing into the darkness and realising there's nothing—nothing good or kind—out there." She searched her sister's face, taking in her lank hair, sunken cheeks and the dark rings under her eyes. "What's going on? Are you depressed? You're not on drugs, are you? I know lots of artists use them for inspiration—"

"Of course not!" Her sister stalked over to her tattered armchair and slumped into its embrace. "I'm fine. Better than fine. I'm finally living my dream."

Sue gestured towards the painting. "Why the hell would someone who's 'fine'"—she made air quotes—"paint something like that?"

"Why? That's the least of my worries." Mel threw her head back and stared up at the ceiling. "At this point, I don't even know how I did it."

"What are you talking about?" Sue frowned.

Mel pulled her knees up to her chest. "Every night since I've moved here, I've slept badly. And when I'd wake, I'd feel drained." She bit her lower lip. "The strangest thing of all was in the morning my body would be streaked with paint, as you see me now. And on the easel would be a painting that hadn't been there before."

"What?" Sue screwed up her face. "That makes no sense."

"Tell me about it." Her sister sighed loudly. "At first, I thought someone was sneaking in here at night after I'd gone to sleep. Yeah, I know. It sounds crazy. Who'd break in and paint?"

"Ah!" Sue drew upright. "So that's why you got me to install the extra lock?"

"But the paintings continued." Mel chewed her lip. "All I can think of is that I must be doing them in my sleep. That I've tried for so long to be this great painter, I've smothered all my talent in my waking life. So my subconscious has taken over and I can only paint when my conscious is dormant."

Sue barked out a laugh. "Really? Sleep painting? Is that what you're going with?"

"Trust you to be so sceptical," her sister spat out. "Don't you remember how I used to sleep walk as a child?"

Sue nodded, feeling a stab of guilt. She'd promised herself she'd be more supportive, but sleep painting? The idea was ridiculous. She crouched down by the armchair and took her sister's hands in hers. "Look. Why don't you come and stay with me for a while? Beauden's put you under a lot of pressure—and living in this . . . this . . . toilet can't be helping your state of mind. My place is big enough. And a damn sight more comfortable."

"Come and stay in your Churton Park McMansion?" Mel's lip curled. "It may be more 'comfortable', but it's got no creative energy. This place inspires me. Since I moved here, I've started to really paint. I've only two weeks and one final artwork to do. Beauden's counting on me. I've got to do that painting. No matter what."

Sue's gaze slid to the canvas and she shivered. "Then at least let me help?" she suggested in a softer voice. "How about I get the techs from my firm to set up a security camera in here?"

Mel snorted. "Are you crazy? I don't want those nerds spying on me."

Sue lent forward. "I'm the only person who'll have access to the feed—and the recordings will remain your intellectual property." She gave an encouraging smile. "Just think—this way we can solve the mystery of how you've been creating your masterpieces."

Mel sat bolt upright, her eyes shining. "What a fantastic idea! We can show the footage at the exhibition—the artist live-streaming her dreams onto the canvas. I can't wait to tell Beauden!"

Sue sighed with relief. At least she'd find out what was really going on with her sister. And she'd bet her McMansion it wasn't sleep-painting.

• • •

Sue stifled a yawn as she drove down the Hutt motorway towards the city. She'd been working 16 hours straight. It was 2.30am and no one else was on the road—just her and the harbour and the glittering lights of Wellington. She idly swiped her finger across her tablet, which sat in its cradle on the dashboard, to bring up the camera in her sister's flat. Not that she expected to see anything. The techs had installed the camera two nights ago and none of the footage so far had shown any sign of sleep painting. She smiled as she saw her sister on screen, fast asleep on the fold out couch, curled in on herself.

"Lying down on the job again?" She barked out a laugh. "What's happened to that busy subconscious?"

The flicker of movement was so unexpected, she didn't see it at first. But then it happened again.

"What the fuck?!"

Sue slammed on the brakes, sending the tablet flying and her car fishtailing across the motorway until it came to a screeching halt mere centimetres from the guard rail. She raised her hands to her chest. Her heart felt like it was trying to stampede out of her rib cage.

"I must be more tired than I thought," she muttered out loud to break the silence.

Sue picked up the tablet and swiped her finger across it to bring it back to life.

Then froze.

The breath caught in her throat and her lungs refused to work, then suddenly she was gasping, like a diver breaking the surface.

The grate in the middle of the room was twisting, moving, rising.

She dialled up the sound, her eyes fixed on the tablet as the thick metal was pushed aside, and then someone—some thing—climbed out of the opening. Sue shrank back into her seat, small moaning sounds coming out of her mouth.

"Good God. What is that?" she whispered.

The creature blinked as though in bright sunlight, even though only shadowy moonlight filtered down through the basement's high windows. It crouched low and swivelled about, as if checking out the room. It was well over six feet in height, with a dark, reptilian head and skin that glistened wetly.

The dark figure made its way across the room, weaving between boxes and paints with practiced ease. It stopped by the bed, looming over Mel's sleeping form and the car echoed with its low sibilant hiss.

"Oh God. No! No!" Sue shoved the tablet back into its cradle and turned the ignition key. She had to save her sister.

Sue floored the accelerator and her BMW leapt forwards. She watched the screen all the while, her jaw slack and a sick feeling growing in her stomach as the creature raised one clawed hand and drew the nightie up to Mel's neck to reveal her pale flesh.

Sue banged her hands against the steering wheel. "Wake up, Mel! Get out of there!"

Then, the breath caught in her throat, as from the thin lipless mouth, a long prehensile tongue flicked in and out as the creature studied her sister's naked form.

"Get away from her, you bastard!" she screamed.

The creature paused. Then turned and moved away. Sue felt a surge of relief. Had it heard her? She shook her head. No, impossible.

Then, a horrible realization dawned on her, as she watched it pace over to the easel.

The creature stared at the blank canvas, its reptilian head cocked to one side. The hisses grew louder. Then it began its work, dipping its tongue into the paint, and sliding the liquid colour onto the canvas.

Sue's eyes widened, as she watched the creature at work. "Oh, Mel. I'm so sorry. The paintings—they're not yours. They never were."

The creature turned and glided back to the bed. It dipped its glistening tongue onto the palette and, as Sue watched in horror, began to mould the colours to her sister's pale body, the gleaming, living brush caressing her flesh with each stroke.

Sue gave a strangled cry, half fear, half nausea. She punched 1-1-1 into the iDrive controller, her car careering wildly across the lanes of the motorway as she headed for the Aotea Quay off ramp.

"1-1-1 Operator. What's the nature of your emergency?"

Sue's jaw hung open. How could she possibly explain?

"Are you there?"

"Police!" she screamed out, as she sent her BMW rocketing down the deserted streets. "My sister . . . there's an intruder . . . "

• • •

The blue and red lights of the police car were flashing like a disco ball in the dark street, as Sue screeched to a halt outside the Dougall-MacMillan Building. She threw the car door open and ran towards the entrance, where a police officer stood, speaking into his walkie-talkie.

"Why are you just standing here?" she all but screamed, her eyes wide and wild. "Where's my sister?"

He looked up, his face impassive. "Are you the person who placed the emergency call?"

Sue pointed at the door with a shaky hand. "Mel lives in the basement. Why are you up here?"

"We've officers down there investigating." He frowned. "But there's no sign of . . . Melanie, was it?"

Sue felt the pavement swoop beneath her and she grabbed his arm, her fingers digging into his flesh. "What do you mean she's not there?"

He shook her off. "Ma'am. I don't think—"

She pushed past him and flew down the spiralling staircase. "Mel! I'm coming!"

The basement door stood open and the room was flooded with light.

"Where is she?" she demanded, as a WPC stepped forwards. "Where's my sister?"

The policewoman frowned. "We can't find any sign of the occupant—or any intruder. But the door was unlocked when we got here. He left the painting behind." She shuddered. "Not that I blame him. Who'd want that hanging on their wall?"

Sue turned to the easel, where the final nightmarish picture squatted. It showed the same reptilian creature she had seen on her tablet earlier. It stood by the open grate and was holding Mel in his arms, staring into her face with glittering avarice, like some horrific parody of a groom with his white-draped bride. Her sister's face was a rictus of fear and her terrified eyes stared out of the painting at Sue as if pleading with her.

"No! Please, no!" Sue raised her hands to her mouth and ran to the centre of the room, where the heavy grill still lay cast to one side. She peered over the rim, into the well going down, down, down.

A flash of white caught her eye and she gasped, hope surging through her.

"Mel? Hang on, chick!" She turned to the WPC. "Give me your torch!"

Sue pointed the beam of light down the shaft. But then the air whooshed out of her lungs. Half way down the well hung her sister's white cotton nightie. It was caught on a nail and fluttered in the fetid air like a banner. While beyond lay only the stygian darkness of that chiaroscuro world below.

•••••••••••

VOX

LISA L. HANNETT AND ANGELA SLATTER

Kate often spoke to grains of rice, flakes of cereal, pistachios waiting to be shelled. She talked to grapes and cherries. Sunflower seeds. *M&Ms.* Sometimes she'd whisper before she ate them, often she wouldn't. Most days, she simply *thought* conversations at them and imagined their mute responses. They never replied using words, only emotions. She *felt* their personalities as a fluttering in her belly. A sensation of warmth beneath her ribs.

This morning, sitting in the waiting room outside Dr Goodman's office, she was muttering to the last pink Tic Tac stuck on the bottom of its plastic case.

'All your friends are already inside me,' she said. The packet had been new—she'd bought it at the corner shop across the road on the way in—but her mouth had been so dry . . . She'd been here, stomach churning, for almost an hour. The mints hadn't stood a chance. 'Don't you want to join them? Won't they miss you if you don't?'

Beside her, Nick chuckled and patted her knee. Giving it a quick squeeze, he went back to the copy of *People* he'd plucked from a glossy heap on the melamine coffee table, smile lingering on his broad face. Kate knew he thought of her as a kook—a loveable kook, but still. She'd never explained to her husband the sympathy she felt for these stupid, inanimate things. How she'd invent stories for the family of Enoki mushrooms about to go into her ramen (they loved to swim, and the tall parents encouraged their skinny kids to stick together when noodle-diving). How the lonely cracked egg, glued by the yolk to its carton, would feel like it'd let the team down. How every kernel of corn on the cob had been raised to burst—so if she missed even *one*, she'd be stealing its only goal, its only dream. How the banana peel she'd accidentally thrown in the garbage bin would be separated, forever, from his wife, who was slowly decaying in the compost, waiting to turn into soil. How the giant strawberry they'd bought at the market had become special, somehow, by being big enough to fill her palm. She couldn't possibly eat it because its red was so bold, so friendly. She'd felt much happier giving it a long life, seeing it age and eventually rot in the fruit bowl, before finally letting Nick chuck it out.

Kate couldn't explain why she cared so much, but she *cared*.

"Come on," she hissed, whacking the little rectangular box against the arm of her chair. The candy didn't budge. She began digging in her purse for something to jam through the hole in the lid—the pens were too fat, but she had a long hairpin in there somewhere—when a soft-shoed nurse stepped, VoiceWorks™ tablet first, into the room.

"Mrs Conway?"

"Yes," Kate said, clutching the container and handbag with sweat-slick fingers. Standing quickly, she fidgeted with her hem to make sure her skirt hadn't ridden up, and grabbed her coat off the seat to her left. Around the low table other women, alone or with partners—husbands, girlfriends, wives—slumped, their names as yet uncalled. With eyes as red-rimmed as her own, they watched Kate inhale deeply, steeling herself. Bundling her belongings and holding them protectively in front of her, she looked to the nurse for guidance.

"Right this way," she said, gaze flicking between Kate's file and her face. Without turning to see if Nick was with her, Kate followed the retreating white leather shoes, white stockings, white polyester dress. Down a brightly-lit corridor, carpeted and painted industrial grey. Past over a dozen closed doors, most with voices murmuring behind them, and into an examination room. All the while, the nurse's tablet had been speaking as the woman reminded herself of who Kate was, of the information she'd given over the phone. The device's volume was low so it couldn't be heard by all and sundry, droning *sotto voce* name, address, age, medical history.

"Have a seat," the nurse said, directing them to a pair of padded swivel chairs next to an oak-veneered desk. Its in-trays were filled with neatly stacked papers, a few more of which lay on the ink-blotter next to a tortoise-shell pen. A coffee mug with cartoon pills dancing around the lip sat empty next to the keyboard. On the double-sized monitor, carefully angled so clients could see it, a single round cell bobbed around in the black, glowing while it split. Within seconds, it subdivided countless times; soon the bubble was filled with hundreds of smaller bubbles, a solid blob forming in the middle. In a blink, the fleshy lump stretched, grew bulbous at one end, grew fronds that became arms and legs, grew an umbilical cord. As the embryo morphed into a foetus, Kate looked away. Pulse racing, she dug her nails into her palms and did her best not to hope.

On shelves hung between cupboards on the walls, colonies of tongue depressors and shrink-wrapped Q-tips sprouted from stainless steel beakers. A single cotton ball sat patiently in the bottom of a round-bellied glass jar. Kate hoped they'd use that last woolly fluff before refilling the pot, otherwise the poor thing would be smothered. And when the new cotton balls discovered him there, a solitary outsider, they might not accept him into the fold.

"Dr Goodman will be with you in a moment," the nurse said, before briskly smoothing the sheet of table paper on the exam bench and draping a crisp blue gown across the pillow. She placed the tablet precisely in the left corner of the blotter on the desk, her thin fingers making sure all edges aligned.

"Thank you," Nick replied. Once the nurse had gone, he leaned over and poked at the tablet, but the screen stayed dark, the voice silent, ID locked. Nick turned to Kate and grinned. 'What's one more minute, after this long?'

• • •

They'd tried everything. Monitoring Kate's basal body temperature. Using the rhythm method. Taking Chasteberry, Black Cohosh and Siberian Ginseng tablets. Making love in the morning, at night, at noon. Once, then twice a day. They'd played out each other's fantasies. They'd used the Kama Sutra. To keep Nick going, after their excitement had petered, Kate bought a few XXX porn mags. On elbows and knees, she read the articles while Nick entered her from behind, skimming the pictures, failing to stifle his yawns.

It had been more than a year—closer to two, if Kate was being honest—and still they'd produced nothing. Not a blip in her cycle. Not even a miscarriage.

They'd found Dr Goodman through a friend of a friend. Not even a friend, really, just a work mate of Nick's who invited them to a BBQ. In the kitchen, trying to find a place on the bench for the quinoa salad she'd so painstakingly made beside all the other quinoa salads, Kate's jealous eye had been caught by the baby bump of a woman in a floaty peach kaftan. The woman noticed and started talking—gushing, actually, about how hard they'd tried and for how long, and wasn't it wonderful they'd found Dr Goodman? Which had, of course, stoked Kate's interest and she'd spent the rest of the afternoon quizzing her new-found friend as intently as a prosecutor.

Kindness was etched into Dr Goodman's face; laugh lines bracketing his wide mouth, crinkles beside his Bassett hound eyes. As he spoke his smile came easily, frequently. There was no pressure, no sense they'd failed more dramatically than anyone else had, no promise he was here to *save* them from barrenness. Soft-spoken, he let the truth flow out in palatable increments, his pauses filled by auxiliary information provided by the tablet, which had responded to his fingerprint touch, its mellifluous voice no longer dampened, but clearly projected. The moderate, though not discouraging, success rates: '17.6% for women your age, Mrs Conway.' The chance of her developing OHSS: 'Ovarian hyper-stimulation syndrome—quite unusual, nowadays, but you should be aware of the possibility. Not overly worried, mind you, simply aware. At worst, it's an outside chance.' Last, with lullaby tones hardening ever so slightly, he discussed the rate of multiple births.

"In recent years," said Dr Goodman, "surrogates—DGUs, Delayed Gestation Units—have effectively carried up to five embryos at once. A combination of genetics and pharmaceuticals has allowed these gifted, temporary mothers to revitalise the population—but surely you've seen the broadcasts. I mention this only as an option; you could certainly employ one of these proxies. Let her bear the burden, save yourself the risk . . . " Dr Goodman stopped, cleared his throat. After sipping his green tea, he continued. "Our facility could make appropriate referrals, get you an appointment within the year. The costs could be offset by health cover—you *do* have insurance, don't you?"

Insurance wasn't the problem. Turning to look at her husband, Kate saw her own thoughts reflected in his slouch, his pinched brows, his subtle frown. Mixing their ingredients in someone else's pot just wouldn't be the same—the baby wouldn't be the same. It wouldn't feel like *theirs*, would it? They'd never know, not for sure, that the creature this stranger gave birth to was the one they'd planted inside her. Would they?

Nick reached over, took Kate's hand, and held tight. *We've waited* this *long* . . . While Dr Goodman went on, outlining the process involved in engaging a DGU, she lifted her gaze. Focused on the lonely cotton ball. Started to shake her head.

"Sorry to interrupt," she said, too loud, too quickly. "But we'd prefer to do this ourselves. I mean, can't we even *try* before dismissing the idea altogether?"

Half a heartbeat, no more, and Dr Goodman relented. "Of course," he said. "Of course. It was merely a suggestion. Only," he slurped at his tea, "you must be prepared. For either outcome—in some cases, success can be as difficult to accept as failure . . . "

"We're listening," Nick said, his cold fingers squeezing the blood from Kate's too-warm ones. Attention turned inward as the doctor brought up charts on his computer screen—the number of fertilised eggs she'd have implanted, the placement of needles and injections, legal definitions of when 'life-proper' began, the probable outcomes, the sentences for soul sacrifices—Kate *knew* they'd be parents soon. Sitting up straighter, she bent her left arm slightly and imagined cradling their newborn. Adding a crook to her right arm, she pictured another child there. With their poor luck at conceiving, it seemed unlikely they'd have more than two. Two would be nice, she thought. Two we could afford. They'd have each other, friends from birth, and we—she couldn't control her grin—we'd be a *family*.

• • •

It wasn't as easy as Kate had hoped, not as easy as Dr Goodman's soothing tone had made it seem. The procedures and treatments chewed through their savings (fees for consultations, fees for preparation and storage, fees for preservation, fees for scans, fees for pathology and, finally, fees for every cycle of fertilisation, every cycle of injection) and by their fourth attempt, their bank account was stretched further than their nerves.

They'd been given a tablet of their own—well, loaned—to record the ins and outs of their attempts: Kate's temperature, Nick's temperature, duration of coitus, position, the combination of vitamins she'd taken that day, how active she was, what she'd eaten. Every morning, and twice nightly, she answered an endless series of invasive questions so Dr Goodman could keep track of their progress. And each time Kate logged in she couldn't help but tap the Results tab; and each time her heart fractured a little more when she heard the machine's voice, sweet yet neutral, kind but uncaring, tell her there was 'no change, no success.'

Ground down, their pockets almost picked clean, there was one last attempt left to them before they were broke, and broken.

But this time, somehow, it worked, though eight weeks had to pass before they would know anything for sure. Eight tense weeks, which Kate spent reconciling herself to a life without children, doing her best to convince herself it was better this way; she could only care for so many things at once. With kids, what love would she have left over for Nick? How could she continue to dote on the objects around her? She'd almost persuaded herself, was almost quite sure she believed, when the little voice on the tablet changed its tune and instructed her to make an appointment with the doctor at her earliest possible convenience.

Dr Goodman finally—*finally*—gave them the good news, and they were stunned. Quietly disbelieving, they smiled dumb smiles, each waiting for the other to say something first. At last, Nick whooped and hugged Kate while she giggled, covering her face with her hands. So happy, they listened with only half an ear to the tablet in Goodman's office as it fairly sang the legal terms for their pregnancy, their rights, responsibilities and obligations. Immediately, Kate loved the cheerful voice, and marvelled at what wonderful things technology could do, imagining how the girl who pronounced those guidelines so carefully and clearly could've been an opera singer one day if . . .

For a split second, the thought gave her pause—the idea that this voice came from an orphaned soul, one of those *not* chosen—but then she shook her head, chastised herself for being such a downer, on this, their happiest day. Even so, she switched off the radio in the car on the way home, switched off her phone, while Nick rushed out to the hardware store to spend their last dollars on paint for the baby's room. It was only for a while, just a very little while, that even the most dulcet of electronic tones struck a sad note deep inside her.

• • •

Kate would never admit she didn't enjoy being pregnant.

It wasn't just the morning sickness, although that was bad enough, or the gradually expanding number of unattractive elasticised pants in her wardrobe. It wasn't just the incontinence. It wasn't just the hyper-alert sense of smell that meant she could tell if Nick farted at the other end of the house, or that its stench set off the vomiting. It wasn't just the grinding in her hips every time she walked, or the sense that her centre of gravity had shifted forever. It wasn't just the walking determinedly into one room then forgetting what she came for. It wasn't just that maternity leave meant no grown-up conversations until Nick came home at the end of the day. It wasn't just Nick patting her arse and whistling the Baby Elephant Walk as she lumbered down the hall. It wasn't just her feet growing a size and a half.

It was the voices.

The chorus of tiny voices that kept her awake at night, all the voices of the lost children's souls, all the voices she'd heard during the day from the devices she'd interacted with. All the voices that had once belonged to someone, somewhere else.

• • •

The gel was cold on her distended belly and the tube made a loud, rude noise as the obstetrician squeezed hard to get the last drops out. Kate winced, imagining him holding a newborn. His hands were stubby, short fingers gripping the probe he pressed below her navel, the hands of a manual labourer, someone who planted cabbages. She decided she didn't like him very much—so little in fact that she hadn't even retained his name, even though he'd told her three times. She couldn't be bothered to ask again. They were in the same medical complex as Dr Goodman's office, which presented a misleading façade when behind it snaked a great alimentary canal of specialist suites.

"Three heartbeats detected," said the console attached to the ultrasound machine. The tone of someone who'd have grown up to be an accountant, Kate thought before she registered what it had said or that Nick had involuntarily clutched her hand too hard, his panic transmitted through their palms.

Triplets.

Trip. Lets.

Kate closed her eyes, trying to block out the screen, the obstetrician's round face. At this stage, they couldn't even afford twins. Their house had been on the market for three weeks, and they'd been desperately looking for a smaller place, with the smallest price tag they could find. Even with Kate's maternity pay, it would be years before they could call their living situation 'comfortable' again. And by then, despite the miracles Dr Goodman peddled, Kate would be far too old to have any more children. The Conways would—could—only, ever, have one.

One is enough, Kate told herself, over and over.

One will have to be enough.

Three little hearts pulsed on the screen, like black mouths gaping then swallowing the lie. Swallowing and swallowing, like they surely would every last cent.

The obstetrician looked at Nick first. Kate noticed.

"As you know," he said, "there's a grace period . . . before life-proper starts . . . You can choose which one to keep and at this stage it doesn't count as a termination, so you don't incur any criminal charges. This early, we call it a *surrender*."

"It's just . . . We can't have . . . We can't afford . . . " Words spilled from Kate's mouth, but they flowed toward Nick, not the medic. "Can we wait to decide? Once and for all, that is. Before . . . I mean, will we even know if they're boys or girls before—"

"Sex as yet undetermined," interrupted the console. "Embryonic sacs, stable. *Funiculus umbilicalis*, secure. Vital signs, strong. Probability of full-term gestation, ninety-seven point eight percent."

"As you know," the obstetrician said sternly, after the devastating stats had been repeated for each of the triplets, "termination is not a real option."

"I suppose it's best not to get too attached," Nick said, talking over the doctor, not quite meeting Kate's gaze. "If we know what they are . . . If we wait that long . . . "

We've waited this *long . . .*

" . . . it'll be that much harder. Better not to find out, I guess."

By the time he'd finished, Nick was whispering.

"Most couples choose randomly," agreed the doctor. "They try not to overthink it."

Taking a handful of tissues from a box beside the bed, Kate wiped the ultrasound gel from her swelling bump, then pulled down her shirt. She grabbed a few more sheets to dry her eyes.

What if they chose the wrong one? What if the one she "saved" was sick? Or horrible? What if the other two were geniuses? What if they would've cured cancer, or colonised Mars, if only she'd picked them? What if the survivor hated her? What if Nick ended up hating her? She was certain she would end up hating him, now, just a little.

Even a little was too much.

She was pulled from her thoughts by the opening of the door, that sliding hiss that no amount of engineering could quite silence.

"What will happen to them?" Kate asked Dr Goodman, as he stepped between her and Nick, between flickering screen and bed. She suspected his proximity was less coincidence and more planned management for moments such as this. "The . . . *surrendered?*"

The good doctor had been in the business long enough to know she didn't mean *physically*. Like all would-be mothers before her, she didn't want details about procedure, implements, how, or when. She didn't want to visualise the evacuation. The wrinkled, nestling features. The blood and mucous. The tiny still limbs.

No, he knew she was concerned with more important, ephemeral matters.

"The souls will be extracted and stored . . . Our facility is sponsored by Sony; their orphanages are nurturing, fair trade environments . . . But if there is a brand of which you are particularly fond, we can certainly recommend Sanyo, LG, Acer . . . "

He sat beside her, balancing one plump buttock on the edge of the examination table, and took her hand. 'Some parents like to set the voices of their surrenders for their own personal use. Kambrook does a whole range of 'Junior' alarm clocks that come highly recommended. And Macintosh is working wonders with wearable tech nowadays . . . Many couples find it most heartening, I'm told, being able to hear specific voices with a simple tap on their wrists. An Apple consultant is available on Mondays, Wednesdays and Fridays—if you like, we can arrange an appointment at the front desk. There would be another fee, of course . . . "

I can't do this, Kate wanted to say, but poverty wired her jaw shut. A few months ago, she'd read an exposé on soul orphanages in *TIME* magazine; the factory-like conditions in distribution centres, staff earning less than minimum wage with no breaks, often sleeping underneath their work stations. The overcrowding in dormitories, young spirits crammed into bits and bytes like so many oversized sows into medieval stalls. The gender realignments in computer labs, the impossible number of boys becoming girls and girls becoming boys simply to suit the manufacturer's product, the colour of its plastic, its design.

But not *all* the facilities were like that; even the article had admitted as much. Some were *clean*—whatever that meant—and others free-range. There was a picture, small but detailed, that Kate had stared at for ages: a series of clear glass domes, each bigger than a football stadium, in which the surrendered could roam until they'd matured, or until they were needed. Out in a field in arable country, this orphanage was a few Ks away from the workshops, so the souls could play in peace. The gravel roads leading between bubbles and concrete buildings were lined with roses and daffodils. There were pinwheels and windmills under the vaults, stirring gentle breezes through which the surrendered could soar.

Closing her eyes, Kate imagined two of her own little souls, flitting like moulted feathers through the air. Surely they'd be happy there? Surely they'd be better off?

"I'm sorry to rush you," Dr Goodman said, tapping his watch until the little boy inside it stopped chattering, *Follow-up with the Belvederes at four*, "but we knew the risks—they were clearly outlined in the agreements and the original product disclosure statement. We absolutely need you to nominate a date so we can ensure it comes under the surrender clause and doesn't incur termination penalties."

Heat bloomed in Kate's sinuses, and leaked from beneath her shut lids. She shook her head. *But they won't know us*, she thought. *We should keep them all. They'll be strangers in the orphanage, they'll be left out. They'll never know us, if we let them go. They'll never know each other. They'll never know me.*

In the end, Nick chose a date from the designated fortnight range Dr Goodman presented. Kate couldn't look at him as they drove home.

• • •

Audra wasn't a fussy baby. She wasn't noisy. She slept for hours at a stretch. She ate whenever she could and plumped up nicely, but didn't often grizzle for the breast. If she had a crying spell, she got over it soon enough. Most of the time. Usually. All morning, she'd lie in her crib and stare up at the Baby Einstein mobile Nick's mother bought, a pink blob with a bright orange starfish, blue turtle and sailor-hat-wearing octopus whirling over her head. She was so sedate, so dull, Kate sometimes forgot she was there.

In some ways, Kate thought the little fleshy girl was to blame. If only she'd made noise regularly, gurgled, giggled, blew spit bubbles in that cute way babies have. If only Audra would proudly own the voice she had been given, the voice she'd been privileged to get. If only she could appreciate what she'd won and the two others lost.

Sitting up in bed, the quilt covered with brown cardboard parcels, some open, some still labelled and taped shut, Kate kept thinking about what Dr Goodman had said, how some parents programmed their surrenders into their own personal devices. Kate and Nick couldn't afford that—they'd arranged no hospital meetings with Apple or Microsoft or any techno-upstarts, and they'd had to hand the medical tablet back to Dr Goodman's nurse once they'd brought Audra home almost three months ago. Soon after, they'd both sold their laptops, one to Kate's nephew and the other to Nick's niece, naming a price well below what they'd paid for them. They'd pawned Nick's gaming consoles, the TiVo, the flat-screen TV—any gadget that was mostly intact, buttons and touchscreens passably good, any frivolous comfort that might fetch a few bucks, quick, because they needed the money, any money, to pay for the baby formula and nappies that Audra was going through at a rate of knots. Nick worked double shifts, he worked evenings and weekends, he worked public holidays, but all they had left was one rattly old desktop, two out-of-date mobiles . . . and Kate's boxes of digital secrets.

The iPods. The Fitbits. The Google hearing aids. The Dell KeyNails™, porcelain and acrylic, for typing, making calls, or even playing piano on any hard surface. The new and improved

Away Mate, only $79.95, doorbell and butler in one small plastic case! The Digideskpal. The Roomba. The Fujitsu sun visor. The IBM wireless headphones in gold, silver and platinum, that even Kate couldn't distinguish from regular pairs of hoop earrings. All second-hand, none top of the line anymore, but every last one more than sufficient to store the voices Kate downloaded from the soul orphanage, courtesy of VoiceWorks™ technology. She bought these—and so many other—devices on eBay, mostly, spending her days tracking down the cheapest ones she could get, saving the bigger portion to spend on downloads.

It didn't matter how cheap these things were, the bargains she'd find; before long, they tore through precious funds, devoured her maternity pay, depleted Nick's salary.

And Kate didn't care.

As soon as her husband was out the door, she purchased and she listened. She listened to all the voices, tracking inflections and tones, cadences and quirks. Sometimes she became convinced she'd found one or both of her surrenders; she would play their files over and over, taking comfort for a few days or weeks, but eventually, inevitably, dissatisfaction set in, a sense she'd been mistaken, misled, cheated. And the search would start again.

'Good morning,' Kate cooed at the new GPS unit clipped on her collar, plotting the route from bedroom to kitchen, telling her to turn left with the prettiest little accent she'd ever heard. The child sounds just like her Nan, Kate thought with a smile, quickly walking past Audra's room. Behind the closed door, the baby was exercising her lungs, wailing at a red-faced pitch. Without pause, Kate marched down the hall. 'Turn right in one point five metres,' said the charming little girl nestled next to her ear. Kate was tempted to play with her, to dart back into the linen closet, take a surprise detour through the laundry room, just to see how the surrender would respond; if she'd show traits of her mother's quick wit, or Nick's silly sense of humour. But she resisted; she was in a hurry. There was a Motorola stopwatch hidden in the pantry that she just knew—she was almost positive this time—*had* to be the GPS's brother. Her possible son. She wanted to introduce the kids properly, and to hear their greetings. She wanted to be there if— when—the siblings finally recognised each other. There would be some sign, she thought, some hint of awareness. There *must* be. A change in register. A blinking Bluetooth connection. An identical chirp. Something, however fleeting, that showed they were family. That they were all family. Not Motorolas, not Sharps. Conways, the lot of them. And that, somehow, they *knew* they were wanted. That they belonged.

"You'll love it here, won't you," Kate said, leaning close to the gadget's speaker, anticipating its reply. "Tell me you will."

Tilting her head, Kate strained to hear the placid voice as it began to speak.

"I'm sorry," she whispered after a second, stopping short just inside the kitchen. She scowled as, down the hall, Audra's crying went from sad to shrill. "I missed most of that. Can you please repeat? Louder, if you can. Full volume."

Covering her left ear, Kate pressed the GPS into her right. Hunched and leaning against the fridge, shoulders bunched up to help block Audra's racket, she listened, anxiously, for her daughter to offer reassurances. For her to give Kate straightforward directions. To tell her to proceed.

• • • • • • • • • • •

DOLLS FOR ANOTHER DAY

RICK KENNETT

Mr and Mrs Merewether were alone in the dining room of Ilbridge House in the English parish of Coxham. The evening meal was over and only wine and glasses were left on the table. They were sat close together, he in blue satin, she in brocade, arranging their plans for later that night.

"So it falls to me to do the deed," said Mrs Merewether in an earnest whisper, her eyes glinting in the light of the single taper burning in its silver candlestick on the sideboard.

"It is your place to give him his medicine," said her husband in a similar low tone. Then, his voice taking on a harder edge, he added, "You do not scruple because he is your father?"

"And the grandfather of my children, which should have made him think better of his intentions. Instead he makes it the crux of his claim on them." Her dark ringlets bobbed as she shook her head. "No, James. I do not scruple. We brought this on ourselves, it is true. Now we must end it while we still can."

"Elizabeth . . . do you regret ever marrying me?"

"A young architect with no prospects above a talent in miniatures?"

"There is no need to wound me with the truth."

"The truth often wounds, one way or the other. That is why lying was invented. James, the truth is that if it were not for my father's . . . *workings*, who can say where we would both now be. We could never have afforded all this." She plucked at her rich clothing, then with a sweep of her hand indicated the cut crystal glasses, the vintage wine on the solid oak dining table, the silverware on the sideboard, and by extension the white stone mansion they possessed. "We sold ourselves, James. Not that I countenance it, especially now with the price being asked of us."

"Demanded of us," he corrected her.

"The children—" She broke off and turned suddenly to the window in an attitude of listening, as did her husband. For a moment they held their breaths; but there was nothing to hear. "I thought I heard the approach of that infernal man."

Mr Merewether flinched at the word his wife had chosen to describe their impending visitor: it had been a little too apt.

"James," she went on, looking out at the night, "do you not feel there are eyes out there, looking in at us?"

He glanced through the windows, at the darkness beyond. "There is nobody there. As to our visitor, men who smell of dust and rat-gnawed book bindings are never punctual. We have yet time to make ready." All the same he went to the window, opened it and put his head out with his hand to his ear. Nothing was heard but the wind in the trees of the surrounding park and the distant cries of owls and other night birds.

He shut the window again and went out of the room, closing the door quietly behind him. Alone now, Mrs Merewether swept up the burning taper in its silver candlestick and held it aloft as if afraid of the shadows, afraid of the dark, afraid of what events the night would bring. It was clear by her strained expression that she was striving to keep down a fear threatening to master her. The consequences of her actions this night, she knew, were awful to contemplate. But the consequences of doing nothing were unthinkable.

Mr Merewether returned then and gave his wife a vial of some dark liquid, pushing it into her moist hand, folding her fingers over it.

"For their innocent sakes," he said, and once more left the room to step out through the front door of the mansion. Here he paused to look out into the night, listening.

The bell of the clock in its Gothic cupola above the stables sounded, and he saw that its hands stood at a quarter to eleven. Yes, there was still time. All the same the feeling of being watched, as expressed by his wife a moment before, came to him now from out of the immense quiet, and he shivered. Then Mr Merewether, the practical man of architecture, dismissed the notion. It was nothing but a twinge of conscience; and conscience, he knew, had no place in what was to be done this night.

He turned to glare up at a lighted window in the upper storey of the mansion and shook his fist.

• • •

Mrs Merewether, the taper in one hand and an uncorked wine bottle in the other, entered the bedroom, all smiles and pleasantries to her white-haired father lying awake in his four-poster. He appeared nervous and anxious from the way he shifted about, his fingers drumming on the coverlet. A nurse was asleep in an armchair by the fireside. Mrs Merewether roused her, giving her the wine bottle. The nurse poured some of its contents into a silver saucepan, adding spices and sugar from casters on the table. While she set it on the fire to warm the old man in the bed beckoned feebly to his daughter.

"If the deal is not struck soon, Elizabeth, I fear I may not last the night," he said in a thin, querulous voice.

She took his wrist, felt his pulse and bit her lip in consternation. Not because it was failing as he feared but because it was as strong as ever. He would last the night. He might last many nights.

"When I sign the pact," her father continued, "the processes and the rituals will be enacted and felicitous results obtained before the morrow. We shall all benefit." Her silence to this and the way she looked at him prompted him to add, "The children, yes. But you were aware of this all those years ago when you agreed."

She turned away and said in a low voice something that might've been, "When you *threatened*."

"Do not fret, daughter," he said, oblivious to her suppressed ire. "They will not suffer. But needs must be done in this desperate hour of my life, and if you and your James are to maintain your fortune. He squandered his talents, such as they were, in the making of these mere models and . . . " His lip lifted in a sneer, "*dolls' houses*. Now he is beginning to create *real* houses and is gaining respect and recognition amongst his peers. If this is to continue . . . truly I am your hope for a better life, just as your children are my gateway to deliverance from death, and in turn yours. Remember that!"

Dropping once more into anxious tones, he asked her to go to the window and listen for approaching carriage wheels. She did so, opening the casement and, like her husband earlier, putting out her head, hand to ear. The night was as quiet as ever.

By this time the saucepan on the fire was steaming. The nurse poured it into a two-handled silver bowl and brought it to the bedside.

"No," said the old man, pushing it away. But the women pressed it on him.

"For your health's sake, sir," said the nurse soothingly, and he took it in several grudging draughts.

• • •

Mr and Mrs Merewether were in the drawing room downstairs when the shrieking began. At once the state of high anxiety they'd been waiting in snapped like a thread, replaced by a coldness in the pit of the stomach and a singing in the heart.

Putting on expressions of alarm like Fifth of November masks, they hurried upstairs. By the time they reached the bedroom the old man was already a corpse, collapsing back under the nurse's hands, foam at his lips, his features contorted with agony and rage—as if he had known the cause of his passing—now relaxing slowly into calm.

As servants crowded in with much bustle, the master and mistress of the house stepped back into the shadows lest they betray themselves with the sly smiles stealing slowly over their faces.

Outside in the carriage drive a coach with flambeaux drove up to the front door. A white-wigged gentleman dressed in black was swift to alight and swift up the front steps of Ilbridge House, though he smelt of slow time, of dust and rat-gnawed book bindings. Under one arm he carried a small leather case holding papers with curious clauses requiring a signature; also a small knife with a fine blade to aid in its signing. Nestling beside these items were two antique volumes, *The Book of the Toad* and *Turba Philosophorum*.

At the door he was met by Mr and Mrs Merewether with their sad faces on once more. Bringing him into the dining room, they explained how his haste had all been in vain.

After a thoughtful moment the gentleman in black said, "Yet there is the matter of our agreement."

"The agreement died with my father," said Elizabeth Merewether in a voice quiet yet forthright.

"Madam," the visitor said patiently, "it is clear you do not appreciate that which has been set in train by your father. His mere death cannot—"

"Nevertheless," James Merewether cut in firmly.

Seeing further argument was futile, their visitor bowed, picked up his small leather case containing knife, contract and tomes of necromancy, and returned to his carriage.

The clock in its Gothic cupola above the stables struck the hour.

• • •

Laughter rilled from the nursery upstairs, the sound of mother and father at play with their children. James Merewether, dressed in the black of mourning, was in animated and happy talk with his son Roger. Both were seated upon a truckle bed playing with a model of a frontier fort: a wall of miniature sharpened logs, ladders to lookout platforms where stood little figures of delicately fashioned wood in proper uniforms, shouldering musketry. Barracks, stables and an armoury completed the establishment. Two lines of toy soldiers stood at attention in the parade ground, flanked by their officers.

On the other side of the nursery Mrs Merewether, likewise wearing the attire of mourning, was likewise showing little sign of it in her demeanour. With her daughter Bessie she was delightedly arranging the furniture, the fittings and inhabitants of a large dolls' house in Strawberry Hill Gothic; a replica in fact of Ilbridge House itself with a chapel with its coloured windows at one side, stables at the other. The finger-small doll of a gentleman in blue satin sat in the dining room; a lady in brocade and a boy and a girl sat in the drawing room; a nurse, a footman and a cook were in the kitchen, while in the stables stood two postillions, two grooms and a coachman. In a four-poster in the bedroom little Bessie found a white-haired man in a long white nightshirt. She held the doll up to her mother.

"Grandpapa," she said in that solemn way only a seven year old can.

Mrs Merewether regarded the doll a moment. Then, taking it gently from the child, she replaced it in the four-poster, sliding the bed curtains shut on their rods all round—and quickly pulled her fingers away as if something had just nipped her.

• • •

Out in the park of Ilbridge House, in the deep of the covering night, a lone figure stood watching the lighted windows and the gaiety within. In one hand covered in blood he held a freshly killed toad; in the other hand, clenched tight, were two rag dolls of a boy and a girl. His gaze moved to the coloured windows of the chapel, to the coffin draped with a black velvet pall lying upon a bier, candles in tall candlesticks flickering at each corner. He raised his hands with what they held as his gaze became a rigid stare and began muttering dire, dread words.

Now one tall candlestick lay toppled on the floor beside the crumpled heap of the pall, and the lid of the coffin was open.

Down the passage connecting the chapel to Ilbridge House a grey light not of lamp or of candle but pallid and ugly receded as something moved away.

• • •

In the nursery, while his son was absorbed in extracting cavalry from the stables of his little fort, Mr Merewether quietly left the room. In passing he took a white garment that hung on a peg by the door.

A minute passed and the door of the nursery opened once more. A muffled head poked around it. A bent form of sinister shape, all in white, advanced on the children, their mouths agape, their eyes wide. It stopped, raised its arms and revealed itself—as their father, laughing. But young Roger was already under the blankets in a shrieking agony of terror, and little Bessie had flown wailing into her mother's arms.

"James! Really!" his wife scolded him, but not without merriment, and swatted ineffectually at him with a pillowslip. Then, taking the children on their laps, mother and father patted and consoled them, showing their terror to be nothing but a white gown. Calmed at last, they were put to bed, their parents bidding them goodnight as they left.

They shut the door and stole quietly away.

For some moments all is dark in the nursery, and silent. But now around the door-case there dawns that pallid and ugly grey light that had earlier advanced along the chapel passage. It washes into the room as the door opens and the smell of nine days dead enters, and with it a figure, wrinkled and toad-like, with scant white hair about its head. It looms a deliberate moment above the truckle beds so that their occupants may see and cry out before cold and wrinkled hands reach down and work among the pillows.

The clock above the stables tolls one.

• • •

Ilbridge House stood in an almost knowing silence, broken only by the sound of weeping. For twelve nights running Elizabeth had retreated to her room alone. Though she never said as much outright, James knew she blamed him for what had happened. And now they wore their mourning raiment without pretence.

The daily tours of the estate farms James Merewether now carried out in a mechanical way, neither heeding his workers' condolences nor his overseer's reports. At night he lay awake listening to those intermittent stretches of quiet he hated which preceded the sobbing from his wife's own room. It was the anticipation, the waiting that strung out his nerves the most. Not that he hadn't done his own weeping. "We acted for the best," he would whisper into the dark.

Not that it made any difference.

For on that twelfth night there came another sound to his ears, a softness as of naked feet moving stealthily down the passage outside his room, heard in the silences between the sobs. He realized he'd been hearing the soft noise of their approach for several minutes, but had been deigning its existence to himself. As he stared out into the darkness for a moment a darker shadow crept slowly past his open doorway. He sat up in his bed, heart racing, telling himself it was imagination, that it was a waking dream, that it was anything than what he knew it to be. The smell of death was in the night air.

Then from the next room he heard his wife say in a small, cracked voice, "James, he is here."

As James scrambled in the dark for a candle and a tinderbox, managing only to knock them to the floor, he heard his wife continuing to speak—not now to him but to some other, and her voice came intermittent and in rising pitch: " . . . not let you take . . . insidious design . . . flesh . . . life . . . *monstrous* . . . "

Her words crescendoed into a long, loud shriek. James leapt from his bed, catching in the bed curtains, colliding with a cabinet, rushing headlong into something cold and wrinkled in his wife's bedroom doorway. He recoiled an instant and dim candlelight came into view as something moved away into the dark.

The candle burning on her bedside table flickered ghastly shadows over her prone body dragged half out of bed. Her mouth gaped open in that last despairing cry now silent in her throat, and her eyes were wide with what they had seen.

As he bent to her, knowing in his heart that she was dead, he realized pale light now streamed from behind. He turned sharp about—to see the footman in his nightshirt standing in the doorway holding a candle in a china candlestick.

"What was it, sir?" he gasped.

"You saw it?"

"I saw . . . *something*," said the man, his face bloodless and white.

"Fool!" said James Merewether in a sudden spasm of passion and, snatching the candlestick from his hand, pushed the man aside to race out into the passage, shielding the flame with his hand as he ran. And as he ran he was dimly aware of running down the wake of some disagreeable odour which grew stronger with every flying step he took. He was not surprised to find the trail leading to the nursery.

Its door was firmly shut, as it had been firmly shut since that day twelve nights ago. Yet the odour of death led here; there was no mistake. Stepping forward, he threw the door open, then for some moments stood looking narrowly into the interior, holding the candle in one hand, the candlestick upraised and ready in the other. He did not know—or did not want to know—what he expected to confront in there, though he was conscious of surprise at the nursery not smelling as of a charnel house in summer. There was only the mustiness that any room closed off for a prolonged period might produce. But for all that it was midnight, all was not entirely dark within.

The children's toys, lying between the truckle beds, and all of them works of love by their father, were illuminated in a dirt, grey glow. It seemed to seep from Rodger's frontier fort, its officers and soldiers standing ready, its sentries still at their posts, looking for the return of their young master. It clung like a visible miasma to Bessie's dolls' house, all Gothic arches and turrets and windows, with its population poised within.

The soldiers in the fort turned stiffly like awakening puppets to face James Merewether, and the people in the dolls' house filed out its front door and regarded him steadfastly. They raised their tiny arms and pointed their tiny fingers at him: the officers and soldiers, the gentleman in blue satin, the lady in brocade, the little boy and the little girl, the nurse, the stable staff, the old man in his white nightshirt who alone of the dolls was laughing silently.

"No!" said James Merewether, staring. "No!"

The dolls' house was not now a four roomed model with a movable front, but a living image of Ilbridge House, to one side its stables with turret clock, to the other its chapel of coloured glass windows. Here the gentleman and the lady talked earnestly in the dining room, though not a word could be heard; now the gentleman stood on the front doorstep, shaking his fist at a lighted upper window; now the lady entered that upstairs bedroom to smile and give poison to the old man anxious in his four-poster.

A moment of darkness intervened, then the house lit into new activity with the old man starting up in his bed, hands clutching at his heart, uttering a cry unheard. Now the servants rushed in, and with them the gentleman and the lady who then backed into the shadows to hide their expressions of quiet glee.

Once more darkness fell on the scene and once more the house relit itself.

James gave a gasp of bitter sweet surprise at the sight of his children in happy play with Elizabeth and himself on that fateful night now reliving itself before him. Then with a groan of some unnameable emotion he saw into the chapel and to what was now happening there.

With one last look at the nursery within the dolls' house, where a dirty grey light now dawned around the door-case, James Merewether raced from the room, fearful of meeting what he had glimpsed entering it as he ran through that self same door.

Somewhere behind him a clock bell tolled one.

• • •

Elizabeth's funeral, much to her husband's surprise and dismay, was attended by the white-wigged gentleman in black, arriving in his coach, its flambeaux burning against the night. Still carrying his small leather case he stood in the dark at a respectful distance from those gathered about the torch-lit gravesite, a smile lurking at his mouth.

• • •

Days afterwards James Merewether returned to the nursery—then returned again and again to watch in perverse fascination the re-enactment of his sins, those of his wife, and their awful consequences.

"We acted for the best," he once beseeched the dolls' house with hot tears rolling down his face as it relentlessly replayed the plotting, the poisoning, the joyful play, the vile retribution. At another time he stood over it with an axe, but could not bring himself to destroy it. What if its destruction should be replicated in reality? Or if in some occult manner the blow kill himself? Was it not his own handiwork, physically and spiritually? No, he could not do it, though he often felt now that his life was not worth living. The punishment enacted on his wife and children had been lenient compared to his own.

Trusting no servant to help him, he carried the dolls' house alone and with much difficulty to the lumber room immediately below the roof, placing it in a far corner, covering it with a sheet. He then locked the door and threw away the key, leaving the dolls' house to tell its tale to the dark and to the dust of the years. But wherever he was throughout those years he could always feel it repeating the deeds done, the crimes committed—a conscience of painted wood and coloured glass and moving shadows best kept hidden.

• • •

James Merewether soon afterwards retired to the seclusion of Ilbridge House, a failed and broken man, having never accomplished any real recognition in architecture. Growing pandemoniously fearful of the creeping dirty-grey light of winter sunrises, and firmly convinced all windows were watching, in his later years he became known in Coxham parish as Old Mad Merewether.

• • •

John Merewether, heir to the estate on his uncle's decease, could scarce credit the shameful family secret played out by the dolls' house discovered in its place of concealment on the demolition of Ilbridge House. He eventually secreted it away in the lumber room of his own residence where it remained until sold many years later and thankfully by his descendants to a travelling buyer of antiques.

Who, after watching the hideous pantomime one, two, and three nights running, sold it for a quick ten pounds to an antiques dealer named Mr Chittenden.

Who, professing he needn't waste money on the picture palace when he and his wife could view a drama of the olden times performing in their own household every one o'clock in the morning, sold it on without warning or explanation to an avid collector, Mr Dillet, the owner of a motor car, a fine house and a keen eye for bargains.

Who, frightened into a disquieting state of nerves requiring sea air medically prescribed, had the dolls' house covered with a sheet and conveyed to the loft.

John Merewether sees his late uncle and aunt in murderous conversation in the dining room, lit by a single candle.

The antiques buyer sees the man in blue satin shake a fist at the upper window.

Mr Chittenden and his wife watch the old man start up in his bed, face flushed, eyes glaring, hands at his heart, foam at his lips.

Mr Dillet sees a coach with flambeaux pulling up before the front door, a white-wigged man all in black alighting.

A figure, wrinkled, toad-like with scant white hair about its head, peers into the dolls' house windows as in the nursery a figure, wrinkled, toad-like and with scant white hair about its head, looms a deliberate moment above the truckle beds so that their occupants may see and cry out before cold and wrinkled hands reach down to work among the pillows . . .

● ● ● ● ● ● ● ● ● ● ●

OF GOLD AND DUST

MICHELLE GOLDSMITH

NORTH OF BALLARAT, VICTORIA, 1853

It darts amidst the river gums, an amorphous shadow flickering in and out of visibility between the twisted trunks. No sound heralds its passing, not the crack of a twig, nor the rustling of leaves.

Instead, a slight lull in the usual forest noises accompanies its presence, a strange faraway quality to the hum of insects, the intermittent cries of birds and the far-off trickle of a stream.

Yet to the entity itself, the bush abounds with music. It is aware of every sound, the steady song of sap moving through the trees, the soft snuffling of nocturnal creatures sleeping in hollows and crevices, the sigh of bark sloughing off trunks, and the thrumming of rock and metals buried deep below the earth.

Its progress slows as it nears its destination. It hovers among the boughs, enveloped in the shadows of the treeline. Silently it watches the strange beings around the river. They are humans; yet unlike those it has known before. These behave strangely, constantly digging and searching, like ants, but with less obvious purpose.

Too many, it decides. Too many separate bodies, minds and motives for it to leave the cover of the trees and investigate.

It waits and observes.

• • •

Nothing, thinks Tom, sifting through a handful of river grit. *A whole lot of bloody nothing. As usual.*

He casts the grit back into the ditch at his feet and leans on the handle of his shovel as he waits for his heartbeat to slow. His muscles ache, every sinew in his body seeming to cry for rest as beads of sweat trickle down between his shoulder blades. The song of bellbirds rings out over the sound of his heavy breathing. Otherwise, silence. His gaze falls upon a lone shovel protruding from a pile of earth. Nearby, the cradle, which his brothers should be using to sort gold from slurry, sits still and abandoned.

"Will? Jack?"

No answer.

Tom sighs. *Lazy buggers. Just like them to wander off while I'm working my arse to the bone.*

He straightens his aching spine and sets off to find them.

• • •

Things had been different when the brothers first arrived at the goldfields. The township of Ballarat, once too small to mark on a map, had become a bustling population centre, ringing with the sounds of tools, trade and harness. Excitement crackled almost palpably through the atmosphere, and every hour brought with it more men, eyes bright and feverish with dreams of untold wealth.

Tom watched his brothers' faces as they traversed the hectic main street. Will walked in a daze, his eyes wide with wonder, while Jack laughed, and clapped his younger brother on the back.

"Ha! You hear that Will? That's the sound of wealth. We'll be filthy rich within a year!"

He turned to his elder brother with a smirk. "And to think I had so much trouble convincing you to leave the old farm."

Tom grunted noncommittally.

We'll only be rich if you don't squander any gold we find on grog, dice and women, he thought. He had not forgotten the debauchery they'd witnessed passing through Melbourne. Rampant gambling, booze and decadence. Fortunes made in a day and lost in an instant. Tom also recalled the hungry gleam in Jack's eyes as he'd taken it all in. Keeping the deathbed promise he'd made to his mother to keep 'her boys' out of trouble seemed more impossible each day.

Yet he still clung to a small hope that some hard work might do his brothers good.

Unfortunately, barely a week had passed before it became evident that the reality of the goldfields was far from the romantic ideal Tom's brothers had envisaged, involving far less riches and far more hard work, dirt, disease, sweltering hot days and freezing cold nights. Just as Tom had feared, Jack was the first to tire of the labour, and where Jack led, Will soon followed.

• • •

Tom finds his brothers some way up the river, sitting on a log with the remains of a meal at their feet. They barely acknowledge him, their attention entirely absorbed by the inhabitants of a nearby claim.

"Look at those yellow bastards," says Jack. "They've gotta have plenty of gold by now. It ain't right."

"First the bloody licence fee, and now this," agrees Will.

Nearby, a middle-aged Chinese man shovels earth from the riverbed as if fatigue is an entirely alien concept. Dirt and sweat encrust his weathered features, testament to long hours spent digging. Beside him, a younger Chinese man works tirelessly at the cradle, sorting earth and picking out likely specks with deft fingers.

As he looks on, Tom can't help but wish his own brothers were half as efficient.

"What do they even want with it?" says Will. "It's not like they're gonna set up here permanently. Are they?"

"How would I know?" says Jack. "I hear they send it back to China and use it to build shrines to their gods. Or burn it to send it to their ancestors, or something."

"That can't be right," says Will. "Gold don't burn."

"Who cares what they do with it,' says Tom. "Maybe if you two layabouts spent less time worrying about them and more time working we might find some gold of our own!"

"What's the point?" says Jack. "Bastard Chinaman's probably taken it all. You know they say his daughter's a witch?" He glares over to where a small girl can now be seen handing over what appear to be packages of food to her father and brother.

"Don't be an idiot," says Tom, unable to contain his frustration. "Ain't no such thing."

"How would you know?" says Jack. "And still, it ain't right. Someone ought to do something about it."

"Less talking, more digging," says Tom, hefting a shovel into his brother's hands.

Scowling, Jack returns to work.

• • •

It was hard to forget the day the first Chinese miners arrived.

It had been a hot December afternoon back when surface gold was still plentiful, and men would dig yards from their camps in a sprawling tent city that stretched on for miles.

As always, a steady stream of new arrivals trickled into the goldfields, barely noticed by the men already hard at work.

Tom had been passing through on his way to town for his fortnightly supply run, winding his way through the maze of campsites and stopping to chat with a familiar face here and there, when an unexpected lull fell over the usual goldfields cacophony. Shovels stopped digging and cradles stopped rocking one by one. Conversations ceased mid-sentence as men looked around, searching for the source of the diversion.

A group of strange figures approached on the road, the other travellers giving them a wide berth. At the head of the party was an elderly Chinese man who, despite his age and diminutive stature, appeared to carry twice his bodyweight slung across his shoulders in baskets tied to either end of a wooden pole. After him came a crowd of others. Dozens of men, a few women and one small girl, no more than seven years of age.

Strangely shaped pots and pans, shovels, bedrolls, wrapped canvas tents. It seemed they carried all their worldly possessions on their backs.

"Who the bloody hell are they?" said the man Tom had been talking to.

He was not alone in the sentiment, a speculative murmur rumbled across the diggings.

Seemingly oblivious to the stir they had caused, the Chinese miners continued on until they reached an unoccupied patch on the far edge of the main diggings. Here they stopped and began to pitch their tents.

Slowly the other men returned to their own tasks, although not without the occasional hostile glance shot towards their new neighbours.

In the months that followed more Chinese miners arrived. They came in the dozens or the hundreds, setting up their own growing community. Whispers of their alien customs, their strange foods, tongue and gods, slowly spread. And while most of the men tried their best to ignore them, others became paranoid, scared for their gold or fearful that their wives and daughters might be seduced away with strange oriental magics or promises of wealth.

Jack especially was displeased when a Chinese family began to work a nearby claim.

"It's like they're trying to rub it in our faces," he said. "Bloody heathens."

Tom couldn't help noticing that, most of all, it was the Chinese family's success at finding gold that did little to endear them to their neighbours.

• • •

Tom works tirelessly, hefting shovelful after shovelful of earth long after both Will and Jack have turned in for the day.

Probably already half-drunk starting fights in some filthy sly grog den, he thinks.

Willpower alone staves off the fatigue lingering on the edge of his perception, and drives his limbs to keep moving far beyond their usual limits. He dares not pause lest his muscles finally give in to the inevitable.

Despite his efforts, he barely has enough gold specks in his pouch for the next week's supplies. And even then only if the brothers agree to ration. Tom can guess who will end up having to go without when they run out of flour to make damper. The necessary sacrifices of being the eldest, he tells himself. They're your brothers. And out here, if you ain't got family what else have you got? Yet he can't repress the resentment brewing in his stomach like some cheap, bitter ale.

He casts his shovel aside and crouches down on a nearby log, wiping sweat from his eyes and taking a long swig from his water skin.

When he looks up, he finds he is no longer alone. The small Chinese girl hovers nearby, watching Tom with wide eyes, bright and curious. Her long hair is black and silky, her skin is smooth and unlined and seemingly impervious to the dirt and dust all around her. Had he not seen her often at a distance, Tom might have mistaken her for an apparition of youth personified, come to bid farewell to a weary man.

Nevertheless, Tom is glad for any company to distract him from his aching muscles and growing frustration.

"Hello," he says. "What's your name?"

The girl takes a step closer, but doesn't reply. Wrinkles furrow her brow.

Of course, Tom thinks. She doesn't know much English. If any.

"Tom," he says, thrusting a thumb towards his chest.

A smile breaks out across the child's face.

"Li," she says, copying the gesture.

"Leah," repeats Tom.

His mother had been called Leah.

That's not so strange and unpronounceable.

"Well, Leah," says Tom. "It was nice to meet you, but I've got a lot of work to do. Wanted to have this lot sorted by sundown." He gestures to the pile of freshly dug earth.

Li smiles again and skips over to the cradle.

"Alright, so you're going to stay a while?" says Tom. "I guess we can deal with that."

Wincing as he stands, Tom sets back to work.

To Tom's surprise, the child does not soon grow bored and leave. Instead, she darts to and fro, attempting to help him in her own small ways. She scoops handfuls of dirt to replenish the cradle or sorts through the discarded grit to find small gold flakes that Tom's older eyes have missed.

Some distance away her father pauses in his own work and looks on. Eventually, seemingly satisfied that Tom is not angered by Li's company and poses her no threat, he returns to his digging.

Later, Tom and Li sit on a log by the river and share a scant afternoon meal. They watch the trees swaying gently in the breeze of early evening and listen to the intermittent song of small finches hidden deep in the brush.

As they begin to fold away the cloth that once wrapped their stale bread, Li stops suddenly, staring intently at something in the trees.

"What's wrong?" Tom asks.

Her eyes dart to and fro as through following something Tom cannot see. Then, she darts to the riverside and starts sifting through the grit in the shallows.

"What you looking for?" says Tom.

Li pulls something from the water and reaches out to Tom.

A nugget the size of a coin rests in the centre of her palm.

"For you!" she says, dropping it into his hand.

Tom turns the lump of metal over and over in his fingers, staring in wonder. It's gold alright. Unmistakable.

"But you found it," he says. "It's yours."

He tries to hand it back.

Li just shakes her head and smiles. Then she runs off back to her family as they begin to pack away their things for the night.

• • •

Over the weeks, Tom and Li's friendship grows. Tom finds himself growing less bothered by his brothers' increasingly frequent absences. He even begins to look forward to them, as only when they are away does Li visit. Tom talks to her as he works, finding it makes the demanding physical labour more bearable. And although they do not share much language, over time an understanding develops between them. Her easy company is especially welcome as Tom's arguments with his brothers grow more heated with each passing day, Jack returning home drunk most nights to accuse Tom of sequestering coin and holding out on him.

One afternoon as he and Li sit by the river eating lunch, Tom hears a rustling in the nearby bush. A foraging wombat shuffles out from amidst the undergrowth on the opposite side of the stream. Tom and Li stay still and silent as it ambles by, snuffling through the leaf litter before finally vanishing back into the forest.

Tom notes the delight on Li's young face.

That evening he begins to carve the creature's likeness for her. Each night he takes his knife and whittles away at a block of wood by the campfire.

When the toy wombat is finally finished he presents it to her. The workmanship is undoubtedly crude, but Li seems to think the gift is wonderful.

Tom admits that she can be strange at times, watching things that aren't there. But aren't all children like that? Always imagining things and getting lost in their own little worlds?

He's heard the rumours of course. About Li being a witch and consorting with demons to find gold. Yet he doesn't give them a moment's thought. *She's just got a nose for it*, he thinks. *Besides, she and her family work hard.* Unlike others he could name.

Sometimes Tom thinks that if he ever escapes this place and has a family, he would hope his daughter would be a lot like Li.

One afternoon Tom is digging when he senses something wrong, a softening of sound and a strange quality to the air around him. Beside him Li is silent, staring at a spot in the shadow of the river gums some distance away.

Tom follows the direction of her gaze. He looks on with shock as a nebulous shape resolves in his vision.

It's like nothing he's ever seen before. A strange shifting mass of fur, feathers, bark and scales, diaphanous as though composed of smoke and emitting a soft light, like some luminous fungus. Something that by all logic shouldn't exist.

Yet Tom feels surprisingly calm in its presence. It gives off no sense of enmity. It merely is.

So this is what Li has been seeing.

As if sensing his recognition, the creature shifts forward to hover purposefully over a nearby section of riverbed.

Then it begins to fade, its form slowly ebbing away until no trace remains.

Li runs to the riverside, gesturing Tom to follow. He picks up his shovel and digs into the indicated spot. Hope leaps in his stomach as he feels the blade connect with something hard. He lifts the shovel free to find a gold nugget, almost twice as large as the one Li had found for him, resting amidst the grit and pebbles.

• • •

Later that night, as he lies restless in his tent, Tom tries to make sense of what he's seen.

It couldn't have been real, could it?

The gold in his pouch testifies otherwise.

Why not? he eventually decides. After all, hadn't the native folks said the bush was full of spirits?

Besides, Tom thinks, *if a bush spirit was lingering around here, why wouldn't it choose Li to befriend? The rest of us had dismissed it as primitive nonsense. And to an ancient spirit we're probably all newcomers, European and Chinese alike.*

Satisfied in this conclusion, Tom sleeps at last.

• • •

The next morning Tom leaves for Ballarat on his fortnightly trip for supplies.

Walking to town by foot, exchanging their meagre gold findings for coin and negotiating provisions often keeps him overnight, which means leaving Jack and Will to their own devices. And thanks to Jack and Will's rampant spending, even with the extra gold he and Li have found Tom will barely be able to afford enough to see them through. Yet as much as Tom hates to leave the claim in his brothers' careless hands, his desire to keep them away from the many temptations of town is stronger. Especially lately. He's heard talk of drunken brawling and although both his brothers vehemently deny any such thing occurred, Tom is sure the scrapes on Jack's knuckles aren't there from digging. He can just imagine having to spend his last coin bailing someone out of the lockup.

Best to leave before either of them get a mind to make trouble.

• • •

It's the early hours of the morning, the darkness hot, still and heavy. Moonlight dances off the surface of the river, the reflected light as pale and fluid as the creature that moves amidst it. It sways to the gentle rhythm of beating moth wings and the far off call of a tawny frogmouth.

The girl however, stares intently at the riverbed. Searching.

The creature senses her intent: to help a friend in need.

It can taste the man's weariness imprinted on the earth he's turned, frustration and desperation potent in his fallen sweat. Although it cannot fathom whatever strange motives keep the man digging, the creature recognises these emotions and is drawn to their resonance.

It follows the song of gold beneath the river's silt down to where it's loudest, where the metal is closest to the surface. The girl follows, her gratitude and anticipation brushing against the creature's perception.

As the girl crouches down and begins to search through the river grit, the spirit detects other humans approaching. Two men stagger through the night, the scent of alcohol seeping from their pores and rising on their breath.

"Told you we wouldn't need much coin," says the older. "Mrs. Higgins serves only the finest!"

"Don't know about finest," the other replies, laughing. "But it was certainly some of the strongest."

Subtly, the spirit nudges at their minds, attempting to cloud their sight and direct their notice away from the child by the river's edge.

It is too late.

"Well, would you take a look at that," says the older man. He points to the place where the girl crouches, still searching amongst the silt.

"Ain't right," he mutters. "Someone oughta do something."

The younger man snorts quietly and nods in agreement.

A cruel smile breaks out across the elder's face. "Reckon it's about time someone taught the little chink witch a lesson." He stalks towards the small figure.

Though it cannot understand the man's words, the creature senses his malice. The long simmering resentment it detects within him flows unchecked under the influence of alcohol and the cover of darkness. Yet there is little it can do. The girl is far too intent on her task to notice as the spirit grasps at her mind, trying to direct her notice to the man creeping up behind her, urging her to run.

She leans over, reaching further into the water.

The man shoves her hard from behind.

The girl plunges forward with a small cry. There is a loud splash, and a sickening crack as her head hits a partially submerged rock. She twitches once, then goes still, a dark stain seeping into the water around her.

The younger man stares at the body in mute horror. The elder looks frantically around for witnesses. "Shit, shit, shit."

The creature looses a mournful cry, an undulating keen that reverberates throughout the surrounding bush land, as if taken up by every tree, hill and stone. Despite the mildness of the night, goosebumps rise on the men's skin.

"Quick, let's get out of here!" says the younger.

"Wait, not yet," says the older. "We need to move her away from our claim."

The younger man complies, hands shaking, and together they heave the girl's body from the water and set it down slightly upstream. A chill wind picks up, stinging their skin and whipping angrily at their clothing. Then they run.

• • •

Tom knows that something is wrong before he even reaches camp. A distinct feeling of unrest radiates throughout the atmosphere. The familiar working noises of the goldfields have been replaced by the discordant notes of raised voices. He crests the rise and surveys the scene below, quickly spotting the gathered crowd.

His innards twist like black snakes in his stomach. Abandoning his wheelbarrow of supplies he hurries down the hill towards camp.

There, in a circle of spectators, stands his brother Jack. And there, just a few feet away, is Li's father, struggling in the grip of two brawny miners. His wife and son are held nearby, the younger man similarly restrained and sporting a fresh black eye. Tears trace winding patterns down their dust-coated cheeks.

Li is nowhere to be seen.

The man's voice cracks as he screams words in his own tongue. "Xuè'àn! Xiōngshǒu!"

"God damn it! For the last time, I had nothing to do with it," yells Jack. "Don't know how you got it into your bloody yellow head that I did!"

"That's right," comes a voice from the crowd. "Not this bloke's fault you folk can't look after your own."

A murmur of agreement runs through those assembled.

"What the hell's going on here?" Tom demands, trying vainly to push his way through the crowd.

A man grabs his arm and mutters to him. "Chinaman's little girl was found dead in the river this morning and now the crazy heathen's got it in his head your brother had something to do with it. Bloody insanity. She obviously slipped on the rocks. Can't see in the dark with them slanty eyes."

Tom's legs grow weak beneath him. He looks through the mass of bodies to his brother and feels a wave of bile rise in his stomach.

That moment, Li's father breaks free and lunges towards Jack. "Murderer!" he screams.

Jack shoves the smaller man back into the waiting arms of the two big miners. One lands a punch straight into the bereaved father's midsection before the other shoves him, winded, to the ground. The man lies still, face down in the mud.

Sensing the spectacle has come to an end, the miners begin to disperse.

Tom breaks through the crowd just as Li's father finally struggles to his hands and knees. His face is plastered with dirt and blood. All the fight seems to have bled right out of him, replaced by grief and despair.

"I'm sorry," says Tom weakly. "I'm so sorry."

The man turns away.

She's gone, Tom thinks. *She's really gone.*

• • •

The next morning Tom wakes early, takes the remaining gold from his pouch and goes in search of the Li's family. Yet, when he reaches their camp, they are gone.

He wonders if they took Li's body with them. He hopes so. Her final resting place shouldn't be somewhere she had suffered and been unwelcome. Tears begin to leak from his eyes as he wanders towards the river where they spent so many days together. For a moment, he thinks he detects a familiar presence, a tell tale shimmer near the riverbed, but when he blinks the space is empty once more. Almost.

He leans down to find the wooden wombat he carved for Li, half buried by gravel. When he looks more closely he detects a dark stain on one of the rocks in the shallows. A wave of nausea threatens to overcome him. He staggers to his feet and makes his way back to camp.

• • •

"I'll have nothing more to do with you," says Tom, shoving clothes and other possessions violently into a pack. "You'll be damned in God's eyes and mine!"

"Come on, Tom. You don't really think I had something to do with that China girl do you?" says Jack. "Told you I don't know a bloody thing about it!"

"Damn you, Jack!" cries Tom. "You think after all this time I can't tell your lies? And now you damn well want to work her father's claim?"

"There's gold there, I know it."

"Is that all you think about?" says Tom. "All the gold in the world won't make you any less of a murdering bastard."

"Prove it. If you have proof go to the troopers, see if they'll hear you."

Tom stands silent, fists clenched and teeth gritted.

"Didn't think so. Even you're not that stupid. Who'll miss one less chink?"

Rage surges through Tom, hot and urgent. His fist connects loudly with flesh and his brother stumbles back, hand clasped to his face.

"Fine," spits Jack through a bloodied nose. "We don't need you anyway. But I won't see you come begging when we're living like kings and you're dirt poor on your beloved farm."

Tom ignores him, turning instead to his youngest brother.

"Will?"

Will looks down at his feet, unable to meet his elder brother's eye.

Tom casts his brothers one last disgusted look, then grabs his swag, ducks out the tent flap and storms off, not once looking back.

• • •

The spirit rushes through the forest, the wind hissing angrily through the eucalypts as it passes. It is not alone. Leaves rustle and twigs snap beneath the hooves of a dozen horses. Subtly nudging at their riders' intentions, it leads the group on a winding path through the scrub.

On the road up ahead, a coach rounds the corner. Pulled by four horses, It's accompanied by a trio of armed guards, one to each side and the last trailing behind.

The spirit shifts forward, placing itself in the coach's path.

It begins to sing.

With a slow deep thrumming like the sound of plants growing and rock eroding, it calls water from deep below the earth. The road grows rapidly muddy, catching at the coach horses' hooves, slowing their progress. A wheel comes loose on an axle.

"Shit," says the driver, reining in his horses.

A curtain is pulled back in the passenger compartment, revealing the faces of two men at the window.

"What's wrong?" says one.

"Wheel's come loose," says the driver. "Won't take too long to sort."

"This isn't good enough," says the passenger. "Got a cheque here worth more than your living and I better bloody well be in town spending it by tonight or—"

"Wait, Jack. You hear that?" says his companion.

The sound of movement amongst the scrub grows gradually louder, a cacophony of breaking sticks and snapping foliage. All other noise seems to cease, the silence like an indrawn breath.

"We're about to be murdered by savages!" cries the younger passenger.

"Shut up! You'll guide them to us."

On cue, a group of armed riders burst from the undergrowth. Rapidly they surround the coach.

"Hands in the air!" cries the leader, his voice accented with a slight Irish brogue. "This 'ere's a holdup."

Outnumbered, the guards lower their firearms.

• • •

Tom returns to the abandoned homestead. He pulls the planks off the door and wanders the musty, dust-shrouded rooms. They smell of dirt, mice and home.

He makes his way to the back veranda and looks out over dry, empty paddocks. It will take a lot of work to get the place up and running again. But now more than ever, Tom is no stranger to hard work and heartbreak.

VICTORIA, 1860

The man in the tunnel digs furiously. He digs through the day and late into the night when all the other miners are gone. His back is bent, his hands are raw, his nails bloodied, his face lined and old beyond its years. He eats little and rarely sleeps, skin stretched tight over sinew and bones. All the while his eyes shine bright and wild, and he mutters to himself—"We'll find it again. Just one more shovel. One more and we'll find it. You'll see." The same words on endless repeat. His obsession is all-consuming, almost unnatural, as though exacerbated by some external force. He digs alone. Even his younger brother will have naught to do with him now. Yet from the dancing shadows of the torchlight, the spirit watches. As it often has.

Finally, it begins to sing. It calls to rock and to soil, coaxing them to wake and move from their slumber. It calls to the wooden sleepers that support the tunnel, coaxes them to splinter. Slowly but surely, it sings the earth down upon him.

• • •

A hot, parched wind sweeps over the fields to rattle against the old weatherboard farmhouse, causing shutters to bang and walls to groan. A chorus of cicada song farewells the setting sun and an electric tingle runs through the atmosphere; a hopeful herald of rain to come.

Tom exhales wearily, taking the carved wombat from its place atop the fireplace and sinking into his weathered armchair, bones aching and muscles throbbing from another long day tending the fields.

It's been seven years since he left the goldfields and returned to scrape a living upon the dusty earth. It is hard, backbreaking work. His hands are calloused from the plough and his face weathered from the sun. Dust and grime seems to have ingrained themselves in his every pore. Yet he cannot bring himself to regret his choice. Not now. Not ever.

He turns the wooden toy over and over in his hands.

He's heard the rumours of unrest on the goldfields, of violence between the Chinese and European miners. Yet while the newspapers decry the invading yellow menace, all Tom can picture is Li, who died so young, and the look on her father's face as he rose from the mud.

He recalls the gloating letter from Jack, received soon after Tom arrived home, announcing that his brothers had stuck a large lode on Li's father's old claim and were rich.

The chorus of insects slowly fades to silence, and Tom detects a familiar shifting presence by the half open window.

"Is it done?" he whispers, his breath catching.

A sense of alien satisfaction brushes against his consciousness. For a moment Tom is sure he detects a faint scent of disturbed earth and blood. Then the presence slowly dissipates, leaving him alone in the night once again. He feels cold. Numb. His hands shake.

Outside, the storm breaks, the first patterings of rain resounding against the corrugated iron roof.

• • • • • • • • • • •

METEMPSYCHOSIS

JASON FRANKS

Layne had spent the entire morning hunched over the pinned-out vellum leaves and all he had to show for it was a crick in his neck.

He'd filled two pages of his notebook with beautiful cursive, but that was entirely because he enjoyed exercising his fountain pen. He had produced little more than a continuous ink line. There was no greater meaning in it than there was in the old manuscript.

Layne put the pen down and let out a long breath. "This isn't prose." The insight surprised him as he said it.

"What?" Trimby looked up from his workstation, across the lab and near to the window.

"It's not prose."

"Of course it's prose," said Trimby, pushing at the cuffs of his tweed jacket as if ready to engage in fisticuffs. Layne wanted to laugh almost as much as he wanted to punch him. "The wallet clearly states that it's a diary."

The document, sealed in a leather enclosure, had been found in a Tipperary bog not far from the famous *Faddan More* site. The leather had been dated to 400CE, which made the wallet a major archaeological find in its own right. An inscription in the Ogham alphabet identified its contents as the journal of a druid named *Edraghodag*. The journal inside the wallet was 500 years older yet. Trimby and his colleagues could not identify the script the druid had employed and assumed it to be some kind of cipher. That was why they had engaged the dubious services of Layne Hutchings.

"I doubt whoever inscribed the wallet could read these pages any better than we can," he said.

"Why would such a person lie?"

"Dunno," said Layne. "Not my area."

"Your area is the translation of gibberish," said Trimby. "Perhaps you should stick to it."

"The druids had no written language," countered Layne. "How can it be prose?"

"Yes, well," said Trimby, bristling. "Perhaps that's less true than we first believed. The Gaulish tribes could and did write in Greek and Latin—"

"But this is neither. If Eddie the Druid could write, maybe he—"

"*Edraghodag.*"

"Oh, yeah," said Layne. "I've been meaning to ask you about that. What does 'Edrag-odac' mean, anyway?"

"It's pronounced *Edraghodag.*"

"I don't care how you say it. What does it mean?"

"It is a bit unusual," conceded Trimby.

"It's a bunch of nonsense syllables," said Layne. "It doesn't even sound like Gaelic."

"Are you now an expert on Celtic languages?"

"No, but I *am* an expert on gibberish."

Layne knew he was on shaky ground. He wasn't an historian or a linguist; he wasn't even a proper cryptologist. Layne was a puzzle-solver: sub-literate in ten different languages, talented at maths and logic, but strictly amateur league in any single discipline. Layne's abilities lay in the narrow intersection of all those areas: intuiting solutions to unusual symbolic problems.

Trimby's group had come to him out of desperation. They'd flown him up to Dublin and put him up in a four-star hotel, hoping that he could shed some light on this mystery among mysteries: a 2100 year old document written in an unknown alphabet, authored by an obscure figure belonging to a secretive sect of a culture that had long been extinct.

"Mr Hutchings, your job is to help us decode the document, not to argue with known fact."

"I . . . but . . . " Layne sighed. "Ah, whatever." He had a feeling that his contract was not going to be renewed.

Trimby turned back to his screen. Layne sighed again and returned his attention to the manuscript. He moved the magnifying lamp over the leaves again and stared down at the rows of angular characters. Some of the figures looked as if they might be pictograms; others were joined in a cursive. The orientation of the letters changed from page to page, sometimes from paragraph to paragraph: here they went left-right, top-bottom; there it was bottom-top, right-left. The author's hand was confident throughout. Layne supposed that Edraghodag had been ambidextrous.

"Eddie the Druid, you are one fucked up individual."

Trimby snorted without looking up. The academic was still trying to master Facebook and it appeared to be occupying all of his attentive resources.

Layne looked at his watch. "I'm going for lunch," he said.

• • •

The lab was empty when Layne got back. The hamburger and two pints of Guinness sat heavy in his stomach, but not heavily enough to account for the sinking feeling. When he opened his email he found an itinerary for his flight back to Melbourne sitting in his inbox. They were shipping him out at the end of the week. He scowled when he saw that they'd routed him through Heathrow.

Trimby returned eventually, accompanied by his boss, Quinnel. "I need a report on your findings by noon tomorrow."

"It's not going to be very long," said Layne. "I've only been here a week."

"The department wants to evaluate what you've got so far," said Quinnel. "If the Dean thinks it's worthwhile, we'll get you working on this from home."

Trimby made a doubtful face, but said nothing.

"Great," said Layne. Work from home, fuck. He would have to get the internet reconnected. The McDonalds across the road from his flat had cottoned on to him stealing their wifi and blocked him. Or maybe his ancient laptop was dying—that was also a distinct possibility.

Thinking of home made him think about Libby. He wondered if she'd even noticed he was gone.

"You better get on with it," said Quinnel.

"Don't forget to spellcheck," said Trimby.

• • •

The flight to Heathrow was easy, but getting to the Qantas gate from the Aer Lingus terminal required a grilling at Passport Control and two more security screenings. At the first screening, a customs guard confiscated Layne's toothpaste and shaving gel. At the second, an officious prick with an earpiece engaged him in a long and vigorous debate as to whether or not his fountain pen constituted a weapon.

Layne had finished the Sudoku and the word puzzles in the in-flight magazine before the flight was fully boarded. He flipped restlessly through the duty free catalogue. He examined the safety card. He even read some of the adverticles in the magazine. None of it held his attention for long.

Not that Layne was in a hurry to get home. It was winter in Melbourne, and he had no heating in his single bedroom flat. He hadn't enjoyed Dublin particularly, but he had liked living in a hotel and being able to expense claim the cost of restaurant meals. Most of all, he liked the paycheque . . . but it wouldn't be long before he was back to two-minute noodles and dry cereal. Work was scarce for a freelance puzzle solver.

Layne turned the airline magazine upside down and flipped through it again, finding patterns in the white-space; playing Tetris with the word shapes. He wanted to work.

Layne did not miss the lab, or the company of Trimby and Quinnel. He did not particularly care about the secret history of Eddie the Druid. Layne just wanted the challenge of a problem to solve, and Edraghodag's journal was a doozy.

When the 777 reached cruising altitude the in-flight entertainment came on. It took Layne about ninety minutes to clock each of the dozen videogames on his TV unit. He tried to watch a movie, but the poor contrast on the tiny screen hurt his eyes. He flipped through the music channels, but that just annoyed him into further restlessness. The fingers of his right hand were twitching. Layne sighed and fished inside his carry-on for his pen and a notepad. His neighbour stirred, but did not waken when he turned on the reading light.

Layne doodled in the pad to get the ink going. A tree, a heart, a skull, a dagger. A pentagram, a star of David, an ankh, a swastika, a cross, a crescent moon. He put a circle around the cross to make it a Celtic gravestone. He scratched it out.

Layne wasn't much of an artist, but he often doodled like this when he was working; manipulating the pen mindlessly while his attention wandered around the edges of a difficult problem. He inscribed a tessellated pattern around the border of the page. He was bone weary, but sleep just would not come.

When the pilot announced that they were descending towards Melbourne, Layne had filled up the entire notebook. Some of the pages appeared to be transcriptions from Eddie the Druid's journal, but most of it was meaningless scribble.

When he looked down at his hands he noticed that both of them were speckled with ink.

• • •

Layne's flat was a mess—just the way he'd left it. Empty beer bottles, piles of books and discount DVDs, plastic shopping bags and dust. The smell of it shocked him, as it always did when he'd been away.

Layne dumped his bags in the bedroom and turned on the space heater. He crouched shivering in front of it for a few minutes, and then went to put on the kettle. He pulled a chipped mug off the shelf, put in a teabag, and waited for the water to boil.

Eventually he noticed that the kettle was unplugged—and so was the phone.

Layne picked up the phone while he waited for the water to boil. The dial tone skip-stuttered: he had voicemail.

Layne couldn't remember the last time he'd heard Libby's voice on the phone. She never answered a call, never returned a message. Libby would usually communicate by SMS or not at all.

"Layne, you bastard, what are you up to? Want to meet me for coffee? Bye."

The message was ten days old. She'd probably forgotten she'd left it already. He dialled back anyway.

Libby's voice over the phone surprised him. "Don't you listen to your messages?"

"I was overseas."

"You didn't tell me you were going." She always sounded angry over the phone.

"I tried. You didn't return my call."

"Well, you're back now. How about that coffee?"

"I just got off the plane. I need a shower and about fifty hours of sleep."

"Tomorrow, then? Café Moro at 10?"

"Better make it 11."

She hung up without saying goodbye.

• • •

Libby was pacing outside Café Moro when he arrived, even though he was five minutes early. When she saw him coming, her scowl changed to a grin and she rushed over.

"Layne! How are you?"

"Same as always," he said. "Scraping by. You?"

"I'm great."

Libby paid for the coffees, although she was usually just as broke as he was. She had a part-time job, told him, as well as some freelance. She talked about all the new bands he hadn't heard of; all the movies he'd avoided watching on the plane.

"I'm trying to be positive, do positive things," she told him. "I'm tired of being so fucking *glum*, you know?"

"That's great," he replied, without conviction.

When their empty cups were cleared away and the staff were putting up the chairs for closing, Libby said "Hey, you wanna go see that new Takashi Miike flick?"

"Is it out already?" Layne wasn't sure if he'd seen any of the old Takashi Miike films, but he'd almost definitely heard the director's name before.

"Opens next Thursday at the Kino."

"Sure." Or was Miike an actor? He'd have to double-check on Google.

"Call me?"

"I will."

They parted with a hug and a handshake.

• • •

When Layne called her the following Thursday, she didn't answer the phone. He left her a message. She didn't reply.

• • •

Trimby's phone call woke him Saturday morning at 4am. Funding cuts, Global Financial Crisis, other priorities, blah blah blah. Layne could keep working on the manuscript if he wanted to—the funding 'might come back'—but Trimby couldn't guarantee he'd be paid. If Layne found anything he would, of course, be properly attributed when Trimby published.

Like hell.

• • •

On Thursday he tried Libby again; left a message suggesting a trip to the Melbourne Show. Saturday she texted back that she would think about it.

In the meantime Layne pottered around the flat, flipping through his dog-eared copy of Edraghodag's journal. He copied it out by hand, doodled and diagrammed all over it, but he still couldn't see any pattern.

He hadn't intended to work on the diary, but he had nothing else to do. His TV didn't work now that they'd stopped broadcasting in analogue.

• • •

The following Monday, Layne went to the Melbourne Show by himself.

He was loath to spend the thirty bucks for the ticket, but he'd been cooped up in the flat with Edraghodag for so long he had started talking to himself. Or to the druid, he wasn't sure. Or perhaps it was to someone else entirely.

Well, it wasn't talking exactly; more like making meaningless sounds. They felt good on his tongue, but there was neither language nor music in them.

He never could hold a tune.

Layne hunched into his threadbare mechanic's jacket and plodded through the showgrounds. He watched punters lose their money at the game stalls, listened to a salsa band playing on a small stage. The streets were thronged with fat teenagers: girls wearing hotpants despite the chill; boys in low, skinny jeans. Young parents with urgent business forced their ways through the crowds, battering their prams against the shins and ankles of the milling hordes.

Layne walked amongst the spinning, rearing, shrieking carnival rides. He stood at the back of a pavilion where a group of woodsy types competed in a chainsaw carving competition. The crowd around the diving pig's marquee was so thick that he couldn't get close enough to see the platform, let alone the animal. He wandered through the reeking livestock pens without bothering to look at the cows and swine.

The wind was cold. Layne pulled on the hood from the sweatshirt he wore under his jacket. A dozen seagulls wheeled across the sky in ominous formation.

He snorted. Omen? They were only fucking seagulls.

Layne looked at his watch. Still an hour before the stunt show—the only thing he actually wanted to see. Dirt bikes and monster trucks, yeah. He looked up at the sky again . . .

Spots before his eyes. Jesus, he'd been staring at the sun. Layne blinked and lowered his head, pinched the bridge of his nose. He couldn't remember the last time he'd eaten.

He went looking for food, but none of the deep-fried, sugar-coated wonderments looked appetising. He bought a burnt-tasting coffee and carried it into the pet pavilion. Rabbits . . . He wanted to buy a rabbit.

He wanted to take it home and cut it open, leave it dead and bleeding with its guts wound around the foot of a great oak tree.

Layne stopped so fast he spilled coffee on himself.

Cruelty to animals? What the fuck was wrong with him? Besides, he wasn't sure he could tell an oak from a eucalypt. He threw the remains of the coffee into a recycling bin, spilling lukewarm fluid all down the outside of the receptacle. A bearded hipster who was apparently the guardian of the trash glared at him. Layne snorted and walked away.

Next door to the pet pavilion was a gardening expo. Layne looked disinterestedly at bags of fertilizer, wheelbarrows, spades, pot plants, ride-on lawnmowers. He had no garden; no use for any of that. What Layne needed was a sickle.

There weren't any sickles, but he did find a tree surgeon's pole saw at the forestry display. It had a telescopic haft and it could be fitted with a number of different attachments. Layne chose a 460mm impulse-hardened blade. It cost more than he could afford, but he spent the money anyway.

Layne took the pole saw home without giving a further thought to the stunt bikes and monster trucks.

• • •

Libby hadn't been a serious runner since she'd done her knee, but she still liked to get out for a jog. Long distance: anywhere from 10K to half-marathon distance. Her new job kept her busy during the day and she was . . . not a morning person . . . so Libby ran in the evening, when the streets were empty and the moon was high.

Layne knew her route, or at least the start of it. He'd tried to run it with her once, but she'd lost him less than a kilometre from the share-house where she lived. He knew the route, and he was waiting for her.

She jogged right past the oak tree where he was standing, hooded in his army surplus poncho. She didn't see him. Her eyes were on the road ahead, her breathing loud and regular. Layne stepped out and swung the pole saw.

Libby never saw it coming. The blade made a flat, whistling sound as it sliced into her neck. He pulled it back towards him and the reverse-angled teeth made a more determined cut; tearing through the skin, severing the pipes in her throat, grating on her spinal column. He changed his grip and clubbed her down with the butt of the weapon.

"Obey the law," said Layne. "Uphold the faith."

• • •

Layne shook all the way home.

He tried to pour some tea, but his fingers wouldn't grip the cup. It exploded on the side of the counter, splashing scalding water all over his legs.

The big square Johnny Walker bottle was easier to handle. He pulled it down off the shelf and took a slug that spilled as much down his neck as into his mouth.

Layne started to sob. Jesus fuck—what was he doing?

Layne was a loser; he knew it. He was a self-obsessed arsehole with anti-social tendencies, but there were thousands, millions like him; in this city and in every other. Layne was an ordinary loser. He wasn't the kind who went out and killed the girl who wouldn't return his calls.

Or at least he hadn't been, until tonight. Until the sun had demanded it. Layne put his face in his hands.

He told himself this wasn't about Libby; it was about *access*. Libby lay dead and disembowelled beneath that stunted oak tree because Layne had better *access* to her life than he did to anybody else's. He knew where she lived; he knew how to find her alone. She was the closest thing to a friend he had. The sun had demanded blood, and Libby had been the easiest for him to bleed.

He told himself it was about access, but some buried part of him felt that Libby owed him something. He had taken it from her and given it to the sun.

He remembered how it felt to see her fall. The weapon suddenly weightless in his hands. The sharp smell of eucalyptus on the air, and the rising stink of blood. The moon had emerged from cover to exalt him with its light. He had honoured his gods and taken his vengeance and he had never, ever, felt so good.

And now the shame and the guilt, but still . . . still he felt the joy of it.

It wasn't him. It was someone else.

Layne had knowledge, now, that was not his own. He knew the birds and the trees. The gods spoke to him—the sun and the moon—and though they would not answer his questions they were not shy about issuing commands. There was knowledge, there was art, but there were no memories. There was no name but his own. There was no will but his own.

But this Layne was somebody else.

• • •

The sun awoke Layne early the next morning.

He didn't want to get up, but the sun demanded it. With a pounding hangover, with eyes red and raw, he sat down at his desk and put his nose to the Edraghodag manuscript.

He still couldn't read it, but today he found a kind of music in its pages. There was a rhythm, although there wasn't a beat. There were changes of pitch, but they were strung together in a way that did not create a melody. It took a conscious effort not to gibber the song out loud.

He could feel the text twitching inside him, catching in his lungs; shivering its way out of his subconscious through his fingers, his feet, his lips.

The manuscript documented truths that could not be described with symbols; truths that could not be parsed with a grammar or determined with any kind of calculus. Truths that stripped reality of context; that drove the meaning out of words. Truths that transcended nature; that denied science and contradicted reason.

Truths that proved only magic.

At midday, it was time for him to take sustenance. Hunger and thirst had become physically painful, but the imperative that drove Layne from his desk was not a biological one. The noonday meal was an offering.

Layne walked a kilometre to the local shopping centre, as he had many times before. There, he bought a box of stale sushi and a litre of water, which he consumed without pleasure.

In a Chinese grocery store behind the food court, he found a sickle with a factory-forged blade and a sturdy wooden haft. It cost barely thirty dollars. The proprietor of the store took his money without curiosity and gave him the instrument in a used plastic bag.

It was exactly what he wanted.

Layne stumbled out of the automatic doors and staggered down the street, the sickle swinging heavily in its bag. There weren't many pedestrians out in the mid-afternoon drizzle, but those few he encountered gave him a wide berth.

There was some green up ahead. A public park. Trees, a garden bed full of hydrangeas and rhododendrons, a wall of bushy wattles. Layne sat down on an empty bench and put his head back, looked up at the sky through the reaching limbs of a ghost gum.

Crows and magpies lit on its pale branches. The sky darkened slowly; black ink spilling into a bowl of grey water. Hours flowed over Layne without their usual viscosity, diluted by some strange new air. Night fell.

There were no stars in the cloudy, light-polluted sky. Even the waxing moon seemed inconstant when he rose from the bench and went staggering on his way.

There were three police cars parked outside his building. Layne drew up behind a jacaranda tree, two addresses from his home and across the street. The lights were on in his apartment. Where the manuscript was.

A pair of cops were posted at the front of his building. One of them spoke into a radio. From where he stood Layne couldn't make out what she said, but he could hear the squelch and squawk of the reply. The copper shifted uncomfortably and turned her head.

She was looking directly at Layne, but it took her a good half a minute to notice him: a hooded figure in a khaki jacket, standing unmoving in the shadows of the jacaranda with a sickle in his hand. She lowered the mike and put her hand on the holster at her belt. Her partner looked at her, then turned his head and followed her gaze towards Layne.

Both cops pulled their revolvers. Layne turned and ran.

Down the hill, feet slapping on the hard concrete footpath. Left into the narrow pedestrian alley behind a three-storey apartment block. Hedgerows loomed on either side; leaning in to shelter him. The cops were yelling after him, their voices ragged behind their pounding footfalls.

Layne heard his own voice intoning some rhythmless nonsense. Wings beat and foliage rustled in reply.

Layne came out of the alley into the bright glare of a service station; the stink of oil and exhaust. He swerved, scrambled over a narrow guardrail and darted across the main road. Stumbled on the lip of the kerb, caught himself. Right, and then left up a hilly residential street. The cops had stopped yelling. They were closing fast.

There were big, spreading trees in this street, and Layne told them what to do. Their limbs waved to protect him; filling the air with leaves, battering at his pursuers with twigs and low-hanging branches. Roots tore free of the ground; bursting open the asphalt; grabbing at the coppers' feet. One of them tripped, fell sprawling. Layne did not wait to see if she got up again.

Layne's chest was burning. His legs and feet ached. He lurched onwards, up the hill, cursing a stringybark for its failure to act with the resolution of the oaks, the conviction of the beeches. These species were strange to him, and did not take well to his commands.

Layne could not hear the gunshot over his own toneless singing, but he felt the air part when the bullet rushed past his face. He hunched lower and scrambled on, looking for cover. Here at the top of the hill the properties were better maintained; the trees were too staggered, the garden hedges too groomed to be of much help.

Layne screamed some more nonsense and a motley flock of magpies and crows swooped down upon his remaining pursuer. The cop stumbled about, yelling and waving his arms in the sudden cloud of feathers and beaks and bird-cries.

Layne kicked through a plastic mesh into the wild front yard of a building still under construction: a three-storey, heavily-buttressed structure with a steeple roof and a pair of spires. Perhaps it was going to be a church. Oaks and wattles leaned over the neighbours' fences into its front yard, which was tangled with briar and brambles.

More gunfire. The shrieks and wing beats crescendoed as the cloud of birds dissipated, screaming and squawking and flapping. Layne turned to face his enemies, his back to the half-finished temple.

The cop came into view, following his pistol. He drew a bead on Layne, but before he could get off a round the brambles caught him. The cop staggered and kicked as thorny tendrils wrapped around his ankles, curled up his legs, and lashed across his torso and his arms. They pulled him screaming to the ground, twisting and thrashing until his joints popped apart and his skin split open.

The other cop stepped cautiously over the plastic mesh, pointing her weapon around. She'd skinned her knees in the fall and still seemed unsteady. The pistol shook in her hands. Layne was on her in three steps.

He swept past the revolver and swung the sickle, but the blade skidded off her Kevlar vest. She took a step back, grunted and tried to bring up her gun. Layne adjusted his grip and swung again. The curved inside-edge of the weapon opened her throat and the cop went down in a spray of blood. The gun in her hand discharged.

Red and blue light spilled into the yard. Layne turned towards the squealing sirens and the trees turned with him, reaching . . .

The sickle spilled from his loosening fingers and he fell to his knees. He looked down—his neck could no longer support the weight of his head. His belly, his jeans were drenched with blood. He couldn't feel his legs.

Layne tried to raise his head as he pitched forwards, but the sun had turned its face away, and the moon had nothing more to say to him.

• • •

The department had screwed up what should have been an open-and-shut case, so they handballed it to Detective Roland Neilly.

There wasn't any doubt that Layne Hutchings had killed all three of the victims, but difficult questions remained about how and why. That made Neilly the ideal detective for the case. Whether the department's flakiest figured out the finer points or not, this was a case they could definitely close. Hutchings was already dead and was therefore unlikely to provoke difficulty at the trial.

The crime scene photos and the lab reports showed that Elizabeth Milan had been killed with a serrated blade. Hutchings had practically severed her head with it, and then ritually disembowelled her at the base of a standing oak tree. It was possible that there had been two assailants, since some of the cuts had been administered left-handed, but the left-hand cuts were clumsier and Neilly was pretty sure Hutchings had simply switched his grip.

The weapon had been recovered from a garbage truck two postcodes away and, although Hutchings had made an attempt to wipe it clean, they'd pulled some good prints off it. The tree surgeon's pole saw was not the strangest weapon Neilly had seen, but it was right up there.

The second murder site was a disaster. With two cops down, backup and the paramedics had trodden all over the place before forensics had arrived. Nobody was quite sure what had happened there, but it was *weird*. Broken concrete, littered with fallen trees and dead birds. It looked as if an earthquake had joined Constables Benrith and Harriman in the pursuit, followed by a cyclone.

Benrith had died from a throat slash administered by a sickle. They had lifted another clear set of fingerprints from the weapon. The bramble trap that had killed Harriman was a different story. There were no springs or tripwires or nets; no evidence at all to describe the mechanism that had enveloped Harriman in brambles and then ripped him apart.

At least Hutchings' apartment had been left more or less inviolate. The one-bedroom flat was a mess, but that was a good thing. More chaos. Neilly's gift was to find the pattern where there did not appear to be one. Usually, he arrived at the key insight by an obscurely lateral process that he couldn't properly explain. Neilly's methods yielded results that were barely good enough for the department to keep him around.

It was dusty in the apartment. Books and papers and dirty clothes everywhere. Not much in the fridge or the rubbish, no dirty dishes in the sink. Neilly found a travel wallet with papers showing that Hutchings had recently been on a trip to the Republic of Ireland.

There was a heavily-annotated photocopy of a coded manuscript laid out on an imitation-Ikea writing desk in the living room. The characters in the manuscript did not belong to any language that he recognized. Hutchings had copied out the contents of the manuscript half a dozen times. His first copies were crude, but his fluency with the bizarre alphabet (if it was an alphabet) improved visibly as he went along. The third copy was close to the original. The fourth and fifth copies started to diverge again, and the sixth was completely different.

Hutchings had written in the notebooks using both hands, but everything else in the apartment suggested that he had been right-handed. Had he secretly been ambidextrous? Could he suddenly have become so? Hutchings' penmanship with his left hand improved visibly from book to book.

What a strange individual. Neilly could barely write his own name with his good hand.

There were a couple of messages on Hutchings' answering machine. One was from Hutchings' first victim, Libby Milan. Another was from an Englishman named Trimby, who claimed to have new information and another contract for Hutchings. He sounded like an arsehole. Trimby had left a number with the country code for Ireland. Neilly called him up on Hutchings' phone.

"Ah, Mr. Trimby? This is Senior Detective Roland Neilly from the, ah, Victoria Police."

There was a pause.

"Victoria, Australia?" Pause. "Is this about Layne Hutchings?"

"Afraid so."

"Has something happened?"

"Ah, yes, there's been a . . . well, there has been an incident. Mr Hutchings has, ah . . . he's no longer with us."

"That's awful news." Trimby didn't sound particularly upset. "If there's anything I can do to help, Detective . . . "

"Mr Trimby, I wonder if you could tell me what you and Mr Hutchings were working on?"

"*Professor* Trimby."

"I'm sorry. *Professor* Trimby."

"I'm currently seconded to the University of Dublin to investigate an ancient druidic manuscript. Mr. Hutchings is . . . *was* assisting us with some cryptographic analysis."

"Druidic? As in, the *druids*?"

"Yes."

"Like, the guy with the beard who mixes the potion that makes Asterix really strong? That kind of druid?"

"A bit like that, yes."

"So, sort of, ancient tree-huggers?"

Trimby took a long breath, audibly winding himself up. "Detective Neilly, the druids were priests and warriors and judges and bards and sorcerers. They were pagans who believed in metempsychosis—transmigration of the soul—and who engaged in human sacrifice, a practice for which they were exterminated by the Roman emperor Tiberius. I do not believe there was a lot of *tree-hugging* involved."

Neilly let the silence hang for a few moments, until he was sure the academic was done. "What's the significance of this document, Professor Trimby?"

"There are no proper records of the druids. They were destroyed over two thousand years ago and they kept an exclusively oral history. Or so we believed, until we discovered this particular document."

"Which is?"

"It's said to be the journal of a druid named Edraghodag, but we have been unable to decode it. That was Mr Hutchings' job, before he returned to Australia."

"He was still working on it when he died."

"He was? Had he made any progress?"

"Dunno," replied Neilly. "His notes are in code."

"Of course they are." Trimby sounded bitter.

"In your message, you said that you had some new information?"

"Yes, some local folklore about Edraghodag. Apparently, he was under geas . . . "

"Geese? Like ducks, but stupider?"

"*Geas*, Detective Neilly. An obligation set by druid gods, to be obeyed on pain of death. Edraghodag's geas was to instruct the people in the ways of his faith."

"That doesn't sound too difficult."

"It must have seemed rather mild, until Edraghodag was captured and tortured by a Roman garrison. He escaped, but not before they had removed the tongue from his head."

"Nasty."

"It's typical. Many of the heroes of Celtic myth died because they were given geasa by their various gods that conflicted with other customs."

"Alright. And then what happened to Ed . . . Edra . . . to the Druid?"

"*Edraghodag.*" Trimby sounded angry now. "There's nothing else. That's all we know."

"And the manuscript?"

"We now believe it to be Edraghodag's teaching notes, but we don't know for sure. The Druids were forbidden to write, but Edraghodag was required to teach, even after losing his powers of speech. That may account for the code."

Neilly thanked the professor and hung up. He sat back, yawned, stretched, and began to flip through the photocopied pages. He stared at the misaligned rows of characters until his eyes lost focus. Shapes resolved and dissolved out of the text, the white-space.

It was nonsense. The script showed no words or numbers, no pictures or maps or diagrams. Gibberish.

Neilly shook his head and growled. There was something hidden in there, and he was going to find it.

"Obey the law," he said, suddenly. He wasn't sure who he was talking to. "Obey the law. Uphold the faith."

Neilly snorted. *Geasa.* Was that the plural that Trimby has used? Surely 'flock' was more correct?

He thumbed through Hutchings' notebooks again. The most recent one seemed more approachable. Some parts looked almost like English, if you squinted at them. He worked at it for about thirty minutes, but it was tough going. Before long he found himself fidgeting with Layne's fountain pen. He changed the cartridge and tried it out in a blank notepad. Neilly's handwriting had always been terrible and now, with the fountain pen, it was also blotchy and smudged. But, he had to admit, it was fun. He liked the feel of it when he got a nice line going.

Neilly copied a couple of lines from Hutchings' notes onto his fresh pad. They looked good. He switched hands and copied a couple more. It was all a lot more satisfying than he'd expected. Before long, he began to speak the words as he wrote them.

He wondered where Hutchings had purchased the sickle.

• • • • • • • • • • •

SHEDDING SKIN

ANGELA REGA

Tonight, my skin is itchy. It burns and prickles where red, anthill mounds sprout on my inner thighs. "Ingrown hairs," he says to me. "You've got ingrown hairs."

I try to squeeze the hair out. The skin is rough and has grown what looks like a purplish lid to keep it in. It hurts but I keep squeezing until the swellings change shape from round anthills to pointy cones and a little pus and water seeps under my fingernails from the squeezing. But no hair comes. "You're very hairy," he says to me. "I didn't know women were so hairy."

I don't answer. I stopped answering him a few months ago when I realized that we weren't compatible. Instead I step into the bathroom, close the door, step onto the cracked and moulding tiles of the shower recess, grab my loofah and scrub my skin.

I scrub and scrub until the skin is chafed and raw, until I feel the hair coming through the skin. The bathroom is small and steams up easily; I push the window open to let the cool air in and stand on tipee-toe to see if anyone is out there getting a good glimpse of me naked. Sometimes he does that to piss me off.

The new girl in the brothel next door is sitting on the bench in the concrete yard, smoking. She looks up at the opening screech of my window; I duck my head so that she doesn't see me. I noticed her for the first time last week. She's got the kind of beauty that makes me feel self-conscious.

Overhead, a plane screeches; it descends over my rooftop and drowns out the noise of the neighbour's Hindi radio program, the hoon boys' cars down the M9 highway and him, wanting to know how long I'll be in the shower. I suppose there is something positive to be said for living *directly* under the flight path.

He bangs loudly on the bathroom door, muttering about how long I take in the bathroom. "You should wax your legs, you *work* at a waxing salon," he persists. "Then the hair becomes sparrow and it won't give you so much trouble when it grows back."

Sparse, I say to myself, *becomes sparse.*

I don't answer. I've been waxing for years. It always grows back.

The coarse blonde hair clogs up the shower cistern. I turn the tap on full pressure and push it down the drain with my toes, so I don't block the water flow, and watch it wash away.

• • •

When I was a kid, there was a story my grandma would tell us. She'd take the three-hour trip on the slow rattler train with big olive green vinyl seats from her home, the Northeast National Park, to City Central. I remember the smell of grease and rusty iron when the train pulled in. We'd pick her up on the crowded platform, travellers carting pillows and blankets, and she'd arrive, carrying a battered suitcase with not much in it except for a change of underwear, some clippers and a story about her childhood. It was always the same story.

"Jen," she'd say, "You know we're related to the dingo."

The only place you see dingoes in Sydney is in snippets in the news about them attacking children at camp sites. You never see a stray dog in this city, let alone a dingo. But Grandma said they were still roaming the Great Dividing Ranges, just a few hours away, up where she lived. She said she went walking in the Northeast National Park and would sit with her back against the sandstone rocks to sing with them. "They're the wolves of our country," she said, "only howling, never barking." And then she'd tell the story about how the women in our family were related to the dingo. I'd shake my head in disbelief and she'd get angry and tell the story again.

"Once a month, the men locked the women relatives up. Locked 'em up in the barn to stop 'em from roamin' free. When I was a child, I remember being tucked into me bed an' hearin' me father lock me mother an' aunt in the barn, threatening 'em with his rifle, firin' shots in the air."

She would use her long, skinny, storytelling fingers to mimic a gun.

"Why didn't your father lock you up, then?" I'd ask, skeptical but reluctantly drawn into the tale.

She'd poke me with that finger gun to shut me up. "Cos the dingo within waits for the moment you become a woman. I was still a little girl when the story I'm tellin' you 'appened. You'll stay 'ere til the dingo goes back to the forest within youse, my father would scream to 'em behind the locked door."

Then she'd bang on my bed head as if she was her father, banging on that door.

"They'd howl through the night, poundin' the doors so that it sounded like a harsh wind was tryin' to escape. But it was them dingo women. *It was always them.*"

My Grandma's eyes were wide and unblinking on that last sentence and it made the thick hairs on my forearms bristle.

Then she'd tell me once how her aunt escaped. Great Aunt Daisy managed to climb through the window and jump out to the open fields. She ran through to a neighbouring farm and killed a sheep. The bleating was heard by an angry farmer who came out and shot the yellow dingo straight between the eyes. In the morning, he hollered and cried when he saw my aunt lying where the dead wild dog had been, a bullet right between her head leaving a mark like a third eye and a blood stained face. The nails on her hands were still claws and the tips of her fingers covered in white fur.

Grandma's father nailed up the windows.

"It's for yer own good," my grandma heard him say to her mother and then sighed like he was tired. "Dingoes are a menace to a farmer's life."

"How long are you going to take in there?" He banged on the bathroom door and knocked me out of my remembering.

"Hold your horses," I said and toweled myself off. I wiped the steam off the bathroom mirror and stared at my reflection. At seventeen, I was changing. My nose was getting longer and the hair on head was becoming such a sandy colour. Just like my grandmother's.

When she became a woman, Grandma knew to hide her dingo ways. She tied herself to her bed at the time the dingo within came calling on her. She didn't want to be shot by a strange man's bullets, let alone her own father's. She wore long skirts and long sleeved tops to cover the hair that grew at that time of the month. She worked hard on the farm and soon met a man related to the crows. There was a tree she'd climb to get away and one day she found a man sitting in her branch plucking feathers from his shoulders. He understood the need to shed skin and they loved each other's fur and feather from the minute they met each other. My Grandma used to say dingoes and crows are good together.

But that was a long time ago. Now, all that is left of Grandma is that story. I'm glad she told it to me so many times. At seventeen, with not much more than a pissy apprentice pay packet and a bed-sit rental at the back of the salon where I work, that story is pretty much the most valuable thing I have.

Squeezing at this ingrown hair hurts. It resists. It is stubborn, building a cocoon of pus that now lives on my inner thigh.

I come out of the bathroom and he's lying on my bed, legs crossed, exhaling smoke rings and texting on his second mobile he uses for the business that he never discusses with me.

"Give us a flash."

When I don't respond, he gets up, tucks his shirt into his jeans, cigarette dangling from his mouth and ash falls onto my carpet. "Fuck, you're a bore. I'm off."

He tries to give me a wet kiss on the lips and when I move my head away he grabs at the back of my neck and forces my face towards his so that my jaw clenches.

"Don't do that," he says, his eyes goring a hole through mine. "Ever." He lets go, pushing me back, the flat of his hands on my sternum. I want to get the courage to tell him I'm leaving but the words don't come out.

I collapse onto the bed and watch him pull out my last $20 from my jeans pocket before he leaves. I don't react. My heart has gone to sleep just like a foot or leg that has been immobile for too long. To compensate, my inner thigh throbs from the pain of my attempts to draw the hair out.

• • •

The waxing salon where I work is in a crumbling one-storey terrace on Sydenham Road with cement instead of lawn in the front and two plastic palms on either side of the fuchsia pink front door. I rent the bed-sit at the back. It is nestled between the 24-hour kebab shop and the "Rub and Tug" massage parlour that doesn't bother to camouflage its entrance. Instead, the brothel adorns its front door with flashing fairy lights and the windows radiate a red hue even at 9 am in the morning. Each day on my break I sit out the front and hope I'll get a glimpse of her again. That girl. TJ. Her name is TJ. I heard one of the girls calling for her out the back the other night asking her for a cigarette.

This morning the salon smells like a combination of cheap potpourri and wet dog. The appointment book is full of girls booked in for body waxes. If a girl waits too long between waxes, she is forced to wear long skirts and pants just like the wild dog women in my Gran's story, like I did this month. They'll get looks of disdain if their skirt flashes a hairy leg; the city is such a judgmental place.

"You need to do something about that hair on your legs!" A rude woman said to me on the bus this afternoon when I lifted my leg up from under my skirt to scratch at my hairy skin. Why do I have to remove it, if it just keeps growing back?

Sometimes our boss Li Li writes up on her special's board: "Get your Booty! Only $25," and then we're inundated with customers. Not the women that want to rip the wild dog out of the private parts but the men that think that *we* are the massage parlour. They think the booty is some kind of special rub and tug session instead of pouring hot wax between bum cheeks and lips, ripping the wild hair out. They leave after we point them next door, slightly embarrassed and looking confused.

But they're not dingo. They're the hunters, the men with the 10-80 bait, the bullets. They remind me of grandma's tales of her father with the rifle, locks and chains, and make my legs tremble so I have to clench my knees to keep them still.

And I work here six days a week to earn some money to live and get my apprenticeship in all aspects of beauty and hair removal. I have learnt to use hot wax strips to spread over legs and rip it off. It's amazing what women need to get waxed to keep the dingo within: legs, labia, upper lips, chin, eyebrows, arms and even the tops of the toes. Now I can wax my own. Each time, it's like ripping a part of me away.

But it keeps growing back. The dingo within is stubborn.

And as I scratch at my inner thigh furiously, apply antiseptic cream to this sore large ingrown hair that has reached the size of a cherry, I know that the dingo within is trying to tell me something. But her voice, the planes overhead, the Hindi radio and the car horns and him have made me hard of hearing for her howl in the distance.

• • •

I've worked out the days TJ works at the Rub and Tug next door. I try and make sure I'm around the window to get a glimpse of her each time she comes into work always hoping she doesn't notice my attentions. She looks the same age as me but her eyes are older. Unlike my blue ones, they are dark. Almost charcoal. I've noticed her and sometimes, the image of her pulling her iPod out of her ears as she walks under the fairy lights into the fuchsia front door of the brothel is the image I see in my mind before I go to sleep.

She has an appointment today to get a full Brazilian. The wind chimes tingle as she enters the salon and I run my finger down the list of names, pretending I don't know who she is, even though I know it's the girl I saw from the shower. "TJ? 11 a.m.?" I ask, trying to look like I'm reading the list so that I don't look at her, and she doesn't see the heat rising in my cheeks. "Full leg and Brazilian?"

She nods and smiles. My heart beats quicker and feels like it's lowered an inch in my chest cavity and my breath shortens. I smile back at her and beckon her to follow me.

"This way."

I go to prep the room while she changes into her gown. When I walk in, she is lying on the waxing bench, with the gown covering her legs. Without her coat on, I see her arm is in a sling. Her dark eyes speak of wild things and freedom. "What happened?" I ask her. But she shakes her head and cries silently.

"Is it broken?"

"Nah, it's not broken. I am," she says.

I push her gown up above her knees, revealing her shins to begin waxing. There are feathers sprouting, through little black bumps of what look like sore ingrown hairs. *You are the other half of me,* I want to say to her but a girl can be silent in the face of true beauty even though the dingo wants to howl it out to the moon.

Beautiful crow girl.

TJ lies down on the bed and lifts her gown up over her belly button for me to wax the feathers off but I put the spatula down. "I'm sorry, I can't."

I put my hand on her shins and stroke the new feathers. They are soft and downy. She lets me. She doesn't flinch.

"I can't work next door anymore until my arm gets better." "I know," I say. "Tell him—you need a couple of days off." And there is silence between us.

In her eyes, I see the reflection of the crow. In mine she sees the reflection of the dingo. She does not look away but smiles.

But I say nothing. Not yet. My hair has not yet fully grown back. And I know, that if her pimp has not hurt her arm when they fought, that once she knows the strength of being a crow girl, she will heal her arm, sprout feathers on them, too, spread her wings and fly.

Come with me.

• • •

"You need a wax," he says to me. "I've never had a girlfriend so hairy."

I walk to the kitchen to put the kettle on and he follows me. "Jen, you gotta keep this package here, all right? But hidden."

"What is it?"

"Ask no questions, babe, and I'll tell you no lies."

"I'm not keeping anything here illegal. I'm renting the bedsit from Li Li. If cops came here, I'd lose my job and home."

He drops the parcel on the bench, grabs both my arms and squeezes tight. "I need it here for a little while. Maybe you're not the girl I thought you were. Maybe I can't trust you. You know the rule—wife for life, keep silence or violence."

"I'm not your wife and I don't want to be your girlfriend anymore." He squeezes my arms so tightly I wince from the pain.

"You didn't mean that." His pupils are large and his grip unrelenting. He goes to my handbag and grabs my keys and wallet. "What are you doing?"

"I'm taking them," he says and walks out, locking the door behind him.

My boyfriend. He smells different to me now, like milk gone rancid. I start to cry and the skin on my legs gets hot and itchy, making me scratch furiously at my shins. The hair breaks through the skin and as each follicle opens, the hot itch starts to subside and my senses heighten. He smells differently and I see him differently. He is the hunter, the enemy.

And I'm scared he has locked me up. This man that came from neither fur nor feathers. Just raw skin.

I didn't inherit the feathers from my grandfather, only the fur from the women in my family. If I had, I would have had the power to fly away. Instead, like a dingo, my travels always bring me back to my home. To the same place.

I am grounded, trapped and fenced in.

But tonight I will remember Gran's tale and believe it like I should have. I will let the hair grow and return to where I've never been.

He has locked the doors but not the windows. I climb onto the toilet seat and propel myself up to the bathroom window and scramble through. The bricks on the outside scratch my palms and my ribs feel bruised from pressing against the sill but I make it to the floor. I'm in the yard of Li Li's waxing salon now and make my way through the backdoor and into the reception area. I hear the sound of Li Li ripping wax and creep to the register.

"Who's there? Jen? Is that you?"

"It's me," I call out, trying to sound casual and I grab $50 from the register and shove it in my pocket. "Jen, you work tomorrow? Early shift?"

"I'm sorry, Li Li," I say, "I'll pay you back."

"Eh?" The sound of the wax stops and I hear her hurried footsteps down the corridor.

I push my hoodie over my head and push through the front door of the salon, leaving the wind chimes clanging, and break into a sprint. It is quiet at night in this city of tar and brick, of highways, playgrounds and garbage. A light rain has made the asphalt on Sydenham Road glisten; there is the strong smell of tar and petrol but I can smell wet grass and rotting leaves underneath. I run to the rhythm of my heartbeat and then I'm on all fours. An even saunter and I'm faster than the Emo kid pedaling his bike with the imitation shrunken head on his handlebars.

Freedom.

Grandma said one day it would be time for me to find my own way.

She'd say that when she was gone and I was grown her spirit would know where to find me. It's not in the city. A dingo doesn't like the routine of working under fluorescent lights ripping out the soul of other wild dog women, doesn't like the sound of the buses and the trucks. A dingo can't walk fast enough in high heels. And now, I am running barefoot.

• • •

As I run, the rest of the ingrown hairs disappear and in their place, my short-coated yellow dust pelt protects my skin. There is a rush of relief that floods my body as the itch has vanished with the cherry sized pustule; the last of its blood and pus now running down my leg. My ears are tuned to the background noise of footsteps and cicadas, of distant cars and wind through branches that rustle leaves.

I smell her.

TJ is in the park behind the tire factory sitting on a kid's swing, swaying back and forth. Her shins are covered in black feathers and her long curls are wings of ebony that flutter about her bare shoulders.

She is crying but the presence of a dingo in the park does not scare her; when she looks into my eyes, she sees the reflection of me, the woman.

"I knew you'd come," she says.

I rip at the bandage and lick her arm to heal it. And the feathers grow. She spreads her arms wide and the wind lifts her. She hovers above me.

I can run fast but she can fly far above me.

We travel all night. Down the motorway to O'Dell's Ferry and then I swim as she soars across the water on the night wind to cross the Ranges River to Northeast National Park.

Where my grandma's stories came from; where my grandma lived. Where wild dog women suckled dingo pups, because their mothers had been poisoned or killed by farmers.

I crouch down, pick up a twig and scrawl into the dirt with its pointy edge: *Dingo and Crow Sanctuary*. I look up and smile at TJ. My crow girl reads the message in the soil then laughs softly, tossing her head so that ebony feathers flitter to the floor.

We will settle here. Return to where we've never been. To freedom.

• • • • • • • • • • •

ABOUT THE CONTRIBUTORS

ALAN BAXTER writes dark fantasy, horror and sci-fi, rides a motorcycle and loves his dog. He also teaches Kung Fu. He lives among dairy paddocks on the beautiful south coast of NSW, Australia. Read extracts from his novels, a novella and short stories at his website **www.warriorscribe.com** or find him on Twitter **@AlanBaxter** and Facebook.

JAMES BRADLEY is an award-winning writer and critic. His books include the novels *Wrack*, *The Deep Field*, *The Resurrectionist* and *Clade*, a book of poetry, *Paper Nautilus*, and *The Penguin Book of the Ocean*. He blogs at **cityoftongues.com**.

IMOGEN CASSIDY is a mother of two from Sydney's inner west, currently juggling parenting, dog ownership and writing. Imogen's fiction has appeared in *Devilfish Review*, *The Colored Lens*, *Aurealis* and *Toasted Cake*. Other writings can be found at her website **imogenwrites.tumblr.com** or on **patreon.com/imogenwrites**.

DAVID CONYERS is a science fiction and horror author and editor from Adelaide, South Australia. His Harrison Peel series is collected in *The Shoggoth Conspiracy* with more stories to follow. Anthologies he has edited include *Extreme Planets*, *Cthulhu Unbound 3*, *Cthulhu Detective*, *Cthulhu's Dark Cults* and *Undead & Unbound*. *The Nightmare Dimension* is his collection of horror fiction while *Nanofabrica*, a collection of best science fiction stories will be released by Aeon Press in 2016. **david-conyers.com**

TERRY DOWLING is one of Australia's most respected and internationally acclaimed writers of science fiction, dark fantasy and horror, and author of the multi-award-winning Tom Rynosseros saga. The *Year's Best Fantasy and Horror* series featured more horror stories by Terry in its 21-year run than by any other writer. Terry's horror collections are *Basic Black: Tales of Appropriate Fear* (International Horror Guild Award), Aurealis Award-winning *An Intimate Knowledge of the Night* and the World Fantasy Award nominated *Blackwater Days*. His most recent books are *Amberjack: Tales of Fear & Wonder* and debut novel, *Clowns at Midnight*. Terry's new collection *The Night Shop: Tales for the Lonely Hours* is due from Cemetery Dance Publications in 2016. terrydowling.com.

THORAIYA DYER is an Aurealis and Ditmar Award-winning, Sydney-based science fiction and fantasy writer. Her short story collection, *Asymmetry*, and time-travel pirate novella *The Company Articles of Edward Teach* are available from Twelfth Planet Press, while the first book in her *Titan's Forest* fantasy trilogy is forthcoming from Tor. Thoraiya is an archer and a lapsed veterinarian. Follow @ThoraiyaDyer or peruse thoraiyadyer.com.

JASON FRANKS is the author of the occult rock'n'roll novel *Bloody Waters* and the writer of the *Sixsmiths* and *Left Hand Path* comicbook series. His short fiction has been published in *Aurealis*, *Midnight Echo*, *After the World*, *SQ Mag*, and other places. Franks's work has twice been short-listed for an Aurealis Award.

MICHELLE GOLDSMITH resides in Melbourne, Australia, where she works as a writer and editor and is completing a Masters degree in publishing. She also has a degree in Zoology/Evolutionary Biology, which she mainly uses for story inspiration. After selling her first story at the age of 21, her short fiction has appeared in various journals and anthologies and been translated. She was shortlisted for a Ditmar Award for Best New Talent in 2014 and 2015. She can be found online at vilutheril.com, or on Twitter as @vilutheril.

MICHAEL GREY was born and grew up in Yorkshire and now lives in Melbourne with his wife and two boys. His work has been featured in print and online. He is currently taking applications for the role of 'Writer's Cat'. Candidates can contact him at michaelgrey.com.au or on Twitter @Mikes005.

STEPHANIE GUNN is a Ditmar-nominated writer of speculative fiction. In another life, she was a (mad) scientist, but now spends her time writing and reviewing. Her short stories have appeared in anthologies such as *Bloodstones, Epilogue, Grant's Pass* and *Kisses by Clockwork*. She is currently at work on several contemporary fantasy novels and too many shorter works for her own good. She lives in Perth with her son and husband and requisite fluffy cat (and too many books). You can find her online at **stephaniegunn.com.**

LISA L. HANNETT has had over 60 short stories appear in venues including *Clarkesworld, Fantasy, Weird Tales, Apex,* the *Year's Best Australian Fantasy and Horror,* and *Imaginarium: Best Canadian Speculative Writing.* She has won four Aurealis Awards, including Best Collection for her first book, *Bluegrass Symphony,* which was also nominated for a World Fantasy Award. Her first novel, *Lament for the Afterlife,* was published by CZP in 2015. You can find her online at **lisahannett.com** and on Twitter **@LisaLHannett.**

GERRY HUNTMAN is a speculative fiction writer based in Melbourne, living with his wife and young daughter. He writes in all genres, and most sub-genres of speculative fiction, having sold over 50 stories to date. Recent sales include *Night Terrors III* and *Creepy Campfire Stories (for adults).* Gerry published a young teen fantasy novel, *Guardian of the Sky Realms,* through Cohesion Press late in 2014. He is Managing Director and Chief Editor of IFWG Publishing Australia, which includes the popular speculative fiction e-zine, *SQ Mag.*

RICK KENNETT'S horror and SF stories have appeared in magazines, anthologies and podcasts including *Dunesteef, Pseudopod,* and the young adult orientated *Cast of Wonders.* He won two Parsec Awards for podcast stories in 2013, the same year the novel *The Devil and the Deep Blue Sea* was published. He is the podcast reporter for the *Ghosts & Scholars M.R. James Newsletter.*

DAVID KERNOT is an Australian author living in the Mid North of South Australia. He writes contemporary fantasy, science fiction, and horror, and is the author of close to sixty published short stories throughout Australia, the US, and Canada. This is his fourth collaboration with David Conyers. More information can be found at **davidkernot.com.**

CHARLOTTE KIEFT lives in Wellington, New Zealand with her husband and two small dogs. She has several short stories published, in 2013 was awarded a New Zealand Society of Authors' Mentorship (mentor David Hill), and in 2015 was shortlisted for the Sir Julius Vogel Award for Best Short Story. She is currently working on an historical novel, and loves travel and scuba diving.

S. G. LARNER is a denizen of Brisbane, Australia, where she complains about the heat, wrangles three children, and explores the dark underbelly of the world in her writing. Her work has appeared in *Apex*, *Aurealis*, *Dimension6* and *SQ Mag*, among others. She's currently studying a Masters of Information Science. You can find her at **foregoreality. wordpress.com** and on Twitter **@StaceySarasvati**.

CLAIRE MCKENNA is a Melbourne-based genre writer and tragic fangirl. The story of "Yard" came about after moving from a comfortable house in the Western suburbs to a Bayside house built by a former high-ranking member of the Nazi Party. (This in fact is a true story. The house was demolished due to evil and termites, but the grass continues to grow . . .)

ANDREW J. MCKIERNAN is an author and illustrator from the Central Coast of New South Wales. First published in 2007, his stories have since been short-listed for multiple Aurealis, Ditmar, and Australian Shadows awards and reprinted internationally, and in a number of Year's Best anthologies. His short story collection, *Last Year, When We Were Young*, was awarded the 2014 AHWA Australian Shadows Award for Collected Work. **andrewmckiernan.com**

FAITH MUDGE is a Queensland writer with a passion for fantasy, folk tales and mythology from all over the world—in fact, almost anything with a glimmer of the fantastical. Her stories have appeared in various anthologies, including *Kaleidoscope*, *Phantazein* and *Hear Me Roar*. She posts reviews and articles at **beyondthedreamline.wordpress.com**. Somewhere in the overcrowded menagerie of her mind, there are novels. She is even writing some of them.

JASON NAHRUNG'S work is often set in Australia and invariably darkly themed. His most recent books are the seaside Gothic *Salvage* (Twelfth Planet Press) and outback vampire duology *Blood and Dust* and *The Big Smoke* (Clan Destine Press). A PhD candidate in creative writing at The University of Queensland, the former Queenslander lives in Ballarat with his wife, the writer Kirstyn McDermott, and lurks online at **jasonnahrung.com**.

EMMA OSBORNE is a fiction writer and poet from Melbourne, Australia. Her short fiction has appeared at *Bastion SF*, *Aurealis* and *Shock Totem* and is forthcoming at *Pseudopod*. Her poetry has appeared in *Apex Magazine*. Her essay "So Say We All" was included in Lightspeed's *Queers Destroy Science Fiction*. She can be bribed with whiskey and ribs. You can find her on Twitter as **@redscribe**.

ANGELA REGA is a belly-dancing school librarian in love with folklore, fairy tales and furry creatures. She is a Sydney based writer and graduate of Clarion South. Her stories have appeared in publications including *Crossed Genres*, PS Publications and the *Year's Best Australian Fantasy and Horror*. She drinks way too much coffee, often falls in love with poetry and can't imagine not writing. She keeps a very small website here: **angierega.webs.com**.

TANSY RAYNER ROBERTS is an Australian fantasy author, blogger and podcaster. She won the 2013 Hugo for Best Fan Writer. Tansy has a PhD in Classics, which she drew upon for her short story collection *Love and Romanpunk*. Her latest fiction project is *Musketeer Space*, a gender-swapped space opera retelling of *The Three Musketeers*, published weekly as a web serial. Tansy also writes crime fiction under the name Livia Day.

CAT SPARKS is a multi-award-winning author, editor and artist whose former employment has included: media monitor, political and archaeological photographer, graphic designer and manager of Agog! Press amongst other (much less interesting) things. She's currently fiction editor of *Cosmos Magazine* while simultaneously grappling with a PhD on YA climate change fiction. **catsparks.net @catsparx**

Brisbane-based writer **ANGELA SLATTER** has won five Aurealis Awards and one British Fantasy Award, been a finalist for the Norma K. Hemming Award once and the World Fantasy Award twice. She's published six story collections, has a PhD, was an inaugural Queensland Writers Fellow, is a freelance editor, and teaches creative writing. Her novellas, *Of Sorrow and Such* (Tor.com) and *Ripper* (in *Horrorology*, Jo Fletcher Books), will be out in October 2015, and Jo Fletcher Books will publish her debut novel, *Vigil*, in 2016, with its sequel, *Corpselight*, coming in 2017.

ANNA TAMBOUR'S latest book is a collection, *The Finest Ass in the Universe*, from Ticonderoga Publications. Her novel *Crandolin* was shortlisted for the 2013 World Fantasy Award. She lives in the bush in New South Wales.

KYLA LEE WARD is a Sydney-based créatif devoted to all things dark and beautiful. Co-author of the Aurealis Award-winning *Prismatic*, *The Land of Bad Dreams* is her solo collection of dark poetry. Her short stories have appeared on *gothic.net*, *Shadowed Realms* and the Stone Skin Press anthologies, amongst others. RPGs, films and plays—she's been there, as well as a whole lot of cemeteries.

Bram Stoker, twice-World Fantasy Award Nominee and Shirley Jackson Award winner **KAARON WARREN** has lived in Melbourne, Sydney, Canberra and Fiji. She's sold over 200 short stories, three novels (the multi-award-winning *Slights*, *Walking the Tree* and *Mistification*) and six short story collections including the multi-award-winning *Through Splintered Walls*. Her latest short story collection is *Kaaron Warren: Cemetery Dance Select*. Kaaron just completed a Fellowship at the Museum of Australian Democracy at Old Parliament House, where she researched Prime Ministers, artists and murderers. The resulting crime novel should see print in 2016. She was a special guest at Genrecon 2015.

JANEEN WEBB is a multiple award winning author, editor and critic who has written or edited ten books and over a hundred essays and stories. Her short story collection, *Death At The Blue Elephant*, was released by Ticonderoga in 2014 and is currently short listed for the 2015 World Fantasy Award. Janeen is a recipient of the World Fantasy Award, the Peter MacNamara SF Achievement Award, the Aurealis Award, and the Ditmar Award. She holds a PhD in literature from the University of Newcastle, and divides her time between Melbourne and a small farm overlooking the sea near Wilson's Promontory, Australia. janeenwebb.com.au

RECOMMENDED READING LIST

Liz Argall, "Soft Feather Dance", *Apex Magazine*
Alan Baxter, "The Darkness In Clara", *SQ Mag*
James Bradley, "Skinsuit", *Island magazine*
Jay Caselberg, "Bite Marks", *Noir*
Rjurik Davidson, "Night-time in Caeli-Amur", *Tor.com*
Terry Dowling, "The Four Darks", *Fearful Symmetries*
Alice Godwin, "Scarlett Fever", *Subtropical Suspense*
David Grigg, "This Too, Too Solid Flesh", *Cadavers*
Lisa L. Hannett, "A Girl of Feather and Music", *Postscripts 32/33:*
    Far Voyager
Lisa L. Hannett and Angela Slatter, "The Female Factory", *The*
    Female Factory
———— "Baggage", *The Female Factory*
S.G. Larner, "Shades of Memory", *Suspended in Dusk*
Tracie McBride, "The Truth About Dolphins", *disquiet*
Kirstyn McDermott, "By the Moon's Good Grace", *Review of*
    Australian Fiction, Vol.12, Issue 3
Ian McHugh, "Apricot Finds a Treasure", *Angel Dust*
Andrew J. McKiernan, "Last Year, When We Were Young", *Last*
    Year, When We Were Young
Robert Mammone, "Suffer The Children", *Amok!*
Paul Mannering, "The Princess and the Flea", *At Hell's Gates:*
    Volume One: Existing Worlds
Faith Mudge, "Descension", *Kisses by Clockwork*
———— "Twelfth", *Phantazein*
Lee Murray, "Inside Ferndale", *SQ Mag*
Ian Nicholls, "Mister Lucky", *Use Only as Directed*
Shauna O'Meara, "Beneath the Surface of Two Kills", *Writers of*
    the Future (Volume 30)

Anthony Panegyres, "The Tic-Toc Boy of Constantinople", *Kisses by Clockwork*

Rob Porteous, "A Drought of Tears", *The Sea*

Dan Rabarts, "Children of the Tide", *AHWA Online*

Angela Rega, "Cloaks and Hoods", *Black Apples*

Carol Ryles, "Siri and the Chaos-Maker", *Kisses by Clockwork*

Leife Shallcross, "Music for an Ivory Violin", *Aurealis 74*

Angela Slatter, "Let The Words Take You", *Dreams of Shadow and Smoke: Stories for J.S. Le Fanu*

—————— "St Dymphna's School for Poison Girls", *The Review of Australian Fiction*

Cat Sparks, "The Seventh Relic", *Phantazein*

Leah Swann, "Of Life Below", *The World To Come*

Cameron Trost, "Lauren", *Of Devils and Deviants: An Anthology of Erotic Horror*

Kaaron Warren, "Eleanor Atkins Is Dead and Her House Is Boarded Up", *SQ Mag*

—————— "The Nursery Corner", *Fearsome Magics*

Janeen Webb, "Skull Beach", *Death at the Blue Elephant*

—————— "The Sculptor's Wife", *Death at the Blue Elephant*

Suzanne J. Willis, "Rag and bone heart", *Phantazein*

AUSTRALIAN & NEW ZEALAND FANTASY & HORROR AWARDS

THE AUSTRALIAN SF "DITMAR" AWARDS

BEST NOVEL

Thief's Magic, **Trudi Canavan** (Hachette Australia)
The Lascar's Dagger, **Glenda Larke** (Hachette Australia)
NOMINEES
Bound, Alan Baxter (Voyager)
Clariel, Garth Nix (HarperCollins)
The Godless, Ben Peek (Tor UK)

BEST NOVELLA OR NOVELETTE:

"The Legend Trap", Sean Williams (*Kaleidoscope: Diverse YA Science Fiction and Fantasy Stories*)
NOMINEES
"The Darkness in Clara", Alan Baxter (*SQ Mag* #14)
"Escapement", Stephanie Gunn (*Kisses by Clockwork*)
"The Female Factory", Lisa L. Hannett & Angela Slatter (*The Female Factory*)
"The Ghost of Hephaestus", Charlotte Nash (*Phantazein*)
"St Dymphna's School for Poison Girls", Angela Slatter (*Review of Australian Fiction* Vol 9, No. 3)

BEST SHORT STORY

"The Seventh Relic", Cat Sparks (*Phantazein*)
NOMINEES
"Bahamut", Thoraiya Dyer (*Phantazein*)
"Vanilla", Dirk Flinthart (*Kaleidoscope: Diverse YA Science Fiction and Fantasy Stories*)
"Signature", Faith Mudge (*Kaleidoscope*)
"Cookie Cutter Superhero", Tansy Rayner Roberts (*Kaleidoscope*)

BEST COLLECTED WORK

Kaleidoscope: Diverse YA Science Fiction and Fantasy Stories, **Alisa Krasnostein & Julia Rios, eds. (Twelfth Planet)**
NOMINEES
The Year's Best Australian Fantasy and Horror 2013, Liz Grzyb & Talie Helene, eds. (Ticonderoga)
Phantazein, Tehani Wessely, ed. (FableCroft)

BEST ARTWORK

Cover art by Kathleen Jennings for *Phantazein* **(FableCroft)**
NOMINEES
Illustrations by Kathleen Jennings for *Black-Winged Angels* (Ticonderoga)
Illustrations by Kathleen Jennings for *The Bitterwood Bible and Other Recountings* (Tartarus Press)

BEST NEW TALENT

Helen Stubbs
NOMINEES
Michelle Goldsmith
Shauna O'Meara

AUREALIS AWARDS

FANTASY NOVEL

Dreamer's Pool, **Juliet Marillier (Pan Macmillan Australia)**
NOMINEES
Fireborn, Keri Arthur (Hachette Australia)
This Shattered World, Amie Kaufman and Meagan Spooner (Allen & Unwin)
The Lascar's Dagger, Glenda Larke (Hachette Australia)
Afterworlds, Scott Westerfeld (Penguin Books Australia)
Daughters of the Storm, Kim Wilkins (Harlequin Enterprises Australia)

FANTASY SHORT STORY

"St Dymphna's School for Poison Girls", Angela Slatter (*The Review of Australian Fiction*, **Vol 9, No. 3**)
NOMINEES
"The Oud", Thoraiya Dyer (*Long Hidden*, Crossed Genres Publications)
"Teratogen", Deb Kalin (*Cemetery Dance*, #71, May 2014)
"The Ghost of Hephaestus", Charlotte Nash (*Phantazein*, FableCroft Publications)
"The Badger Bride", Angela Slatter (*Strange Tales IV*, Tartarus Press)

BEST HORROR NOVEL

Razorhurst, **Justine Larbalestier (Allen & Unwin)**

NOMINEES
Book of the Dead, Greig Beck (Momentum)
Obsidian, Alan Baxter (HarperVoyager)

BEST HORROR SHORT STORY

"Home and Hearth", Angela Slatter (Spectral Press)
NOMINEES
"The Executioner Goes Home", Deborah Biancotti (*Review of Australian Fiction*, Vol 11 No. 6)
"Skinsuit", James Bradley (*Island Magazine 137*)
"By the Moon's Good Grace", Kirstyn McDermott (*Review of Australian Fiction*, Vol 12, No. 3)
"Shay Corsham Worsted", Garth Nix (*Fearful Symmetries*, Chizine)

BEST COLLECTION

The Female Factory, **Lisa L Hannett and Angela Slatter (Twelfth Planet Press)**
NOMINEES
Secret Lives, Rosaleen Love (Twelfth Planet Press)
Angel Dust, Ian McHugh (Ticonderoga Publications)
Difficult Second Album: more stories of Xenobiology, Space Elevators, and Bats Out Of Hell, Simon Petrie (Peggy Bright Books)
The Bitterwood Bible and Other Recountings, Angela Slatter (Tartarus Press)
Black-Winged Angels, Angela Slatter (Ticonderoga Publications)

BEST ANTHOLOGY

Kaleidoscope: Diverse YA Science Fiction and Fantasy Stories, **Alisa Krasnostein and Julia Rios eds (Twelfth Planet Press)**
NOMINEES
Kisses by Clockwork, Liz Grzyb ed. (Ticonderoga Publications)
Amok: An Anthology of Asia-Pacific Speculative Fiction, Dominica Malcolm ed. (Solarwyrm Press)
Reach for Infinity, Jonathan Strahan ed. (Solaris Books)
Fearsome Magics, Jonathan Strahan ed. (Solaris Books)
Phantazein, Tehani Wessely ed. (FableCroft Publishing)

BEST CHILDREN'S FICTION

Shadow Sister: Dragon Keeper #5, **Carole Wilkinson (Black Dog Books)**
NOMINEES
Slaves of Socorro: Brotherband #4, John Flanagan (Random House Australia)
Ophelia and the Marvellous Boy, Karen Foxlee (Hot Key Books)
The Last Viking Returns, Norman Jorgensen and James Foley (ILL.) (Fremantle Press)
Withering-by-Sea, Judith Rossell (ABC Books)
Sunker's Deep: The Hidden #2, Lian Tanner (Allen & Unwin)

YOUNG ADULT SHORT STORY

"Vanilla", Dirk Flinthart (*Kaleidoscope: Diverse YA Science Fiction and Fantasy Stories*, **Twelfth Planet Press**)

NOMINEES

"In Hades", Goldie Alexander (Celapene Press)

"Falling Leaves", Liz Argyll (*Apex Magazine*)

"The Fuller and the Bogle", David Cornish (*Tales from the Half-Continent*, Omnibus Books)

"Signature", Faith Mudge (*Kaleidoscope: Diverse YA Science Fiction and Fantasy Stories*, Twelfth Planet Press)

BEST YOUNG ADULT NOVEL

The Cracks in the Kingdom, **Jaclyn Moriarty** (**Pan Macmillan Australia**)

NOMINEES

The Astrologer's Daughter, Rebecca Lim (Text Publishing)

Afterworld, Lynnette Lounsbury (Allen & Unwin)

Clariel, Garth Nix (Allen & Unwin)

The Haunting of Lily Frost, Nova Weetman (UQP)

Afterworlds, Scott Westerfeld (Penguin Books Australia)

BEST ILLUSTRATED BOOK/GRAPHIC NOVEL

Mr Unpronounceable and the Sect of the Bleeding Eye, **Tim Molloy** (**Milk Shadow Books**)

NOMINEES

Left Hand Path #1, Jason Franks & Paul Abstruse (Winter City Productions)

Awkwood, Jase Harper (Milk Shadow Books)

"A Small Wild Magic", Kathleen Jennings (*Monstrous Affections*, Candlewick Press)

The Game, Shane W Smith (Deeper Meanings Publishing)

BEST SCIENCE FICTION SHORT STORY

"Wine, Women and Stars", Thoraiya Dyer (*Analog*)

NOMINEES

"The Executioner Goes Home", Deborah Biancotti (*Review of Australian Fiction*, Vol 11 No. 6)

"The Glorious Aerybeth", Jason Fisher (*OnSpec*, 11 Sep 2014)

"Dellinger", Charlotte Nash (*Use Only As Directed*, Peggy Bright Books)

"Happy Go Lucky", Garth Nix (*Kaleidoscope*, Twelfth Planet Press)

BEST SCIENCE FICTION NOVEL

Peacemaker, **Marianne de Pierres** (**Angry Robot**)

NOMINEES

Aurora: Meridian, Amanda Bridgeman (Momentum)

Nil By Mouth, LynC (Satalyte Publishing)

The White List, Nina D'Aleo (Momentum)

This Shattered World, Amie Kaufman and Meagan Spooner (Allen & Unwin)
Foresight, Graham Storrs (Momentum)

AUSTRALIAN SHADOWS AWARDS

NOVEL

Wolf Creek: Origin, **Aaron Sterns and Greg McLean (Penguin)**
NOMINEES
Suicide Forest, Jeremy Bates (Ghillinnein Books)
Book of the Dead, Greig Beck (Momentum Books)
Dark Deceit, Lauren Dawes (Momentum Books)
Davey Ribbon, Matthew Tait (HodgePodge Press)

PAUL HAINES AWARD FOR LONG FICTION

Dreams of Destruction, **Shane Jiraiya Cummings (self-published)**
NOMINEES
Ghost Camera, Darcy Coates (self-published)
"The Shark God Covenant", Robert Hood, *Dimension6 #3*

COLLECTION

Last Year When We Were Young, **Andrew J. McKiernan (Satalyte Publishing)**

EDITED PUBLICATION

SQ Mag #14, Sophie Yorkston ed. (IFWG Publishing)
NOMINEES
SNAFU, Geoff Brown and Amanda J. Spedding eds (Cohesion Press)
Suspended in Dusk, Simon Dewar ed. (Books of the Dead Press)

SHORT FICTION

"Shadows of the Lonely Dead", Alax Baxter, *Suspended in Dusk* **(Books of the Dead Press)**
NOMINEES
"Mephisto", Alan Baxter, *Daily Science Fiction*
"Mummified Monk", Rebecca Fung, *Daylight Dims Volume 2*
"Bones", Michelle Jager, *SQ Mag #14*
"Last Year When We Were Young", Andrew J. McKiernan, *Last Year When We Were Young* (Satalyte Publishing)

SIR JULIUS VOGEL AWARDS

BEST NOVEL

Engines of Empathy, **Paul Mannering (Paper Road Press)**
NOMINEES
Dreamer's Pool, Juliet Marillier (Pan MacMillan)
The Sovereign Hand, Paul Gilbert (Steam Press)
The Caves of Kirym, Derrin Attwood (Worldly Books)
The Seventh Friend, Tim Stead
Onyx Javelin, Steve Wheeler (HarperCollins Australia)

BEST YOUTH NOVEL

The Caller: Shadowfell, **Juliet Marillier (Pan Macmillan)**
NOMINEES
Tantamount, Thomas J. Radford (Tyche Books)
Wee Mac, Linda Dawley (Little Red Hen Community Press)
Donnel's Promise, Anna Mackenzie (Longacre Press)
Watched, Tihema Baker (Huia Press)

BEST NOVELLA

Peach and Araxi, **Celine Murray** *Conclave: A Collection of Science Fiction and Fantasy*
NOMINEES
"A Mer-Tale", Jan Goldie *Conclave: A Collection of Science Fiction and Fantasy*
Trading Rosemary, Octavia Cade (Masque Books)
Ranpasatusan, Shelley Chappell
The Last Homely Housekeeper, Rolf Luchs
In the Spirit, J. C. Hart

BEST SHORT STORY

"Inside Ferndale", Lee Murray *SQ Mag*, **Issue 12**
NOMINEES
"The Watch Serpent", Eileen Mueller, *Disquiet*, (Creativa)
"Chiaroscuro", Charlotte Kleft, *Disquiet*, (Creativa)
"Water", Lee Pletzers, *Disquiet*, (Creativa)
"Santa's Sack", Simon Fogarty, *The Best of Twisty Christmas Tales* (Phantom Feather Press)

BEST COLLECTED WORK

Lost In The Museum, **Phoenix Writers Group**
NOMINEES
Corpus Delecti, William Cook (James Ward Kirk Publishing)
Dreams of Thanatos, William Cook (King Billy Publications)

The Best of Twisty Christmas Tales, A. J. Ponder, E. Mueller and P.
Friend eds (Phantom Feather Press)
Write Off Line 2014: They Came In From The Dark, Lauren Haddock
and Jessica Harvey eds (Tauranga Writers Publishing)
Beyond The Briar, Shelley Chappell

BEST PROFESSIONAL ARTWORK

Cover for *Lost In The Museum,* **Geoff Popham**
nominee
Cover for *The Best of Twisty Christmas Tales,* Geoff Popham

BEST DRAMATIC PRESENTATION

What We Do In The Shadows, **Directed by Jemaine Clement and Taika
Waititi, Produced by Chelsea Winstanley and Taika Waititi (Shadow
Pictures)**
NOMINEES
The Hobbit: The Battle of the Five Armies, Directed by Sir Peter
Jackson, written by Peter Jackson, Fran Walsh, Philippa Boyens,
Guillermo del Toro.
Housebound, Directed by Gerald Johnstone

BEST PROFESSIONAL PRODUCTION/PUBLICATION

Weta Digital: 20 Years of Imagination On Screen, **Clare Burgess with
Brian Sibley**
NOMINEES
The Hobbit: The Desolation of Smaug, Chronicles: Cloaks and Daggers,
Daniel Falconer (Weta Workshop)
*The Hobbit: The Desolation of Smaug, Chronicles: Unleashing the
Dragon,* Daniel Falconer (Weta Workshop)
Cosplay New Zealand, Sylvie Kirkman
Weta Workshop: Celebrating 20 Years of Creativity, Luke Hawker

OTHER AWARDS AND ACHIEVEMENTS

The Norma K. Hemming Award for excellence in the exploration
of themes of race, gender, sexuality, class and disability in
Australian speculative fiction was won by Paddy O'Reilly for her
novel *The Wonders* (Affirm Press). *Galactic Suburbia Podcast,* run
by Alisa Krasnostein, Alexandra Pierce, Tansy Rayner Roberts,
and Andrew Finch, won the Hugo Award for Best Fancast.

Three Australians have been nominated in the World Fantasy
Awards. For Best Short Story is Kaaron Warren, "Death's Door

Café" (*Shadows & Tall Trees*), and in Best Collection are Angela Slatter, *The Bitterwood Bible and Other Recountings* (Tartarus Press) and Janeen Webb, *Death at the Blue Elephant* (Ticonderoga Publications).

ACKNOWLEDGEMENTS

"Shadows of the Lonely Dead" copyright © Alan Baxter 2014. First published in *Suspended in Dusk*, edited by Simon Dewar (Books of the Dead Press).

"The Changeling" copyright © James Bradley 2014. First published in *Fearsome Magics*, edited by Jonathan Strahan (Solaris).

"Soul Partner" copyright © Imogen Cassidy 2014. First published in *Aurealis 74*, edited by Dirk Strasser (Chimaera Publications).

"The Bullet and the Flesh" copyright © David Conyers and David Kernot 2014. First published in *World War Cthulhu*, edited by Brian M. Sammons and Glynn Owen Barrass (Dark Regions Press).

"Corpse Rose" copyright © Terry Dowling 2014. First published in *Nightmare Carnival*, edited by Ellen Datlow (Dark Horse Books).

"The Oud" copyright © Thoraiya Dyer 2014. First published in *Long Hidden*, edited by Rose Fox and Daniel José Older (Crossed Genres Publications).

"Metempsychosis" copyright © Jason Franks 2014. First published in *SQ Mag #15*, edited by Sophie Yorkston (IFWG Publishing).

"Of Gold and Dust" copyright © Michelle Goldsmith 2014. First published in *Andromeda Spaceways Inflight Magazine 60*, edited by Sue Bursztynski (ASIM).

"1884" copyright © Michael Grey 2014. First published in *Cthulhu Lives: An Eldrich Tribute to H.P.Lovecraft*, edited by Salomé Jones (Ghostwood Books).

"Escapement" copyright © Stephanie Gunn 2014. First published in *Kisses by Clockwork*, edited by Liz Grzyb (Ticonderoga Publications).

"Vox" copyright © Lisa L. Hannett and Angela Slatter 2014. First published in *The Female Factory* (Twelfth Planet Press).

"Of The Colour Turmeric, Climbing on Fingertips" copyright © Gerry Huntman 2014. First published in *Night Terrors III*, edited by Theresa Dillon, Marc Ciccarone, and G. Winston Hyatt (Blood Bound Books).

AVAILABLE FROM TICONDEROGA PUBLICATIONS

WWW.TICONDEROGAPUBLICATIONS.COM

LIMITED HARDCOVER EDITIONS

978-0-9806288-1-4   The Infernal BY Kim Wilkins
978-1-921857-54-6   Black-Winged Angels BY Angela Slatter

EBOOKS

978-0-9803531-5-0   Ghost Seas BY Steven Utley
978-1-921857-93-5   The Girl With No Hands BY Angela Slatter
978-1-921857-99-7   Dead RED Heart ED Russell B. Farr
978-1-921857-94-2   More Scary Kisses ED Liz Grzyb
978-0-9807813-5-9   Heliotrope BY Justina Robson
978-1-921857-36-2   Dreaming of Djinn ED Liz Grzyb
978-1-921857-40-9   Prickle Moon BY Juliet Marillier
978-1-921857-92-8   The Year of Ancient Ghosts BY Kim Wilkins
978-1-921857-28-7   Bloodstones ED Amanda Pillar
978-1-921857-04-1   Damnation and Dames ED Liz Grzyb & Amanda Pillar
978-1-921857-31-7   Midnight and Moonshine BY Lisa L. Hannett & Angela Slatter
978-1-921857-44-7   The Bride Price BY Cat Sparks
978-1-921857-60-7   Everything is a Graveyard BY Jason Fischer
978-1-921857-64-5   The Assassin of Nara BY R.J. Ashby
978-1-921857-78-2   Death at the Blue Elephant BY Janeen Webb
978-1-921857-82-9   The Emerald Key BY Christine Daigle & Stewart Sternberg
978-1-921857-57-7   Kisses by Clockwork ED Liz Grzyb
978-1-925212-06-8   Angel Dust ED Liz Grzyb
978-1-925212-17-4   The Finest Ass in the Universe BY Anna Tambour
978-1-925212-37-2   Hear Me Roar ED Liz Grzyb
978-1-921857-38-9   Bloodlines ED Amanda Pillar

THE YEAR'S BEST AUSTRALIAN FANTASY & HORROR SERIES
EDITED BY LIZ GRZYB & TALIE HELENE

978-0-9807813-8-0   Year's Best Australian Fantasy & Horror 2010 (hc)
978-0-9807813-9-7   Year's Best Australian Fantasy & Horror 2010 (tpb)
978-0-921057-98-0   Year's Best Australian Fantasy & Horror 2010 (ebook)
978-0-921057-13-3   Year's Best Australian Fantasy & Horror 2011 (hc)
978-0-921057-14-0   Year's Best Australian Fantasy & Horror 2011 (tpb)
978-0-921057-15-7   Year's Best Australian Fantasy & Horror 2010 (ebook)
978-0-921057-48-5   Year's Best Australian Fantasy & Horror 2012 (hc)
978-0-921057-49-2   Year's Best Australian Fantasy & Horror 2012 (tpb)
978-0-921057-50-8   Year's Best Australian Fantasy & Horror 2010 (ebook)
978-0-921057-72-0   Year's Best Australian Fantasy & Horror 2013 (hc)
978-0-921057-73-7   Year's Best Australian Fantasy & Horror 2013 (tpb)
978-0-921057-74-4   Year's Best Australian Fantasy & Horror 2010 (ebook)
978-0-925212-18-1   Year's Best Australian Fantasy & Horror 2014 (hc)
978-0-925212-19-8   Year's Best Australian Fantasy & Horror 2014 (tpb)
978-0-925212-20-4   Year's Best Australian Fantasy & Horror 2010 (ebook)

THANK YOU

The publisher would sincerely like to thank:

Alan Baxter, James Bradley, Imogen Cassidy, David Conyers, Terry Dowling, Thoraiya Dyer, Jason Franks, Michelle Goldsmith, Michael Grey, Stephanie Gunn, Lisa L. Hannett, Gerry Huntman, Rick Kennett, David Kernot , Charlotte Kieft, S.G. Larner, Claire McKenna, Andrew J. McKiernan, Faith Mudge, Jason Nahrung, Emma Osborne, Angela Rega, Tansy Rayner Roberts, Angela Slatter, Cat Sparks, Anna Tambour, Kyla Ward, Kaaron Warren, Janeen Webb, Donna Maree Hanson, Robert Hood, Pete Kempshall, Karen Brooks, Jeremy G. Byrne, Kim Wilkins, Marianne de Pierres, Jonathan Strahan, Peter McNamara, Ellen Datlow, Grant Stone, Sean Williams, Simon Brown, Garth Nix, David Cake, Simon Oxwell, Grant Watson, Sue Manning, Steven Utley, Lewis Shiner, Bill Congreve, Jack Dann, Lucy Sussex, the Mt Lawley Mafia, the Nedlands Yakuza, Shane Jiraiya Cummings, Angela Challis, Kate Williams, Andrew Williams, Kathryn Linge, Al Chan, Brian Clarke, Alisa and Tehani, Mel & Phil, Jennifer Sudbury, Paul Pryztula, Helen Grzyb, Hayley Lane, Georgina Walpole, Rushelle Lister, Nerida Fearnley-Gill, everyone we've missed . . .

. . . and you.

IN MEMORY OF
Eve Johnson (1945–2011)
Sara Douglass (1957–2011)
Steven Utley (1948–2013)